WHAT BECAME OF GUNNER ASCH

Full of expectation, Kamnitzer left *La Paloma*. He was strolling along the dark street when he heard a sound. "Who's there?" he asked.

"It's Rammler, Sergeant-Major Rammler."

"Anyone could say that," said Kamnitzer. "Come out where I can see you."

"I can't. I've been set on, left without a stitch."

"You're beginning to annoy me." said Kamnitzer reprovingly. "If you really are stark naked you're creating a nuisance. I'll have to report you to the police."

The sergeant-major saw no alternative but to show himself. "I order you to recognise me," he said menacingly.

Kamnitzer sounded amused. "Since when do people issue orders in the altogether? That makes two offences you've committed – indecent exposure and masquerading as a sergeant-major in the German army . . ."

HANS HELLMUT KIRST

What Became of Gunner Asch

translated from the German by
J. Maxwell Brownjohn

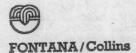

FONTANA/Collins

Originally published in Germany under the title 08/15 HEUTE
First published in Fontana Books May 1966
Second Impression August 1967
Third Impression May 1968
Fourth Impression December 1971
Fifth Impression June 1975

© 1963 by Verlag Kurt Desch
© 1964 in the English translation
by Wm Collins Sons & Co Ltd

Made and printed in Great Britain by
William Collins Sons & Co Ltd Glasgow

Recently—it might have been yesterday or the day before—a trial took place in a West German town. The defendant, a private soldier charged with having assaulted a superior officer, was convicted and sentenced.

While this was not a miscarriage of justice, it was a direct result of failings within the Bundeswehr. Some of its members had apparently mistaken illusion for idealism and blind obedience for discipline, an almost invariable characteristic of the Bundeswehr's predecessors. Once again, the consequences proved to be extremely dangerous.

Nevertheless this story of two equally unfortunate men, Grenadier Recht and Captain Ahlers, is far from being the whole story of the Bundeswehr. It merely tells of men in uniform and of their private lives, which they tried to lead in as uncomplicated a fashion as possible. If their story is not without its more humorous aspects, the final outcome remains a catastrophe.

Grenadier Recht flung open the window and leapt into the night. He landed in a narrow back-yard, knocking over a dust-bin in the process. The accumulated garbage spilled across the flagstones and lay there in a stinking heap. Martin Recht breathed heavily.

"Stop!" called a powerful, beery voice. It had a benevolent, almost wheedling tone, like that of a mother coaxing a reluctant child to eat.

Martin Recht had no intention of stopping. He blundered on until he came to a gate, which gave under his weight with a crash of splintering boards. Before him, like a long dark tunnel, lay a deserted street. From behind him, as though in the far distance, came the wail of a juke-box, whose languishing strains oozed through the open window like artificial honey. The sergeant-major was still standing there, peering over the sill. "You there, stop!"

But Recht plunged into the darkness, feeling as if he were diving off a spring-board into a pool of unknown depth. Although he was stationed in the town, its topography was still a mystery to him. He only knew the location of his barracks, the main square and the Espresso bar known as the *La Paloma*—or, as his fellow-recruits called it, "the passion parlour." It was from a first-floor window of the latter establishment that he had just made his escape.

"Stupid clot!" said the sergeant-major in charge of the regimental police picket, resentfully. "Who does he think he is, running off like that?"

"Let him go," said the sergeant who was acting as second-in-command. He had no wish to take part in a prolonged chase. In his experience, such ventures resulted in nothing but sweat, and his thirst needed no added stimulation.

The sergeant-major, however, was outraged. "He just wouldn't stop, the artful bloody grass-hopper." An order—

his order—had not been complied with. Besides, the man had directly flouted a regimental police picket instituted by the garrison commander himself.

"Get after him!" he called in rousing tones.

"It's no use," the sergeant temporised. "He's got a good turn of speed, and I'm no four-minute miler."

"Don't worry, he's running in just the right direction."

The sergeant-major, who was well-versed in picket work, knew the small town like the back of his hand. He listened contentedly to the sound of pattering feet as their owner sped due south, parallel to the Koenigstrasse. He was making for a district which could be easily combed, like a model on a sand-table.

"We'll get him, never you fear," he said confidently.

"Why all the fuss, for God's sake?" demanded the sergeant, snorting indignantly, but his snorting was in vain and his appeal to the deity inappropriate at this juncture. By now the sergeant-major was wrapped up in his role as picket commander and firmly resolved to catch the miscreant who had dared to evade his clutches.

"I'm going to have his guts for garters, that's why," the sergeant-major declared with something akin to solemnity. Then, hastily reflecting that expressions of this sort were now frowned upon in higher quarters, he corrected himself:

"We'll show him what discipline means."

And, so saying, he set off in pursuit.

Reaching the outskirts of a housing estate, Grenadier Martin Recht paused for a moment. He strained his ears for sounds of nocturnal movement, but all he could hear at first was his own breathing.

He was in full uniform, which was as it should be. Recht was still a relatively new recruit and recruits were not allowed to wear civilian clothes on week-ends—or not, at least, in his battalion, whose members were known locally as the Ironclads in deference to their C.O., a man of iron determination.

Recht clutched his head. His cap was askew, his hair

felt damp and he was sweating like a race-horse. He tried to calm down, forcing himself to inhale and exhale slowly.

"Damn it all," he muttered, "how did I get into this mess?"

He was always getting into messes, or so it seemed to him—at least since he had donned uniform. Ever since that day he had been oppressed by a sense of having hitherto seen the world in a false light. Suddenly there were no more curves, only angles, and he had to conform to them. His locker was too small, his rifle too big, his boots too tight, his shirt too baggy and his handkerchief never clean enough. Quite a few of his superiors regarded him with suspicion, a sentiment which he reciprocated.

Guided by the dim light of the street lamp, Recht's gaze turned to a gleaming brass plate suspended from a gate post. On it, in bold capitals, was the name "Turner," and beneath it, smaller but no less bold, the word "Colonel." He shrank back, and as he did so his ears caught the sound of an approaching car. It was the sort of harsh, grinding sound which only a carelessly driven military vehicle would emit. Simultaneously there came the noise of hurrying, clattering feet. Recht realised that the picket had split up and was executing a pincer movement. He set off again down the dark empty tunnel of the street. The beery voice of the sergeant-major floated after him. It still sounded genial, though slightly laboured. It was extremely unusual for the picket commander in his garrison to have to indulge in nocturnal sports of this kind. One word normally sufficed to bring the lads to heel.

Mindful of this, the sergeant-major once more brought his most highly developed organ into play. Even at a considerable distance, his voice sounded as though it had been amplified by a loud-hailer. "You, there!" he called. "This is your last chance! Come back!"

The next sentence might have been: "Or I'll fire!"—but it was never uttered, or else Recht never heard it.

He boldly veered left and crossed the next sizeable street— the Koenigstrasse, not that he realised it. Here, however, he was brought up short by a wall. It was smooth and plastered, and looked greyish white in the meagre light of the moon—a wall of compressed cotton wool, but uninvitingly high.

Martin Recht could hear the raucous voice of the sergeant-major again, bawling now, but largely drowned by the noise of the swiftly approaching engine. He was dominated by a panicky urge to run for his life.

Panting like a wrestler in the closing round, he skirted the wall at a trot but suddenly slid to a halt when his eye was arrested by something out of the ordinary. Outlined against the smooth, forbidding surface of the wall were two bold vertical lines connected by a number of other horizontal lines. It might have been a mirage, but it proved to be a ladder—a rope ladder.

Recht found time to shake his head in astonishment before scrambling up the mirage with trembling knees and bursting lungs. Gasping like a steam locomotive at full throttle, he reached the top of the wall.

Beneath him, not very far away, he could see two figures. They swam before his eyes like fish in an aquarium, but he recognised them as the garrison picket: the sergeant-major, bulky as a cabin-trunk, and the sergeant, round as an inflated balloon. They were both staring up at him like twin allegories of unbelief.

But Recht was already hauling up the ladder.

Recht pulled up the rope ladder and let it down the other side of the wall. Secure for the time being, he descended cautiously, step by step, until, to his relief, he felt solid ground beneath his feet once more. He had absolutely no idea where he was.

Then he heard a voice behind him say: "Who have we got here?"

The voice sounded entirely friendly—a veritable 'cello by comparison with the sergeant-major's bass trombone. Recht turned hopefully to face his unexpected interlocutor, only to see a man in uniform. It was a uniform like his, and it belonged to an officer.

"This is an unexpected pleasure," said the man in officer's uniform. "Welcome, my dear fellow."

Martin Recht could muster no reply. He stood there like a rabbit who runs happily into a clover-field and finds himself struggling in a snare. Now that his eyes had grown accustomed to the light he saw that the man was wearing the insignia of an air force captain.

"Follow me," said the captain, in tones of invitation rather than command. He opened a near-by door, and blinding light pierced the gloom.

The captain entered, followed by Recht. By rights, he should have been feeling like a lamb led to the slaughter, but he had reached the stage where everything was of consummate indifference to him.

"Make yourself at home," said the captain with disconcerting bonhomie.

He dropped into a chair, waving Recht into the chair opposite him. His clear blue eyes scanned the young soldier's agitated face appraisingly. Then he began to smile.

The figure before him was that of a boy, smooth-skinned, mild-eyed and awkward. He looked as nervous as a greyhound before the start—ready to spring, but painfully aware that he had no idea which way to turn.

"My name's Ahlers," said the captain. "I'm a squadron-leader in the transport wing here. This is my office. As you can see, I'm doing some overtime."

The captain's voice sounded sympathetic, but his lean features were stern, grey and fine-drawn. Deep lines furrowed his brow and cheeks, and skirted the corners of his mouth. He looked as though he had spent many long and sleepless nights in the course of his career.

"And who are you?" he inquired gently.

"Grenadier Recht—Martin Recht." The youngster opened his breast-pocket and fumbled for his pass with trembling but eager fingers. By now, he had reconciled himself to the idea that his nocturnal adventure was at an end, though he dared not reflect on its possible consequences.

Captain Ahlers waved the pass away. "No need to rush things," he said easily. "You look as though you could do with a stiffener, Recht. How about a whisky? I brought some back from Scotland last week—duty-free, of course."

Recht, who was buttoning up his breast-pocket, managed a nod. He exuded mistrust from every pore as he incredulously watched the captain fill two glasses and push one across to him.

Ahlers raised his glass. "Visitors are always welcome here," he said with a smile. "The bonds between the army and the air force should be strengthened whenever possible— for the greater good, if you like. Let's drink to that."

They had hardly drained their glasses when the door was pushed open and a warrant officer appeared, a tall lean man with the craggy features of a Hollywood sheriff. He paused in the doorway, blinking at Captain Ahlers in the bright light.

Martin Recht waited for the customary ritual to unfold : the warrant officer, or subordinate, would come to attention, cap clasped to his chest and right hand raised in salute. Only when this performance had been completed, and not before, would the reason for his presence be voiced.

But nothing of the sort happened. Without preamble, the warrant officer burst into an indignant torrent of words. "What a lousy cock-up! I've gone and lost my bet."

Martin Recht regarded the strange apparition with dismay. He was breaking all the rules. Such a thing was quite impermissible, at any rate in a Grenadier battalion, which constituted Recht's only field of military experience. He stared at Captain Ahlers in bewilderment.

The latter's smile did not fade. He even seemed to be enjoying the situation. "May I introduce you two gentlemen? Warrant Officer Vossler of my squadron : Grenadier Recht, an unexpected guest."

"Sorry, didn't notice you sitting there," said the warrant

officer, going over to Martin Recht and extending his hand. "At the moment all I can see is red, but if you knew what had happened you'd sympathise."

Vossler sat down uninvited and reached for the whisky bottle. He poured himself a glass and drained it.

Martin Recht's bewilderment grew with every passing minute. To one accustomed to the rigid discipline of the Ironclads, this warrant officer was behaving as though he had never heard of the correct relationship to be maintained between a subordinate and his superior.

"Hell and damnation!" Vossler continued. "It's too bad I lost that bet. I'm half a dozen bottles of bubbly to the bad, though that's not what I'm annoyed about. It's the thought of that fat slug Langhorn beating me back to barracks. Some idiot hauled up my rope ladder. Was it you, Ahlers?"

"I'm afraid it was our young friend here," said the captain, indicating Recht. "Apparently his need was greater than yours."

The warrant officer looked searchingly at the disconcerted grenadier. "Since when do visitors climb in over walls?"

"Since people started leaving rope ladders around, I imagine," commented Ahlers.

"He must have had a pretty good reason," Vossler said, looking intrigued. "What was it?"

"Our young friend seems to need some enlightenment, too." The captain's tone was kindly. "I have a feeling that the world's tumbling about his ears to-night—to be exact, the world his superior officers in the Ironclads cultivate so carefully. Isn't that so, Recht?"

"I don't know," the grenadier said with an effort, and his face seemed to indicate that he didn't know anything any more.

"He really does look as though he could do with an explanation," the warrant officer agreed.

Captain Ahlers nodded. "On one point in particular. Our guest is evidently puzzled by the way warrant officers treat captains in this establishment. Well, that's easily explained. Vossler and I served together in the war. We made a hundred sorties in the same crew."

"Successful ones, of course," supplemented Vossler.

"But it wasn't an unmixed pleasure. We've always been more interested in flying itself than in the possibility of being shot down while doing so. Anyway, here we are together again, and my old friend Vossler is the best pilot we've got."

"Come off it," said Vossler cheerfully. "You only say that so you can saddle me with tricky missions you ought to fly yourself. You're a better pilot than I ever was."

They both laughed, and even Martin Recht ventured a diffident smile. His spirits rose slightly. He hadn't deserted the frying pan for the fire, it seemed, although caution was still indicated. After all, the two men were his superior officers.

Their cheerful laughter was cut short by the buzz of the telephone. Captain Ahlers picked up the receiver and listened in silence. Eventually he said: "Tell the gentlemen to wait."

He replaced the receiver on its cradle with a thoughtful expression, seemingly avoiding the others' gaze. Then he picked up his glass and drained it.

"It's a funny business altogether," remarked Vossler, refilling his squadron-leader's glass with whisky, "your paying us a visit across the wall like that. Surely the gate would have been more convenient."

"More convenient, certainly," said Ahlers, "but not so appropriate in this case—am I right?" He regarded Recht quizzically.

Recht realised that he was expected—not required—to tell the truth. If only because of this slight but important difference in approach, he felt impelled to be completely honest.

"I was trying to get away from a regimental police picket," he said. "I don't know this town yet—I've only been out of barracks a few times before, so I had no idea the wall bordered air force property. When I saw the rope ladder I used it. I didn't know where it would lead to."

"It led you to our whisky, among other things," the warrant officer remarked dryly. "What's more, you've done me out of half a dozen bottles of champagne. That rope ladder was mine. It was put there to help me win a bet."

"We'll talk about that later." Captain Ahlers sounded suddenly businesslike. "First, I'd be interested to know why you were running away from the patrol. Not just for fun, I imagine?"

"No," Recht conceded. "I'd been in a coffee-bar called the *La Paloma,* in the back room."

"The so-called passion parlour," Warrant Officer Vossler interjected knowledgeably. "It's off limits to army personnel."

"There were seven of us." Recht seemed to have lost all his inhibitions now. "Seven—a friend of mine, an air force corporal, an American soldier, three girls, and me."

"The usual thing, in fact," explained Vossler. "They sit around in rows, exchanging small—ah—tokens of mutual affection in a dimly-lit room."

"Just that?" inquired the captain.

The warrant officer answered for Martin Recht, who only had to nod his assent. "You can't do much more in that dump. Hence the nickname."

"And that's all there is to it?"

"Yes. Too bad, isn't it?" Vossler gave Recht a sympathetic grin. "Places like that are a positive threat to normal relations between the sexes. If things don't change radically, I foresee a dangerous decline in local morale."

"Anyway," Recht went on, "then the picket turned up. They forced their way in and I—well, I ran for it."

"Why?"

"I can't say why, exactly. Perhaps because I remembered all the black marks I'd earned already and realised I mustn't get caught. Not that anything very terrible happened, but

I'd have been embarrassed to get picked up in a place like that. Well, when the picket arrived I grabbed my cap and raced up the back stairs with them after me. I jumped out of the first-floor window into the yard."

"I'd probably have done the same myself," said Vossler, turning to Ahlers. "After all, why should the lad risk getting booked and reported? Not for the sake of the tarts who patronise the passion parlour, surely?"

"Anyway, sir, that's what happened," Recht concluded.

Captain Ahlers rose, paced up and down the office and halted beside his desk. "That phone call I had just now was from the duty officer. He tells me there's a military police picket at the barrack gates. They say that a soldier they were chasing climbed over our wall."

"Ridiculous!" Vossler said gaily. "Since when have the Ironclads been in the habit of sticking their noses into our business? Surely they're not thinking of trying to introduce their methods here? We ought to leave them standing there until they take root."

"Unfortunately," Captain Ahlers said with deliberation, "there's one thing that can't be dismissed : the existence of a rope ladder—your ladder, Vossler. It's a concrete fact, and I'm not sure that I can invent a plausible explanation for its presence."

"I didn't use it, though, did I?"

"No, but you put it there. That makes you a sort of accessory after the fact—and me too, for having sanctioned your little game with Langhorn. Of course, we couldn't reckon with complications of this kind."

"You'll think of something," Vossler said confidently. "Anyway, what if we do have a rope ladder, and what if it was hanging on the wall? We might have been planning a night exercise or something. The main things is, any explanation you give must sound strictly official."

"And what shall we do with Recht here?"

"Quite simple—chuck him back over the wall." Vossler evidently saw not the slightest difficulty in this. "He can vanish into the night and double back to barracks, conveniently forgetting everything that's happened here. Isn't that right, Recht?"

"I'm awfully sorry about it all," said the grenadier. The past few minutes had brought him into contact with two men whom he would gladly have followed to the ends of the earth. "I'm ready to give myself up and take the blame."

"He suffers from noble impulses, this lad," said Vossler. "We'll have to do something about that, don't you agree, Klaus?"

*

Outside the gates of the air force barracks, which were adjacent to the air-field with its four hangars and two runways, stood the regimental police picket: the sergeant-major in a commanding pose beneath the lamp over the gate, and behind him, yearning for his bed and surreptitiously yawning, the sergeant. The sergeant-major presented a picture of adamantine fortitude, faithful to his battalion commander's idea of dogged determination in the face of overwhelming odds.

As luck would have it, they had come up against a sentry of horrendous obstinacy, an air force lance-corporal who was possessed by the simple conviction that an air force base existed for air force personnel. It had nothing to do with the army, let alone those professional bullies the Ironclads, who sometimes referred to their air force colleagues as "the brilliantine brigade," "the slop-merchants" or simply "the armchair warriors."

In short, the sentry showed not the least inclination to take orders from the Ironclads. He merely informed the guard commander, who informed the duty officer, who informed the squadron-leader, Captain Ahlers, who always seemed to be on call at any hour of day or night.

"Tell the gentlemen to wait," Ahlers had said. "They're to wait," the duty officer told the guard commander, who told the sentry, who relayed the message to the picket.

"You're to wait," he announced indifferently, like a butler shaking off a couple of importunate vacuum-cleaner salesmen at the tradesmen's entrance.

"How long are we supposed to wait for?" the sergeant-major inquired resentfully.

"Don't ask me, mate," the sentry replied, grinning insolently. To him, the Ironclads were a lot of dim-witted louts. Two of them had tried to muscle in on his girl-friend the Saturday before, a piece of impertinence which he was glad of a chance to repay.

"Listen here," the sergeant-major said majestically. "I don't think you realise who you're talking to."

"What makes you so sure?" the sentry asked, unabashed.

Seeing the sergeant-major draw in his breath and prepare to fire a salvo, the sergeant pulled him aside. With some difficulty, he managed to smooth his superior's ruffled plumage. "After all, this isn't the Grenadiers."

"Worse luck," growled the sergeant-major.

"But," went on the sergeant, who was of a practical turn of mind, "that's got its advantages too. An outfit like this is always up to its elbows in fresh coffee—cigarettes, too, straight from Greece and Turkey. What about seeing if these armchair warriors can show a little fellow-feeling from that point of view?"

"Haven't you got any pride?" the sergeant-major asked reprovingly.

"Of course I have, but I've got a thirst too." The sergeant gazed longingly at the electric percolator on the guard-room window-sill. "It wouldn't hurt to get them to pour us a cup."

"Yes, it would," snapped the sergeant-major, who had never felt less thirsty in his life. "Do you want to let the side down in front of these half-civilised buffoons? That's all we need!"

Meanwhile, Captain Ahlers was trying to arrange matters. In the first place he believed Martin Recht's story; secondly, he had taken to the boy, who reminded him a little of his own dead son; and, thirdly, there were his own personal responsibilities. His friend Vossler's rope-ladder operations were not entirely above reproach, certainly as seen through the eyes of an iron-willed Ironclad. Awkward investigations would have to be avoided as far as possible.

" We must try to take the wind out of these supermen's sails," he said meditatively.

" Splendid! " cried Vossler, winking at Recht. " It's one of his favourite occupations, you know. He's got a secret passion for taming the mad military."

" I'm merely concerned with human relations," said Ahlers.

Vossler chuckled. " That's one way of putting it. You're a born clearer-up of messes, anyway. What's the first move?"

" The first move," said Ahlers, " will be to put through a call to Colonel Turner."

Warrant Officer Vossler emitted an admiring whistle. Colonel Turner, the wing-commander and area commandant, was a sort of demi-god who sat enthroned behind his desk most of the time. Normal mortals—that is, men of junior rank—seldom if ever set eyes on him. His decisions had scarcity value, mainly because a great deal had to happen before he came to a firm conclusion about anything. In addition, Turner was a philosopher of a sort. Legend even had it that he was working on an original, and doubtless important book. He had settled on a title—*Soldiers and Society*—five years ago.

The Colonel answered the 'phone promptly in a voice at once sonorous and benevolent. Ahlers began by apologising for making such a late call.

" Please, please! " Turner replied cordially. " I'm always at the service of my colleagues. Besides, I was still working on my book. What can I do for you?"

Captain Ahlers reported the presence of a military police patrol outside the gates of the air force barracks, allegedly waiting to arrest a runaway soldier " on our territory, sir." It was a highly questionable and precipitate action undertaken with insufficient justification and absolutely no prospect of success—in short, an intrusion.

"I understand," said Colonel Turner in his best bedside manner. "From what you say, it appears to be a clear enough case. I have the fullest confidence in your judgment."

"Then I have your authority to take the appropriate steps, sir?"

"But of course, my dear chap—within regulation limits, which are familiar to you all, I trust. I also trust that you will show tact and discretion. You're aware of the slightly strained relations that exist between us and our army friends, I imagine?"

This was a question which demanded an affirmative answer, and Captain Ahlers supplied one. "So I can act on your behalf, sir—as deputy area commandant?"

"Of course you may, my dear Ahlers. I'm certain you won't disappoint me, just as I'm certain you won't let yourself be influenced by certain prevailing prejudices. After all, the methods employed by our army colleagues in achieving their training objectives don't concern us. Such things are their affair. We merely act according to the rules laid down by higher authority."

Such was Colonel Turner—invariably courteous, slippery as an eel and the most agreeable commanding officer imaginable—so long as no one saddled him with any unpleasantnesses. He would have allowed his subordinates to get away with murder, provided that it was committed exactly in accordance with standing orders.

Captain Ahlers imbibed some strong coffee and made some more telephone calls.

First, he instructed the duty officer to inform the military police patrol, firmly, that air force territory was outside their jurisdiction—which was equivalent to telling them where they got off. Then he put through an urgent call to the C.O. of the Panzergrenadier battalion.

The latter, Major Bornekamp by name, was widely known

as a fire-eater and widely respected in consequence. Having been one of the heroes of the last war, he intended to give a repeat performance in the next. Hence it was one of his brass-bound principles to be ready for action at any moment, even in the depths of peace.

At present he was in the Mess, coaching some of his younger officers in *savoir-vivre* as he understood it. The Y.O.s called him " Old Leather-face," and his manner was correspondingly tough.

" So you're at it again, are you, Ahlers?" Bornekamp asked, chuckling harshly into the telephone. " Well, fire away."

Ahlers delivered his broadside and then rang Herbert Asch, the local burgomaster and most influential civilian for miles around, being not only the town's first citizen but president of its thriving sports club and proprietor of the Hotel Asch, a centrally located establishment with café, restaurant and public house attached. Ahlers requested an interview with him as well.

" Certainly," was Asch's terse reply.

" Now for some in-fighting!" Vossler said expectantly.

Martin Recht was still standing there, confused and un-certain what to say. Ahlers gave him an encouraging nod. " Don't worry, we'll arrange things."

" It'll be a pleasure, what's more," Vossler assured him, adding confidentially: " There are some people we don't mind making trouble for."

Ahlers frowned slightly. " You can forget that remark. I'm merely concerned with a few fundamental issues, one of them being the simple recognition that a soldier is a human being and ought to be treated as such."

A few minutes later Captain Ahlers climbed into an official car. Warrant Officer Vossler acted as driver, and Grenadier Recht was enjoined to sit in the back and stay there.

The car turned out of the barrack gates, rolled smoothly along the Koenigstrasse, crossed the market-place and headed for the Grenadier barracks. Here the gates were flung wide in deference to prior notification of arrival issued by the C.O. in person. No passes were demanded.

Grenadier Recht had—or so it seemed—been brought to safety.

*

Ahlers's interview with Major Bornekamp, commander of the local Grenadier battalion, began satisfactorily and without formality. It took place in the Mess. Bornekamp shooed a couple of subalterns away from his table and invited Ahlers to drink a glass of champagne and beer, mixed.

"You would come disturbing me in the middle of the night, wouldn't you!" growled Bornekamp with apparent good humour, scrutinising Ahlers like a man studying enemy dispositions. "I can think of better things to do at this hour. Would you like me to be more explicit?"

Captain Ahlers did not press for details—he could imagine them. Bornekamp set store by being known not only as a dashing warrior but as a lady-killer—two roles which, in his estimation, went hand in hand. Ahlers surveyed the hero of many and varied battles with a certain amusement.

"The would-be soldier," Bornekamp declared stoutly, "must always be ready to test his mettle." He laughed raucously at his own remark, watching to see whether his visitor appreciated its enormous subtlety, and was gratified to see Ahlers smile.

"I'm here," Ahlers said, "in the role of deputy station commander, Major."

"We've always worked well together," Bornekamp said promptly, though with slightly less volume than before. There was no need for the young officers seated respectfully in the background to hear everything, no need to rub their noses in the fact that even he, the father-figure of the battalion, was occasionally forced to make concessions. "Our co-operation has never been in doubt, has it?"

"Of course not, there's been no cause for complaint," Ahlers assured him. "Not until now, that is."

Bornekamp screwed up his eyes like a marksman focusing on a target. Then he broke into a booming laugh. " Well, let's have a drink first," he said, clinking glasses with Ahlers and draining his at a gulp. " You're not proposing to make difficulties, are you, my dear chap?"

" I'm here to eliminate them," Ahlers hastened to explain, not unaware of the latent menace in the C.O.'s question.

" Good," said Bornekamp. His boisterous bonhomie had given way to an expression of alert watchfulness. " Well, what's the trouble?"

" A military police patrol tried to force its way into the air force barracks this evening."

Bornekamp's reaction was swift. " Bloody fools!" he snapped. " What do they think they're up to? They must have been out of their minds. I hope you kicked them in the crutch."

" In a manner of speaking," said Ahlers. " I told them to get lost."

" Good for you," the Major said approvingly, though his mien, even at the juncture, wholly befitted one who commanded the Ironclads : tough, resolute and unyielding. " Well, do you expect a personal apology?"

Ahlers hastened to avoid a head-on collision. " There's no question of that, Major."

" What did you come for, then?"

" Partly to create a better climate of co-operation. Colonel Turner sets great store by that. I spoke to him on the 'phone just now, and he was most insistent on the point. Little misunderstandings will always occur, he said, but they mustn't be allowed to mar our team-spirit."

" He said that, did he?" Bornekamp uttered the words with vague displeasure. He was determined not to be cajoled by these " tailor's dummies," as he termed a large proportion of the air force. It was sheer impertinence to provoke him like this. " I resent the implication."

" It was a misunderstanding," Ahlers interposed, slightly taken aback by the Major's sudden indignation. He had intended to clear the air in the pleasantest possible manner, but Bornekamp seemed determined to smash up the proverbial china-shop. "In my opinion, the proper course is to take note of such misunderstandings and then forget them again as quickly as possible."

"That," said the Major, inaccessible as a castle keep, "may be the air force attitude, but it's not one that prevails in the units under my command. I don't tolerate misunderstandings, let alone forget them—I investigate and eradicate them. Any other course is idle compromise, and if there's one thing I abhor it's that. Good night, Captain."

*

"Herr Asch," said Captain Ahlers, "I think you were an officer, weren't you?"

"Are you appealing to my esprit de corps?" Herbert Asch asked with a faintly ironical smile. "I wasn't an officer the whole time, you know. I spent a far greater proportion of my army career in the ranks, and I haven't forgotten the fact."

"All the better," Ahlers assured him. "You'll find it that much easier to understand me."

"In what respect, Captain?"

"I need your support."

"As a hotel-keeper, as a mayor—or as a man?" Herbert Asch laughed. "Or perhaps you mean as a soldier? Preferably not that, Captain. I've always been in favour of plain-speaking, and I can afford to indulge in it these days." Captain Ahlers had always felt free to speak his mind in the mayor's presence, but he phrased his next question with care. "You don't think much of the army, do you?"

"I learnt to avoid generalisations very early in life, Captain. What soldiers are or aren't depends entirely on what's beneath their uniforms—and the uniforms of the men who lead them."

"Exactly." Ahlers sensed that he was expected to make a statement of principle at this stage, but Asch was opening

a bottle of carefully cooled Franconian wine, a sure sign
that there was no need to rush things.

Thus encouraged, Ahlers launched into a lengthy preamble.
Its gist was as follows: anything which wants to exist
must be prepared to defend its existence; consequently,
soldiers are a fact of life. The world is not a perfect
place, and soldiers of any nationality are anything but perfect beings. Every military organisation has its shortcomings,
the Bundeswehr included. The main words, to effect im-
provements wherever possible, even when this involves—as
it sometimes does—clashing head-on with incorrigible elements.

"Not badly put," commented Asch. "But I assume your
remarks aren't intended merely as a theoretical exercise.
Presumably you're about to draw some practical conclusions.
Well, Captain, what do you expect of me?"

"This evening," said Ahlers, "a military police patrol
raided a local place of entertainment—the *La Paloma*—
you probably know it."

"I know it," Herbert Asch said with some amusement,
"and I know what goes on there."

"Disregarding that, Herr Asch, do you imagine the patrol
marched in there purely by accident—that it was just a
chance raid? It's quite possible that there may be an attempt
to put other establishments under surveillance to-morrow—
establishments belonging to you, for instance. What then?"

"They could try it," Asch said coolly, "but the results of
such a step might well prove surprising—and not only for
the patrol."

"Then you agree that one can't just let such things
pass?"

"I'm beginning to understand you, Captain. In fact, I'm
pretty sure I know what you want me to do." Herbert
Asch lifted his glass and sipped it without removing his
eyes from his visitor. "I assume you wouldn't take it amiss
if a protest were lodged by so-called authoritive circles of
the civil population against such methods of control—an

effective protest, preferably delivered by me in my capacity as mayor. Am I right?"

"Yes," said Ahlers. "I appreciate your having spared me the need to express myself too clearly. I should have found it embarrassing."

"All the same," Asch said thoughtfully, "I can't take the whole weight off your shoulders. I'm not saying I won't do it, but I've no intention of taking sides prematurely. What I mean is, I haven't the least desire to be played off against the army by the air force—or vice versa, for that matter."

"There's absolutely no question of that, Herr Asch."

"I hope not," Asch replied. "Your internal squabbles are nothing to do with me. Besides, I prefer to play my own game."

"Thank you, Herr Asch. I have a feeling you want to help. I hope you're satisfied that my motives are of the best."

Asch smiled. "We've known each other for some time now. I think we both know what to expect from one another."

"If I may say so," Ahlers ventured, "you're one of the few people I should like to count among my friends."

"Please do that, Captain." Asch toasted his guest with a look of genuine pleasure. "I've often wished you would come and see me as plain Klaus Ahlers, not Captain Ahlers, deputy station-commander. How does the idea appeal to you?"

"You're very kind." Ahlers's face had changed. His eyes looked weary and the lines in his cheeks seemed to have deepened. He clasped his hands together as though they needed mutual support. "I know what you mean, Herr Asch. You're aware of my private circumstances, but let's not discuss them now. Don't worry, I'll manage."

Asch nodded. He knew what Ahlers meant by private circumstances. He knew that his son, the apple of his eye, had died in a frightful accident the year before, and he also knew the tragic story of his daughter, who had suffered from a malformation of the spine since her birth during the closing months of the war. She had been forced to undergo several major operations which had cost, if not a fortune, sums which an ordinary air force captain must have found it hard to scrape together.

"All right, we'll leave the subject," Asch said. "But if the occasion ever arises, please remember that I'm your friend. Will you promise me that?"

"Of course," Ahlers said gratefully.

"And what else can I do for you, apart from pouring you another glass of wine?"

"May I send a young soldier to see you?"

"Why not?" Asch said. "What am I supposed to do with him?"

"He's a Grenadier and his name is Martin Recht. He needs a little looking after—deserves it, I should say. I'm afraid he's got into bad company. Would you mind keeping an eye on him occasionally?"

"A relative of yours?" asked Asch, looking interested.

"No, no—I got to know him quite by chance." Ahlers hesitated before continuing, with a hint of embarrassment: "To be honest, he reminds me a little of my son."

"Then go ahead and send him to me. You've whetted my curiosity."

*

"On your feet, gentlemen!" came the orderly sergeant's friendly bellow. Throwing the door wide and flinging open all the windows with an eye to the health-giving properties of fresh air, he proceeded to strip the recumbent inmates of Room 13 of their bedclothes, keeping up a stream of cheerful encouragement as he did so.

"Don't catch cold, lads!" he shouted.

Room 13 demanded his special vigilance, being the home of "Kamnitzer's Commandos," who had already driven more than one N.C.O. to the verge of a nervous breakdown. Lance-Corporal Kamnitzer, it should be explained, was the company's leader of fashion and made a habit of sleeping with a copy of Army Regulations under his pillow.

The orderly sergeant had more or less mastered the comparatively new-fangled rules of the military game. Grinning, he rattled the window-frames, shifted chairs around with a noise like thunder and drummed cheerfully on a locker. Not even the hard of hearing could have slumbered on in the face of this carefully organised barrage of noise.

"Anything else I can do for you, lads?"

"Yes," muttered Lance-Corporal Kamnitzer, heaving himself upright with a groan, "you can tell me why everyone looks so bloody stupid at this unearthly hour of the morning."

"Everyone?" asked the orderly sergeant with sudden asperity. Six bleary faces regarded him with interest. Although he sensed the challenge behind Kamnitzer's remark, he quickly realised what was required of him. The only way to remain master of the situation was to refuse to be provoked.

"Always good for a laugh, aren't you, Kamnitzer," he said, retiring hastily.

Corporal Streicher, who was the room senior and had a bed by the door said: "You might be a bit more careful, Kamnitzer. Your behaviour leaves a lot to be desired, and the whole room has to suffer for it."

"You most of all, I suppose," Kamnitzer said boldly. "Shut your trap or I'll shut it for you."

Corporal Streicher did not reply. He grimaced scornfully, but not before turning his back. Kamnitzer was insufferable in the early morning, and the best thing was to ignore him.

The first inmate of Room 13 to make for the ablutions was Grenadier Martin Recht. Weary but willing, he trotted down the corridor with his wash-roll clamped under his arm and a towel thrown over his shoulder.

"Hang on, mate!" Kamnitzer called after him. "Don't wear your legs out, it's not worth it."

Recht paused to let Kamnitzer catch up with him. He

was a short wiry youth with a thin, humorous face illumined
by a pair of sharply observant eyes. He moved lithely, like
a cross between a dancer and a wrestler. In addition, he
was the owner of a powerful voice which could sink, when
he chose, to a whisper as soft as a sea-breeze.

"Well, how was it?" he whispered. "Did you give the
R.P.s the slip yesterday?"

"By the skin of my teeth."

"How did you get back into barracks?"

"Professional secret, Karl."

Karl Kamnitzer, always a creature of boundless curiosity,
pricked up his ears.

"What?" he asked with interest. "Do you mean to say
there's a place where even a novice like you can climb over
the wall safely? If there is, I'd like to know where."

"I came in through the barrack gates, Karl, I promise
you." To whet Kamnitzer's curiosity still further, he changed
the subject. "How about you? Did they catch you?"

"That'll be the day!"

They were in the wash-room by now and had laid out
their things on two adjoining basins. Kamnitzer lathered
his face thoughtfully. "You did the right thing, clearing
off like that when the picket arrived. Me, I just sat there
—moved away from the girls, stuck my paws on the table
and sat there looking like a village idiot. It comes easy to me.
I know those R.P.s like the back of my hand. When they
saw you run for it they went after you like a dose of salts
and left us to carry on necking in peace."

"Bright and cheery this morning, aren't we?" came
a voice from behind them. It had a companionable, slightly
ingratiating note, and it belonged to Corporal Streicher.

Martin Recht hastened to disabuse him. "Not particularly."

"Push off, you garden gnome," Karl Kamnitzer told
Streicher with brutal relish. "I don't fancy you this morning."

"No harm in asking, is there?"

Kamnitzer turned the water full on and stuck his thumb in the tap, directing a knife-like jet into Streicher's face.

Streicher jumped back, wiping his eyes. "You've got a nerve," he said indignantly. "I warn you, I won't be treated like this. After all, I'm in charge here."

"Not as far as I'm concerned," replied Kamnitzer. "I wouldn't put you in charge of a roll of lavatory paper, even if I had two."

Corporal Streicher withdrew, watched belligerently by Karl Kamnitzer. Kamnitzer seemed to be fighting back an urge to kick him in the hind quarters, but he was no stranger to the impulse. "That chap would report me if I told him what I really thought of him."

"You're exaggerating as usual. What have you got against Streicher? He always seems very friendly to me."

"Precisely," said Kamnitzer, reaching for the soap. "That's what makes me suspicious."

Martin Recht towelled his chest meditatively. "Karl," he said at length, "if you were asked who you were with in the *La Paloma* last night, would you mention my name?"

"Come off it," Kamnitzer expostulated. "You're not trying to appeal to my better nature, are you?" He grinned. "Still, you do sleep in the bunk above me, so I suppose that gives us some claim on each other."

"Then I can count on your keeping quiet?"

"You're a bit naïve, aren't you?" said Kamnitzer. "I'm not a welfare organisation. I'm a faithful defender of the Fatherland, and I intend to be demobbed in one piece." He patted Recht on the back. "Don't worry, you're in luck. Some of these animated uniforms get on my tits. I enjoy doing them down—just for the hell of it."

*

"I'm going to crucify those two." Major Bornekamp addressed these words with grim composure to his adjutant, who stood there like a block of stone. "I'll show those dead-beats what happens to people who overstep the mark."

"Yes, sir," the adjutant said deferentially. As the third officer to serve Bornekamp in this capacity within the past twelve months, he was resigned to anything. Even the choicest products of the Major's vocabulary had lost their power to irritate, although they were reserved mainly for him. When a third party was present the Major managed— if only for a limited period—to create an impression of breeding, not to say culture.

"Blithering idiots like that should be hung, drawn and quartered," Bornekamp went on. "Dunderheads who undermine the army's reputation deserve no mercy. I'll show them what's what."

At this juncture, shepherded by the adjutant, the regimental police picket for the previous night marched in: the sergeant-major with the cabin-trunk physique and the sergeant who looked like a balloon on the point of bursting. Both men stared woodenly at the C.O., who stared back at them as though from a great height—no mean feat, in view of the fact that he was appreciably shorter than either of them.

"Well, gentlemen!" Bornekamp rasped. On the walls around him hung maps, plans and directives, but no pictures —not even one of the Federal President or the Defence Minister of the day—nothing but the symbols of a stern and purposeful devotion to duty. "Well, gentlemen!" Bornekamp repeated scathingly.

In Major Bornekamp's idiom, no more awesomely framed reprimand could have been conceived. It was one of his basic maxims that the man he did not call "friend" was not one, and the very air about him was expected to freeze to attention. After all, he commanded a battalion which was —in his eyes—destined to become an élite unit. The Americans had their Leathernecks: the Germans would, if he had anything to do with it, have their Ironclads.

"I am grieved, gentlemen," the Major continued sarcastically. "I would never have believed you capable of such a blunder, and I don't intend to let it pass." He refrained from uttering the other, riper, version of this sentence which sprang to his mind.

The sergeant-major attempted to defend himself.

"Sir, it was brought to our attention by a junior N.C.O. that certain nuisances were being committed in the *La Paloma* Espresso bar."

"Well, did you see them for yourself?"

"One man ran away, sir, and we tried to catch him. We chased him as far as the air force barracks."

"But you failed to arrest him," said Bornekamp, which, being interpreted, meant: so you couldn't even catch one idiotic runaway, you half-witted nincompoops. "That's what I call a really successful night's work," he commented.

The fat sergeant was oozing sweat at every pore, but the sergeant-major stood his ground bleakly like a bare tree on a winter's night.

"There was this ladder, sir," he said finally. "A ladder, hanging from the wall of the air force barracks."

"Balls and bang-me-arse!" exclaimed the C.O. "I mean," he amended quickly, "that's quite incredible. Since when do ladders grow on barracks walls?"

At this point the adjutant intervened. "Perhaps we ought to check the sergeant-major's statement, sir," he suggested with due diffidence, "—just as a matter of form. It may have been a piece of training equipment which someone left lying about by accident, or an optical illusion. There are any number of possibilities."

"Not in this case," the C.O. announced emphatically.

Bornekamp was a firm believer in the principle that what is impermissible is impossible, especially when the object in question happens to be a ladder allegedly suspended from a barrack wall. What could be more absurd!

"There's only one thing that carries weight with me, and that's success. Anything else is rank failure or wishy-washy theory. So you didn't catch this long-distance runner' —I mean, you failed to arrest the man who tried to evade arrest. What about the other patrons of this sink of iniquity? Did you get any of them?"

"No, sir," stammered the sergeant-major. He felt as if he were drifting away into the arctic night like a wounded seal on an ice-floe.

The sergeant puffed and blew violently. He opened and closed his mouth twice before speaking. "We went after the man who ran away," he blurted out, "but there was another grenadier who stayed behind. I'd remember his face anywhere. Perhaps we can find him, sir."

"What's the use?" Bornekamp demanded balefully. "You ought to have caught him yesterday—on the spot, red-handed." The case was closed as far as he was concerned. All that remained was to put his two scapegoats through the hoop.

"All the same, sir," the adjutant remarked, discreetly curious, "it would be interesting to know what our men get up to in that place."

The sergeant-major could supply the answer to that. "They sit side by side on benches, one man to each girl, listening to decadent music—jazz and so on. And they fumble with each other."

"What's that? How do you mean, fumble?"

"They fumble with each other, sir."

"What the devil do you mean by that?"

Here the adjutant intervened once more. "I believe," he said, "that the technical term for this activity is "petting" —an American expression, sir, if I'm not much mistaken."

"Explain yourself, damn it!"

"I'm not particularly well-informed on the subject," said the adjutant, "but I believe that the word petting implies manual caresses—below the waist included. It does not, however"—he cleared his throat—"imply going the whole hog, as I think it is called."

"That's right, sir," the sergeant-major corroborated, "they just fumble with each other, like I said."

"Ugh!" ejaculated the C.O. He was outraged, knowing

B

from his long experience of army life that no true soldier would behave in such a fashion. "We'll soon put a stop to that. I won't tolerate pig-sty behaviour in my battalion. Find me the men who were there."

*

When the order requiring the battalion to parade at full strength eventually reached No. 3 Company, the first man to lay hands on it was Company Sergeant-Major Kirschke. This might have been described as an accident, since Kirschke had recently developed the habit of taking lengthy naps during working hours.

"What's all this balls?" he drawled.

"Orders from Battalion," the corporal clerk replied tersely.

"Well, what of it?" demanded Kirschke, yawning with expertise. He emitted several more yawns—justifiably, in his opinion. What had lately been going on in No. 3 Company was more than could be readily endured by any normal modern man and soldier—and God knew he regarded himself as such. He had been quite prepared to enter wholeheartedly into the new army spirit, but the past few weeks had encouraged him in the belief that it was pointless. Extended spells of sleep appeared to be the just man's last resort.

Wearing an air of extreme weariness and indifference, Kirschke betook himself to the company commander's office, the order from Battalion fluttering sadly from his hand like a flag at half-mast.

"Your salute," said Lieutenant Dieter von Strackmann, "could do with a little smartening up."

Kirschke considered it beneath his dignity to reply. In his eyes, Lieutenant von Strackmann was a complete novice who had still been wetting his nappies when he, Kirschke, was commanding a gun-crew in a close support artillery unit—though his troop-commander got the Iron Cross that should have gone to him.

"Deal with it," said Lieutenant Dieter von Strackmann, casting a cursory glance at the order. "Get the company there on time, Sergeant-Major."

"It's not as simple as that," Kirschke said.

"Simple or not," snapped the lieutenant angrily, "an order's an order—and that goes for you too."

Kirschke's eyes closed, though not from weariness. He looked far more as if he were trying—if only for a brief instant—to blot out the sight of the uniformed dilettante at the desk.

Ever since young von Strackmann had assumed temporary command of the company in place of the regular company commander, a captain who had been in hospital for some weeks, suffering from jaundice, he had done his best to be the most iron-bound Ironclad of all.

"Some of the men are out on firing practice," Kirschke explained patiently, "and some are in town collecting stores. The M.T. class is swanning around somewhere in the area, and No. 2 Platoon is doing field training."

"I couldn't care less," said Lieutenant von Strackmann with mounting annoyance.

"But I could," said Kirschke in the tones of an indignant schoolmaster. "I'm not a miracle-worker."

"Kindly do as I tell you, Kirschke!" von Strackmann yelped. His youthful features, coarse-grained, angular and prematurely seamed by devotion to duty, tried to don an air of authority. To him, Kirschke was a clandestine saboteur, at least of the von Strackmann career. "If you wish to remain C.S.M. of this company, you will obey my orders."

These words seemed to afford Kirschke some amusement. He had difficulty in suppressing a broad grin. The fact was that he had been classified—on the strength of rigorous aptitude tests—as a warrant officer of outstanding ability, whereas von Strackmann's record as an acting company commander was still a blank page. He was the one who had to prove himself, not Kirschke.

"How you organise it is your business," the lieutenant continued. He rose and walked to the door, unable to endure Kirschke's presumption any longer. "The main thing is that the company turns out at the stated time."

The company turned out on time. All C.S.M. Kirschke had to do was to mobilise a number of junior N.C.O.s, still yawning incessantly with the easy assurance of a virtuoso who could manipulate the controls of the military machine in his sleep. Punctually to the minute, the members of No. 3 Company streamed in from all directions.

They thronged the parade-ground docilely, not inquiring why they had been summoned because they were not interested in knowing. The only thing that still aroused interest in the company since von Strackmann had taken over was the prospect of an evening off.

Only Martin Recht, standing in the front rank next to Karl Kamnitzer, felt any nervousness.

"Look, here's the picket!" he whispered excitedly. "They're making straight for us. I can guess what'll happen now."

They were still some distance away, being shepherded along by the battalion adjutant. Looking positively cheerful in the absence of Bornekamp, the adjutant almost danced along, with the picket trotting at his heels like a pair of bloodhounds. Von Strackmann strutted out to meet them with peacock strides.

"Get into the rear rank," Kamnitzer told Recht. "I'll give these lads something to chew on."

Martin Recht needed no second bidding. Corporal Streicher tried briefly to make difficulties, but a menacing look from Kamnitzer quelled him.

The adjutant and the acting company commander, both lieutenants, exchanged salutes, whereupon C.S.M. Kirschke negligently reported that the company was ready for inspection.

The next command was: "Open order, march!"

When this manœuvre had been completed, von Strackmann nodded to the adjutant. "All right," said the latter, addressing the picket in a slightly bored voice. "You can repeat the process, and let's hope we have more luck this time."

The sergeant-major propelled himself forward, followed

by the sergeant. Portentously, they started to pace along the front rank.

"I'll stake my life it wasn't a member of this company," von Strackmann assured the adjutant in an undertone.

"Steady, my friend," said the adjutant, a man of humane impulses when he was out of the C.O.'s reach, "you may be courting death."

Meanwhile the picket pursued its slow and deliberate course intent on doing a thorough job. Sergeant-major and sergeant looked from one indifferent face to the next, from eyes which regarded them with cool appraisal to others which shone with humble devotion. Cows, bulls and calves, thought the sergeant-major, but cattle one and all.

Suddenly both men paused, rooted in astonishment. A grinning, expectant face had swum into view. It belonged to a lance-corporal.

"Are you looking for me?" he inquired.

"That's the fellow!" the sergeant cried exultantly.

"Name?" asked the sergeant-major.

"Kamnitzer," the lance-corporal replied, "Christian name Karl. What can I do for you?"

"Were you in town last night?"

"Certainly I was." With satisfaction, Karl Kamnitzer sensed that every eye had turned in his direction. Even Lieutenant von Strackmann stared at him with his mouth slightly open, possibly recalling his pledge of two minutes earlier.

"I was in the *La Paloma* yesterday evening," Kamnitzer volunteered. "I was sitting there with a few friends of mine and some girls when you gentlemen walked in. I just went on sitting there."

"Right, follow me," commanded the sergeant-major.

"With pleasure," replied Kamnitzer, sounding as if he meant it.

"We've got him, sir!" the sergeant-major reported to the adjutant. So complete was his triumph that he loftily ignored the scepticism written on a couple of faces, among

them those of the adjutant and Lance-Corporal Kamnitzer.
" Perhaps we can get to the bottom of this, now."

" Getting to the bottom of this " took the form of a semi-
official interrogation. This was limited to the basic facts
and took place in the battalion reading-room, known to
all and sundry as " the lending library."

" Well, out with it!" prompted the sergeant-major.

" Out with what?" Karl Kamnitzer looked eager to oblige
but slightly puzzled. " I don't know what you want me to
say."

Lieutenant von Strackmann subjected Kamnitzer to a gaze
of searching inquiry which was apparently lost on him.
The adjutant, meanwhile, stared out of the window. En-
countering nothing more interesting than a blank wall,
his eyes turned to the bookshelves, which were crammed
almost to bursting-point with an impressive array of books.
The " Democracy " section contained various works by Heuss,
memoirs by Churchill and de Gaulle, *Gedanken und Erin-
nerungen* by Bismarck, and the standard works *Great Germans,
German Generals* and *Soldiers of the German Nation*. All
gleamed with cleanliness, fresh as the day they emerged from
their wrappers, since the majority of the Federal Republic's
citizen-soldiers preferred such staple fare as Karl May and
Ludwig Ganghofer.

" So you were in the bar in question yesterday evening?"

" Yes, I told you that already," Kamnitzer's tone was
conversational, like that of a guest at a tea-party. " You
could have had a word with me last night if you'd wanted,
but you didn't seem particularly interested. You steamed
through the place so fast I hardly had time to salute."

The sergeant gave a suppressed snort and glanced warningly at the sergeant-major, but the sergeant-major pressed
on regardless, the flames of his enthusiasm fanned by an
encouraging nod from Lieutenant von Strackmann. Only the
adjutant preserved an attitude of indifference. He was
still examining the bookshelves, and had now reached

the fiction section entitled " World Literature ": *Gone with the Wind, The Count of Monte Cristo, Quo Vadis. . . .*

"Who was the man who ran for it?" asked the sergeant-major.

Kamnitzer's face betrayed utter astonishment. "You say someone ran for it?" He shook his head. "All I know is, someone made for the lavatory in a hurry just as you came in. Quite a natural reaction, I thought."

"Who was this man?" pursued the sergeant-major.

"How should I know? I didn't take any notice, but if you were so interested in him you could have asked him his name—or wouldn't he tell you?"

"Are you trying to make a fool of me?"

"I wouldn't dream of it, Sergeant-Major."

"That's enough of that!" Lieutenant von Strackmann said incisively. He pushed the sergeant-major to one side and stationed himself in front of Kamnitzer, who eyed him with a look of pleasurable anticipation. The adjutant had interrupted his inspection of the bookshelves and was now wearing a thoughtful expression.

"Well, come on!" von Strackmann demanded impatiently, convinced that the lance-corporal had merely misconstructed the situation. "Let's have some names!"

"You want the girls' names, sir?" Lance-Corporal Kamnitzer smiled. "I'm sorry, I only know their Christian names, and I can't give you their addresses."

"Fiddle-faddle!" shouted the lieutenant. "I want the name of this man!"

Kamnitzer inclined his head slightly as if to get a better view of von Strackmann, whom he appeared to consider worthy of close scrutiny. "Sir," he said with deliberation, "when I visit a place of that sort it's not because of the other chaps there. I'm not interested in them off duty—least of all on Saturday nights. I only go there for the girls."

"This is intolerable," declared the lieutenant.

"My attitude towards girls? Surely not, sir. It's quite natural, really."

" I meant, it's intolerable that you won't give a straight answer to my question."

" I don't see how I can make myself plainer, sir."

The adjutant considered it advisable to intervene at this stage. He drew his brother officer aside and presented him with a cogent résumé of the situation. The lance-corporal either knew nothing or declined to say if he did. Coercion seemed inopportune, and the C.O. was waiting for results.

Major Bornekamp was indeed awaiting the outcome of the interrogation, and awaiting it with impatience. He received the two officers standing beside his desk. Propelled forward by the adjutant, Lieutenant von Strackmann summarised the results of the investigation, striving for well-disciplined brevity.

In conclusion, he reported : " The man who attempted to evade arrest was a member of the armed forces—of this battalion, what's more—but his name could not be elicited."

" You've exhausted all possibilities?"

" In regard to Lance-Corporal Kamnitzer, sir?"

Bornekamp answered von Strackmann's query with a vigorous nod, and the lieutenant hastened to cover himself. " Well, sir, his attitude is rather mystifying. He's a hard nut to crack, if you'll pardon the expression. I just can't understand the man. He strikes me as secretive, obstinate and downright difficult. It may take a little time to convince him where his duty lies."

" I want concrete results," Bornekamp cut in, " and I want them quickly. To achieve this, I suggest we issue a sort of appeal to the men's conscience—to their sense of honour."

The adjutant gazed at the office ceiling—whether in veneration or resignation it was hard to tell—but Lieutenant von Strackmann gave an emphatic nod of approval, effectively conveying that he understood the C.O. as well as, and probably better than, any officer under his command.

" A proclamation to the battalion ! " Bornekamp dictated to the adjutant in sovereign tones. " One of my men has attempted to evade the regimental police picket instituted by me. This may have been understandable in view of the circumstances, but the man in question has been identified. I therefore call upon him to come forward voluntarily, and I shall regard his voluntary surrender as a mark of confidence in myself."

Major Bornekamp nodded contentedly. "That ought to do the trick, don't you agree, gentlemen?"

*

A quarter of an hour later a duo-tone Porsche 1600 drew up outside the gates of the Grenadier barracks. At the wheel sat Herbert Asch, who informed the sentry that he wished to speak to the Commanding Officer in his capacity as mayor.

This request was conveyed to the adjutant, who transmitted it to the C.O. without delay. "Any idea what the fellow wants?" Bornekamp asked thoughtfully.

"No, sir," said the adjutant. "It's never easy to tell what Herr Asch has in mind, but I imagine you'll have to see him."

"Of course I will," boomed the C.O. "You don't think he scares me, do you? I've had breakfast off better men than him before now. I even gave the Führer a piece of my mind once."

This episode was widely known, having been more than adequately publicised by Bornekamp himself. Apparently, the Russian campaign would have turned out quite differently if Hitler had taken his advice—which he didn't, as events had since proved. The adjutant retired at speed.

Major Bornekamp advanced a few steps to meet his visitor, extending his arm to deliver the iron handshake which the occasion warranted. Herbert Asch endured it without blinking an eyelid.

The C.O. had a certain weakness for the local mayor, who had always proved helpful and generous. Quite apart from that, Asch had a pronounced feeling for the soldierly way of life, as he proved—yet again—by reporting the arrival of a new consignment of Chablis and Meursault from France.

" I'll send you round a selection," promised Asch.

" Please do," said the C.O.—an entirely official request, since Bornekamp, besides being commander of the Grenadier battalion, was also senior member of the Mess and, as such, responsible for the welfare of his officers. Only the best was good enough for them, and Asch could be relied upon to produce it.

Even so, the C.O. could not entirely banish a sense of mistrust. There was virtually no one in his entourage whom he did not mistrust, and only concrete achievement could persuade him otherwise.

" But you're not going to tell me, Herr Asch," he said, with a mixture of geniality and wariness, " that the sole reason for your visit was to sell me some white Burgundy."

" Did I say it was?" Asch asked with a smile.

" Of course not." The C.O. laughed raucously. He was convinced that he knew Asch, and equally convinced that the man had only become mayor in order to feather his nest with greater facility. " You've got something on your mind, I can see."

Herbert Asch had come across a wide variety of officer-types in the course of his not unduly long life, but the Mayor appeared to be a new sub-species—a buzzard who sometimes endeavoured to coo like a dove. The Bundeswehr's pre-occupation with democracy had made him something of a quick-change artist, though a comparatively primitive exponent of the art.

" You see," Bornekamp went on, " it didn't escape me that you expressly announced yourself as ' Mayor' Asch." His eyes narrowed. " Well, let's have it!"

" I had a long and not altogether agreeable telephone conversation with the proprietor of the *La Paloma* this morning."

" Aha!" barked the C.O., lowering himself into his chair with an air of expectancy. " So that's the way the wind blows."

Herbert Asch selected a turn of phrase which neatly side-stepped the awkward fact that he had contacted the proprietor of the coffee-bar on his own initiative. The C.O. would infer that the owner of the "passion parlour" had contacted him, the mayor.

"It's simply ludicrous," Bornekamp continued loftily. "There's no point in wasting words on a chap who owns a knocking-shop like that. The place sounds like an utter pig-sty to me. You haven't come here to complain about my patrol, surely?"

"More than that, Major—I must request that you refrain from using such methods of surveillance in future."

"Come off it, Asch!" the C.O. exploded, contriving to mitigate the effect of his outburst with a confidential wink. "After all, it can't do you anything but good if I wipe out one of your competitors."

"It would be a very short-sighted policy, Major. Setting aside the fact that I'm not worried about competition from a pig-sty, as you call it, where do you propose to draw the line? What goes for the 'passion parlour' to-day may apply to my hotel to-morrow."

"I understand—you want to cover yourself."

"All I want to do is clarify the situation as far as possible. I've no wish to meddle in your affairs, I assure you. Why not return the favour? The barracks are your sphere of operations, places of entertainment in the town are ours— that is, unless you're prepared to see misunderstandings arise between the garrison and the civil population, or between us personally?"

"Of course not," the C.O. assured him. "But I'm puzzled, to say the least. I never thought you'd try to hold a pistol at my head in this way. Have you studied the implications carefully?"

"I merely want to avoid unnecessary complications."

Bornekamp scrutinised Asch like a military map. The mayor was not the sort of obstacle to be taken by frontal assault. The best course for the moment was a tactical detour. "Don't worry, Herr Asch, we'll arrange something."

" I'm delighted to hear it."

" Well, let's get down to business. What do you want, precisely?"

" Not want, Major," said Asch, " just a polite request— a suggestion, if you like : call off your dogs. Cease fire. Demonstrate your generosity and understanding. The civil population will be grateful to you, I'll see to that."

" Agreed," Bornekamp said with well-simulated heartiness, but his slightly narrowed eyes remained cool as ice. " I'll get him yet," he told himself. " I'll get him yet."

*

Corporal Streicher sat next to Grenadier Recht at lunch —purely by chance, or so it seemed. " I'm junior ranks' welfare representative for No. 3 Company, you know," he began. " I'm just reminding you so you'll know you can trust me."

" Fair enough," said Martin Recht. " You're welcome to the job as far as I'm concerned. It doesn't worry me."

Corporal Streicher thoughtfully dissected his veal cutlet. " Did you see the C.O.'s announcement, Martin?"

" I did," said Recht, chewing vigorously on his own cutlet, which was as tough as old boots, and telling himself—as one who was always ready to look on the bright side—that it was good for his teeth.

" The C.O. expects the man to come forward voluntarily."

" I know," said Recht, ruefully reflecting that if there was one veal cutlet in the dining-hall which was as tough as a rubber tyre, it was inevitable that it should turn up on his plate.

Things like that were always happening to him. The sweat-band in his helmet was made of corrugated iron, his denims let in water like a sieve and his boots might have been designed as instruments of torture, but he always did his best to be adaptable.

" You can talk freely to me," Corporal Streicher declared. His own cutlet spurted with juice and cut like butter.

The dining-hall was crowded. Its long tables were packed with soldiers, most of whom ate silently and with mechanical fervour. Many of them had eaten worse in the course of their short lives, but their main object was to fill their bellies, it didn't much matter what with.

"I'm not stupid, you know," said Corporal Streicher, pleasurably inhaling the scent of the dessert. This was vanilla pudding with raspberry syrup, humorously known in the battalion as "blood and matter." "I make it my business to keep my ears open, so I know you were in the *La Paloma* yesterday evening."

"In that case, either report me or shut up about it."

"I want to help you, that's all," Streicher explained in friendly tones. "I hope you appreciate that."

As though seeking inspiration, he gazed at the mural which dominated the dining-hall. It depicted a battle waged with lance, sword and mace, and had been commissioned from a patriotic artist of guaranteed academic pedigree—for a fee, so it was rumoured, of thirty thousand marks. The central figure was an anonymous super-hero with a bare chest of ochre hue and mountainous proportions which seemed to be attracting showers of spears like a lodestone. Beneath his firmly planted feet lay piles of corpses—symbolic, presumably, of the sacrifices which have to be made when democracy is in peril. Unfortunately, few of the munching soldiers lavished more than a single glance on this instructive tableau.

"Not much escapes me, you see," Corporal Streicher pursued. "I need hardly tell you that you can rely on me, and if you're wise you'll take advantage of the fact."

Martin Recht parried the remark. "Perhaps I will, if the occasion arises."

"You did go to the *La Paloma* with Kamnitzer, didn't you?" Streicher insisted.

"It's possible," said Recht. He pushed the remains of his lunch away, his untouched pudding included.

Corporal Streicher pulled the plate in front of him. Sweet things, he told himself, fortified his nerves and meant more to him than tobacco and alcohol. It was a matter of taste, of course, but he liked to subscribe to a set of definite principles.

"Martin," he went on, having devoured his second plate of pudding, "I appeal to your conscience. Be absolutely honest—you were in the *La Paloma* when the patrol arrived, weren't you?"

"It's none of your business," Recht advised moodily.

But Streicher was not to be deterred. "When Kamnitzer pushed you into the rear rank just before the patrol came round—that's when it dawned on me."

"Then keep your trap shut."

"You don't appreciate the situation," the corporal said mildly. "You've put me in an awkward position. We all make mistakes, I know, but we ought to own up to them. Don't you agree?"

"Is that what you insist on my doing?"

"I'm not insisting on anything, Martin. I only want what's best for you. I'm your friend, after all. Also, as I told you, I'm the company welfare representative. Please remember that. You see, under certain circumstances I should have to report what I know—it would be my duty to."

"I can see you doing it, too."

Corporal Streicher looked aggrieved. "I'll tell you this much, Martin. That chap Kamnitzer is not the right sort of company for you. He's always trying to involve you in his escapades, can't you see that? If you're not careful he'll get you into serious trouble one day—mutiny, even. Believe me, the only thing to do is own up voluntarily. The C.O. will take it into account."

"Are you trying to force me?"

"Who said anything about forcing? I'm just offering you some advice. If I were you I'd take it."

"Well," Martin Recht said resignedly, "it looks as though I've got no alternative."

Grenadier Martin Recht was in no hurry to lodge his

report—voluntarily or involuntarily. He decided to speak to Kamnitzer first, in the hope that he could assuage the welfare representative's over-sensitive conscience.

Karl Kamnitzer was nowhere to be found, however, having left barracks during the lunch-time break. He had been put on " stores detail," for the afternoon and had vanished into the town prematurely to avoid getting involved in duties of a more arduous nature. Ever since von Strackmann had been in charge of the company, training programmes and duty rosters had been subject to lightning alteration, and Kamnitzer had no taste for surprises of that kind. Being " on stores," he was not expected back before the end of working hours.

" Been to the C.S.M. yet?" Corporal Streicher demanded, when Recht returned to Room 13.

Recht shook his head and told him that Kirschke was not in the Company Office.

" Then you must go and look for him, Martin. I'll be happy to help you." Streicher seemed genuinely worried. " You must get this business over as quickly as possible. Don't wait too long—it'll make a bad impression."

Eventually, worn down by Streicher's tireless solicitude, Recht left the room and made reluctantly for the company office.

C.S.M. Kirschke, however, was enjoying his siesta. His usual custom before retiring to bed was to inform the office staff that he was going to change his trousers. In the normal way, this took about two hours.

After Martin Recht had waited patiently in the corridor for a considerable period, Kirschke actually emerged. He sauntered along to the office, yawning heartily, with Recht at his heels.

" You wanted to see me?"

" Yes, Sergeant-Major."

" Couldn't it wait till to-morrow?"

Kirschke sensed that Recht wanted to lodge a report, and reports of any kind were distasteful to him. If they had to be lodged at all, the right time to lodge them—in his opinion—was the morning. And the next morning was to-morrow morning.

However, Grenadier Recht would not be put off. After listening wearily to everything that Recht deemed it necessary to tell the C.S.M. closed his eyes as though urgently in need of further sleep. Then he said: "Not a bad yarn, Recht."

"It's the truth, Sergeant-Major."

"It's a load of poppycock," said Kirschke, with an un-abashed yawn which revealed his tonsils. "What's the matter with you—got a hero-complex, or are you just feeling suicidal? Whatever it is, I'm not the man to help you. Besides, you're in luck. My hearing's pretty poor sometimes —like now. I didn't hear a word you said."

"But what about the C.O.'s announcement?"

"God Almighty!" exclaimed Kirschke. "You're begin-ning to bore me. You look overtired. Get a good night's kip and come and see me to-morrow."

He was on the point of turning away when Lieutenant von Strackmann strode up, his rubber-soled boots thumping the ground like pile-drivers. He stared past Kirshke, glad of an excuse to ignore his salute, which would have done credit to a cripple, and focused his attention on the young grenadier's agitated face.

"What's going on here?" he demanded imperiously.

"Nothing special," C.S.M. Kirschke replied in casual tones. "This man's got a bee in his bonnet about something. Push off, Recht, and stop wasting my time."

"Stay here!" called Lieutenant von Strackmann.

Kirschke's manner was provocative in the extreme, he told himself, but there was something of a challenge in having been selected to deputise for a company commander who seemed—with Kirschke's help—to have turned his unit into an indisciplined rabble. "Well, what does he want?"

The C.S.M. shrugged his shoulders and abandoned Recht to the ever-eager lieutenant, whose first step was to transfer the proceedings from the corridor to his office. Kirschke

lolloped after him like an amiable St. Bernard, less from
curiosity than as a safety-measure.

Martin Recht repeated his voluntary statement from the
beginning, watched by von Strackmann as a hawk watches
its prey. When he had finished, the lieutenant exhaled
audibly and told him to wait in the outer office. Then he
drew a deep breath and looked at C.S.M. Kirschke as though
he were seeing him properly for the first time.

" This is absolutely outrageous ! " he said at length.

" A piece of stupidity, that's all."

" I was referring to your behaviour, Sergeant-Major. It's
incredible ! Scandalous ! Someone brings you information
which the C.O. is urgently waiting for—and what do you
do ? "

" The only thing to do, sir, under the circumstances—
wait and see. Never rush things, that's what the company
commander always says."

" Your conduct is alarming in the extreme ! " the lieutenant
exclaimed furiously. " It's little short of sabotage."

The C.S.M. remained imperturbable. " Orders are hardly
ever final. Even written orders often turn out to have been
superseded by the time they reach this office. If I were
you I'd start by asking Battalion whether the C.O.'s announcement still stands."

" But you're not me ! "

Kirschke's face registered no sign of retreat at this mis-
fortune, but Lieutenant von Strackmann was already on the
line to the C.O. " The man in question has been found, sir,"
he reported, not without pride. " His name is Recht, Martin.
Rank : grenadier."

Von Strackmann heard Bornekamp growl like an infuriated
dog. Then he barked : " For God's sake, man, don't
bother me with all that nonsense ! "

" But," von Strackmann stammered in bewilderment, " the
announcement which you personally . . ."

The C.O. cut him short. " It's been countermanded, and
I must request you not to trouble me with matters which

have already been settled. Concentrate on bringing your company up to scratch instead. You seem to have an unusual number of dead-beats in your outfit. Do something about them, Strackmann, and don't take too long about it!"

"Yes, sir!" cried the acting company commander, still bewildered but eager to demonstrate his zeal. However, a short, sharp click on the line told him that Bornekamp was no longer listening. It was like a slap in the face.

Von Strackmann was painfully embarrassed. He refrained from looking at his company sergeant-major, correctly gauging that the latter must be grinning like a Cheshire cat—and he could not have endured the sight.

"I'm surrounded by dead-beats!" he growled eventually, in a fair imitation of the C.O.'s voice. "Lay-abouts, the lot of them—but things are going to change round here. We'll lay on a field exercise, for a start."

*

Field exercises could not be held often enough. Such, at least, was the view of Major Bornekamp, who would have preferred every form of training—drill parades, P.T. and educational classes included—to be transferred to open country. However, he told himself, things had not yet reached that stage in the Bundeswehr, which still laboured under the regrettable influence of certain self-styled democratic elements.

Nevertheless, as an old war-time commander, he fundamentally approved of sudden practice alerts and unexpected field exercises. All that was required was a brief word to the adjutant, who merely reported that the company in question was moving off. Since Lieutenant von Strackmann had been deputising for its jaundice-stricken commander, No. 3 Company's itinerant habits had earned it the name of "The Hiking Club."

"What's the form this time?" inquired Sergeant-Major Rammler, a recognised expert in hand-to-hand combat training and one of No. 3 Company's warrant officer platoon commanders. "How long is this little tea-party likely to last?"

"How should I know?" Kirschke replied equably. "I'm only the C.S.M. here. Anyway, since when have you been interested in the duration of an exercise? I thought you were a glutton for that kind of punishment."

"I like stretching out somewhere else occasionally—not just in a slit-trench." Rammler laughed coarsely. "I'm on the track of something really big. The hottest bit of stuff for miles around—you've never seen such a pair of beauties, not even on the films. I tell you, if I'm back in barracks by muster parade it'll be a bloody marvel."

"You're otherwise engaged this evening, I take it," Kirschke said dryly.

"You're telling me! First the flicks, then a couple of quick ones, and then the Municipal Gardens. You'll probably still be out on the moors. Don't forget you're wearing full marching order."

"That doesn't mean we'll be out half the night. It may just be ballast."

Ballast it certainly was. The men were loaded like packmules with rifles, light machine-guns, bazookas, shovels, field-telephones, walkie-talkies, smoke-bombs, practice ammunition, water-bottles, iron-rations, ground-sheets, sleeping-bags, semaphore flags, ropes and snipers' rifles complete with telescopic sights. No motor transport had been laid on.

Lieutenant von Strackmann, too, turned out in battledress, but all he carried was a pistol, a map-case, a whistle and a packet of paper handkerchiefs. He naturally considered it a point of honour to conduct any field exercise in person.

Before giving the order to march off, von Strackmann went in search of C.S.M. Kirschke.

"You're coming too, of course!"

"I'm afraid not," Kirschke said stolidly.

"I'm afraid you are!" countered the lieutenant. "A little fresh air won't do you any harm."

"I wouldn't suffer, perhaps, but my work would."

"To-morrow's another day, Sergeant-Major."

"Precisely, to-morrow's the day when we've got to produce the clothing store inventory. It's due at Battalion first thing to-morrow morning and we've hardly started on it yet. All the same, if you say it can wait . . ."

"All right, get shot of it," von Strackmann said furiously, "but catch us up when you've finished."

"I may get there pretty late," Kirschke remarked amiably. "Very late, in fact—if at all."

Von Strackmann strode off, seething with rage, to rejoin his heavily laden company. The C.S.M. watched his superior's retreating form with a bland smile. Then, yawning heartily, he informed the company clerks that he was going to change his trousers again.

*

Lance-Corporal Karl Kamnitzer, meanwhile, was still in town on "stores · detail." The official object of his mission was a radio set priced at approximately two hundred marks and destined for the Junior Ranks' Canteen.

No one was better suited to such a task than Kamnitzer. He proposed to expend a mere half-hour on buying the radio and divide the remaining four or five hours between the cinema and the Café Asch—an enjoyable afternoon which he planned to follow up with a no less enjoyable evening.

The Café Asch was little frequented at this hour, a fact of which Kamnitzer could only approve. He stood in the entrance and surveyed the interior with a look of anticipation. But evidently failed to find what he was looking for.

Strutting up to the counter, he raised his hand to the peak of his cap in a salute of gaily exaggerated precision.

"Good afternoon, ma'am," he said brightly. "May one inquire the state of your esteemed health?"

The woman behind the counter, who was sorting cash slips, looked up and smiled when she recognised Kamnitzer. It was Frau Elisabeth Asch, who normally supervised the café while her husband looked after the hotel side when he was not involved in his mayoral duties. Asch was universally respected, but his wife was venerated—even by Kamnitzer.

"Disappointed it's only me?" she asked with a smile.

"Madame!" Kamnitzer protested gallantly, "I can't imagine a lovelier sight. If you were still a free woman I wouldn't leave you alone for an instant."

Elisabeth Asch smiled, and Kamnitzer was struck yet again by her charm. No man was worthy of her, he reflected, not even her husband.

"Take a seat over there on the right, near the window," she suggested. "You're bound to get the best service there."

Kanmitzer did as he was bidden, pulling his chair round so that he could survey the entire establishment. He noted with grateful satisfaction that Frau Elisabeth had opened the door to the kitchen. "A customer for you, Fräulein Wieder!" she called.

After a moment or two the object of his visit appeared. Helen Wieder was probably the most efficient member of the Asch staff and certainly the most decorative. She sauntered up to Kamnitzer's table, swinging her sturdy but pneumatic hips.

"There you are at last!" he cried rapturously.

"I know, don't tell me," Helen Wieder said, unimpressed. "You lie awake every night thinking about me. Well, I'm on duty now. What can I get you?"

"I leave it to you."

"I shouldn't—you might get nothing at all."

Helen Wieder studied Kamnitzer as if he were a troublesome insect. "It'd serve you right if I simply ignored you. Where were you yesterday evening? I thought we had a date."

"I was officially detained," Kamnitzer said. "By a regimental police picket. I realise how much I missed, believe me, but we can make up for it. What about this evening?"

"Sorry, I've already got a date this evening."

Kamnitzer looked outraged. "You must be joking! I don't think you understand what it means to be a forces' sweetheart. Are you trying to undermine our morale? I'm held up by a patrol for once, and you go making dates with other men. Do I know him?"

"Do you mind?" Helen Wieder said grimly. "We're not married—we're not even engaged, so I can make dates with anyone I choose. Come on, let's have your order."

"Are you trying to keep me on ice for a while, or is this the big brush-off?"

"One coffee, then," said Helen. "Anything else?"

"This evening, when you're finished here, I'll explain the whole thing to you. All right?"

"I'll be busy then," Helen said coldly, and flounced off.

"What do you mean, busy?" Kamnitzer called after her. "Who's been poaching on my preserves, that's what I'd like to know!"

*

The Grenadiers' field training area was comparatively easy to get to. It began a bare twenty minutes' march from the barrack gates and extended for some miles north of the town. It was an ideal mixture : bare scrub, dense woodland and low-lying marshes—no place for tanks but a veritable paradise for iron-willed infantrymen.

"This afternoon," Lieutenant von Stackmann told the company when they had reached the edge of the woods, "we'll start with some basic procedures like digging-in and camouflage."

He radiated martial comradeship, convincing almost everyone that he would have liked nothing better than to set an example by attacking the ground himself, entrenching tool in hand.

First, however, he summoned the platoon commanders together. There were three of them : two downy-cheeked subalterns and Sergeant-Major Fritz Rammler, the battle-scarred expert on hand-to-hand combat.

"Gentlemen," the lieutenant said, "a company is a unit. It's like a human body, each organ of which must function efficiently. If they don't, the body is sick. Transferring the analogy to this company, we might possibly speak of soft, flabby or destructive elements. I don't say there are any, but I say that, if there are, they must be spotted and dealt with! This exercise is part of the cure. Any questions, gentlemen?"

Although the inquiry was meant to be purely rhetorical, it evoked a response, surprisingly enough, from Sergeant-Major Rammler.

The lieutenant nodded, not over-graciously, to indicate that Rammler had permission to speak. Rammler spoke: " Is the exercise likely to last very long, sir?"

Von Strackmann looked disagreeably surprised. He had not expected an indisciplined interjection of this sort from anyone, let alone Rammler. He was saddened by the thought that even a reliable instructor like the sergeant-major was subject to human failings and symptoms of flabbiness. The unit certainly needed to be brought up to scratch—and quickly, too, as the C.O. had so rightly said.

" The exercise will last for as long as I deem it necessary," the lieutenant replied coldly. He might just as well have said " for an indefinable period," which effectively dashed Rammler's hopes of an enjoyable night on the tiles.

Removing the members of his platoon from the gaze of Lieutenant von Strackmann, Rammler deployed them over a wide area and shooed them into the nearest patch of woods. From there he pushed on in the direction of a signalman's cabin on the railway line that skirted the heath. A few hundred yards short of his destination, he stationed himself in the middle of his platoon, legs apart and hands on hips. His expression seemed genial and his voice gentle as that of a favourite uncle about to tell a fairy-tale, but all he said was: " Nuclear attack."

He had no need to say more. These two words meant: " Dig in!", and thirty entrenching tools swung into action. Rammler's platoon would be fully occupied for the next half-hour at least.

Rammler himself stalked through his human moles and plunged into the undergrowth as though he intended to check their progress from a hidden vantage-point, but he emerged on the other side and made for the signalman's cabin. There was nothing for it but to telephone his new discovery, warn her that he might be late and beg her to be patient.

*

Helen Wieder served Karl Kamnitzer with his coffee, slamming the crockery down in front of him as though he had already been convicted of evading payment.

"I'm the easiest person in the world to get on with," Kamnitzer ventured. "It's just that I'm always being misunderstood."

"Misunderstood? Seen through, you mean—and not before time, either."

"I'm the soul of gallantry," Kamnitzer pursued. "I desert my platoon in broad daylight, just for you, and what thanks do I get?"

Helen Wieder retired, but not before emitting a scornful laugh. Kamnitzer eyed her rear view with rapture. He could have watched her for hours on end, but he was not permitted to.

"I trust you're not trying to keep my staff from their work," came an amused voice from behind him. He turned and saw Herbert Asch.

The two men had met some time before, the day Karl Kamnitzer had discovered Helen Wieder, in fact, though "discovered" was not quite the right word. He felt like a ship-wrecked mariner who had been cast ashore on some palm-fringed, silver-shored island of delight. One look, and he had known that she was the girl for him—and then Herbert Asch had materialised, just as he did now.

Asch sat down opposite him, as he had done before, and smiled. "Well, how's the market doing?" he asked, meaning the Grenadier barracks, which seemed to hold a certain degree of interest for him.

"Alarums and excursions over a regimental police picket,"

Kamnitzer volunteered. "A false alarm, probably. You know what a fuss they make over things in our mob, but the R.P.s behaved like bulls in a china shop. It was 08.15 all over again, and even our revered C.O. gets worried about that sort of thing."

"It almost sounds as though you were there," Asch said intently.

"Of course I was. Trust me to be in the thick of it. I haven't seen a stupider bunch of faces for a long time."

"Tell me more," demanded Asch, but Kamnitzer's attention was distracted by the appearance of Frau Elisabeth.

"There's a 'phone call for Fräulein Wieder," she said. "Isn't she with you?"

"No, worse luck," said Kamnitzer. "She's avoiding me like the plague, and she won't let me explain."

"I'm sorry," Frau Elisabeth said sympathetically. "The 'phone call sounds urgent, though. It's a Herr Rammler."

Kamnitzer's eyebrows shot up. "Who?" he asked.

"Rammler—a sergeant-major, so he says."

"Leave him to me!" said Kamnitzer cheerfully.

He hurried over to the counter, picked up the receiver and said briskly: "Yes, what can I do for you?"

He identified the answering voice readily enough, though it lacked its usual harsh imperious note of parade-ground superiority. "May I speak to Fräulein Wieder, please?" it cooed into Kamnitzer's ear.

"Sorry," said Kamnitzer, grinning, "completely out of the question at the moment. What do you want with her?"

Sergeant-Major Rammler seemed to hesitate. He breathed heavily. Eventually he said: "I have an engagement with Fräulein Wieder this evening, but I probably won't be there at the time we agreed—I'll be on duty. Would you be kind enough to tell her?"

"I beg your pardon!" Kamnitzer exclaimed in a husky, assumed voice. "We're not a call-girl establishment here, you know. This is a reputable house, and we resent being used like a brothel."

"Who am I speaking to?" demanded Rammler, suddenly

hoarse with rage. "Your voice sounds familiar. I know you, don't I? Who are you?"

"You know what you can do?" Kamnitzer inquired with relish. "You can take a running jump at yourself, with my compliments."

With that, he slammed the receiver back on its hook, confident that he had won a battle but forgetting that it takes more than one battle to win a war.

*

Sergeant-Major Rammler reeled out of the signalman's cabin like a man who has just been hit over the head with a club. Feeling in need of moral support, he reached for his hip-flask.

Almost mechanically, he elbowed his way back through the undergrowth to his platoon. The men were still digging, supervised by their section commanders.

Rammler stationed himself near by and studied them like an animal trainer watching his charges go through their paces. He felt embittered, and started to ask himself who was to blame.

The conclusion he reached was not devoid of a certain logic : the guilty party was the man responsible for this performance—some flabby individual who had landed the company, i.e., his superior, of a promising evening.

But Rammler's logic did not stop there. If it weren't for this wet fish, this " destructive element," he reasoned shrewdly, they wouldn't be here now. If they weren't here, he would be in town, and if he were in town he would have been spared that embarrassing telephone call. Consequently, if someone had done his best to make mincemeat of him on the 'phone, only one person was to blame, and that was the man he was going to track down.

"Excuse me, Sergeant-Major, but is it advisable to take the direction of the wind into account when siting a slit trench—even when there's no wind?"

Rammler turned on the questioner in surprise, certain

that he was being got at. Then he saw that it was Corporal
Streicher, and the sight was as welcome as a glass of beer
in a heat-wave.

"Streicher," he said, not unkindly, "a rectangular slit
trench should always be sited so that the short side faces
the wind. That's the rule. But when there's no wind, like
now, you can dig whichever way round you like, as far as I'm
concerned."

"All I wanted to do," said the corporal, "was to take
into account the direction of the wind normally prevailing
in this area at this time of year. Even though there's no
wind at the moment, one might spring up at any moment.
Isn't that right, Sergeant-Major?"

"Dead right," Rammler agreed, nodding approvingly.

"Right," said Streicher, addressing his section. "Short
side facing east—north-east, to be more exact."

One or two of the men near by stopped digging and
seized the opportunity for a short breather. Fortunately
for them, Rammler was not watching. He drew Streicher
to one side and began to pace up and down with him.

"Streicher," he said in what, for him, were honeyed
tones, "you're the company welfare representative, and you're
quite a useful soldier as well. If it was up to me, you'd
have your third stripe by now. Tell me quite frankly: have
you any idea why this jaunt was arranged?"

"It's possible, Sergeant-Major." Streicher studiously hesitated for a moment before registering eagerness to respond
to the confidence reposed in him. "I can't say for certain,
of course, but I've got a theory—only a theory, mind you."

"All right, all right, Streicher," Rammler said. "Let's have
it."

Streicher launched into an account of the facts as he
knew them: the raid by the picket, the chase through the
streets, the rope ladder, the investigation and its possible
consequences. The man in question was ready to own up,
but it was probably too late by that time.

"Who?" Rammler asked.

Corporal Streicher pointed to a towering mole-hill some

yards away. The man behind it was throwing up earth like a machine, rhythmically, vigorously and with astonishing regularity—pile upon pile of it. It might have been the work of a mechanical excavator.

Rammler walked over and peered into the trench. Grenadier Martin Recht's grimy face peered back, glistening with sweat.

"You there!" called Rammler, after subjecting Recht to intense scrutiny. "You're reassigned to tree-sniping."

Recht knew what that meant. Springing out of the weapon-pit like a cork from a bottle he seized a rifle with telescopic sights and climbed the nearest large tree. He scrambled through the branches, monkey-like, until he reached the top, where he tried simultaneously to clear a field of fire and camouflage himself. Below, he could feel the sergeant-major's searchlight gaze focused on him.

"That's the wrong tree," Rammler called mildly.

Martin Recht clambered down and doubled to the next tree, but no sooner had he reached the top than he again heard Sergeant-Major Rammler's voice, still comparatively mild, calling: "Not enough field of fire."

Rammler's verdict on the next tree was: "Not enough cover," and on the fourth: "Too much cover and hardly any field of fire." His voice had taken on a slight edge.

It was not until he reached the summit of the fifth tree, gasping for breath and drenched with sweat, that Recht formed some idea of what the sergeant-major was trying to do. He clung to the bough on which he was squatting with trembling hands. The branches swam before his eyes like a barbed wire entanglement.

"What are you doing up there, having a kip?" Rammler called in tones of suppressed fury. "A lively lad like you! Come on, come on, don't tell me you're tired! Next tree!"

It struck Recht with staggering clarity that there must be dozens of trees in a wood of that size.

*

The Café Asch was full by this time, its tables crowded with chattering, cake-gorging, coffee-swilling customers.

" I think you said you were present when the patrol raided the *La Paloma*, Herr Kamnitzer?" Herbert Asch put the question with the innocuous expression of a dentist approaching a patient.

Kamnitzer looked up from his gargantuan slice of cherry flan in some surprise. He had accepted the proprietor's invitation all the more readily because it meant that Helen Wieder had to serve him, but she continued to treat him like part of the furniture.

" I said I was there when the patrol arrived," Kamnitzer replied through a mouthful of flan, " but I didn't say anything about the *La Paloma*. Who told you that, Herr Asch?"

" This Martin Recht—what sort of chap is he?"

Kamnitzer choked violently. " Who else knows?" he spluttered. " Just you, or is it all over town? If it is, I might as well pack my bags."

At this point a man in a shabby civilian suit came up. Asch greeted him warmly and introduced him to Kamnitzer as Herr Ahlers. Kamnitzer took him for a sales representative, possibly in washing-machines.

" Herr Kamnitzer," Asch said, inclining his body slightly in Ahlers's direction, " seems to know your friend Martin Recht fairly well."

Kamnitzer nodded. " He sleeps in the bunk over mine."

" Are you a friend of his?" asked Ahlers.

" Friend's a big word. You might call him a mucker of mine, but perhaps that doesn't go far enough."

" The choice of words doesn't matter," Ahlers said amiably. " You seem to like him, that's the main thing. May I ask why?"

Kamnitzer glanced discreetly at Asch, who nodded as if to imply that frankness was in order.

" Sometimes," said Kamnitzer, " Martin's like one of the

Babes in the Wood—you know, always getting lost and whistling to keep his spirits up. I suppose there are a lot of people like him in the world—many more than you'd suspect, anyway."

" He's not just a sheep?"

" No, far from it, though he may look like one sometimes. That's why he's such a challenge to the sheep-dogs—and there are plenty of them in the army."

Ahlers leant forward a little. " You're not fond of soldiering, I gather?"

Karl Kamnitzer hesitated. Then, reflecting that the man was in civilian clothes and seemed to be a friend of Asch, he decided to treat him as a civilian. " Give people a chance to ride over other people rough-shod or lead them up the garden path, and most of them will, if it's required or expected of them. If you go one better, and persuade them that they're doing it for the sake of an ideal—patriotism, liberty—it doesn't matter what—then they'll really put their backs into it. People ought to realise that—and that's just where Martin Recht falls down."

" I'd like you to introduce me to Martin Recht sometime, Herr Kamnitzer," said Asch. " Invite him here—this evening, if you like."

" You're up to something, aren't you?" Kamnitzer said, intrigued.

Asch smiled. " If I am, it's nothing that will hurt Recht."

" Then I'm all for it," Kamnitzer declared, and wolfed the rest of his flan.

*

Major Bornekamp usually lingered in the battalion offices for a considerable time after the end of duty hours. He leafed through files, studied plans and directives, nosed through the contents of his underlings' desks and made surprise checks by telephone. The adjutant stood by, mute for the most part, like a well-trained sheep-dog.

The Major's appetite for work was generally construed

as an unwearying love of efficeincy. Those who knew him better, however, realised that he was prompted by quite another motive : a straightforward reluctance to go home, which was entirely comprehensible to anyone who knew the Mayor's wife.

"Call my house," Bornekamp commanded the adjutant.

"Yes, sir," said the latter. He needed no telling what to say—it was always the same : the Major was still working and didn't know when he would be through.

Bornekamp betook himself to the outer office. This was a favourite haunt of his because it was where the civilian typists worked, and he derived immense pleasure from teasing them in a robust, virile way.

"What—not gone home yet?" he boomed jovially. "You must have a crush on me!"

The object of his attentions, a spinster of forty, essayed a blush, but without success. She had already had ample opportunity to get to know the C.O. In her eyes, Bornekamp was a perfect cavalier in the old tradition, and it was almost a pleasure to do overtime for him.

"So you can't tear yourself away from me, eh, beloved?" bellowed the Major, assuming what he imagined were the tones of a Lothario. "Go on like this, and I may yield to temptation!"

The adjutant smiled indulgently. He read Bornekamp like a book, every page of which was identical. As far as these women were concerned, the Major might chaff them heartily, but he would never do more than that—not, at any rate, in his official domain.

"I'm still waiting for a report from No. 3 Company," the secretary explained. "It's already completed, C.S.M. Kirschke says, but it's still got to be signed by the Company Commander."

Cocking an eye at the vast time-table which filled one wall of the office, Bornekamp saw that the blue card referring to No. 3 Company's activities that day had been criss-crossed with red diagonals. This signified that duties in camp had been replaced by external duties.

"That's news to me," Bornekamp said to the adjutant. "Why wasn't I informed?"

The C.O.'s genial, jocular tone had abruptly become cold and incisive. The adjutant did his utmost to avoid an internal collision by drawing attention to a standing rule which the C.O. himself had laid down. Its gist was that field exercises were to be welcomed, and that to alter the training schedule accordingly required no express approval from Battalion, only a routine report to the adjutant.

"But not in this case!" Bornekamp cried furiously. "I made it very clear that I regarded a certain matter as closed. I don't like arbitrary behaviour. It encourages people to think that they can start special operations in my command, without a by-your-leave."

"In that case, sir," the adjutant said humbly, "there must have been some misunderstanding on Lieutenant von Strackmann's part."

"Kindly ensure that he packs up his picnic immediately. He's to report to me in the Mess as soon as he gets back."

The adjutant transmitted this order verbatim to Kirschke, who listened delightedly to the expressions "pack up," "picnic" and "immediately." Then he mounted the Company bicycle and pedalled off, at considerable speed, into the country.

He found Lieutenant von Strackmann in a small birch-wood, discoursing to a group of N.C.O.s on the methods to be adopted when bivouacking in trees in an emergency. He had just moved on to the problem of how to live off roots and weeds when cut off from supplies, when he caught sight of Kirschke's pedalling figure.

"Ah, there you are at last," he called. "You can join No. 3 Platoon."

"For the march back to barracks?" Kirschke inquired, grinning.

"That mayn't be until to-morrow morning," the lieutenant said with authority.

"Within the next quarter of an hour at latest," Kirschke

gently corrected him. "Orders from Battalion. You're to pack up this picnic immediately."

Not without an effort, Lieutenant von Strackmann gave a perfect display of self-control. For almost ten seconds he stood there, rigid and unspeaking. Then he drew a deep breath, stared past Kirschke, and ordered: "Cease operations!"

When this order reached No. 3 Platoon—by runner—Sergeant-Major Rammler appeared to be standing by himself on the edge of the wood. His men were all up trees, and in the tallest of them cowered Grenadier Martin Recht, clinging precariously to a swaying branch.

A glance at his watch told Rammler that it was already too late for him to keep his date, but he had not yet taught Recht the lesson which, in his opinion, he so richly deserved.

"Close on me!" he yelled up at the trees.

While the platoon members were scrambling down and gathering round him in open formation, Rammler had been devising a brief final manœuvre. Time was short, but the terrain was favourable and a small river flowed invitingly close at hand.

"Enemy has occupied edge of wood," Rammler announced. "Platoon will advance in nor'-nor'-westerly direction to relieve units at present engaged. Speed essential!"

There was nothing wrong with this move, tactically speaking, but it meant that the platoon had to advance, screened from the eyes of an imaginary enemy by trees and bushes, straight across the river—and the sweat-soaked Martin Recht had been singled out for the special privilege of carrying a light machine-gun.

Obediently, the platoon trotted through the water, knee-deep at first, then up to their chests. Martin Recht gasped. He was a non-swimmer, and panic flickered in his eyes.

"Come on," Rammler exhorted him from the bank. "Not scared of a little water, are you?"

It was Rammler's last enjoyable moment of the day, how-

ever. A minute later Lieutenant von Strackmann appeared.
"You're holding us all up!" he yelled at Rammler.
Unpleasant visions of the C.O. waiting for him in the Mess
flitted through his head. "The exercise is over—didn't you
understand my order? No more detours, Sergeant-Major!"

Rammler stood stiffly to attention until the lieutenant had
departed. Then he glowered at Martin Recht, up to his
neck in water but still on his feet. "The things I have to
put up with," he growled to himself "—and all because
of a little sod like that!"

Back in barracks, Rammler went straight to C.S.M. Kirschke's
room. "That chap Recht is a shit of the first order," he
announced.

"Could be," said Kirschke. "There are plenty around."

"He needs a dose of extra guard duty—to-night, what's
more."

"No reason why not," Kirschke said equably. "But
to-night's guard is already detailed."

Rammler refused to give in. He demanded, he requested,
he even pleaded. In the end he appealed to Kirschke as a
brother warrant officer, and Kirschke, whose prime concern
was a quiet life, finally consented. "All right, if you're so
mad keen."

Grenadier Martin Recht, however, was not to be found.
Apparently he had gone into town as soon as the field
exercise was over.

"That's that, then," said Kirschke.

"He's got to be found at once!" Rammler insisted. "He
can't just piss off like that!"

"Why not?" asked Kirschke in mild amusement. "You
don't expect him to ask your permission every time he goes
off duty, do you?"

Rammler, who felt as though he were floundering helplessly in a sea of mud, experienced a vague sense of betrayal.
Even the warrant officers' trade union seemed to have
stopped functioning.

"This lousy outfit!" he mumbled resentfully. "Just a lot of dead-beats, that's all they are."

So saying he retired to his room, where he changed his shirt, sprayed himself with eau-de-cologne and smeared his hair liberally with brilliantine. A glance in the mirror reassured him that he was a fine, upstanding figure of a man, which raised his spirits. To raise them still further, he treated himself to a small tot of schnapps (brand name; Strong Man's Milk) in his tooth-mug.

Thus stimulated, he marched off into town at high speed and steered straight for the Café Asch. On arrival he asked in ringing tones for Helen Wieder, only to be informed politely by the woman behind the counter that Fräulein Wieder had already left—with a soldier.

Rammler gave a snort of indignation. "Who's in charge of this knocking-shop?" he inquired belligerently.

The woman behind the counter, who happened to be Elisabeth Asch, retained her good humour. She gestured invitingly towards a table near the window, where two men in civilian clothes were sitting, namely Herbert Asch and Klaus Ahlers. Their laughter sounded downright provocative to Rammler, who could not dismiss the possibility that they were laughing at him.

Resolutely, he marched across to them. He diagnosed them as two typically frivolous civilians, devoid of martial sternness, dignity and poise. Not, of course, that he was fundamentally ill-disposed towards the civil population, but his world was the barrack-room world—what was more, the barrack-room world of to-morrow, as he envisaged it, rooted in the traditions and experiences of yesterday.

"What can we do for you?" asked one of the civilians.

"Who," Rammler demanded, "is in charge here?"

"In charge of what?" asked Herbert Asch.

"That telephone, for one thing." Rammler's expression was a blend of disdain and condescension, as befitted a soldier confronted by a lounge-lizard.

The lounge-lizard had the effrontery to smile. "What's the trouble exactly?" he asked.

" When I rang this place earlier, some objectionable bastard answered."

" It's quite possible," Asch agreed. " The telephone is a much-abused instrument."

" Don't try to dodge the issue!" Rammler thundered. The amused smile on the other man's face gave way to a hearty laugh, which rang provocatively in Rammler's ears. "Who the hell are you, anyway?" he demanded rudely, as the café transformed itself under his irate gaze into an extension of the barrack square. It was his conviction that the town lived off the garrison, and it didn't live badly. A little gratitude was the least that could be expected. " I don't like your attitude," he pursued grimly.

" I can't say how my attitude strikes you," Asch said, still unruffled, " but I'll gladly tell you who I am. Among other things, I'm the owner of this establishment."

" There you are, then!" Rammler said triumphantly, determined not to be impressed by such a display of self-confidence on the part of a civilian. " That means you're responsible for the misuse of your telephone, blast you!"

" Perhaps you could do with a black coffee," Asch suggested. " Be my guest, if you're agreeable."

Rammler haughtily dismissed the suggestion. " What do you take me for—a sponger?"

" I don't know what you take me for," Klaus Ahlers mused, " but you're probably wrong. It's easy enough to make a mistake."

" You keep out of this. I wasn't talking to you."

" But I'm talking to you," said Ahlers. " It may interest you to know that I'm an air force captain."

Rammler was nonplussed for a moment, but an expert on unarmed combat is always prepared for tricky counter-moves on the part of an opponent. " Anyone can say that," he parried.

" Would you care to see my identity card?" Ahlers inquired affably.

Rammler hesitated again, this time for an appreciable span. After about five seconds he delivered what he conceived to be a short rabbit punch. "This has got nothing to do with you. I'm speaking to the owner of this dump, so there's no need for you to interfere. All I'm interested in is this telephone call. Besides, I'm here as a private individual."

"I'm glad to hear that," said Herbert Asch, "but I suggest you behave accordingly."

"I want to know who I was speaking to on the 'phone!" Rammler persisted. "I'll find the bloke if it's the last thing I do."

*

"Sit down," said Major Bornekamp. "It's about time I told you a few home truths."

This invitation was addressed to Lieutenant von Strackmann. The C.O. studied him closely, not without deriving mild satisfaction from his air of eager endeavour and willing deference.

"If I hadn't sent for you, Strackmann, what would you have been doing at this hour?"

"Working, sir."

"And when you had finished your work?"

"There's always something to do, sir."

Bornekamp imbibed some of the ruby-red contents of his glass. It was Turk's Blood, equal parts of native German champagne and French red wine. "Have you got a girl-friend, von Strackmann?" he asked.

Von Strackmann repudiated the idea almost as if he were dismissing an unworthy suspicion. "No time for that sort of thing, sir. I hardly ever get out of barracks."

"My dear young friend," the C.O. said didactically, "there are some things one simply has to make time for, like shaving or personal hygiene. And there are certain young officers' activities which can be classified as part of personal hygiene."

Lieutenant von Strackmann tried to look amused. Everyone knew that when the C.O. indulged in turns of phrase like these it was advisable to humour him.

Having thus created what he felt to be a pleasant atmosphere of confidence, Bornekamp went so far as to pour the young officer a glass of Turk's Blood.

" I want to be able to rely on my officers," he continued, " especially those who work closely with me, like company commanders."

Von Strackmann nodded with alacrity. He was passionately eager to prove himself, and looked up to experienced superiors with quasi-religious fervour.

" Our world," said the C.O., " is a world apart. We must avoid letting outsiders exert an influence on our way of life. They must be given no occasion to do so."

This struck him as a peculiarly subtle piece of phrasing. What he really meant was : civilians, mayors included, have got no control over what we do here. Even so, they can't simply be slapped down when they dare to interfere with us. We just give them a friendly grin and leave it at that. No other visible reaction of any kind—let alone a hastily organised field exercise.

" Do we understand one another, Strackmann?"

" Yes, sir," the lieutenant assured him eagerly.

" Good," said Bornekamp. " Carry on like that, my dear chap, and you'll find yourself something more than an acting company commander in the near future."

Von Strackmann glowed, less with Turk's Blood than with pride. " Thank you, sir!"

" Would you do me a personal favour?" Bornekamp asked, almost confidentially.

" Name it, sir!"

" Go and see my wife—this evening if possible, and take a bottle of cognac with you. I promised her one. Give her my regards and tell her I shan't be home until very late, if at all. I have several things to check on and a stack of papers to look through. All right? Then I won't detain you any longer."

*

Sergeant-Major Rammler crouched over his table in the Café Asch like an ornamental lion. He had commandeered a seat where he could watch the entrance and was lying in wait for Helen Wieder.

"You're probably wasting your time," Elisabeth Asch told him. "It's highly unlikely that Fräulein Wieder will be back to-night."

"But it's possible, isn't it?"

"It's not out of the question, certainly, but you may have to wait a very long time."

"I'll wait," Rammler said with dour determination. "I've got time, and I don't give up easily—anyone'll tell you that. Bring me a double, and make sure it's the brand I like."

"I'll pass your order on," said Frau Asch, gladly leaving her unwelcome guest to his own devices.

Rammler stared suspiciously at the fashionable café's smart décor until a waitress brought him his double dose of Strong Man's Milk. He inspected her carefully. She did not rate comparison with Helen Wieder in any respect, and was thus incapable of dispelling his mood of exasperation.

And then, in the doorway, he caught sight of a feminine apparition who seemed to be well worth a second look. The girl, who had a lithe, athletic figure, stood there, taut as a steel spring, surveying the café like a sprinter about to perform on a cinder track.

She strode across the room, apparently making straight for Rammler, and sat down at the next table. She was a chic little thing, he noted expertly, with plenty of spirit and a smart turn-out that would have done credit to a soldier.

Blithely ignoring the fact that the table next to him was the only free table in the café, Rammler construed her proximity as an invitation to dance.

"Well, what about it?" he asked, leaning forward confidentially.

Everything about the girl was cool and bright: her hair, her eyes and her dress. Her voice was no exception. "Have we met?" she inquired.

"We have now," Rammler said adventurously. In the first place, the girl appealed to him, and in the second place, that artful bitch Helen Wieder deserved a lesson. He'd show her she wasn't the only pebble on the beach!

"Will you come to my table, or shall I sit with you?"

"Neither," said a male voice over Rammler's shoulder. "Don't bother, friend—the lady already has a date."

Rammler looked round indignantly to see a slim man of medium height dressed in civilian clothes. "My name's Vossler," he said with a cheerful smile.

"It could be Adenauer, for all I care. I was speaking to this young lady, not you."

"My answer to that," said the girl in tones of relief, " is : get lost."

It was an unmistakable brush-off, and a man with less self-confidence would have accepted it as such—but not Rammler. He was slightly taken aback but far from discouraged.

Observing the couple at the next table with some resentment, he noted that she called him "Viktor" and he called her "Gerty"—presumably a shortening of Gertrud—and that they behaved like a couple of turtle-doves. Wresting his exasperated gaze away from them he focused it on the counter, and what he saw there exasperated him still further.

Grenadier Martin Recht was standing there—Recht, the very person responsible for his disappointing day. He had already taught him a preliminary lesson, but the boy was looking cheerful enough. He chatted casually to the woman behind the counter until, almost as though he felt Rammler's gaze on him, he glanced in the sergeant-major's direction. Rammler drew himself up in his seat to ensure that Recht caught sight of him, and the grenadier, with a sudden start, saluted in a most irregular manner.

Rammler did not deign to return the compliment. Instead, he waggled the index finger of his right hand, and Recht moved obediently in his platoon commander's direction.

"What do you think you're doing here?" demanded Rammler.

Realising that there was no satisfactory answer to this sort of question, Recht remained mutely at attention, his eyes pleading for at least a modicum of human decency.

"I'll tell you what you're doing," Rammler pursued ruthlessly. "Skiving, when you're supposed to be on guard duty."

"I had no idea . . ."

Rammler glowered at the grenadier, still casting around for the best course to adopt.

At this point the man in the civilian suit at the next table had the effrontery to intervene for a second time. He interrupted his billing and cooing, stood up and walked over to Recht. "Hello!" he exclaimed. "Who have we got here? It's last night's visitor, isn't it?"

"Hello, sir," said Recht, feeling immeasurably relieved. "How are you?"

"Fine," said Warrant Officer Vossler. "I'm enjoying an evening out. You ought to do the same—don't let anyone put you off."

Recht smiled gratefully at Vossler and clasped his outstretched hand like a drowning man clutching a life-line. "Won't you join us, Herr Recht?" Vossler asked cordially. "Fräulein Ballhaus and I would be delighted."

"Do you mind!" said Rammler with barely suppressed fury. "Who do you think you are, sticking your nose in like this? My conversation's got damn-all to do with you."

"Keep your hair on, chum." Vossler regarded Rammler placidly. "You've got the wrong end of the stick: you're the one who's barging in. I shouldn't, unless you want to make an exhibition of yourself."

"What do you mean—'chum'!" shouted Rammler. "I'm talking to one of my men on an official matter. I won't tolerate any interference!"

Viktor Vossler placed one arm protectively round Martin Recht's shoulders, and his voice took on the quiet but incisive tones of a muted violin. "Calm down, my friend. Take a few deep breaths and count up to ten—and don't forget the old soldier's motto: things are never as bad as they seem."

"Cut it out!" Rammler shouted irascibly, his blood pressure rising several points as he registered the impudent smile on "Gerty's" face. "I won't be talked to like that, do you hear!"

At this point, Herbert Asch bore down on the group, unerring as a hawk, and stationed himself between the adversaries like a referee. "Do you mind turning the volume down a bit, gentlemen?" he asked. "This is a café, not a barracks."

"Maybe," thundered Rammler, "but I'm dealing with an official matter. It's got nothing to do with anyone except Grenadier Recht and me."

"You're mistaken," Asch said calmly. "This is my sphere of jurisdiction, not yours."

Martin Recht stood there like a forlorn sheep in a deserted field. He could hear the wolves howling all round him, but somehow he felt safe.

"Listen, you!" Rammler hissed at Asch. "I'm warning you—don't stick your nose into army business."

"Better let me handle this," Vossler suggested. "It's far easier to settle these things if you talk the same language."

"Quite unnecessary," said Asch. "I'm in charge here, no one else. That being so, Herr Rammler, I must regretfully ask you to stop annoying my customers and leave at once."

"You're not serious!" Rammler eyed Asch incredulously. "You're not chucking me out?"

"Call it what you like."

"All right, I'm going," Rammler said menacingly. "But you'll regret this, I promise you!"

He departed without paying his bill, Asch ordered it to be debited to his personal account as running expenses, and then devoted himself to Martin Recht. He invited the slightly bemused grenadier to his private quarters, partly so that Recht could renew his acquaintanceship with Captain Ahlers, and partly so as to leave Vossler and his girl-friend in peace.

Sergeant-Major Rammler, meanwhile, strode through the swing doors determined to endure his heavy lot with dignity. He felt himself to be the victim of malicious and uncomprehending civilians, of fellow-N.C.O.s without any sense of solidarity, and of women who lacked all appreciation of real values.

Smiling contemptuously, he started down the stairs that led to the street, then stopped as though rooted to the spot. Helen Wieder was on her way up, accompanied by Karl Kamnitzer.

"Good evening, Sergeant-Major!" called Kamnitzer. "Not leaving, are you?"

"You!" the sergeant-major croaked. "You're the one I spoke to on the 'phone!"

"Am I?" Kamnitzer asked, eyes twinkling. "When was that? And if it was, did you enjoy it?"

Helen Wieder pushed past Rammler. "Fine behaviour, I must say," she remarked in quiet but challenging tones, "shooting a big line with a girl and then standing her up. I'm not used to that sort of thing, I can tell you."

Rammler felt that he had been abruptly forced on to the defensive. Instead of venting a flood of accusations, as he had meant to, he was now being called upon to justify himself. Helen Wieder evidently doubted his goodwill, his tried and proven reputation for reliability.

"But I sent my apologies," he said. "I was held up by work—an unexpected field exercise."

Helen Wieder stared at him incredulously, and Rammler turned, with a mixture of reproach and entreaty, to Kamnitzer. "Didn't you tell Fräulein Wieder that?"

"Me? Why should I have?"

"We talked to each other on the 'phone, for God's sake!"

"Did we?" Kamnitzer looked mightily surprised. "Was that really you?"

"Of course! Who did you think it was?"

"That's funny," said Kamnitzer, "I could have sworn it was someone trying to pull my leg. He called himself Sergeant-Major Rammler, but I've been had like that before."

"Who do you think you're fooling?" Rammler demanded furiously. "I know your type, don't worry."

"You're not being fair, Sergeant-Major," Kamnitzer said with an ingenuous smile. "Put yourself in my place. Some chap rings up and gives your name, bellowing something about a field training exercise—to me, when I happened to know our training programme backwards and could have told him there was no field exercise scheduled for to-day."

"It was changed without warning, you clot!"

"Really? But how could I have known that? Besides, your voice sounded different from the way it does in barracks —quite charming, it was."

"This is too stupid!" said Helen Wieder. "I can't stand around here all night."

"But I'm only trying to explain, Fräulein."

"I've heard quite enough," she snapped, and made her way up the steps.

The sergeant-major and the lance-corporal stared after her, reduced to rapt silence by the sight of her undulating posterior, which might have fulfilled any soldier's dream of home and beauty.

"I hope you'll excuse me," said Kamnitzer, "but I'm a bit pushed for time. You see, Sergeant-Major, I've offered to entertain Fräulein Wieder—as your deputy, so to speak. I couldn't let her just sit there, all dressed up and nowhere to go. I'm the persevering type, too. I'll do my best to go on entertaining her, if that's all right with you. It's the least I can do."

So saying, Kamnitzer deserted the sergeant-major and started up the steps after Helen. Rammler stood there open-mouthed for some time, as though turned to stone. Then he clamped his jaws shut, shook his head ponderously and stamped away, telling himself that people couldn't treat him like that with impunity.

*

The following morning opened with the daily but ever-enjoyable spectacle of Lieutenant von Strackmann personally cleaning his boots, a task which he performed in the corridor outside the door of his room, where his example could be observed by all.

At the same time, he summoned the duty N.C.O. and asked, still polishing busily, for his report. " Nothing special to report, sir," was the form it took, morning after morning, to which his invariable reply was: " I'd like it even better if there were."

After the duty N.C.O. had feasted his eyes sufficiently on the person of the acting company commander, it was the C.S.M.'s turn to appear.

Kischke was late as usual, but he turned up in the end, looking comparatively rested at this early hour of the day. The two men eyed each other with mistrust.

" Well," said the lieutenant, " what's on to-day?"

" The usual," Kirschke replied laconically.

The lieutenant demanded details. He knew the day's programme like the back of his hand, but he wanted to know if the C.S.M. was equally well-informed. Kirschke drew a mimeographed sheet from his pocket and prepared to read its contents aloud.

" Don't bother with that!" Von Strackmann's contempt for the refractory sergeant-major was so intense that he forgot to polish his boots for a moment. " I want to know what you—you personally—intend to do to-day."

" The usual," Kirschke delivered himself of this remark with unremitting indifference. " Routine jobs, that's all."

" Company Sergeant-Major Kirschke," the lieutenant said acidly, " I expect my senior N.C.O.s to produce at least one good idea a day."

Kirschke would have had no difficulty in producing the

requisite good idea, but he sagely kept it to himself. Von Strackmann behaved as though he were in the Boy Scouts, he reflected. If he had seen the light of German day twenty years earlier the Hitler-Jugend could scarcely have gained a more promising recruit, but he had been born into a democracy and was—according to his lights—making the best of it.

The indefatigable von Strackmann spent the first few hours of this particular day playing the sheep-dog, as Kirschke termed it. He watched over his flock, circled it alertly and intently, shepherded stragglers back into the fold and generally kept things on the move. While he did so his thoughts returned repeatedly to the C.S.M., who seemed, quite apart from anything else, to be one of the stiffest hurdles in his path to professional success. There were, he told himself, ample reasons for removing the said hurdle. Its elimination was imperative not only in his own interests but in the interests of all.

At last, when he could withstand the voice of decision no longer, the lieutenant went to the Company Office. The C.S.M. was not there, but von Strackmann's persistent inquiries as to his whereabouts elicited the information that he was " in his room, probably, changing his trousers."

Kirschke had actually announced his intention of changing his trousers two hours before, but no one thought to inform the lieutenant of this fact and he omitted to ask.

Borne along on wings of suspicion, he made for the C.S.M.'s room, which gave off a downstairs corridor. He did not get further than the door, however, because it was locked. His knocking, discreet at first, like that of a chambermaid, produced no response.

" Sergeant-Major Kirschke!" he called imperiously. " Open up!"

The door remained shut.

" Open up, Sergeant-Major!" he repeated, this time thundering on the panels like a detective armed with a warrant. " This is Lieutenant von Strackmann! I know you're in there!"

He beat a few more tattoos, but his only answer was continued and provocative silence.

Quick as a flash or, as witnesses later agreed, like a dose of salts, the lieutenant raced along the corridor, out of the door and round the block to the spot where he judged Kirschke's window to be.

The window was about ten feet above the ground, but von Strackmann was an athletic young man. Leaping up, he grasped the window-sill and performed a text-book pull-up —much to the delight of several watching grenadiers.

Looking through the window with his chin on the sill, von Strackmann was rewarded by the sight of a plump posterior clad in underpants. While von Strackmann was peering through the window into the room, Kirschke was peering through the key-hole into the corridor.

This vision seemed to rob von Strackmann of his remaining reserves of strength. He dropped to the ground, panting slightly. Then he marched off at speed, round the block, along the corridor, and up to Kirschke's room. The door was now open, and the C.S.M. was looking out.

"You haven't heard the last of this," said von Strackmann, still breathing heavily.

"What's up?" Kirschke demanded. "Can't a man change his trousers these days?"

"Behind locked doors?" the lieutenant asked sternly.

"Certainly, sir. I always lock the door before changing my trousers. One of the lady cleaners might walk in."

"We'll see about that," von Strackmann said grimly. "I shall conduct the requisite investigation in person."

"By all means, sir." Kirschke appeared unimpressed. He was satisfied that he was more than a match for an unblooded ignoramus like von Strackmann. On the other hand, he was capable of making a nuisance of himself, so it might be advisable to distract his attention. "All the same, there are more urgent matters to attend to."

"Kindly allow me to decide that!"

"Of course, sir. But there was a call for you earlier from a Herr Asch, proprietor of the hotel of the same name. He wanted to know whether you could persuade members of your unit not to behave like animals in his establishment."

Von Strackmann drew himself up stiffly, like a wax effigy. " He said that—to you?"

" That's right, sir. He wanted to speak to you at first, but you were too far away to be reached."

" The man actually said that?"

Kirschke noted the lieutenant's expression of outrage with gratification. Herbert Asch had not employed such a harsh turn of phrase, of course, but Kirschke's rendering was an accurate interpretation of his meaning, and von Strackmann was evidently prepared to accept it at its face value.

The lieutenant immediately recalled his momentous conversation with the C.O. on the previous evening, particularly the disguised injunction not to be pushed around by civilians.

" Who does he think he is?" he demanded unsuspectingly. He knew very little about conditions in town. His life was dedicated exclusively to the army, and he seldom looked beyond the confines of the barracks—except in the direction of the training area. Consequently, he had no idea who Herbert Asch was and cared less.

" Here's his telephone number," said Kirschke, proffering a slip of paper.

Von Strackmann snatched it as a pike snaps at a minnow. " I'll show him where he gets off!"

Five telephone calls ensued in the next few minutes. Their echoes were destined to dislodge an avalanche and bring it down on the unwitting lieutenant's head.

First, von Strackmann called the hotel and asked the switchboard to connect him with Herbert Asch. He told him, among other things, that indirect accusations were valueless and that any complaints should be communicated in writing through official channels.

Herbert Asch was slightly taken aback. " I hope you realise who you're speaking to," he said mildly.

" As long as you know who you're speaking to," von Strackmann replied, " that's good enough for me."

Herbert Asch did know, and it was he who conducted the second conversation in the series, this time with Captain Ahlers.

Asch told him of his precautionary telephone call to No. 3 Company. His sole intention had been to curb the high spirits of a sergeant-major named Rammler and thereby protect Martin Recht. He had first spoken to a Sergeant-Major Kirschke, who appeared to be a calm, congenial and understanding person, but had later been telephoned by another man, Lieutenant von Strackmann by name.

" I know him slightly," Ahlers said. " He's a bit officious, but he probably means well."

" I'm glad to hear it. He dressed me down as though I was a pick-pocket."

" Did he," mused Ahlers. " We'll see about that."

The third 'phone call was made by Ahlers to Colonel Turner. " Deal with it, my dear chap," said the latter, after listening in attentive silence. " Deal with it for me—in the regulation manner, of course."

Captain Ahlers pointed out that the situation was not so straightforward this time. " You see, sir," he confessed, " I was the one who advised Herr Asch not to lodge an official complaint. I thought it better to settle the matter as unobtrusively as possible."

" Nothing wrong with that," Turner said approvingly. " I consider that your advice was most apt, under the circumstances."

" Except that it was addressed to the mayor of the town by the deputy area commandant, in a sense, so Herr Asch regarded my suggestion as semi-official. Lieutenant von Strackmann's brusque manner was extremely ill-judged, to say the least. I think a word to his commanding officer wouldn't be out of place, and it can only come from you, sir. Your experience of inter-service diplomacy is infinitely greater than mine."

Although Colonel Turner found some difficulty in swallowing this, he saw no alternative but to make the suggested telephone call.

He picked up the receiver and asked to speak to Major Bornekamp. It was not his habit, he said, to offer unsolicited advice, and he did his best not to interfere in other spheres of command—"but a commanding officer is responsible for his officers, as I'm sure you'll agree."

"Are you speaking in general terms, Colonel, or have you a particular case in mind?"

"One of your officers, a Lieutenant von Strackmann, has made a serious blunder. He spoke to the mayor, Herr Asch, in a manner which I can only describe as inconsiderate in the extreme. I can't believe that you would have approved, Major. After all, Herr Asch is the local civic leader—at least until the next elections. As area commandant, I'm rather concerned, but I'm sure you'll deal with the matter in a correct and befitting manner."

The Major received this gentle but unmistakable reprimand with a grinding of teeth. He knew that the Colonel would now compile a report giving the place, date, time and exact details of their conversation. Apart from that, he felt that von Strackmann had let him down. He had credited the lieutenant with more intelligence, but he must have been deceived. At all events, it was von Strackmann who had called down this unpleasant rebuke upon his head.

Thus it was Major Bornekamp who made the fifth telephone call. Summoning Lieutenant von Strackmann to the 'phone, he pulverised him—as Kirschke later described it—like a tank running over a frog.

"Sheer idiocy—that's what it was!" the C.O. bellowed. "Iron things out immediately, or you'll find yourself out on your neck!"

Lieutenant von Strackmann stood there like a block of stone while C.S.M. Kirschke, who had heard every word, grinned happily.

"Do you want me to put myself on a charge now," Kirschke inquired, "for sleeping during the hours of duty?" He might have added: "At least a sleeping man doesn't make idiotic 'phone calls," but this would have been superfluous. Von Strackmann could guess what the C.S.M. was thinking.

"All because of this miserable shower!" he muttered dispiritedly.

*

"You must excuse my husband's absence, Herr Recht. He seems to have been detained."

Frau Ahlers smiled at her guest as she spoke, and there was no hint of resentment in her voice.

"We live very simply," she continued, "but I don't need to tell you that—you can see for yourself."

Martin Recht could, but it didn't embarrass him. The furniture was simple and functional, the materials tasteful but obviously cheap, the carpet a plain, inexpensive broadloom. Recht knew a little about such things because his mother owned a shop which sold modern furnishings.

"I must get back to the kitchen," Frau Ahlers went on, "but my daughter will keep you company in the meanwhile."

Her thin, serene face appealed to Recht. She hesitated for a moment, then asked: "Did my husband tell you that our daughter is an invalid—I mean, that she has a disability which hasn't been cured yet?"

"Yes, he did mention it."

"Did he say what it was?"

"No."

"You're bound to notice," said Frau Ahlers, "but I'm sure you'll know how to treat it."

Carolin Ahlers appeared a moment or two later. Looking at her, Recht became aware that her eyes were bright and her skin the colour of white roses bathed in evening sunlight. Her long sweeping hair was like a silken curtain and her smile, he noted blissfully, reminiscent of a princess in a fairy-tale. In short, Martin Recht experienced a brief moment of poetic rapture.

He couldn't help himself. There was a sort of enchantment about the girl which gently but irresistibly fired his imagination. Then he saw her walking, and was jolted back to reality. She walked carefully, uncertainly, as though not in full command of her limbs. It might have been said that she limped, but that was not an entirely apt description of her deliberate but somehow tentative movements. Although he registered all this objectively, Martin Recht knew at the same time that he would not have been unduly surprised if she had risen into the air and floated slowly towards him.

She noticed his expression and smiled—not a brave smile, but one which seemed to contain more sympathy for Recht than herself. Watching her visitor closely, Frau Ahlers was happy to see that he quickly overcame his surprise.

"Can I help you?" he asked, hurrying forward to meet the girl.

"Oh no, thank you!" she replied with unexpected gaiety. "I can walk quite well by myself. You must just try to get used to it—or don't you like sick people?"

"What makes you think that?" he said, pulling a chair forward for her. "My sister had polio, and she did her best to exploit us all—had the family running around like slaves."

"What about you—did you let her exploit you?"

"Of course, I enjoyed it." Recht took Carolin's arm without undue hesitation. "Do let me. You mustn't discourage my chivalrous instincts."

Frau Ahlers smiled at her daughter and nodded at Martin Recht with a mixture of gratitude and encouragement before leaving the room.

Recht drew up a chair and placed it next to Carolin's. At first he found it slightly disconcerting to be gazing into that gentle, radiant, smiling face at such close quarters. This time it reminded him—borne away on another flight of fancy—of a spring morning, but he forced himself to concentrate on her disability.

"How do you come to walk like that?" he asked, frankly curious. "What's the trouble exactly?"

"Partial paralysis of the legs," Carolin replied. "There's something wrong with my spine."

"I'm so sorry," said Recht, trying to sound as matter-of-fact as possible. "How long have you had it?"

"Ever since I was born."

Martin Recht could not conceal his surprise. He looked at her inquiringly.

"I'm a sort of hang-over from the last war," Carolin went on. "I was born in Lübeck in nineteen forty-five, during the treck from the East. The hospital was packed and the doctors were working round the clock. Anyway, they made a mess of me."

"What can I say?" Recht said gently.

"Nothing. There's nothing to be said. I'm like that—and that's all there is to it." Carolin leant back in her chair looking resigned and a little tired. "It's not as bad as all that, is it? I'm quite used to it."

"What about the doctors? Can't they do anything?"

"They've done a lot already. I've had several operations, you know. It was much worse in the old days. I used to sit in a wheel-chair the whole time, but now I can walk." She added, smiling: "A little, anyway. That's something."

"It's a lot!" Martin Recht broke in. "It's a great deal—and a good beginning. Do you ever go for walks?"

"Sometimes, with my mother. In the Municipal Gardens, usually."

"Does it tire you?"

"No, not if people are patient with me."

"Splendid," Martin Recht said firmly. "Then you can come for a walk with me some time."

Carolin eyed him dubiously. "Do you mean it?"

"Why shouldn't I?"

The rosy flush on her cheeks seemed to deepen. "You're just saying that to be polite, or to cheer me up—or perhaps because you feel you owe something to my father. But you've no need to, really you haven't."

"Listen to me," said Recht, drawing a deep breath and searching for the bluntest way of expressing what he wanted

to say. He had always found it the best way of handling
his invalid sister. "You're talking nonsense. I like you—
that's all that matters. Or doesn't the idea of my company
appeal to you?"

"It's not that."

"Then it's settled."

"Maybe."

"When are we going for this walk, then?" he persisted.

"Some time soon."

"Why not this evening, after supper?"

Carolin shook her head doubtfully. "I don't know—we
oughtn't to rush things."

"There's no point in waiting. Is it a date? Please say
yes."

Carolin Ahlers smiled. "Yes," she said.

*

"You ought to install a waiting-room," Lance-Corporal
Kamnitzer suggested. "I feel as if I were visiting the
dentist."

"What dentist," asked Asch, "would supply his patients
with free drinks?"

"Am I a patient of yours?"

"Let's say I regard you as a sort of guinea-pig."

"What's the experiment?"

"I'm interested in finding out whether common sense ever
prevails in the army."

"You've come to the wrong man, Herr Asch. It doesn't
need any common sense to do what I do occasionally—just
instinct. I hope you don't think I'm hell-bent on throwing
a spanner into the military works, because that's the last
thing I want to do. It's an entertaining sight, army life—
like a circus. I sit back watching it and waiting for the
end of the performance."

Herbert Asch regarded Kamnitzer benevolently. There
were moments when he saw the young man as a reincarna-

tion of himself, but things had changed a good deal since he last wore uniform. Or had they?

Asch had invited Kamnitzer into his office so that he could wait there quietly, and without charge, for Helen Wieder.

"Go on like this," said Kamnitzer, "and you'll find yourself running a soldiers' canteen."

"Surely you don't regard everyone in uniform as a soldier?"

Kamnitzer grinned. "You want me to stick my neck out, don't you?"

"Don't you trust me?" Asch asked, looking amused.

"It's not that, exactly," Kamnitzer replied casually. "But I can put two and two together, and I know the garrison brings you in a fair amount of business."

"You mean I make money out of it?"

"Of course. Quite a bit, too—not that I grudge it to you."

"I'm happy to hear it."

This conversation, which Asch seemed to be enjoying, was rudely interrupted by the appearance of Viktor Vossler, who walked in without knocking, stalked over to Asch and halted in front of him with an expression of mock severity on his face.

"Oh, dear!" Asch chuckled. "Have you come to read the riot act? I've already had one lecture."

"The way you treat your employees," Vossler said pleasantly, "verges on slavery. Overtime seems to be the order of the day with you lately."

"I second that," said Kamnitzer. He regarded Vossler, whom he had not met before, with interest.

"Don't be too hasty, my friend," Herbert Asch rubbed his hands gleefully, and those who knew him well could have forecast that he was about to make one of his little jokes. "After all, you may both be waiting for the same girl—what then?"

Vossler and Kamnitzer, each in civilian clothes, eyed one another with mounting distrust. As men of similar calibre, it occurred to them that they might well appeal to the same girl, despite their difference in age.

"Don't you gentlemen know each other?" Asch asked amiably. "Allow me to introduce you: Warrant Officer Vossler—Lance-Corporal Kamnitzer."

"I won't say I'm delighted to meet you because I don't know whether I am yet," said Kamnitzer without rising from his chair. "But I'd like to point out—just in passing —that I'm here as a private individual."

"So am I," said Vossler, extending his hand after a moment's hesitation.

Asch enjoyed watching the two men jockeying for position in ignorance of the fact that Kamnitzer was waiting for Helen Wieder, still on duty in the café, and Vossler for Gertrud Ballhaus, Asch's private secretary, who was finishing off some letters for him.

Kamnitzer took Vossler's hand and shook it casually. "Maybe you'd prefer me to salute?" he said.

"Forget about it," said Vossler, dropping into an armchair.

"What do you mean—forget about it?" Kamnitzer asked. "I'm here privately, I'm in civvies and I'm a guest of Herr Asch, so you can't expect me to salute. I don't expect you to, either."

Vossler felt slightly worried. He was taken aback by Kamnitzer's cool effrontery because he knew it was what appealed to Gerty in himself. He smiled uneasily and made no reply.

Kamnitzer, however, pressed on regardless. "If you want to know, it doesn't matter to me whether a man's a warrant officer or a postman. I couldn't care less."

"That makes two of us," said Vossler.

"Then we're all agreed," Asch interposed, pushing a brimming wine-glass towards each of his guests. Before they drank he enlightened them about his little joke, deriving as much amusement from their relief as he had from the mutual hostility that preceded it.

"All the same," Vossler confessed, "for a moment I really thought you'd been poaching on my preserves."

" I'm honoured," Kamnitzer said. " The same goes for me."

Vossler smiled. " Glad to have met you, anyway."

Herbert Asch leant back contentedly in his chair. It pleased him when his friends got on well with each other.

" Tell me something," Kamnitzer said after a pause. " For a warrant officer, you're almost human. Don't you feel a bit lonely in your mob, or are there more where you come from?"

" Plenty," Vossler assured him.

" And you're not regarded as undesirable types?"

" We're in the majority. It's the others who are the undesirables."

" That's terrific!" Kamnitzer exclaimed. " You're not pulling my leg, are you?"

" Pay us a visit some time," Vossler suggested. " Any time —I'd be happy to show you round."

" I'll take you up on that," said Kamnitzer. " I always find it a bit hard to believe that all barracks aren't identical." A look of sudden distrust flitted across his face. " Or do you look on yourselves as a sort of feudal club?"

" We're flyers," Vossler said. " That's all we're interested in—flying."

" Ah!" said Kamnitzer. " And it doesn't matter to you whether you fly around carrying bombs, medicine, ammunition or underpants?"

" The types you dig up!" Vossler said, turning to Asch. " Who does our friend think he is—a frustrated missionary or something?"

Asch smiled almost affectionately at Kamnitzer. " He suffers from attacks of conscience sometimes, only he won't admit it."

" Oh, well," Kamnitzer shrugged, " let's not go into that. Whatever you do in the air, Herr Vossler, I've a feeling we mightn't get on badly on the ground."

*

" How nice of you to find time to drop in again," said Frau Bornekamp, opening the front door wide.

Before her stood Lieutenant von Strackmann, Christian name Dieter. Holding the upper part of his body rigid, like a sack stuffed with sawdust, he described a series of movements which might have been interpreted as something between a correct military salute and a deferential greeting. " I hope I'm not disturbing you, ma'am," he said courteously.

" What do you think ! " Elfrieda Bornekamp cried with the spirited graciousness of one born to command. " No false modesty, now ! You know you're very welcome."

Von Strackmann expressed his gratitude in what he deemed to be the regulation manner. Not for nothing had he passed the officer cadets' course entitled " Social Etiquette," a success which was recorded in his personal file.

Docilely, he followed the C.O.'s lady inside, circling her attentively in an effort to keep on her left side. Before he could unwrap his bottle of cognac—the second he had delivered (at the C.O.'s suggestion) within a week—he found himself in the drawing-room, and not only in the drawing-room but on the couch.

Elfrieda Bornekamp switched on a table lamp and extinguished the centre light. " We can chat better like that. It's much cosier, don't you think?" Then she sat down beside him at a distance of approximately twelve inches.

" This is a great honour for me," the lieutenant declared manfully. " I'm most grateful for all your kindness and generosity."

Von Strackmann did indeed feel privileged. Not only had he, a young officer, been appointed to stand in for an ailing company commander, but the C.O. had made him a repository of his personal confidence. He had conversed with him privately and introduced him to his family circle.

To Frau Elfrieda, there was something endearing about the young officer's fresh, idealistic approach. She shifted four inches closer, conscious that the subdued glow of the table lamp behind her enhanced her charms.

"My husband," she said without resentment, "is so busy all the time."

"Duty comes first with him," the lieutenant declared. "He never spares himself. It's remarkable."

"Remarkable," Frau Elfrieda agreed. "But he never neglects me. Look at the way he sends you to see me."

"I regard it as a great honour," said von Strackmann. He was determined to prove himself worthy of the C.O.'s trust, and it occurred to him that the most effective way of doing so would be to reveal some of his personal plans. Frau Bornekamp would undoubtedly tell her husband about them. "I started a debit-and-credit book to-day."

"A what?" Frau Elfrieda had been on the point of sliding another four inches closer, but she stopped in her tracks.

"A debit-and-credit book," repeated von Strackmann. "You know, an assessment of individual merit, based on a points system. The C.O.'s extremely receptive to new ideas, but he tries to combine them with traditional methods of training. I think it's a first-class principle."

Frau Elfrieda sank back as though slightly exhausted. As she did so, her left knee brushed Dieter's right. "I beg your pardon!" he said politely, withdrawing the offending limb in haste. Then he cleared his throat and went on : "I always do my utmost to follow the C.O.'s suggestions."

"Do you really?"

"In every respect," he assured her. "Hence my debit-and-credit book. By keeping it, I'm implementing one of the C.O.'s most stimulating suggestions. You see, traditional methods of character assessment ignore some of the finer psychological points."

"And you feel you're a good judge of character?"

"I try to be. Anyway, I shall do my best to observe the requisite gradations as accurately as possible in future. For instance, do you know the difference between an admonishment and a reprimand?"

"No," said Frau Elfrieda, almost tartly.

Quite oblivious, von Stackmann plunged into greater detail. He spoke of the severe reprimand, which does not exclude the possibility of improvement, and expatiated at some length on the "warning," which was equivalent to disapproval and implied that the recipient might be reported to a superior. Finally——

"You're being a bore," Frau Elfrieda said bluntly.

Von Strackmann was dismayed. "I'm so sorry," he said, trying to master his embarrassment. "Please tell me what I can do. . . ."

"Open that bottle of cognac," commanded Frau Elfrieda, "and come here."

*

Major Bornekamp, meanwhile, was indulging in his favourite pastime : war. It was only a paper war, of course, but —in default of the real thing—it seemed to be claiming his fullest attention.

A reporter named Flammer from the local *Town and Country News* had been waiting outside for a considerable time, but Bornekamp let him wait. To the Major, Flammer was just a cheap penny-a-liner who produced half a page of marketable padding for forty or fifty marks. A few years back he had probably been churning out articles entitled "Peace in our Time," but now, no doubt, he was writing decent German again. Reflecting that he was not one to bear a grudge, Bornekamp waited a while longer and then asked Herr Flammer to come in.

"Well, fire away, my dear chap," the C.O. said indulgently, leaning back in his chair with the air of a grand seigneur. "What do you want to know?"

His sovereign sense of superiority was so complete that he omitted to ask another, equally important question : namely, what had inspired the journalist to come and see him in the first place. Flammer might, of course, have attributed the interview to general public interest, but he might also have answered, more truthfully, that he was following up a suggestion made by Mayor Asch.

In fact, Asch had done more than inspire Flammer to visit the Major. He had even worked out the various questions to be put at the interview. The first of these sounded entirely innocuous.

"What is your opinion of the latest intake of recruits?"

Bornekamp gave a superior smile at this naïve inquiry. "I'd describe them as first-rate material," he said without hesitation. "Young men free from false, airy-fairy idealism. Down-to-earth, realistic, clear-thinking—and fundamentally reliable as a result. They've got their feet firmly planted on democratic soil."

The journalist did not look up from his notebook as he put the second question.

"How would you describe the relationship between your men and the civil population?"

The Major was secretly amused. Naïve wasn't the word for this hack, he told himself. The man was a blithering idiot. What was more, he doubted whether Flammer had ever seen service. You could tell that just from the slovenly way he sat, hunched up like a sack of potatoes.

"Relations with civil population . . ." Bornekamp knew all the appropriate clichés on this subject, and he reeled them off like a gramophone record. "Improving day by day, thanks to increased understanding on both sides. The men like it here. Occasional isolated and trivial incidents make no difference. We still have to overcome the after-effects of certain slanderous allegations levelled at the army in the past—but overcome them we shall!"

Flammer scribbled away busily. He had a whole string of similar questions in stock, and Bornekamp's answers bubbled forth like spring-water. He quoted whole pages from army periodicals, interspersing them with choice extracts from his own lectures to officers' instructional classes.

Flammer's pencil continued to race across the paper. He gave no indication of whether he understood the finer points of the Major's discourse, but simply wrote down whatever was said. Little by little, his questions coaxed the C.O., by now in full spate, out on to the thin ice of politics.

"Do you consider that traditional barrack-square methods, as generally understood, have been abolished?"

"There was no need to abolish them," Bornekamp asserted, "because they never existed—except in a few isolated cases which had no bearing on the army as a whole. It should be realised that the stories one heard about such things in the old days were often concocted by irresponsible idiots or deliberate liars. They were either exaggerated or based on rare and exceptional cases. Any allegations to the contrary are slanderous falsehoods put about by left-wing intellectuals for their own nefarious ends."

Major Bornekamp had got the bit firmly between his teeth by this time, but he was bolting in the desired direction. Flammer only needed to put one last question, and he did so with a well-simulated air of innocence.

"What is your opinion of conscientious objectors?"

This, as Herbert Asch knew, was one of the Major's pet subjects. The red rag having been unfurled, the bull launched himself at it with predictable ferocity. "Conscientious objectors? Either Communists or cowards. Stick 'em into a striped suit and you'd soon see the last of 'em!"

"Thank you, Major," said Flammer, closing his notebook. "I'm sure your remarks will arouse great interest—very great interest indeed."

*

Sergeant-Major Rammler was paying another visit to the Café Asch. His objective, needless to say, was Helen Wieder, but he had not come alone this time. The privilege of accompanying him had fallen to Corporal Streicher.

"They don't make soldiers like they used to," Rammler declared, looking about him scornfully. "You're not up to standard either, Streicher, but you could be. You've got the makings. You know how to treat your superiors properly."

Although Streicher knew better than to attach too much importance to such figures of speech, he experienced a certain sense of gratification. Sergeant-Major Rammler obviously had a weakness for him, and that could be useful, especially as he wanted to rise to the rank of sergeant.

"It won't be long before you get your third stripe," Rammler told him confidentially.

"Really, Sergeant-Major?"

"If I say so." Rammler stared across the café to where Helen Wieder was standing. "Just between you and me, Streicher, you've already been recommended for promotion."

Streicher was not unaware of this, either, but he feigned pleased surprise. Discreetly, he asked if he might order a round.

"Two or three, if you like," said Rammler, raising his hand. Helen Wieder ignored the gesture. She publicised her refusal to serve him by sending over the stringy female who had incurred his displeasure once before.

"This world stinks," Rammler said darkly. "Take it from me, Streicher."

Streicher concurred, even though he was an optimistic person who brimmed with orthodox ideas. "All the same, Sergeant-Major, there are constructive forces at work too."

Rammler gave a nod of agreement, but his excursion into philosophy was not over yet. "Artificial, that's what this world is," he brooded. "A lot of nancy-boys, that's all they are these days, and the women fling themselves at them— God knows why."

Still meditating on this gloomy prospect, he tore his gaze away from Helen Wieder and looked towards the swing doors. Martin Recht, that milk-sop of a soldier with his typically civilian mannerisms, was just entering, accompanied by a girl who walked with a slight limp.

"Look what Recht's dug up!" exclaimed Rammler. "Just his type, I reckon."

Martin Recht's whole attention was chivalrously concentrated on Carolin Ahlers. He had eyes for her alone, and her slight air of helplessness only strengthened his tender feelings for her. He found a table near the entrance, oblivious of the fact that Rammler was sitting near by.

He held Carolin's chair and sat down opposite her, with his back to the sergeant-major. Then he reached for her hand, which was trembling slightly, and covered it with his own.

"You see," he said cheerfully, "it wasn't as bad as all that."

"You made it easy for me, Martin."

Recht looked a little shy. "Keep up the good work," he said hurriedly, "and we'll soon be able to take quite long walks together."

"That would be lovely," Carolin said, looking down at the table, where his hand lay on hers.

Rammler, who heard every word of this conversation, snorted contemptuously as he watched the neighbouring table being subjected to a sort of invasion.

The first to appear was Helen Wieder, who gave the couple a cordial welcome and took their order—a bottle of mineral water for Carolin and a coffee for Martin. Rammler watched her retreating form in an agony of frustration.

A moment later Frau Asch arrived. She greeted the young couple like old friends—more than that, she sat down at their table and chatted to them for some minutes until Helen Wieder reappeared with their order. "I'll leave you to yourselves now," she said, rising. "I hope we'll be seeing a lot of you both in future."

No one paid any attention to Rammler, although he was a regular customer. Helen Wieder seemed to have a penchant for inferior forms of life, he reflected savagely. What was worse, she concentrated her attentions on the less admirable members of the species. He decided to make it a matter of principle.

Turning portentously in his chair, he tapped Recht on the shoulder and said, more parenthetically than severely : "Your eyesight bad, or something?"

Martin Recht gave a start of surprise and swung round to

face the sergeant-major. Flushing to the roots of his hair, he said: "I beg your pardon, Sergeant-Major, I didn't see you." He rose, saluted and sat down again.

"Too busy, I suppose?" asked Rammler, feigning amusement. "Your eyes really must be bad, though—mistaking me for a chair and a lame duck for a swan." He laughed as if he had just made a coarse but good-natured jest.

Martin Recht sprang to his feet again, this time as though he were about to throw himself at the sergeant-major, who sat there with a gleam of anticipation in his eyes. Almost simultaneously, Corporal Streicher leapt into the breach, presumably in his capacity as room-mate and welfare representative.

"Don't do anything foolish, Martin!" he said, gripping his arm.

Martin violently shook off the corporal's restraining grasp and bent over Rammler with clenched fists.

"Martin," said Carolin, and her voice, though soft, was clear and distinct, "you were just going to tell me about to-morrow evening. Where did you say we were going?"

Martin Recht straightened up. He relaxed, turned slowly to look at Carolin and resumed his seat. "Thanks, Carolin," he said with a half-hearted smile.

Now it was her turn to put her hand on his.

Sergeant-Major Rammler exhibited grim amusement. "What was all that about?" he demanded of Streicher. "Wanted to wring my neck, did he? Well, that takes the bleeding biscuit! Never mind, we've got ways of dealing with his sort."

That evening, later known as "Gloomy Thursday," appeared to end on a successful note as far as Sergeant-Major Rammler was concerned. He was not a man who gave up easily, and he also knew the value of the strategic withdrawal.

His first move was to make an obtrusive exit from the Café Asch. He did not wait for Herbert Asch to put in an appearance, nor the delinquent Kamnitzer, nor the unsoldierly Vossler, his air force rival of the previous evening. He

D

marched out, grandly ignoring both Helen Wieder and Martin Recht, who reluctantly saluted him for the second time.

"Types like that," he announced to Streicher, who retained the privilege of escorting him, "ought to be shot."

"It's not that I like playing the nursemaid, Sergeant-Major," Streicher remarked cautiously, "but he doesn't find soldiering easy."

"Then he ought to pull his finger out!" snapped Rammler. "Though it doesn't matter what a bloke like Recht does—he'll never amount to more than a pinch of chicken-shit."

"Perhaps he feels at a disadvantage, Sergeant. They say he's half-Jewish."

"So what?" Rammler had heard this before. "What am I supposed to do—give him preferential treatment? Lay off the subject, I'm sick of it."

Streicher did not regard Rammler as anti-Semitic, but it seemed unwise to pursue this theme further. All he wanted to do was register a small, discreet warning.

By this time they were standing in the middle of the market place. Rammler gazed about him like a boxer with victory in his grasp. "What is there to do in this Godforsaken dump?" he demanded.

The houses of the little town stared mutely back, their sturdy half-timbered façades softly illumined by the moon. It would not have seemed unduly surprising if a night-watchman had materialised, complete with lantern and staff.

"There must be something to do here!"

"Maybe it would be better if we went home," Corporal Streicher suggested vaguely. By "home" he meant barracks.

"Balls," said Rammler. "I'm nowhere near ready for bed yet. What about paying a visit to the *La Paloma*?"

Streicher tried to talk him out of the idea. "It's hardly the place for senior N.C.O.s, Sergeant-Major."

"You poor fool," Rammler said, undeterred, "get this straight: as soon as we walk into a place, it belongs to us. We set the tone wherever we choose to park our arses, get it?"

Sweeping into the Espresso bar with a proprietorial air, he

made straight for the so-called " passion parlour," taking the steps two at a time. Streicher followed him reluctantly.

All Rammler could see to begin with was a cloud of smoke, so thick that it might have been emitted by a smoke-bomb. Then he made out a densely packed throng of figures, preponderantly male, ranged round the small tables and along the miniature bar counter. The juke-box was churning out a sentimental ballad about the deep blue sea.

Rammler, who was wearing civilian clothes, cleared a path by pushing Streicher along in front of him like a battering-ram. When he reached the bar counter he ordered his favourite drink—" Strong Man's Milk, and make it a large one!"—and proceeded to take stock of the situation.

" At least three blokes to every bird," he announced. " That means two-thirds of them are in the way."

" It's not always like this," a youth beside him remarked moodily. " The Italians got here first to-night."

" The who?" Rammler asked in astonishment. " I didn't know we were on the Adriatic."

The young man was happy to enlighten him. It seemed that there was a factory on the outskirts of the town where insulating materials were manufactured with the aid of im-ported Italian labour. The foreigners weren't badly paid, either, especially by comparison with the average soldier.

" Fair enough," Rammler said indulgently. " They can make as much insulating tape as they like, but what right have they got to muscle in on our women?"

The youngsters round him shrugged. " That's all very well, but what can we do about it? They were here first."

Rammler, who had realised at a glance that his bar companions were servicemen in civilian clothes, was outraged. " What can you do? What a bloody stupid question! You must be air force blokes, aren't you?"

They nodded.

" That explains it." Rammler ordered himself another double ration of Strong Man's Milk, turning his broad back on the airmen as he did so.

He then embarked on a stentorian conversation with

Streicher, doing his best to fan the flames he had already kindled. When frequent use of the expression "macaroni-merchants" failed to have any effect, Rammler resorted to war-time reminiscences.

The Italians gradually caught on. Three of them deserted their German dates and elbowed their way towards the men at the bar. Mildly, at first, they demanded an explanation.

"Cheeky sods, aren't they?" said Rammler. "But then you air force boys let people get away with murder." So saying, he moved in the direction of the Gents, noting as he did so that Corporal Streicher had already beaten a retreat. On the way, he shoved two or three airmen aside with rough camaraderie. It apparently escaped him that one of them ricocheted into an Italian, just as it escaped him that the Italian took umbrage and shoved the airman in return.

A moment later Rammler was standing in the Gents, listening with satisfaction to the growing tumult outside. Judging by its intensity, the airmen were making a take-over bid.

When Rammler re-emerged some minutes later, the place looked emptier but considerably more comfortable. Two-thirds of the customers had disappeared, and there now seemed no reason why he shouldn't bring his day to a successful conclusion.

"Do you mean to say our friends from Italy have deserted us already?" he asked with a wink.

The others laughed. They were enjoying the situation, and continued to do so until the air police picket arrived.

*

Grenadier Martin Recht was still smiling happily when he got up next morning.

"What's the matter with you?" said Kamnitzer, watching him closely. "You look as if you'd won the pools or found your demob papers in your pocket."

"That's just about how I feel, Karl."

Karl Kamnitzer went on making his bed, but he continued to observe Martin Recht. Apart from the fact that he could make his bed with his eyes shut, Recht seemed far more worthy of his attention. The boy's evident sense of well-being worried him.

"Yesterday evening," Recht went on blithely, "I got the urge to knock Rammler's teeth down his throat."

"I get it all the time," said Kamnitzer, "but I make sure I don't give way to it. I just grin at him—he knows what I think of him just the same."

"If Carolin hadn't stopped me," Recht continued, "I'd have clouted him."

"You must be dreaming. What did you have to eat last night?"

Martin Recht was not to be deterred. "It was a relief, believe me, Karl. Just for a few seconds, I felt like a different person."

"You'd better tell me all about it," Kamnitzer said, frowning. They sat down together on the lower bunk and Recht launched into an account of the scene in the Café Asch. The longer Kamnitzer listened, the fewer questions he asked. Eventually he relapsed into silence.

"Well, what do you think of that?" asked Recht.

"I think you're crazy," Kamnitzer said dryly.

"What did you expect me to do," Recht expostulated, "let him insult the girl?" His face darkened. "Lame duck! It was a lousy thing to say. Anyway, he's wrong—she's not a lame duck."

"Of course she isn't," said Kamnitzer, "but some remarks are best ignored." He appeared to be thinking deeply. "I reckon your best plan is to lodge a complaint."

"What's the point? I'd only be making a mountain out of a mole-hill."

"You've no choice, laddie! Rammler won't let anyone get away with that sort of thing, least of all you!"

"The matter's closed as far as I'm concerned. Maybe he thinks so too. He must have a conscience, after all."

"Yes, but not our sort. The way he looks at it, you've assaulted a superior officer—at least in spirit. That's why he'll have your guts for garters if you don't book him first. You stand a good chance, too, especially as the girl's a captain's daughter. You've got to report him—you've no alternative. I'll act as middle-man, if you like, just to get things under way properly."

"Maybe you're right," Martin said reluctantly. "But Carolin may get dragged into it—for questioning, say—and I don't fancy that idea. I couldn't ask her to do it."

"You're not in love with the girl, are you?"

"Yes, I think so."

Karl Kamnitzer clicked his tongue. "That's bad—I mean to say, it may make it harder to deal with Rammler, but we'll have to try all the same. Let's leave it up to him: if he has a sudden attack of decency and apologises, fair enough, but if he's still mad for the sight of blood we'll make sure it's his own."

*

Lieutenant von Strackmann, once more engaged in polishing his boots to the delight of all, was gratified to receive what he took to be signal confirmation of the confidence reposed in him by his men: Sergeant-Major Rammler appeared, gave an immaculate salute, and asked for permission to speak.

"I'm listening," von Strackmann said benignly. The more he saw of Rammler in recent days, the more favourably he compared him with Kirschke. Rammler knew the meaning of discipline and his platoon was regarded as one of the smartest in the battalion. Substitute Rammler for Kirschke, and No. 3 Company would soon be on its feet.

"Quite by chance," Rammler reported, "I entered the *La Paloma* Espresso bar yesterday evening."

"Not exactly the sort of place for you," von Strackmann commented with an indulgent smile.

"I was thirsty, sir, but my real object was to gain some information," Rammler stated with an unclouded brow. "I wanted to find out if any members of my platoon used the place. For that reason, I took one of my most reliable men with me—Corporal Streicher."

Lieutenant von Strackmann nodded. Streicher was of the clay from which acceptable sergeants could be moulded.

"While I was in the urinal, sir, a fight broke out between some foreign workers and air force personnel in civilian dress."

"Most regrettable." Von Strackmann reached for a duster and began to impart a final shine to his handiwork. "But I infer from your account that you had nothing to do with it."

"Nothing whatsoever, sir," stated Rammler. "Corporal Streicher can confirm that. In fact, when the air police arrived I did my best to assist them." `

This was the literal truth. Rammler had at once placed himself at their disposal, brandishing his identity card.

"I'm sure your behaviour was entirely above reproach. It's only what I should have expected of you."

"Anyway, sir, I thought I'd report the matter at once."

Von Strackmann nodded approvingly. "I appreciate your frankness, Sergeant-Major."

He surveyed his boots—the best-polished in the battalion —with satisfaction. "We must be able to trust one another," he went on. "Mutual trust is the only thing which can provide a sound basis for the restoration of esprit de corps which this company so urgently needs—and which I mean to give it. I'm relying on people like you, Sergeant-Major. I'm confident you won't let me down."

*

Captain Klaus Ahlers was having breakfast with his family. Very often, it was the only half-hour in the day which he was able to spend with his wife and daughter.

Ahlers always enjoyed this brief interlude, but to-day he found it particularly enjoyable. Carolin, looking unusually cheerful and relaxed, chattered away vivaciously about her outing of the previous evening. "We walked quite a long way," she said proudly. "It did me good."

Ahlers shot an inquiring glance at his wife, but she smiled reassuringly. "Carolin was well looked after, I'm sure. Martin Recht seems such a nice young man. I felt I was leaving her in safe hands."

Carolin launched into an account of her visit to the Café Asch. "It was awfully funny," she said. "A soldier at the next table called me a lame duck."

"And that struck you as funny?"

"Very," she said gaily. "You see, when he said it, I thought : he should have seen me before, when I could hardly move. What would he have said then? And what will he say if he sees me when I can walk properly?"

Ahlers patted his daughter's arm delightedly. He was more than pleased at her reaction to such a tasteless remark. Far from destroying the fundamental serenity of her nature, her disability seemed to have enhanced it.

When the door-bell rang, Ahlers noted with surprise that it was Carolin who rose to answer it. As she went out, he got the impression that she moved more easily than usual. She merely walked like someone who was slightly stiff and tired after taking physical exercise.

Then Ahlers heard Vossler's voice. Not without satisfaction, he gathered that Vossler, too, had noticed the change in Carolin. "What's all this!" he exclaimed. "You'll be cross-country running next! Come here and give us a hug."

Viktor Vossler behaved like a member of the family. After greeting them affectionately he sat down at the breakfast table without waiting to be invited.

"We've got time," he declared. "At least fifteen minutes, and my car's outside. I wouldn't say no to a cup of coffee if someone asked me."

The car outside, a pale blue saloon, was more than smart enough for the officers' married quarters. Not even Colonel Turner possessed a better car, but then Vossler could afford such extravagances. He owned mineral springs on an estate in Franconia and employed a reliable agent to handle his business affairs. All that interested Viktor Vossler was flying—and, latterly, Mayor Asch's secretary, Gerty Ballhaus.

He sipped his cup of coffee, chatted with Frau Ahlers and made facetious remarks to amuse Carolin, offering to race her over a hundred yards in the near future and pretending to be worried about the result.

When Ahlers and he left the house and emerged into the street, the warrant officer suddenly turned into a subordinate. Vossler knew that there were probably onlookers in the married quarters—ladies who had nothing better to do than peer through their lace curtains—so he opened the car door for Ahlers and waited until he had taken his seat. No private chauffeur could have been more attentive.

" Your daughter's becoming more and more of a live wire," he remarked as they drove through the married quarters towards the barracks.

" Yes, let's hope she keeps it up."

" Whether or not it's a permanent improvement, this seems to be a favourable opportunity "—Vossler slowed down slightly—" you know what I mean, Klaus. What about that final operation? The doctor said it would be worth doing when she was strong enough."

" Perhaps," said Ahlers, " but let's not talk about it now."

Viktor Vossler knew what lay behind Ahlers's silence. He was also familiar with a string of figures : six thousand five hundred marks for Carolin's seven-month sojourn in hospital, two thousand one hundred marks for three operations performed by a leading surgeon, and more than three thousand marks for routine check-ups, drugs and medical attention.

" Klaus," Vossler said, " I've offered to help you more than once."

" Thank you, Viktor, but you know I can't accept."

" What nonsense ! I'm not a poor man. Besides, it's beginning to annoy me, the way you always turned me down."

" Cut it out ! " Ahlers said with forced cheerfulness.

" You're my friend, not my money-lender. I'm afraid the two things don't mix, and if I have to choose one or the other I'd sooner have a friend."

*

No. 3 Company had assembled for Military Education. Everyone was in attendance except the officers, those on sick parade, leave and guard duty, and Company Sergeant-Major Kirschke, who knew everything and therefore needed no further enlightenment.

Lieutenant von Strackmann was speaking—with the aid of *Collected Examples of Approved Lessons*—on the subject of loyalty, obedience and courage. He was confident that the men were listening attentively, being unaware that Kamnitzer, for instance, had acquired the knack of sleeping with his eyes open.

" Loyalty," announced the lieutenant, quoting almost verbatim from his manual, " is an automatic prerequisite in any form of organisation. What is meant here is loyalty toward one's employer—in this case——" and here he deviated slightly from the text " —the Fatherland."

The members of No. 3 Company received his remarks much as they would have if he announced that river-water always flows downstream or hot air expands—that is, impassively.

" The soldier," von Strackmann continued, " has, in addition, to show unswerving obedience to the orders of his superiors, who are acting on behalf of the employer—that is to say, the Federal Republic."

This early morning period, the first of the day, was regarded by the company as a welcome extension of its night's repose. Most of the men dozed in attitudes of profound concentration, while Streicher, alone among them all, busily took notes.

" Courage," von Strackmann recited, " should be regarded as a natural attribute in cases where the rights and liberties of the German people have to be defended."

This formula, which appeared on page 86 of the standard work called *The Officer's Manual* seemed to hold particular appeal to the lieutenant. He raised his forefinger to stress the point.

The men below him, Kamnitzer excluded, were finding it difficult to keep their eyes open. The class-room was too small to accommodate the whole company in comfort, so the men sat packed together, almost on each other's laps, like sardines in a tin. A frowsty, sweetish-sour smell pervaded the air.

"Comradeship," von Strackmann continued, still quoting, "forms the basis of any community, especially when its members are obliged to live in close proximity."

At that moment C.S.M. Kirschke appeared. He murmured something in the lieutenant's ear, but not so softly that the men in the front rows, among them the sergeants and other N.C.O.s, could not catch it. "The C.O. wants you immediately."

"The C.O. wishes to speak to me," announced von Strackmann, his tone suggesting that the C.O. was in urgent need of his advice. "I shall be back as soon as possible. Sergeant-Major Rammler will supervise you in the meantime."

Lance-Corporal Kamnitzer perked up at this announcement. "Now we can have some fun," he whispered, digging Recht, his next-door neighbour, in the ribs.

The others evidently seemed to share his view. A general sense of anticipation filled the air, for Rammler, who had only been asked to supervise, seemed bent on continuing the lesson himself. The manual lay open on the lectern, and he could read aloud as well as the next man.

"Take the following example," Rammler read. "Grenadier X habitually turns up late for duty. He also manages to get out of unpleasant routine jobs such as room orderly, guard duty, fatigues, etc. How would you describe this man's conduct?"

Kamnitzer's hand shot up, but Rammler ignored it. "Let's hear what you've got to say, Grenadier Recht."

Recht rose obediently to his feet. He knew what answer was expected of him, having learnt it by heart. "The soldier has committed a breach of faith. Loyalty is shown in the execution of all forms of duty. A soldier who commits a breach of faith in peace-time will not fight bravely in war-time."

Comparing Recht's exemplary answer with the text, Rammler found that it tallied word for word.

"That's all very well," he said peevishly. "Anyone can learn a thing by heart. It's whether you put it into practice that matters."

"Quite right, Sergeant-Major!" Kamnitzer called with spurious approval. He got up without waiting to be asked. "For instance, I wonder why they call guard duty an unpleasant routine job—also, how Grenadier X manages to avoid it. I'd be interested to know that, Sergeant-Major."

Rammler deemed it wise to give a general answer rather than examine Kamnitzer's question in detail. "It's like this," he explained in resounding tones. "You've got to obey—that's what loyalty means."

"Under any circumstances?" Kamnitzer inquired pensively. "Even someone like Hitler?"

"Stop splitting hairs!" Rammler bellowed in outrage. "What's this got to do with Hitler? You're talking about two completely different worlds."

Kamnitzer's voice was mild. "But some people manage to live and obey just as well in either sort of world, wouldn't you say, Sergeant-Major?"

"That's enough of that!" shouted Rammler. "Class is suspended until the company commander gets back. Hands on the table, everyone! Sit to attention! We'll have a bit of singing. I suggest *Westerwald*."

Kamnitzer grinned. "As for you," Rammler said menacingly, "I'm going to report you. You're going to answer for those remarks!"

"By all means, Sergeant-Major," Kamnitzer replied. "I'll be interested to see what happens."

*

Captain Ahlers shook hands with his office staff and wished them good morning, as he did every day. The only civilian employee in his office was a high-spirited brunette known to all and sundry as Monika. Vossler was convinced that she owed her dark beauty to some anonymous ancestor from the Middle East, and called her " Turkish Delight," but she was a highly efficient secretary.

"Anything special to-day?" Ahlers inquired.

"I don't think so," said Monika. "I'm sure Captain Treuberg will have other ideas, though."

Treuberg, equal in rank but junior to Ahlers, was one of the twelve captains on the station—which meant that there were eleven too many for his taste. He was, however, Ahlers's official deputy and a highly conscientious officer.

"He's waiting for you inside," Monika went on.

Treuberg waited for Ahlers every morning, but then he was always waiting for something, if only a chance to demonstrate his worth. Ahlers did not hurry. He had a final word with Viktor Vossler and the sergeant clerk before entering his own office.

"A most unfortunate business," Treuberg began, before they had even saluted each other. "Take a look at this report from the air police picket."

Ahlers read the report through in silence, watched impatiently by Treuberg, who found it hard to endure his chief's untroubled composure.

"I wouldn't shoulder the responsibility for this, if I were you," insinuated Treuberg.

"You don't have to," Ahlers replied. "It's my job."

He sent for the picket commander, a sergeant with an expressionless apple of a face, smooth, round and gleaming.

"I gather from your report," Ahlers said, "that you were alerted by telephone yesterday evening, though the informant didn't give his name. You then proceeded to the *La Paloma*. Am I right so far?"

"Yessir," replied the sergeant.

"In this bar," Ahlers continued amiably, "you found several airmen in civilian dress together with a number of young women, presumably of medium price-range. We are not, however, responsible for commercial transactions of this sort when they are conducted outside barracks. Are we agreed so far, Sergeant?"

"Yessir." The sergeant's piscine eyes rested trustfully on Ahlers. He did not appear to notice Treuberg's presence, but then Treuberg did not count.

"I now ask you the following: who lodged the information? The proprietor? One of the airmen? One of the girls? One of the foreign workers?"

"No idea, sir," the sergeant replied truthfully.

"To resume: was there any direct threat to the garrison's reputation? Did you enter the premises in order to prevent or put a stop to physical violence? Did you observe any definite act of immorality or indecency?"

"No, sir," said the sergeant.

"In that case," said Ahlers, "I think we can regard the matter as closed." He glanced at the sergeant, who nodded. Ahlers tore up the report. "With your permission," he said to the sergeant, who nodded again.

"I don't know if I entirely agree with you there," said Treuberg, when the sergeant had departed.

"That's all right, Treuberg, your agreement's not essential."

The two men exchanged a brief look of mutual antipathy. To Treuberg, Ahlers was a man devoid of any well-developed sense of discipline and military exactitude—practical man, perhaps, but not one who was willing and able to perform administrative duties in an irreproachable manner. To Ahlers, by contrast, Treuberg was merely a deputy who had every intention of stepping into his shoes.

"Without in any way trying to influence you, sir, I should like—with all due discretion, of course—to record my misgivings on this particular subject."

"No one's stopping you, with or without due discretion." Ahlers contemplated his deputy without malice. Treuberg had been assigned to him and was not his personal choice. "But it's part of our job to make decisions. You'll get used to the idea in time."

"Of course, sir, of course. It's just that I don't see why we should take responsibility—precipitately, in my view—for something which may lie outside our jurisdiction. It might have been advisable to notify Colonel Turner."

Captain Treuberg, as Ahlers knew only too well, always did his best to surround himself with an impregnable rampart of directives, regulations, decrees, orders of the day and amendments to the same. He accepted the paper-war which dominated the station as if it were a natural phenomenon.

"In doubtful cases," Treuberg concluded, "it's always wiser to cover oneself."

"For God's sake!" exclaimed Ahlers. He screwed the torn remains of the sergeant's report into a ball and threw it into the waste-paper basket. "Everyone tries to hide behind everyone else in this place. Nobody seems to be willing to accept responsibility voluntarily. It's a second-rate attitude, Treuberg—a bureaucratic attitude."

"Aren't you over-simplifying things a little, sir?"

"Things are simple," Ahlers declared. "At least, they ought to be. The only point to remember is that a grain of humanity is worth a mountain of red tape."

*

Company Sergeant-Major Kirschke sat in the company office, yawning.

"I'm putting that bastard Kamnitzer on a charge!" bawled Rammler. "He had the cheek to compare the Bundeswehr with Hitler during class."

Kirschke shook his head sleepily. "Even you can't believe that, Rammler. Kamnitzer's far too cunning to say such a thing in front of witnesses. He doesn't make bloomers like that."

"He did this time. I can swear to it if necessary."

"I hope it won't be." Kirschke slumped back in his chair and stretched his legs, savouring a sense of superiority. The wild buffalo leaning over his desk might be a first-rate leader of cannon-fodder but he hadn't got the makings of a company sergeant-major.

"You mustn't underestimate Kamnitzer," he said mildly, mollified by this thought. "If I know him he'll swear he said the exact opposite, and find a pal to back him up. In the end, it'll be the same old story—either you misheard him, or he was misunderstood and meant something quite different."

"All right, send for him," said Rammler. "The little swine won't dare deny it to my face."

"Listen here," said Kirschke. "If you really want to hang something on him, my advice is as follows: get him to slap you round the chops—in the presence of at least two friendly witnesses. Then you may get somewhere."

Rammler, however, remained adamant. "I insist!" he bellowed.

"Very well," Kirschke said wearily. "If you're really set on the idea I won't stop you." He turned to one of the company clerks. "Fetch Lance-Corporal Kamnitzer."

"You've been reported to me," said Kirschke, when Kamnitzer had been found.

"As far as that goes," replied Kamnitzer, "I've got a complaint to make myself."

"Against me?" Rammler demanded in amazement.

Kirschke's face broke into a delighted grin. He knew the ropes, and he knew Kamnitzer.

"In the case of this complaint," Kamnitzer explained obligingly, "I'm acting as a sort of intermediary. The actual complainant is Grenadier Recht. His young lady, who is slightly disabled, was described in his presence—and in a crowded restaurant—as a lame duck. I can produce witnesses if necessary."

"Is this true?" Kirschke asked Rammler.

"Well, you know how one says things sometimes," Rammler mumbled vaguely.

"The young lady in question," Kamnitzer went on, "happens to be the daughter of an officer—a captain, to be precise."

Kirschke closed his eyes in ecstasy. His judgment of human nature had scored yet another triumph. He had gauged both men—Kamnitzer and Rammler—correctly.

"How could I have known that?" Rammler expostulated. Kamnitzer's allusion to the captain's daughter had manifestly disturbed his equilibrium. "If I really did pass such a remark, it was only meant as a joke. Anyway, I don't remember. It may be a misunderstanding."

"It was a direct and unmistakable insult," Kamnitzer pursued, "and Grenadier Recht is entirely justified in lodging a complaint."

"But not with me!" protested Kirschke. He saw his well-earned afternoon nap threatened by two pieces of tedious paper-work instead of one, and both seemed equally super-fluous. "I haven't the least wish to get involved in your troubles."

"If you mean," Kamnitzer said obligingly, "that someone's in trouble round here, Sergeant-Major, you're dead right—and I don't think it's me, either."

"Do I have to put up with this?" Rammler demanded.

"In this case—yes." Kirschke winked at Kamnitzer as he spoke, and Kamnitzer winked back.

"Is it going into the waste-paper basket, then?" Kamnitzer asked.

The C.S.M. nodded. "You can go, Kamnitzer. You're back to square one again. Nought plus nought equals nought."

He dismissed Kamnitzer with a gracious wave of the hand.

"I never thought you'd side with a bastard like that," Rammler said bitterly. "Never!"

"There are two ways of looking at it, Rammler," said Kirschke. "I could ask you what choice I've got, when my senior N.C.O.s go around behaving like wild animals. Alternatively, I could ask you when you're going to realise that things have changed in the past few years."

Rammler looked suddenly exhausted. He deposited his

massive haunches on Kirschke's desk and mopped his perspiring brow. "So the little sod's trying to get me, is he?" he muttered. "Well, he's picked the wrong man."

"You can do what you like out in the country," Kirschke said, "—worse luck. But not here in barracks or in my presence. I'm more of a nanny than a boxing referee."

"I'll show those lads," Rammler said doggedly. "There's a map-reading exercise this afternoon."

Kirschke shrugged. "Just watch out you don't lose your own bearings, that's all."

*

"Would you like a quick trip to Athens?" Ahlers asked. "We've got to fly some equipment there."

"No thanks," said Vossler, who was sitting back comfortably in an armchair in Ahlers's office. "It's too hot for me —puts me off my whisky."

"In that case, I could assign you to a flight to Bordeaux." This, as Ahlers well knew, was an extremely tempting offer. Warrant Officer Vossler had a distinct penchant for the *grands vins de Bordeaux*. "You'd have three hours there," he added, implying that Vossler would have plenty of time to lay in a couple of dozen.

Vossler continued to display a marked lack of enthusiasm. "Anyone's welcome to go swanning round Europe as far as I'm concerned," he said. "Personally, I don't feel the slightest inclination to. I've lost the urge, somehow."

This was something new. Vossler normally jumped at any opportunity to fly. He was not only the keenest but the most reliable pilot in the squadron, and Ahlers tended to give him preference as a matter of course, when the choice was left to him.

"I'm sick of the whole business, Klaus," Vossler said. "I'm thinking of handing in my papers. I've had enough offers from civil airlines, God knows."

"But you're not the employee type," protested Ahlers. "It would bore you stiff to operate on a fixed schedule arranged weeks or months ahead. You like a bit of freedom, and you'll only get that here with us."

"But I'm only a warrant officer," Vossler grumbled. "To a lot of people, that means an underling—and I don't always like it."

"You could take a commission any time you wanted."

"I wouldn't dream of it," Vossler said stubbornly. "Can you see me sitting through a training course at my age? And where would it get me? I want to go on flying, that's all, and becoming an officer won't make me a better pilot."

Klaus Ahlers felt slightly at a loss. He failed to see what Vossler was getting at. All he had to do was issue the order "Flight 347 to Bordeaux; usual crew; take-off: 1300 hours" and Vossler would merely say "Yes, sir." But that was too simple.

"Have you had a row with someone, Viktor—Captain Treuberg, say?"

Vossler eyed his friend reproachfully. "I know better than to row with Treuberg. For one thing, a warrant officer is junior to a captain, and for another, he belongs to a different class of society—even if he's called a friend in private."

"That's absolute poppycock," said Ahlers, "and you know it."

"Really? Then prove it sometime. It wouldn't be difficult. If you need money for Carolin's operation, I'll gladly let you have it. How many more times do I have to tell you?"

"Thanks, I know you mean it."

"Then for God's sake behave as if you did!"

Ahlers passed a hand across his brow. "All right, if I can't scrape it together any other way I'll call on you. But there's no getting round it, Viktor, military regulations contain very strict rulings on the subject."

"They don't apply to personal friends."

"Yes, they do—when the friends in question voluntarily submit to the existing military code."

"Come off it! I'm not trying to bribe you—I'm not even giving you a present. You can make it a loan if you like, and pay interest—at the highest prevailing rate, if it'll salve your conscience. Or don't you want Carolin to be cured completely?"

"All right," said Ahlers. "If the doctor thinks it's worth doing the operation now and I don't manage to raise a loan elsewhere, I'll take you up on the offer."

"Done!" cried Vossler. "I'll put a couple of thousand marks at your disposal straight away. You can give me an I.O.U. and pay a steep rate of interest if you like. If it's against regulations for an officer to exploit his subordinates, we'll try it the other way round."

*

"Anything special?" demanded Lieutenant von Strackmann, expecting to hear the C.S.M. produce his usual stereotyped negative.

"Yes, sir!" replied Kirschke.

Von Strackmann had just returned from an officers' conference in the C.O.'s office and was feeling rather exhausted. He had been obliged to take note of seventeen new additions to standing orders, of which fourteen superseded rulings of an earlier date.

"You must be joking, Sergeant-Major. Did I hear you say yes?"

"Yes, sir," the C.S.M. repeated. "I've just received a disturbing report from Sergeant-Major Rammler."

Kirschke took care to say this in the presence of two witnesses : the corporal clerk and a civilian employee. He was determined to spoil von Strackmann's lunch-hour before embarking on his own midday siesta.

"Sergeant-Major Rammler," he continued, "is under the impression that he heard Hitler and the Bundeswehr mentioned in the same breath, so to speak, in front of the assembled company."

Lieutenant von Strackmann's brows contracted and his mouth opened in what was, for a man of iron, a slightly helpless expression. He felt like someone who has been lured on to thin ice and can only move with the utmost caution.

"I hope," he said eventually, "that there's been some mistake."

"It's possible that Sergeant-Major Rammler misheard," Kirschke generously conceded, having laid his egg. The fact that his report had been parenthetical in tone did not make it any less official. What the lieutenant made of it was up to him, at least for the moment. Kirschke could always turn it to account later if he felt like it.

"Has anyone made a written deposition on the subject?" inquired von Strackmann.

"Not to me."

Von Strackmann heaved a sigh of relief. "So it could be just hot air." Then, covering himself in the time-honoured manner, he went on : "Anyway, I can see you didn't take it seriously, Sergeant-Major. I'm sure you handled the matter correctly."

"Begging your pardon, sir, I didn't handle it at all. I merely asked Sergeant-Major Rammler if he had considered things carefully, and he didn't seem too sure. Whether there's anything in his story I'm not in a position to judge." This sort of tug-of-war could have gone on for some time if von Strackmann had not decided to break off the engagement. He didn't want any complications. As one who found it hard enough to cope with the present, he felt that having to cope with hang-overs from the past was asking too much of him.

"As far as I'm concerned, a report which hasn't been submitted doesn't exist." The lieutenant's voice betrayed his conviction that the case was closed, and Kirschke did not disabuse him.

*

Herbert Asch sat opposite his wife, looking at her tenderly
and revelling in his hour of lunch-time privacy. The staff
were forbidden to disturb him, and even the telephone had
been disconnected.

" Have I told you that I love you?" he asked.

Elisabeth smiled. " Not recently, but it's not absolutely
essential."

" Well, it's what I tell myself every day, even if I don't
say it aloud."

" I sometimes wonder how much longer these little lunch-
time idylls are going to last," she said, when their food had
been brought in. " If things go on as they are, there won't
be time."

" You're not worried, are you, Elisabeth?"

" No, just thinking my own thoughts." She pushed the
dish across to him. Asch never needed to state his preferences
on the subject of food because Elisabeth knew them by
instinct. " You spent a long time with that reporter this
morning, didn't you?"

" I couldn't avoid it."

" And your meeting with the council?"

" Couldn't get out of that either. I am mayor, after all."

" And all those telephone conversations with the army
and air force are equally essential, I suppose?"

" One can't ignore the services. They exist, so one has
to deal with them."

Elisabeth refrained from looking at her husband. She
didn't want him to know what she was thinking, though
she was pretty sure he did anyway.

" The trouble is that I've never grown up," Asch went on.
" I'm always interested in things which most people would
say didn't concern me. But can we really pretend that what
goes on in our immediate vicinity doesn't concern us? Look,
Elisabeth—when I was in the army, and serving in this
very town, in the barracks over there, my pals and I often

used to spend the odd evening in each other's homes. Our fathers used to ask us how we were—not what we were doing in there or what they were doing to us. They'd done their own service long ago, and if they'd been treated wrongly or unjustly in the past—well, why shouldn't we have a dose of the same medicine? They couldn't have cared less what happened to us, or so we used to think."

" And how do you propose to change that?"

" I'm not quite sure yet," Asch said thoughtfully, " but the main thing is not to be indifferent. We must make it our business to find out whether they're really doing things better these days. We've got to help and encourage the people who are, and rub the others' noses in the results of past experience. To be frank, I've got an urge to stick my mayoral finger in their little pie."

" Isn't that what you've been doing for some time?"

Herbert Asch realised that his wife had seen through him and admired her powers of perception. "Maybe," he said carelessly, " but it's a temptation I can't resist."

*

Sergeant-Major Rammler thought he knew what was wrong with his men : they weren't in a state of absolute combat readiness. A man's fighting spirit could be impaired by the wrong sort of ideas and modern civilisation was a softening influence, but, whatever the reason, Rammler told himself conscientiously that things had got to change.

" My platoon will assemble on the parade-ground ten minutes earlier than usual," he told the orderly sergeant.

When other platoon commanders made such a request, they were, the orderly sergeant knew, merely making a suggestion designed to cover themselves in case complications arose later on. The others expressed a wish but did not insist on its fulfilment. Rammler, however, was more explicit. " That's an order ! "

Prematurely routed out of their rooms, the members of No. 3 Platoon assembled—in Rammler's jaundiced opinion

—like a gaggle of tourists gawping at the Brandenburg Gate. He found their chatter intolerable.

" Quiet ! " he shouted.

The men fell silent and gazed at him apprehensively as though he were a dangerously overheated boiler with a malfunctioning safety-valve.

" I said quiet," Rammler announced. " I didn't say shut your gob."

" That's just how it sounded," Kamnitzer whispered to Recht.

" Let's see your finger-nails," Rammler continued. " You'll notice I didn't say : hold out your grubby paws."

This was Rammler's favourite way of demonstrating his observance of modern military etiquette. His men extended their hands while he passed down the ranks, face contorted with displeasure.

" An uncultured man," he said, " would call you a lot of filthy dirty scum. All I say is, your general standard of cleanliness leaves a great deal to be desired."

The finger-nails proffered for his inspection were anything but clean, and the clean body, as Rammler knew, was a prerequisite of the clean mind. " If I had hands like that," he declared, " it'd put me off my food."

" We needed the extra ten minutes, Sergeant-Major." The author of this friendly comment was, of course, Kamnitzer. " I didn't manage to clean my boots properly either, if you'd care to have a look."

" On your backs," Rammler commanded. The platoon lay down. " Now let's see your palms."

The palms confronting him were far from clean, thanks partly to dirt acquired when lying down, and Kamnitzer's and Recht's were no exception. Rammler's verdict on the latter sounded comparatively kindly. " Trust you two to catch my eye again ! I wish you wouldn't."

" So do I—Sergeant-Major." Kamnitzer added the last word almost as an afterthought.

Rammler stationed himself in front of the supine platoon.

" Right, on your feet!" he shouted. " The efficient soldier keeps himself and his equipment clean at all times. The same goes for this grass here."

This was not a new subject. Rammler raised it on average about twice a week, asserting that he had seen discarded cigarette packets, spent matches or sheets of newspaper in front of the company block. This time, according to his account, there had been scraps of paper—possibly lavatory paper.

" Spread out and start looking!" he commanded, not forgetting to add : " I won't say it was one of us who made a pig of himself here, but whoever it was—we won't tolerate a speck of filth on our grass. Anyone care to differ?"

If anyone did disagree he refrained from saying so. When Rammler was bitten by the cleanliness bug, nothing could stand in his way, and if he said the grass was covered with garbage that was all there was to it.

Obediently playing the game, the platoon spread out and combed the area. Anyone who found anything had to hand it over to Rammler, who regarded each piece of treasure trove as a sign of diligence on the part of the finder and had been known to await results patiently for anything up to forty-five minutes.

To-day however, he had a bright idea. When three traverses had been made with deplorably meagre results, he shouted : " Right! Success will be rewarded. Anyone who finds any more rubbish can dismiss and push off to the mess-hall straight away."

" A lot of good that is," Recht mumbled, expressing the thoughts of all. " There aren't any more foreign bodies to find."

" Then we'll manufacture some," Kamnitzer said airily, groping around in his hip pocket. He pulled out several sheets of lavatory paper, tore off a strip about two inches long, dropped it on the grass and stamped on it. Then he picked up his handiwork and took it to Rammler.

" May I hand over what I've found, Sergeant-Major?"

Rammler accepted the trophy with extreme reluctance. He examined it for some moments with an air of justifiable suspicion.

" Can I go and get my grub now, Sergeant-Major?" Kamnitzer asked brightly. Without waiting for a reply he saluted with commendable precision, turned about and strutted happily away.

Rammler had no time to glower at Kamnitzer's retreating form because his example had now been adopted by the other members of the platoon. Almost to a man, they rummaged in their pockets and produced objects which they trampled on and alleged that they had found. A substantial heap of rubbish grew at the sergeant-major's feet.

" All right, pack it in!" he yelled furiously. "Go and get your pig-swill!"

No one waited to be told twice. The platoon trotted off, leaving the sergeant-major alone with his pile of refuse.

Rammler was not easily discouraged, however. The day was far from over, and he had inexhaustible reserves of energy. He was a man of ideas, too, and his ideas were not limited to the subject of garbage disposal. There were other ways of raising a platoon's morale.

*

Warrant Officer Vossler, inspired by a wish to help his friend —and no trip to Athens or Bordeaux could have dissuaded him from putting his offer into effect at the earliest possible moment—climbed into his pale blue saloon during the lunch-hour and drove off to see Frau Ahlers.

" We've made it," he told her. "Klaus has agreed to accept my help."

" Did he really say he would?" she asked, looking half hopeful, half uneasy. "That's wonderful."

" I used every trick in the book. I don't know whether he wanted to spare me further effort, but he finally agreed."

Frau Ahlers greeted this announcement with evident relief,

but she realised what was expected of her. Practical arrangements would have to be made.

First, she went to consult Carolin and asked her whether
she would be prepared to undergo another operation.

"Yes," Carolin said promptly, adding, after a moment's
hesitation : "But can we afford it?"

"You needn't worry about that, Carolin. All that matters
is whether you want the operation."

Carolin's enthusiastic response was conveyed to the waiting
Vossler. "That's that, then!" he exclaimed happily. "You
wait, I'll be dancing with Carolin before the year's out—if
the current girl-friend allows it, that is."

Vossler was thereupon dismissed to the kitchen, where
Carolin improvised a mushroom omelette for him. While
he was eating, Frau Ahlers put a call through to Carolin's
surgeon, Professor Martin. He told her that, while such
an operation was never devoid of risk, the decisive factor
was the patient's general condition and mental preparedness.

When Frau Ahlers told Professor Martin that Carolin
had not only agreed to the operation but seemed bent on
having it as soon as possible, he concurred, subject to the
usual reservations. Only then did he broach the subject
of expense. Rather hesitantly, he told her that his fee and
the cost of Carolin's stay in hospital would amount to more
than two thousand marks.

"If that's all it is!" said Vossler, when he heard. "Let's
call it three thousand. That should cover all eventualities."

He took his leave hurriedly, determined that Klaus Ahlers
should get his loan before he had a chance to change his
mind. Apart from that, he mustn't be allowed to think that
Vossler would lose by lending him the money, or that he
was motivated by pure altruism. The only way to ensure
this was to draw up a fairly stiff-looking contract which seemed
to sail close to the restrictions imposed on money-lenders
by law.

Vossler decided to get Gerty Ballhaus to type the contract,
but found that she was snowed under with letters for her
employer.

" Hasn't Asch got anything better to do than supply this town with reading matter?" Vossler demanded indignantly.

In fact, Asch's letters contained an element of interest. Headed " Relations between the Bundeswehr and the Civil Population," they were addressed to Colonel Turner of the air force, Major Bornekamp of the army, members of the town council and certain specified commercial concerns classified under the heading " Catering and Entertainment."

Every one of these letters expressed a lively desire for the maintenance of cordial and harmonious relations between the garrison and the town. They also invited comments, welcomed suggestions for improvement and stressed that complaints, if any, could be made in confidence. The one sentence which recurred in each letter read simply : " We are all citizens endowed with equal rights, whether we wear uniforms or not."

" Can't you make it clear to Asch that your services are urgently required elsewhere?" Vossler asked.

" In the middle of the day, Viktor?" Gertrud Ballhaus looked positively stern, but her eyes sparkled merrily. " You seem to forget I've got a job to do. It's a job I don't want to lose, either. I'm not a married woman, after all. I'm not even engaged."

Viktor Vossler left the Rathaus hastily. Gerty's hints had been a little too broad for his taste, though not, he reluctantly conceded, wholly unjustified. Banishing the thought from his mind, he concentrated on the problem of how to draft Ahlers's promissory note as quickly as possible.

On his return to barracks he was lucky enough to find Monika alone in the office—Monika, that happy blend of Europe and the Middle East. It was pleasant to see such a decorative specimen of femininity in such a nest of officialdom, and Monika was an obliging creature.

" Just tell me what you want me to do, Herr Vossler. I'd do anything for you." She giggled. " Well, almost anything."

" A bit of typing will do for the time being. But it's strictly private, so I rely on you to be discreet."

Vossler proceeded to dictate the note. Its terms made

him, the lender, look more like a usurer, and gave no hint
that he was really an unselfish man who was trying to help
a friend.

When this agreeable task was interrupted by a call from
Ahlers summoning Monika to his office, Vossler used the
opportunity to fetch some cigarettes. The half-completed
document remained in the typewriter, and the office remained
unattended—unattended that is, until Captain Treuberg walked
in.

As he crossed he empty office, Treuberg's eye caught the
letters " I.O.U." at the head of the sheet. Somewhat surprised he read the preamble beneath: *Form of Agreement
between Klaus Ahlers and Viktor Vossler . . .* And finally,
with an incredulity which gave way to growing excitement:
*In respect of a loan in the sum of DM 3000 (three thousand
marks). . . .*

" Very interesting," mused Captain Treuberg, " very interesting indeed."

*

Sergeant-Major Rammler used words very sparingly when he
was in his natural element, and his natural element was the
training area north of the town, which he knew like the
back of his hand.

Out in the country he preferred to beckon with his thumb,
toot his whistle or clap his hands. One powerful sweep of
his arm—not unlike that of a peasant scattering seed—and
his platoon adapted itself to the terrain, pressed its collective
belly to the ground and tried to crawl into the nearest fold in
the ground.

" Looks as though he's got plans for us to-day," Martin
Recht said with foreboding.

" Don't worry," scoffed Kamnitzer, " he's all wind and
piss."

" For Christ's sake shut up!" Corporal Streicher hissed
apprehensively. " There's no need to put his back up."

But Rammler was not so easily provoked to-day. He was

far too sure of himself. He stood there with his legs planted
firmly apart, studying the map in his hand. In front of
him was the platoon, behind him two three-ton trucks, and
around him the open country, which stretched far to the
north. It was his idea of heaven : an expanse of tangled
undergrowth, dense woods, marshy meadows and muddy
fields.

"Map-reading exercise in individual groups!" he announced.

This came as no surprise to the platoon, since all pre-
parations had pointed to it. Each man was in full marching
order and had been issued with a map and compass.

"Now get down and crawl to the edge of the wood!"

Rammler regarded crawling, which formed a branch of
fieldcraft, as a means of improving his men's physical fitness.
The only variable factor was the ground to be covered.
This was an average distance, which meant that Rammler's
ingenious outdoor game would consume about a quarter of
an hour. Satisfied that his schedule allowed ample time for an
additional manœuvre of this sort, he followed the toiling
platoon at a comfortable stroll.

"Grenadier Recht is waggling his bottom in the air,"
he announced after five minutes. "I hope it's not meant to
be an invitation."

Pausing briefly for appreciative laughter, he continued :
"Grenadier Recht will go back and start again."

At the edge of the wood Rammler informed the platoon
of their rendezvous, a disused water-mill about fourteen
miles away. "Time allowed, three hours."

"That means a forced march!" muttered Streicher.

"I call it a dirty trick," said Kamnitzer. "What's the
point? I've already done that stretch twice in the past
three months."

Meanwhile, the sergeant-major was handing out prepared
slips of paper telling the platoon who was marching with
whom and from where. Rammler was a great believer in
getting his men to converge on a common destination from
widely scattered points. He divided the platoon into about

a dozen separate groups and loaded them on to the trucks which were to deposit them at their individual starting-points.

The various groups were to operate under very varied conditions. Some had tracks at their disposal, others had to traverse densely wooded country, and still others had to cope with sand and mud. The members of Group 7 would have to wade through miles of bog unless they were prepared to risk making a long and time-consuming detour.

Group 7, needless to say, comprised Lance-Corporal Kamnitzer, Grenadier Recht and another grenadier named Armke. Armke seldom spoke and scarcely ever registered approval or disapproval. He appeared to remain completely indifferent, whatever the circumstances, a fact which struck his superiors as suspicious in the extreme.

"Every minute under three hours earns you a plus mark," Rammler told them in conclusion. "Every minute over three hours means a minus mark. Lame ducks"—and here he grinned savagely at Recht—"better be prepared to do the whole trip again from scratch."

The trucks lumbered off and deposited the men in their predetermined positions. They jumped out and were soon swallowed up in the surrounding countryside, conscious that every minute counted. Kamnitzer, Recht and Armke disembarked at the edge of a marshy field, and a few seconds later they were standing alone in a wide tract of deserted country.

"All right, let's go," Martin Recht said resignedly. "We've got no choice."

"What about you, Armke?" asked Kamnitzer. "Are you keen on taking a mud-bath too?"

"I don't give a bugger," said Grenadier Armke, truthfully.

"You've said a mouthful." Kamnitzer sat down comfortably at the edge of the road. "Let's start with a break for a fag."

"But we can't afford the time!" Recht protested. "We're going to have to pull our fingers out if we want to make the rendezvous inside three hours."

"Calm down," said Kamnitzer. "Get this straight: you'll

never get into Rammler's good books, even if you march home on your bleeding stumps. Am I right, Armke?"

"I don't give a bugger," said Armke.

Kamnitzer nodded at him appreciatively. "Our pal Armke doesn't say much, but when he does it's always to the point."

"We could have done half a mile while you've been jabbering away here." Martin Recht was consumed with impatience. "I've had enough of Rammler's attentions for one day. I don't want to put his back up again."

Kamnitzer winked at Armke. "Did you hear that? The poor lad's piddling his pants. Never mind, we'll soon cure that." He turned to Recht. "I've got a little brain-teaser for you. Question: who can do fourteen miles across a swamp in three hours? Answer: a hippopotamus couldn't and neither can we. We'd be too late whatever we did. So, if we can't use our legs, we better use these." He tapped his head.

Grenadier Armke had no need to utter his favourite maxim—it was obvious what he thought of the idea—but Martin Recht's uneasiness mounted still further. "You're not working out one of your little schemes, are you, Karl? If Rammler catches on, I'll be the one who suffers."

"Just so we understand one another," Kamnitzer said pleasantly, "I'm the senior here, so I hereby appoint myself group leader. You two are under my command, all right?"

"I don't——" began Armke.

"We know, Armke, we know." Kamnitzer got slowly to his feet. "We're supposed to be going north, aren't we? Right, the first thing to do is move south. There's a pub called the Traveller's Rest a mile down the road. We can have a quiet snack there and put away a couple of mid-afternoon noggins."

"You must be out of your mind!" Recht protested furiously.

"March at ease!" ordered Kamnitzer.

Armke set off without hesitation and Recht saw no alternative but to follow suit, maintaining a reproachful silence. Lance-Corporal Kamnitzer, who had seen *The Bridge on the*

River Kwai, cheerfully whistled a tune which bore a vague resemblance to *Colonel Bogey*.

Fifteen minutes' leisurely stroll brought them to the small Gasthaus which Kamnitzer had mentioned, where they relieved themselves of their packs and rifles and sat down. As the only customers, they received a cordial if slightly surprised welcome from the landlord.

"Three large schnapps and three litres of beer for me and my men," Kamnitzer commanded. "They need fortifying. They've got a lot of work ahead of them."

"And a plate of ham and eggs for me," said Armke.

Martin Recht continued to brood in silence. He saw a host of complications looming before him like a dark storm-cloud, and above it, thunderbolts poised, a god of vengeance with a face resembling Rammler's. A smell of brimstone assailed his nostrils.

Armke, whose appetite seemed unimpaired, munched in silence but not silently. Kamnitzer asked for a paper and read it from end to end with apparent interest, local fat-stock prices included. Then he demanded to hear some music, and the landlord put a record on. After listening to *O'er Hill and Dale* (Folk-songs in March Tempo) for a minute, Kamnitzer protested, and it was replaced by some Neapolitan love-songs.

After about an hour, Kamnitzer rose to his feet and stretched luxuriously. "I suppose it's about time we made a move," he drawled. Then he went to the telephone and ordered a taxi.

*

Lieutenant Dieter von Strackmann, meanwhile, was neither in barracks nor in the country. Instead, he was spending the afternoon with Frau Elfrieda Bornekamp, esteemed wife of the highly-esteemed Major, at her personal request.

"I really don't know whether I ought to be here at this hour," he said, vacillating between duty and inclination.

E

" Why so worried?" She flashed him an encouraging smile.
" Didn't you want to come?"

" I can't think of anywhere I'd rather be." Dieter knew
how to produce text-book compliments with an air of conviction, and Elfrieda revelled in them.

They still employed the formal mode of address, despite
a certain incident that had occurred between them. Even
at the crucial moment, Frau Elfrieda had managed to preserve
formality—at least in spirit—by whispering: " Go on—
Lieutenant!"

As one who considered himself a man of honour, however,
von Strackmann was deeply sensible of the tragedy that
hung in the air. Where would it end—his love for the wife
and veneration of the husband?

" If the C.O. ever questioned me on the subject," he
admitted, " I wouldn't know how to answer him."

" He won't question you on the subject," she said firmly.
" He's not petty-minded."

" Of course not!" von Strackmann agreed. " Major Bornekamp is the soul of generosity."

" And understanding."

" And understanding too, of course."

" Exactly," said Frau Elfrieda, and leaned against him as
though overcome by a fit of weakness.

He scarcely ventured to breathe, but she went on: " You've
no need to worry—he knows you're here."

Von Strackmann jumped like a man seared by a red-hot
iron and released her hastily.

Elfrieda walked over to a small table in the corner of the
room and busied herself with the bottles and glasses that
stood there.

" I told my husband I was asking you over, and he agreed.
As you so rightly say, he's a generous man."

At first, von Strackmann couldn't take in the vista which
these words opened up. The radiant picture which he had
so far entertained of his revered C.O. threatened to fade.

Elfrieda looked amused. " Haven't you caught on yet?"

she said, handing him a brimming glass. "You're here on duty, so to speak."

"On duty!" yelped the bemused lieutenant. His imagination boggled.

Elfrieda decided that it was high time to enlighten her bewildered admirer. "I suggested organising a social evening for the officers of the battalion and their ladies, and my husband agreed. You're to help me arrange it."

Von Strackmann experienced a sense of boundless relief. He drained his glass at a gulp, glowing with pride at this fresh token of the C.O.'s confidence. Bornekamp was now entrusting him with his personal administrative problems.

"If the C.O. plans to hold a Ladies' Night," he mused, "the best place would probably be the Hotel Asch."

"Never mind that now," Frau Elfrieda said petulantly. "We can discuss details later. Come here!"

*

Sergeant-Major Rammler stood beside the disused water-mill with Corporal Streicher at his side. Streicher had been given the job of check-point N.C.O., which he regarded as a special privilege, not to say a definite mark of favour.

Streicher demonstrated his gratitude. "The first groups should be here any time now," he said, looking at his watch. "I'm sure your calculations were absolutely correct, Sergeant-Major."

"As usual," Rammler said confidently.

Having spent years familiarising himself with the district, he now knew every tree and bush, path and by-path.

"Kamnitzer and his shower are bound to be at least half an hour late." Rammler complacently surveyed the dark, glutinous surface of the near-by marsh, which stretched away into the far distance. "Shall we have a bet on it, Streicher?"

"I'm sure you're right, Sergeant-Major."

"I bet you twenty marks."

" I'd be bound to lose, Sergeant-Major."

Rammler was gratified by his trusty subordinate's perception, though he would have enjoyed betting on such a foregone conclusion.

Meanwhile the first groups were beginning to straggle in. They reported to Rammler and then handed their slips of paper recording time and point of departure to Streicher.

" Greyhounds, that's what you are!" Rammler said, not without pride. " But that's the way you've got to be in this platoon—fighting fit and ready for anything! We'll smash all the records when it comes to the autumn exercises."

" It can't be!" Streicher broke in suddenly. " My watch must have stopped!"

Turning, Rammler saw what Streicher meant. Kamnitzer's group had apparently emerged from the swamp and was marching jauntily down the road towards them. The sound of cheerful whistling came to the sergeant-major's ears, and even at a hundred yards he could detect a broad grin on Kamnitzer's face.

" But there's still seventeen minutes to go," Streicher said helplessly.

Kamnitzer trotted up and reported the arrival of his group. Then he jabbed at his watch. " Seventeen minutes before time means seventeen plus marks—not bad, eh?"

" It's only fifteen minutes now," Streicher said officiously.

" You can blather as much as you like," said Kamnitzer, " but not at my expense. I set my watch by the wireless—isn't that good enough for you?"

" Shut up!" shouted Rammler, momentarily losing self-control.

" Did you hear?" Kamnitzer told Streicher. " Just chalk up seventeen plus marks to us and pipe down."

Sergeant-Major Rammler scrutinised Kamnitzer's map-reading group closely. To his experienced eye they looked suspiciously fresh. Neither their boots nor their faces betrayed signs of recent exertion. They were either stout-hearted lads or a bunch of crooked double-dealing skivers, and he knew which alternative he favoured.

" How did you manage it, Kamnitzer?"

" We just marched," the lance-corporal replied laconically, " and now we're here."

Rammler knew from experience that he would get nowhere with Kamnitzer, so he turned hopefully to the next member of the map-reading group. This happened to be Armke —don't-give-a-bugger Armke—and it was easier to get blood out of a stone than extract a sensible answer from him. In desperation Rammler turned to Recht.

" You there!" he commanded. " Get round the back of the mill—at the double! When you get there, dig in. I've got a special job for you."

Confident that he had put his finger on the weak spot in Kamnitzer's group, Rammler left the platoon in charge of a sergeant and trotted after Recht, scenting trouble and determined to get to the bottom of it.

Reaching the back of the mill he looked about him keenly. Beyond the red brick walls he saw an expanse of lush green meadow-land and, in the middle of it, Recht, endeavouring to dig in as ordered. In the background, close to an idyllic-looking birch forest, flowed a stream—waist-deep only, to his regret.

" Into the wood, at the double!" called Rammler.

This was a wise move. He didn't want Recht to excavate too deeply because of possible complaints from the local peat-cutters, who had quickly learnt to enrich themselves at the garrison's expense. Apart from that, the sergeant-major wanted no chance passer-by to witness his unavoidable tête-à-tête with Recht. The obstinate, pig-headed youth had to be softened up with every means at his disposal. Discipline was in danger!

Rammler proceeded to warm Recht up. He chased him across the meadow, through the stream and into the wood. He made him lie down, crawl through thickets and double on the spot. Having driven him through bog, mire and water for upwards of fifteen minutes, he paused.

" Well, haven't you got anything to tell me?" he asked, when Recht lay panting at his feet.

The fact that he received no reply did not dishearten him. He repeated the whole process from scratch : across the field, through the stream, into the wood and back again. " Just to give you time to think it over, you little bastard!"

Rammler normally selected his epithets with great care, in deference to modern army practice, but this was a special case and there were no witnesses in sight.

" Come here, you shit-bag, you blue-arsed baboon! I'm going to put you through it until you beg for permission to tell me the truth, you pool of piss!"

Even now, Rammler felt that he was only yielding to force of circumstance. The last thing he wanted to do was violate human dignity as guaranteed by the Federal constitution. On the contrary : anyone who failed to obey an order or indulged in clandestine acts of sabotage was an enemy of the freedom and human dignity which he was pledged to defend, and, as such, had to be dealt with resolutely.

" I'll tear you limb from limb, you little sod, if you don't start co-operating properly with your superiors. Well, what about it? Either you tell me the truth about your map-reading jaunt or I'll have your guts for garters!"

Even this failed to elicit a reply, much to Rammler's righteous indignation. Half an hour later Recht collapsed in an exhausted heap.

" Revolting!" Rammler ejaculated scornfully. " Revolting, the way some people force a man to do things like this."

❦

Herbert Asch looked forward to the week-end with an unusual sense of anticipation.

The first person to ring him had been Colonel Turner, commander of the transport wing, area commandant and philosopher. The Colonel was something of a phantom. Although Asch had often spoken to him on the 'phone he had hardly ever seen him in person, just as his own men, though familiar with several hundred of his directives, scarcely knew what he looked like. He reigned from a throne in the clouds, like Zeus.

"I have always attached great importance to our friendly collaboration, Herr Asch," Turner told him. "I read your letter with close attention, and I merely wanted to say at once that we are agreed in principle. My sincerest thanks."

Following on Turner's decidedly friendly call came another from his adjutant, who announced that the Colonel would welcome any attempt to widen the social horizons of his officer cadets. "It is proposed to hold a sort of *thé dansant,* inviting specially selected young ladies from the senior form of the local high school. Subject to your agreement, this could take place in your hotel, if you have a suitable room available."

"Aha!" Asch said in some amusement, adding, more audibly, "By all means."

Immediately afterwards, Asch received a personal visit from an officer to whom he had only spoken on the 'phone hitherto. Lieutenant von Strackmann withdrew a list from his briefcase and said, in tones of command: "Major Bornekamp has decided to hold a mixed party for about forty people this Saturday. Kindly be good enough to make suitable premises available."

Herbert Asch hesitated before replying. Herr von Strackmann had a jarring effect on his civilian disposition, and for a moment or two he felt tempted to decline the request flatly. The lieutenant seemed to be in urgent need of a little lesson on how to treat people who were not privileged to wear uniform. However, there would be time enough for that when Saturday came, so he said: "I'll arrange it," and left it at that.

"I was sure you would," von Strackmann replied condescendingly.

Determined to have his little bit of fun, Asch at once telephoned Ahlers. "I've already got two mixed parties booked for Saturday," he told him. "All the mixture needs now is a little yeast, if you know what I mean."

"A couple of pike for the gold-fish pond?"

Herbert Asch chuckled. "Precisely. Can you supply something of the sort?"

"It's quite possible," said Ahlers. "What about half a dozen young officers who've just finished a stiff training course and are itching to celebrate?"

"Couldn't be better! I can guarantee them reduced prices and preferential treatment. Thanks a lot, then, and don't forget—if I can ever do anything for you. . . ."

Asch seldom missed an opportunity to make such an offer because the captain's personal troubles were often on his mind. Officers with a healthy measure of human understanding were a boon—and not only to the men under their command—but how much more effective Ahlers would be, he told himself, if only his financial worries were eliminated.

Asch's next telephone conversation was with Bornekamp. He thanked the Major for enlisting his services as a hôtelier. "I shall devote my undivided attention to your Ladies' Night," he promised. "And as far as the wines are concerned, I shall take the liberty of sending over a few modest samples."

"You're always on your toes, Asch, I'll give you that."

"Would you allow me to make a small suggestion, Major, just between ourselves?"

Bornekamp gave his assent, and Asch revealed that Colonel Turner had suggested holding a small dance for his officer cadets. In the process, he had not only learnt about Bornekamp's plans but—so Asch alleged—evinced a certain amount of interest in them. "Perhaps it might be advisable to invite him, Major."

"Not a bad idea," the C.O. agreed. "I'll do it."

Herbert Asch had now mobilised every influential member of the garrison. Their common destination: his hotel. Estimated time of arrival: Saturday evening. A collision had been set.

*

Sergeant-Major Rammler surveyed his handiwork with repugnance. By collapsing, Grenadier Martin Recht had once more demonstrated his flabby physical condition and shown himself unworthy to belong to an élite unit.

"Gutless bastard!" Rammler said finally. He left the idyllic meadow behind the water-mill and returned to his men, who had all straggled in by this time. The sergeant in charge and Corporal Streicher had supervised their arrival, noting times and awarding plus or minus marks accordingly. Rammler, however, spared no glance for the results of the map-reading exercise. He strode through the assembled platoon and confronted Karl Kamnitzer.

"I'll give you one last chance," he said threateningly.

"To do what—Sergeant-Major?"

"I warn you, Kamnitzer, don't play dumb with me. You know bloody well what I mean."

Lance-Corporal Kamnitzer knew very well what he meant, but if Rammler expected to find out from him what he had obviously failed to learn from Recht, he had another think coming.

"What's the matter, Kamnitzer—aren't you talking to me any more?"

"Of course, Sergeant-Major. What do you want me to talk about?"

Rammler could endure the lance-corporal's affable grin no longer. He turned on his heel and shouted: "Equipment on! Be ready to move off in ten minutes." Then, to Streicher: "Go and fetch Grenadier Recht. He's behind the mill—he slipped and fell over."

"Right, Sergeant-Major!" called Streicher, and trotted off. Kamnitzer followed him without being asked, much to Rammler's increased fury. However, battalion regulations stated that "initiative" was not to be discouraged.

They found Martin Recht alone in the field. His body

drooped like a weeping willow, and his face, where it was visible through its coating of mud, looked white as chalk.

"Pull yourself together." Kamnitzer's tone was deliberately harsh. "In this outfit, anyone who gets himself worked over like that only has himself to blame."

"Come on, Martin," Corporal Streicher said encouragingly. He made a move to help him, but Recht shook off his comradely grasp. "I'll manage," he muttered.

When they rejoined the others they found them drawn up in front of the mill ready to move off. The two trucks stood there, purring gently. Conscious that Sergeant-Major Rammler was studying their reactions closely, the men avoided looking at Recht.

"Embus!" shouted Rammler.

The platoon divided itself between the two trucks. The drivers and co-drivers closed the tail-flaps and laced up the tarpaulin covers. The engines roared and the convoy moved off in the direction of the barracks, nearly twenty miles away.

"I feel sick," said Martin Recht.

Kamnitzer, who sat next him in the second truck, wagged his head disapprovingly. "You could have spared yourself that."

"What was I supposed to do?" Recht asked bitterly. "He had me over a barrel, and he knew it—treated me like a piece of dirt."

"If you will put up with that sort of treatment . . ."

"I couldn't have done a thing, Karl."

"Of course you could."

"What do you expect me to do—report him? He'd deny the lot. We were alone out there, without witnesses."

"That's just it, laddie! There weren't any witnesses— that's precisely why I'm blaming you."

"I don't follow," Recht said dully.

"You say gaily ' there weren't any witnesses '—but what could be better? The fact that there aren't any witnesses works both ways, don't you see? You could have told him to go to hell—among other things. He'd never have been able to prove anything."

Martin Recht closed his eyes. Even if Kamnitzer had put his finger on the truth, he, Recht, wasn't the man to put his theory into practice—certainly not in his present condition. His stomach heaved.

"I feel sick," he repeated.

"Have a good puke, then," said Kamnitzer, opening the tarpaulins.

"Battalion orders," Streicher recited in the background, "expressly state that, in default of instructions to the contrary, opening the flaps while travelling through wooded country or along tree-lined roads is forbidden."

"Belt up!" snapped Kamnitzer. "I don't know of any battalion order that says Recht's got to puke in my lap."

He pulled the flaps apart and helped Recht to crane out. The road danced crazily beneath his eyes as he retched and strained without success.

Suddenly the truck squealed to a halt. Sergeant-Major Rammler leapt out of the cab and ran round to the back, where he drew himself up with an expression compounded of undisguised animosity and barely concealed pleasure.

"That," he said, "is all we needed."

He proceeded to quote the battalion order word for word, just as Streicher had done, but added a footnote of his own. "Orders are meant to be obeyed, especially sensible orders like this. Opening the flaps in wooded areas has often caused accidents, not only to vehicles but to the men inside."

He stood there four-square, like a breakwater, his face a dull puce and his voice throbbing with satisfaction.

"There has been a direct contravention of standing orders," he continued, "not only by the man who leant out but also by the N.C.O. who helped him to do so. Grenadier Recht and Lance-Coroporal Kamnitzer, you will complete the rest of the trip on foot. You've only got three hours to do it in, so get cracking."

The rest of the trip amounted to eighteen miles. Sergeant-Major Rammler ordered Recht and Kamnitzer out of the truck and drove off, leaving them standing beside the deserted road.

"I'm sorry," Martin Recht said glumly.

"Stow it," said Kamnitzer. "You needn't think you're a clot just because someone tells you so."

"All the same, it's my fault if we've got to march back to barracks."

"It's a mistake you're going to pay for in hard cash, don't worry." Kamnitzer gave his friend an encouraging wink. "There's no question of marching back. We'll simply take another taxi and you can pay the fare. I'll claim it back from Rammler the first chance I get."

Before Kamnitzer returned to barracks with his resigned and submissive companion, he made a telephone call from the bar parlour of a public house called the Crown, only three miles from the barrack gates.

"Watch out!" Kamnitzer grinned into the receiver. "Careless talk cost lives. I'll give my report in code: special procedure E, six hundred and five."

No one in the bar parlour seemed to appreciate his charade. The few customers within earshot continued to quaff their beer, presumably unwilling to risk being regarded as eavesdropping foes.

"Is that Blockhead?" Kamnitzer inquired of the mouthpiece. "This is Jackass, escorted by Nitwit."

The recipient of this information was Corporal Ramsauer, commonly regarded as C.S.M. Kirschke's right-hand man in the company office. Ramsauer, who had a weakness for Kamnitzer, said: "Rammler did his nut when he came in. Even Kirschke couldn't calm him down this time. If you two get back to barracks too soon you'll find yourselves on guard duty."

"Forget about that," Kamnitzer told him, "there's no question of our getting back before time."

"They're planning to put you on picket duty when you do turn up."

"I've got plans of my own," Kamnitzer said. "I'll turn up when it suits me—so you can forget about picket duty as well. Got it?"

"Got it," said Ramsauer. "I'll pass that on to Kirschke, on the quiet. He couldn't care less, these days."

"Now listen," Kamnitzer went on, "make out the guard and picket duty rosters for to-day and the next couple of days. Get everything down in writing straight away, but make sure my name and Recht's only appear on to-day's list—not to-morrow or the day after. I like a bit of free time at the week-ends."

"Fair enough," Ramsauer said, "I'll get Kirschke to sign it at once, then it'll be official. All the same, I shouldn't drift in too late. There'll probably be a celebration to-night. Streicher's just been promoted sergeant."

Kamnitzer laughed. "It's about time that non-commissioned nincompoop was removed from our midst. Still, I certainly won't pass up an opportunity to congratulate him in person."

Kamnitzer's course of action was now clear. He and Recht mustn't return to barracks until the guard had gone on duty and the pickets had been checked for the first time. On the other hand, they mustn't be back too late, or he would miss the free beer in honour of Streicher's promotion, and he was determined not to do that.

Replacing the receiver, he went back to the table, where Martin Recht was still sitting in gloomy silence.

"We've got at least two hours to kill," he announced.

"I've got a date."

"With the lame duck?" Kamnitzer inquired with a grin.

Martin Recht shot his friend a surprised and reproachful glance. "You shouldn't say things like that," he said. "You, of all people."

Kamnitzer decided to give Recht a quick course of mental massage. "You'll have to get used to hearing that expression more often in future."

"It's a mean thing to say!"

"Of course, Martin, but people repeat things like that without thinking. They don't mean any harm. You've got to let it roll off your back, don't you see?"

Recht shook his head angrily. "Leave it alone, Karl."

"All right," said Kamnitzer, "we'll leave it for the moment. All I know is, you won't be able to meet the girl in town—now or later."

"I could always 'phone, I suppose."

"Bravo!" cried Kamnitzer. "You're catching on at last. All the best people fight their wars by telephone these days. Go on, then—jump to it! Get yourself cleaned up and see if you can fix something. I'll be downstairs in the cellar."

Kamnitzer hired the downstairs skittle alley for the next two hours. A ball-boy was soon found and Kamnitzer formed two teams, not only acting as the captain and members of each side but refereeing the match as well. According to the slate on the wall, it was a contest between the "Fatherlanders" and the "Internationals." They were so well-matched that the issue remained in doubt for some time.

After about half an hour Kamnitzer was joined by two visitors. Martin Recht, hair combed and face and uniform largely innocent of mud, came down the cellar stairs leading a girl. She had a slight limp, not that Kamnitzer noticed it at first.

"How do you do?" the girl said gaily. "I'm the lame duck."

"Glad to meet you," said Kamnitzer, gazing entranced at her gentle smile and wistful face. "You're just in time to bowl the next ball."

Recht looked worried. "Thanks for the invitation, Karl, but I don't think she ought. . . ."

"It can't hurt to try," Carolin said.

Kamnitzer gave her an encouraging smile. He handed her a ball, explained briefly how to hold and deliver it, and then shouted: "Watch your front! First ball coming up!"

The girl swung the ball to and fro, took two or three

hurried steps and let it go with surprising force. Then she stood back, panting slightly, as the ball rumbled along the gleaming planks.

"Nine!" shouted the ball-boy, discreetly manipulating two skittles with his foot. Carolin's ball had only knocked down seven, but the ball-boy's correction met with Kamnitzer's approval. He decided to give him a bonus.

"Shall we go on?" Carolin asked eagerly.

Kamnitzer nodded. "You look a pretty dangerous customer to me—as a skittler, that is—but I'm always game. We'll play for a bottle—scent for you, schnapps for me. Martin can act as referee."

They played a thoroughly hilarious match. The ball-boy did his stuff so well that after the third game Kamnitzer invested him with the rank of corporal and a five mark piece. Carolin had never felt so happy or so completely oblivious of her disability.

"You're the most athletic lame duck I've ever come across," remarked Kamnitzer.

Carolin smiled gratefully. "I'm so happy Martin's got you for a friend."

"Not only athletic but cunning," Kamnitzer chuckled, "reminding me of my responsibilities like that. Let's have one more game before I indulge in quite another form of entertainment."

*

The festivities held to mark Corporal Streicher's promotion took place in the company office. This unusual choice of venue was partly attributed to Kirschke, who had hinted that his room and, consequently, his bed were more easily accessible from there.

Streicher had been notified of his promotion by Lieutenant von Strackmann, who insisted on performing that pleasant ceremony in person. It took the form of a solemn handshake, an inspiring gaze, and some such words as: "This is a great moment for you, Sergeant Streicher."

The freshly minted sergeant shared that sentiment.

" It's usual to stand drinks all round," Kirschke insinuated.

Streicher reacted promptly. " If you would do me the honour of being my guest in the canteen, Sergeant-Major . . ."

" No need for all that palaver," said Kirschke. " We can send out for some beer—schnapps too. It doesn't matter where the party's held as long as there is one."

The party snow-balled. Rammler, who was an early arrival, congratulated Streicher with bluff bonhomie, hinting that most of the credit belonged to him. He was followed by other N.C.O.s from No. 3 Company, men who had suddenly ceased to be Streicher's superiors and were now his peers. Ramsauer, the veteran company clerk, started to pour out drinks.

Eventually, Lieutenant von Strackmann himself appeared. He announced his readiness to take part in the impromptu celebration " as a fellow-soldier," thus demonstrating his ironclad sense of solidarity. True comradeship knew no rank, provided always that the subordinate was prepared to respect his superior officer. Respect, however, was dependent on personality, and von Strackmann felt himself to be well-endowed with that commodity.

Like his comrades of inferior rank, he opened the nearest bottle of beer and, disdaining a glass, conveyed it to his lips. He had some difficulty in draining it at one go, but Kirschke was an expert and the lieutenant was determined not to be outdone, least of all by his *bête noire*.

Von Strackmann drained his beer, panting triumphantly, and followed it with some of Rammler's staple drink— Strong Man's Milk—successfully concealing its explosive effect. Happily noting what he took to be admiring glances on the faces round him, particularly Streicher's, he felt more than ever convinced that he had promoted the right man.

" The solidarity that exists between the commander of a unit and his junior leaders," von Strackmann informed the seemingly attentive circle round him, " is of great and abiding importance. It must be carefully fostered, and it is based on mutual trust."

From there it was only a step to the subject of welfare representatives, of which the newly promoted Streicher was one.

"He must enjoy the confidence of his superior officers and his fellow-soldiers. He is also responsible for the maintenance of comradely trust within his sphere of jurisdiction. His main duty is to serve the community."

Kirschke grinned broadly. He was acquainted with these stilted phrases, all of which appeared in *The Officer's Manual*.

Before the lieutenant could pursue his enlightening discourse further, Lance-Corporal Kamnitzer appeared, accompanied by Grenadier Recht.

Kamnitzer held himself stiff as a ramrod. His bearing would have done credit to a drill-sergeant and his salute resembled one of the diagrams in a Prussian drill manual. He asked the lieutenant for permission to speak to Sergeant-Major Rammler.

Von Strackmann granted his request with a look of approval, gratified that his unit should contain such a model of soldierly precision. He had obviously misjudged the man hitherto.

Kamnitzer proceeded to make his report to Rammler. "Lance-Corporal Kamnitzer and Grenadier Recht reporting back from special duties, Sergeant-Major!"

"Carry on!" Rammler called hastily. He was not anxious to discuss the two men's route-march in present company, especially as he had omitted to make a full and immediate report on the subject.

"May I request the lieutenant," Kamnitzer ventured, selecting his words with extreme care, "for permission to extend my heartiest congratulations to Sergeant Streicher?"

Address in the third person was not prescribed by any manual of military instruction. Officially, superior officers were supposed to be addressed as "you," followed immediately by their rank, but the third person—sometimes referred to as the "traditional mode of address"—still survived here and there, and Lieutenant von Strackmann was not alone in regarding it as a token of loyalty and obedience.

"Why don't you join us, Corporal?" asked von Strackmann. "Help us to celebrate the occasion."

"Many thanks, sir!" Kamnitzer barked, and sat down.

In between beers, von Strackmann turned to Rammler. "You've obviously got some first-class material in your platoon," he murmured confidentially. "We seem to have over-looked Kamnitzer till now. You must keep an eye on him."

"I've had my eye on him for a long time," Rammler said grimly. The lieutenant's benevolence towards a charlatan like Kamnitzer caused him a spasm of almost physical discomfort—but, as he told himself, to-morrow was another day.

*

The new day was a long time coming. It was preceded by a long night, not devoted exclusively to sleep.

"A creative night," Colonel Turner murmured to himself.

He formed this conclusion while seated at his desk, having just penned a sentence which struck him as pregnant with significance. It ran: "Just as there is an element of indestructability in the human being, so there is in the soldier; for the soldier is a basic constituent of the human being."

His thoughts always travelled along these grandiose and exalted lines, and his work would undoubtedly cause a stir if he managed to complete it before the next war broke out. . . .

"A night like wet sponge," Captain Ahlers remarked to his deputy, Captain Treuberg, as they waited for a transport plane which was on its way from Sicily. The bad-weather front over the Alps might be several hundred miles distant, but it was under an hour's flying time away.

"Nothing can go wrong if we're both on our toes," said Treuberg.

But Ahlers had an exhausting day behind him and was

tired. When Treuberg asked if he could " run the shop "
himself, Ahlers replied curtly: " Better not."

" The best place for us on a night like this," Warrant Officer
Vossler said to Gerty Ballhaus, who was sitting beside him
in his car, " is bed."

" Each to his own," she said enigmatically.

Yet another muffled peal of wedding bells, thought Vossler.
He was a victim of his own freely chosen profession. If
he wanted to fly he had to live in this one-horse hole.
He wished he were in Bali or Hawaii—not parked in a
narrow side-street on the outskirts of a provincial town. At
moments like this, Europe shrank to the size of a nutshell
and the garrison town to a mere pin-head.

" Day and night are all one to me," Major Bornekamp said,
buttoning up his trench-coat. " I'm never off-duty, you ought
to know that by this time."

Frau Elfrieda smiled indulgently in his general direction,
but made no attempt to prevent his departure. She could
very well dispense with his presence at the moment, thanks
to von Strackmann's personal attentions.

" You've got some first-class officers," she said. " Lieutenant
von Strackmann has made a wonderful job of the arrangements
for your Ladies' Night. He's a young man of many parts."

When this sentiment was expressed, Lieutenant Dieter von
Strackmann was already lying on his camp-bed, half-asleep
and smiling to himself. The C.O.'s confidence, Frau Elfrieda's
favours and his subordinates' adulation—all had filled him
with contentment, and alcohol had done the rest.

Elsewhere in the company block, Sergeant-Major Rammler
endeavoured to sleep clad in full uniform and boots. Failing to find sleep but finding his bottle of Strong Man's Milk,
which stood ready to hand beside his bed, he placed it to
his lips, trumpet-fashion, and drank.

A few rooms distant, Streicher was spending the first
night of his sergeant's career lying supine with his hands

folded on his chest like a knight on a medieval tomb. Suddenly he jumped up, pulled his uniform tunic over his night-shirt and hurried out of the room—not for intimate reasons but in order to admire the splendour of his new chevrons in the corridor mirror.

Martin Recht lay in the bunk next to Streicher's, curled up like a child, his face pillowed on his hands as though he were trying to hide it and his breathing rapid and shallow. He was dreaming about a duck—not a lame duck, but one which skimmed ahead of him while he, also on the wing, tried desperately to catch it up.

"To-night," Frau Ahlers told herself as she watched her sleeping daughter's face, "could be the turning-point."

It was true that she felt this almost every night when she peeped in at Carolin, but there really was an air of repose about her slumbering form.

She had come back from her outing full of gay chatter about Martin Recht and his friend, also about the skittle match, which she described in glowing terms. She seemed closer to recovery than she had ever done.

"If only everything goes well," Frau Ahlers murmured silently.

"I can't stand nights like to-night!" Helen Wieder declared roundly. "Everyone gets so restless. You don't dare go out with men when they're in that state."

"Be that as it may," said Herbert Asch, "there are at least three of them waiting for you out there." He took her order book, checked it briefly and passed it to his wife.

"You know Karl Kamnitzer, don't you, Herr Asch?" Helen asked. "What do you think of him? Is he as much of a wolf as all the rest?"

"Not being a woman, I couldn't really say, but I know one thing: he's different from the rest. It might be worth bearing that in mind."

"All I know is, he's the only man who's ever stood me up

twice in the same week," Helen said petulantly. "No one treats me like that. I'll line up six dates for to-morrow evening and see how he likes it."

When Helen had gone, Herbert Asch said to his wife: "We've got a pretty complicated day ahead of us to-morrow," —but his smile betrayed that he was far from displeased at the prospect. Some complications appealed to him, especially the sort that showed people in their true colours. It was high time to know which side everyone was on.

"Tiring, a night like this," C.S.M. Kirschke remarked to Lance-Corporal Kamnitzer. "Sleep's a great thing. The only thing is, it gets a hold on you."

As the sole survivors of Streicher's promotion party they were still drinking his beer, though not still in his honour.

"You're browned off with this mob, aren't you?" Kamnitzer put the question without a trace of embarrassment. "See no evil, speak no evil, that's your motto these days. That's why you go off for a kip whenever you get the chance, isn't it?"

"You've got a nerve!" Kirschke said ponderously. He drew himself up with an effort, looking rather like a Buddha in a specimen cabinet. "Whatever you may think, I'm a soldier, heart and soul!" he announced suddenly. "I never wanted to be anything else. It's the breath of life to me, man!"

Karl Kamnitzer nodded. "The only trouble is," he said softly, "in this circus they put the horses and tigers in the same stable—and it's not a good arrangement."

"True." Kirschke fortified himself with another bottle of beer—his tenth at least—and went on: "I don't say I'm an idealist—you get over that as time goes by—but I've always done my best. And then along comes a would-be hero complete with blinkers and a built-in loudspeaker— the sort that munches regulations and shits directives. . . ."

"You mean Strackmann?"

"I'm not mentioning any names, Kamnitzer. All the

same, when an officer's over-enthusiastic, whatever his motives
—even perverted idealism, if you like—he wears the people
round him down, and most of them let themselves be
worn down."

"Surely we can do something about it, can't we?"

The C.S.M. shook his head pityingly. "You haven't the
first idea how the military machine functions."

"Maybe all one needs to know is how to swap cogs around
—or switch the thing off when it's been running too long."

"You're talking balls, my lad."

Kirschke's show of irritation made no impression on Kamnitzer whatsoever. "People can have entirely different motives
and still be after the same thing, Sergeant-Major. Co-operation
has it's advantages. Why don't we try it some time?"

With that question, which remained unanswered, "Black
Friday," which succeeded "Gloomy Thursday," came to an
end. If Kamnitzer's prayer had been answered, the next two
days might have been christened "Sunny Saturday" and
"Splendid Sunday," but they weren't.

*

The following day's troubles began when Lance-Corporal
Kamnitzer awoke. The first person his eyes lighted on was
comrade Streicher, whom he proceeded to shake vigorously.

"You're the welfare representative here, aren't you?"
Kamnitzer inquired. "What's the matter—still pissed?"

"Take your paws off me," groaned Streicher. "I want to
lie in a bit. It's a sergeant's privilege."

"You mean to say you're a sergeant?" demanded Kamnitzer.
"Since when? Have you got it in writing?"

"Do you mind!" Streicher sat up indignantly, his head
throbbing with the persistence of a steam-hammer. "You
were there last night when we celebrated my promotion—
you even congratulated me."

"I congratulated you? I can't imagine doing that."

Kamnitzer winked at the other occupants of the room,

who had gathered round expectantly but were maintaining a cautious distance.

"Do you mind!" Streicher repeated, by now slightly agitated. "You're talking to a sergeant."

"If you're really a sergeant, where are your stripes? I don't see any on that night-shirt of yours. The only thing I'm interested in knowing is this: are you the company welfare representative or not? I'm thinking of lodging a complaint."

"Another one?" exclaimed Streicher.

"What do you mean—another one? I can put in as many complaints as I like. I know my rights."

"You've got a complaint?" Streicher was wide awake now. He slid hastily out of bed and stood there in his crumpled night-shirt. "Against me, do you mean?"

"Not yet," Kamnitzer said airily. "It's Rammler's turn this time, and as welfare representative you're responsible for seeing my complaint goes through the proper channels."

Having laid his preliminary mine-field, Kamnitzer started to get dressed. Streicher squatted on his bed, debating whether to react as a sergeant or a friend in need. Had he automatically ceased to be junior ranks' welfare representative now that he'd been promoted, or did he keep the job until someone else was chosen to replace him? His brain reeled with indecision.

"Why do you always have to stir it up?" Martin Recht demanded, as he accompanied Kamnitzer to the wash-room. He felt uneasy. "Wouldn't it be wiser to lie low and say nothing?"

"You're hopeless, Martin. Hasn't anyone ever told you that attack is the best means of defence? That's what the brass-hats always say, anyway, so we might as well see if the theory works out in practice."

"All this fuss!" Recht mumbled unhappily. "All I want to do is finish work and go into town. I've got a date with Carolin."

"You'll never make it unless we stir up a bit."

Reaching the door of the wash-room, Kamnitzer handed

Recht the roll containing his soap, tooth-brush and shaving kit with a gesture which meant : book my usual place, the basin on the right, next to the window.

" Do you really have to go through with this?" Recht persisted.

" God Almighty!" Kamnitzer said angrily. " Haven't you caught on yet? Look, I'll explain the situation in words of one syllable : Rammler's bound to try and get us on guard duty—or at least picket duty—let alone any other little treats he's got in store for us, but he won't be able to lift a finger if there's a complaint in the pipe-line. Now do you see?"

Recht began to understand at last. Any punitive measure undertaken against the author of a complaint might be interpreted as a form of pressure or coercion. " Shall I lodge a complaint too, then?" he asked.

" No need. Why use two sticks of gelignite when one'll do the trick? You can be my witness this time."

" What do I have to say?"

" Just tell the truth, whatever they ask you. That's the whole point. We'll give them something genuine to chew on. Let's hope it chokes them."

Meanwhile, Sergeant Streicher had hurried off to put Sergeant-Major Rammler in the picture. Rammler flew into a rage and tried to exert pressure on C.S.M. Kirschke, who endeavoured—yawning—to divest himself of his unwelcome visitor.

Rammler, however, was determined not to be shaken off this time. Having come to the conclusion that Kirschke was a sluggard, he did his best to make his opinion plain— which was where he went wrong.

" Do something for your money, Kirschke!" he exhorted. " Don't sit around doing nothing all day. Clobber that chap Kamnitzer before he opens his trap."

" You haven't got a guilty conscience, surely?"

" What makes you think that?" Rammler glowed with righteous indignation. His conscience was clear, and if his actions ever overstepped the regulation mark—which they seldom did—it was always in the interests of good order and military discipline. "It's just that—well, we're not going to let a bloke like Kamnitzer muck us about, are we?"

"What do you mean—we?" Kirschke's face beamed rosily as though he had enjoyed an unusually good night's sleep. "I hope you're not trying to talk me into perverting the course of justice? Any soldier—I quote—who believes himself to have been unjustly treated by his superiors or by an official department, or to have been wronged by disloyal conduct on the part of his fellow-soldiers, may lodge a complaint to that effect. Army Regulations, Para One."

"I've heard all that cock before! But if I was C.S.M. of this company I'd have shut that bloody malcontent's trap long ago."

"N.B. No soldier shall suffer detriment as a result of lodging a complaint. Ditto, Para Two."

Rammler uttered a few quotations of a less printable nature and retired in high dudgeon. He then sent for Streicher and endeavoured to make it clear that he had to work on Kamnitzer—in the friendliest way, of course—for the sake of company harmony. Streicher, however, knew that Kamnitzer was too hard a nut to crack. "The most I can do, Sergeant-Major, is to show Grenadier Recht where his duty to the company lies."

"If the lad's got a spark of common sense he'll toe the line!" Rammler growled.

But C.S.M. Kirschke, looking for a few brief moments as though he had never yawned in his life, was acting with unaccustomed speed.

The more Lieutenant von Strackmann heard of the distressing news which his C.S.M. was, so to speak, spreading on his morning toast, the more perplexed his expression became. Eventually he asked: "Have we got two men in the company called Kamnitzer?"

Kirschke was obliged to inform the lieutenant that the Kamnitzer in question was the same man who had impressed him so favourably the night before. For a minute or two, von Strackmann felt completely at a loss. His first inclination was to read the riot act to all concerned, but the situation looked tricky. "Do you think it's possible," he asked cautiously, "that Sergeant-Major Rammler really has put his foot in it?"

Kirschke savoured the moment of weakness—temporary, without a doubt—which had prompted the lieutenant to ask his C.S.M.'s advice for the very first time. "Anything's possible," he replied tersely, "in this outfit."

"I must talk this over with the C.O.," von Strackmann said finally. "In the meantime, kindly ensure that nothing happens to make matters worse. I shall hold you personally responsible if it does."

*

Major Wilhelm Bornekamp, Commanding Officer of the local Grenadier battalion, had been looking forward to a pleasant day. After an excellent breakfast came a 'phone call from Colonel Turner, who expressed thanks for his invitation to the Ladies' Night and promised to turn up, punctually and with pleasure, accompanied by "a small party—three in all." He concluded by sending his best regards to Bornekamp's lady wife.

And then Herbert Asch appeared.

At first, he too gave the impression that he had welcome news to impart. "Everything's all set, Major. I've put the Silver Room at your disposal, so the party ought to go with a swing."

"Many thanks," said Bornekamp, with a condescending smile. He always cherished an attitude of superiority toward tradespeople and saw no reason to disguise it. "But you needn't have bothered to call in person—a telephone call to Lieutenant von Strackmann would have done. I've put the entire arrangements for this evening in his hands."

Herbert Asch appeared to ignore this unmistakable hint. He leant back in his chair and said: "Before coming here this morning I happened to drop in at the newspaper office, and there, quite by chance, I caught sight of some galley proofs of an article about you."

"That's right," said the C.O. "Some local hack came and asked me for an interview. He was mad keen to have one—you know the form, democratic practice and so on. Even asked me for a photograph."

"I saw that as well. They've given you a page to yourself, complete with picture. The headline's already set, too, in inch-high capitals : *We know what we want!*"

"I say, that's going a little far, don't you think?" Bornekamp almost bridled, but only for a moment. "Still, it can't do any harm. Why shouldn't the army get a good press for a change?"

"You regard the contents of this article as good?"

The C.O. settled himself comfortably in his chair. "You know, Asch, when I think back—and it's only a few years ago—I remember all the mud that was flung at us. There were plenty of muck-rakers about—mostly inspired by the Americans, I regret to say, until they realised that they'd be in the cart without us. Then the wind changed, and the penny-a-line merchants spun like weathercocks. The day before yesterday it was : 'No more war!' and yesterday : 'Look reality in the eye!' or 'Rearmament is a necessary evil!' To-day it's : 'Freedom and the defence of the West!' Uniform has become a symbol of national pride once more."

"All the same, Major, things aren't quite to your liking yet, are they?"

"It's a question of time. But you must admit we've made pretty good progress already. Take certain books, for instance —plain unadulterated un-German filth. Booksellers have stopped putting them in the window and readers are becoming ashamed to buy them. Or take these chaps on television. They've got tired of burning their fingers. One or two of 'em still have a go at us, I grant you, but they're rare exceptions. Even the film industry is doing its level best to cover us with glamour and glory. What more do you want?"

Herbert Asch appeared to be lost in thought. Some of Major Bornekamp's assertions were not incorrect. The last war was almost twenty years old, it was true, and after twenty years even obituary notices have lost their original impact and graves become over-grown with grass. The human memory was a sieve.

"For all that, Major," he said eventually, "a person can't say absolutely anything he wants to, even to-day."

"Yes, he can at last—if he's got the guts."

"But the Federal constitution still grants a citizen certain rights—and one of them is the right to refuse to do military service."

"In my view," the C.O. reiterated with conviction, "anyone who dares to do that is either a Communist or a coward."

"And all we need do is put them into a striped uniform —i.e. convict's garb—and that'll be the end of them?"

"Precisely!" Bornekamp gave an approving nod. "My view precisely. But how did you know?"

"It says so in your interview with the *Town and Country News*—in bold type." Asch eyed Bornekamp with curiosity. "But what you're saying, in practice, is that you regard the constitution as a shield and buckler for Communists and cowards, and your talk of striped uniforms may awaken memories of concentration camps. Do you really want to create the impression that this is the only way the officers of your regiment think?"

The Major started. For some moments he registered surprise and incredulity, but gradually he seemed to grasp what he had done. Asch gave him time.

"There must have been some misunderstanding," he said at last, breathing hard.

"But you've been quoted verbatim, Major."

"It's a diabolical liberty!" Bornekamp spluttered, realising that the interviewer had tricked him into laying a trap for himself. "Besides, that remark wasn't original—it was made by a senior government official."

"Did you quote the source? No? Then you'll have to

take responsibility for it yourself. And I can tell you one thing: if the local paper publishes that article on Monday there'll be all hell let loose by Tuesday. *Der Spiegel* will be down on you like a ton of bricks, closely supported by a section of the foreign press. The subject may even be raised in the Bundestag by a member of the Opposition."

"Damn it all!" exclaimed the Major, by now thoroughly perturbed. "Something must be done about this twaddle. Can't we simply ban it?"

"Twaddle or not, Major, you were responsible for it, I'm afraid." Herbert Asch smiled. "It's impossible to dictate to a free press what it should or should not publish. We haven't reached that stage yet, regrettable as it may seem to some."

"But what about you, Herr Asch? You must have contacts."

"Possibly," said Asch, bland but wary.

"Couldn't you . . ." Bornekamp searched in vain for the right words, and for a second or two he almost stuttered. "I would be uncommonly obliged if you . . . well, I think you know what I mean. . . ."

"It mayn't be too easy, but I can always try—under certain conditions."

Bornekamp did not immediately learn what these conditions were because at that moment the adjutant came in to report that Lieutenant von Strackmann wished to speak to him on an urgent matter.

"Tell him to go to hell!" bellowed the C.O., enraged at this untimely interruption. "Tell him to deal with his own problems. I've got more important things to do."

*

The adjutant, who was a man of tact, confined himself to telling von Strackmann that the C.O. could not be disturbed under any circumstances. He was in conference and would be tied up for an indefinite period.

Von Strackmann emerged from the administration block

and paused outside, meditating. He came to the conclusion that there was nothing for it but to return to the company office, where Lance-Corporal Kamnitzer's complaint awaited him. Reluctantly convinced that he would have to investigate it in person, he stationed himself behind his desk and ordered Kirschke to bring in the parties involved.

Kamnitzer, who was the first to appear, gave the acting company commander a renewed opportunity to admire his soldierly correctitude. Once again, he looked every inch a model grenadier.

Lieutenant von Strackmann cleared his throat. "Have you thoroughly considered this complaint of yours?"

"Yes, sir, I have."

"You feel you have received unjust treatment from Sergeant-Major Rammler?"

"Yes, sir. I might even go so far as to call it chicanery."

This term, though lifted straight out of Army-Regulations, von Strackmann declined to accept. He appealed to Kamnitzer's better judgment, but without success. Then he announced his intention of clearing the air by means of an exchange of views and summoned Rammler for this purpose.

"My conduct was entirely proper, sir," stated the sergeant-major. "There had been a direct violation of a standing order. Truck flaps are to be kept closed while travelling through wooded areas and along tree-lined roads."

"But this was an emergency," Kamnitzer protested. "Grenadier Recht was sick, that's why the flaps were opened temporarily. And if you'd like to know why Grenadier Recht was sick, sir . . ."

Von Strackmann checked him with upraised hand. It was one of his principles to stick closely to the point. He abhorred digressions into potentially murky details.

"The said grenadier is available to give evidence, sir," Kirschke put in.

"Thank you," the lieutenant said curtly. "I trust that won't be necessary." He got up and began to pace stiffly round the room. "Men," he said, "we're like members of one big family, in a sense, and every family has its share of quarrels and misunderstandings."

"This wasn't a misunderstanding, sir," Kamnitzer interposed. "It was completely intentional."

"It was a direct contravention of orders, sir," Rammler persisted, "and had to be dealt with accordingly."

"Perhaps we ought to call the witness in," Kirschke suggested.

"Nonsense!" snapped von Strackmann. "We'll settle this by ourselves, in the proper way."

He grappled manfully with the situation. On the one hand, contravention of an order, on the other, an alleged emergency—each statement entirely credible and each made by an exemplary soldier. A compromise seemed indicated.

"Men," he said, coming to a halt, "see here. We must try to be realistic. Misunderstandings do occur, and we all make the occasional mistake. Let us assume that Sergeant-Major Rammler has made a mistake. He will apologise for it. Let us also assume that Lance-Corporal Kamnitzer's suspicions are unfounded. He will apologise, too."

Lieutenant von Strackmann stared challengingly from one to the other, sensing that he was on the brink of a satisfactory solution. Even Kirschke seemed to be indulging in a smirk of approval.

"Any man worthy of the name," von Strackmann pursued, now confident of victory, "is big enough to admit his own mistakes. He doesn't hesitate to apologise when necessary. Well?"

"All right, sir," said Rammler.

"What about you, Kamnitzer?"

"I'm not vindictive, sir, and I'm not petty-minded either. I'll be glad to accept the sergeant-major's apology, but who's going to pay the fare?"

"What fare?" Von Strackmann looked slightly bewildered. "What are you talking about?"

"For the taxi, sir."

"What do you mean—taxi?"

"The taxi, sir."

Von Strackmann gaped at Kamnitzer helplessly.

"I might have known it!" Rammler said in a choking voice. "It's just what I'd have expected from you, Kamnitzer."

"That's rich!" Kirschke was almost groaning with delight. "That's one for the book! He took a taxi. If it gets around, the whole battalion will laugh itself sick."

Lieutenant von Strackmann appeared to be prompted by a similar fear. Laughter, whatever its cause, might prove positively fatal, not only to the reputation of the company he commanded but to him personally.

"Silence!" he yelled. "I won't hear another word on the subject. I shall give all concerned ample time to reconsider the situation carefully. In the meantime, I insist on absolute secrecy. Dismiss!"

*

"You're barking up the wrong tree, you know," Sergeant Streicher insinuated. "You think you can rely on Kamnitzer, but that's just where you're wrong."

"Kamnitzer's my friend," said Martin Recht.

They were sitting on their beds in Room 13. The rest of the company were out on the barrack square, and Rammler and Kamnitzer were still closeted in the company office. It had fallen to Streicher to work on Recht—in a comradely way—before he could be called as a witness.

"Kamnitzer is a first-rate chap up to a point," Streicher said, "but he's too often mistaken in his choice of methods. It's hardly surprising some of his superiors think he's a malcontent, and that's dangerous—for you as well as him."

"He's my friend," Recht repeated stubbornly.

"So am I," Streicher insisted. "That's why I want to help you—and you need help, believe me. You don't want to be on extra duties permanently, do you?"

"Of course not."

"You'd like a free week-end, wouldn't you?"

"Yes. I've got a date, and I want to keep it—if it's humanly possible."

"Why shouldn't it be?" Sergeant Streicher radiated boundless assurance. "Everything's very simple in this mob, really, provided you know the rules. Rammler's not a monster, after all."

"Come off it! He worked me over yesterday until I was all in. I've never been treated like that in my life."

"I grant you, he's a tough nut. He can be quick-tempered too, sometimes, but you and Kamnitzer had provoked him. He means well at heart, take it from me. I can understand your attitude, but what happened yesterday mayn't be as pointless as you tend to think. Rammler's bark is worse than his bite. Once he sees that you realise he means well, everything'll be all right."

"He'll do me again if he gets the chance."

"That's just Kamnitzer talking. You've got the wrong end of the stick, I promise you. Rammler's only human. He's a friendly type, really, but discipline means everything to him. Once you accept that, it's easy to get on with him."

Martin Recht sat motionless on his bed. He was impressed by Streicher's remarks and grateful for the efforts which the newly fledged sergeant was making on his behalf. "All I want," he said, "is to be left in peace. And I want to keep my date in town this afternoon."

"You will, Martin—I'll see to that. Trust me, that's all."

"There's one thing, though: I won't do anything to hurt Kamnitzer."

"No one's asking you to. In any case, Kamnitzer hasn't found out which side his bread's buttered. He won't be able to hold his own against Rammler indefinitely—the sergeant-major's too well in with the lieutenant—so the best thing we can do is stop him doing anything rash. We owe it to him as friends."

*

" Are you sure you haven't bitten off more than you can chew this time?" C.S.M. Kirschke asked, with an air of curiosity.

" Quite sure," Kamnitzer said firmly.

They stood facing one another in the company office. Lieutenant von Strackmann had closeted himself in the inner sanctum while Sergeant-Major Rammler paced impatiently up and down the corridor outside.

" That taxi business was absolutely brilliant," Kirschke conceded, " but have you thought it out carefully enough? There's a bit of difference between foot-slogging and riding in a taxi, after all."

" I know, a taxi costs more. However, if the sergeant-major's prepared to refund the fare, I may reconsider my complaint."

" You've got a nerve!" Kirschke said, not without admiration. " Just between us, what makes you so sure of yourself?"

" Lack of clarity when issuing a verbal order." Kamnitzer winked at Kirschke. " When Rammler marooned us, he didn't say clearly and distinctly : march back to barracks. That would have been a straightforward order. Instead, he just told us to hook it. You've got three hours, he told us, so get cracking. He never said anything about marching back."

" That's what he meant, though."

" I'm not disputing that, but I'm not a mind-reader."

Kirschke grinned and disappeared into the company commander's office, where he found the lieutenant engaged in leafing through his *Manual of Military Law,* a thick red tome containing collected texts, notes, cross-references and appendices.

" Must you disturb me, now, Sergeant-Major?"

" Yes, sir," said Kirschke, and repeated—almost word for

word—what Kamnitzer had told him. Von Strackmann re-alised that if the lance-corporal managed to dig up almost any kind of corroborative evidence, which was a fair assumption, Rammler was in the cart and the company's reputation with him.

Lack of clarity when issuing a verbal order was a grave defect. The C.O. himself had repeatedly drawn attention to the fact that if there was one cancerous disease within the Bundeswehr, this was it.

"Fetch Rammler," ordered von Strackmann.

The sergeant-major, who was still lurking in the corridor, appeared, and von Strackmann repeated exactly what his C.S.M. had told him a few minutes earlier. "Well, Sergeant-Major," he concluded, "explain yourself."

"The meaning of my order was unmistakable, sir."

"The meaning of an order is important, of course, but the phraseology must match it."

"I can't remember every last detail, sir," Rammler protested, squirming like an eel, "but I meant the men to march back."

"What do you mean—meant? You should have said so." Lieutenant von Strackmann tapped the bulky volume on the desk before him. "Anyone incapable of issuing proper orders," he declaimed, quoting the C.O., "is not fit to command men."

Rammler had turned as pale as the latest consignments of rifle-grease, popularly known as "dead man's dripping." He made a final attempt to extricate himself. "There's a certain type of subordinate, like this man Kamnitzer . . ."

"That's enough!" the lieutenant broke in. "I don't want any vague excuses or far-fetched explanations. I'm concerned with the facts alone, and they imply—unfortunately—that a full-grown sergeant-major, in my company, what's more, hasn't yet learnt how to issue clear and unmistakable orders."

Rammler tottered on his foundations like a weather-beaten war memorial. He found it hard to maintain his martial poise.

"I should never have expected such a thing from you, of all people," the lieutenant said bitterly. "You're obviously not fit to be trusted with a platoon, let alone a whole company."

With that ruthless *coup de grâce*, Rammler was dismissed. He marched out looking pale and rigid.

"Shall I call Kamnitzer in now, so that we can settle the matter?" Kirschke asked.

"It needs going into thoroughly first," Lieutenant von Strackmann said, still racking his brains for a satisfactory solution. The taxi presented an almost unsurmountable obstacle.

"Right, sir," said Kirschke. He realised that the case had been shelved for the moment, but this state of affairs could not survive indefinitely, especially as Kamnitzer was involved.

The week-end took its course.

Lieutenant von Strackmann continued to pore over the *Manual of Military Law* until his attention was claimed by last-minute arrangements for the Ladies' Night. Sergeant-Major Rammler sat brooding on his camp-bed for a quarter of an hour and then retired to the canteen, and C.S.M. Kirschke changed his trousers yet again.

Sergeant Streicher had worked on Martin Recht so successfully, meanwhile, that the grenadier now seemed to be suffering from loss of memory.

"You know, Karl," he said to Kamnitzer when the latter returned to Room 13, "I really think we ought to avoid unnecessary fuss, don't you agree?"

Kamnitzer looked thoughtfully, first at his friend and then at Sergeant Streicher, who was standing in the background. He didn't find it hard to guess which way the wind was blowing. "So he's been at you, has he? Three cheers for the voice of conscience!"

"I merely gave him some advice," Streicher said. "He doesn't have to take it, but it was well meant."

" We've thought things out very carefully, Karl," Recht said, eager to convince his friend. " The point is why make things unnecessarily difficult? Why go out of our way to make an enemy of Rammler?"

" You're talking rot," Kamnitzer said flatly. " You can't turn a lion into a lamb—not with the best will in the world."

Kamnitzer brushed Recht aside and made for his bed. He lay down, unbuttoned his tunic and stretched out comfortably in preparation for a brief morning nap.

Streicher drew closer, looking worried. " Our mutual friend has come to the conclusion that there may have been a misunderstanding—that Sergeant-Major Rammler really did give you the order to march, even if indirectly. On the other hand, you may have misheard his order or interpreted it wrongly. I'm trying to be fair to both sides."

" I really think that would be the best solution from everyone's point of view," Recht chimed in.

" The best solution would be for you two to get lost," said Kamnitzer. " You're spoiling my beauty sleep. If Rammler refunds our taxi fare I may reconsider the position —and that's a pretty generous offer. On the other hand, if he doesn't pay us promptly I'll present him with a bill for the other taxi."

" What other taxi?" Streicher asked, perplexed.

" The one we took during the map-reading exercise, of course," said Kamnitzer, and rolled over on to his side.

Streicher glared helplessly at the lance-corporal's back. He had proffered the olive branch, only to see Kamnitzer fling him a hand-grenade in exchange. One taxi was bad enough, but two taxis on the same day were catastrophic.

" I don't know what you're talking about," Streicher said, and shot out of the room like greased lightning.

The remainder of the morning passed uneventfully. Kamnitzer snored peacefully to himself while Martin Recht carefully sponged and pressed his walking-out uniform.

Early in the afternoon, the first inmates of the Grenadier

barracks started to stream into town, Lance-Corporal Kamnitzer and Grenadier Recht among them. Kamnitzer was
contemplating a visit to the air force barracks, whereas Recht
intended to have a hair-cut and then call for Carolin.

"Give anything in uniform a wide berth," Kamnitzer
advised his friend. "You're not old enough to play with
big boys yet. I'll look forward to seeing you in the Café
Asch this evening, preferably in one piece."

Kamnitzer's visit to the air force barracks was a series
of surprises. The first came when he presented himself
at the barrack gates and asked to speak to Warrant Officer
Vossler. All the sentry said was: "If you want to speak to
him, you getter go look for him."

When Kamnitzer inquired the best place to begin his
quest he was referred to Captain Ahlers, who, it seemed,
knew everything. Kamnitzer found him in his office, seated
behind his desk with his uniform jacket removed and sleeves
rolled up. The door stood invitingly ajar.

"Good afternoon," said Kamnitzer, agreeably impressed
by such an obvious lack of ceremony in a military establishment. His salute was noticeably casual.

"Good afternoon," replied the captain, eyeing his visitor
with interest. "To what do I owe the pleasure?"

"I'm looking for Warrant Officer Vossler."

"You'll find him in No. 2 Hangar."

"Where do I find No. 2 Hangar?"

"You can't miss it—just make for the control tower and
you'll see it immediately next door." The captain smiled.
"My name's Ahlers, by the way."

"Mine's Kamnitzer," responded the lance-corporal. "I
think I know your daughter—Fräulein Carolin Ahlers, isn't
it? I played a brisk game of skittles with her and my friend
Martin Recht yesterday afternoon."

"Ah, so it was you!" Ahlers looked pleased. "Sit down
for a moment, if you've got time. What about something
to drink? We're fairly well stocked at the moment. I can
offer you Scotch, Irish, rye or bourbon."

Kamnitzer sat down with alacrity. Nothing like this had

ever happened to him before. After a moment's hesitation he decided to test the resources of the transport wing by asking for raki. Five minutes later a glass was in his hand, brought by a sergeant who served him as if it was the most natural thing in the world.

Ahlers and Kamnitzer continued to chat like members of the same club until a lieutenant strolled in and asked Ahlers if he needed him any longer. If not, he was thinking of going fishing. "No objections," said Ahlers, and the lieutenant strolled off again.

"You mustn't judge our outfit by army standards," Ahlers told Kamnitzer. "We haven't time for them here."

"When do you knock off, usually?"

"Whenever we get the chance," Ahlers said promptly. "It's not unheard of for us to fly transport missions several nights on the trot, week-ends included. To make up for it, we occasionally take a mid-week break—two or three days, sometimes."

"So there's no set routine?"

"What do you mean, Herr Kamnitzer? We merely fly when we have to fly. You don't imagine wars are fought on a time-table basis, do you?"

"Then your chaps have to be ready for action all the time—without a break? That's even worse than our lot."

"Hold hard," Ahlers said smiling. "We concentrate on essentials and we make a thorough job of them, but we leave all the superfluous details to other people."

Ahlers's account of air force procedure appealed to Kamnitzer, but further surprises were in store for him when the captain took him to see Warrant Officer Vossler at work.

They found Vossler standing in the middle of No. 2 Hangar surrounded by a group of young men, all of them officers.

"Advanced pilot's course," Ahlers murmured.

Vossler had a notebook in his hand and was asking questions. He looked as casual as ever, but his questions were crisp and to the point, and the young officers' replies equally so.

" Well, how are things going?" asked Ahlers.

Vossler nodded cheerfully at the captain without saluting, and passed him his notes. " Fair to middling," he said.

While Ahlers was looking through the notes, Vossler caught sight of Lance-Corporal Kamnitzer. He walked over and greeted him like an old friend. " Nice of you to drop in. I'll be through in about ten minutes."

Then he devoted himself once more to Captain Ahlers and his young officers. " Well, gentlemen," he said, " if no one's got any more questions, I think we'll call it a day."

Rather naturally, none of the officers had any more questions, but one of them said : " We're having a celebration at the Hotel Asch this evening, and you're cordially invited, Herr Vossler. Will you look in?"

" Thanks," the warrant officer replied. " I'll see if I can manage it."

When the class had dispersed, Vossler turned to Kamnitzer. "Well, what brings you here?" he asked. ". Business or pleasure?"

" I always try to combine the two. I could say I was keen to take a look inside this place, just for interest's sake—and it wouldn't be a lie, either. There was another reason, though. I wondered if you could lend me a few marks."

Vossler chuckled. "Do I look like an easy touch?"

"Yes," said Kamnitzer with disarming frankness.

" How much do you need?"

" Thirty?" This was only a suggestion, but when Kamnitzer saw Vossler reaching for his wallet he added : " You could make it fifty, of course. I've had a lot of official expenses recently. I had to take a taxi on a map-reading exercise yesterday."

" A taxi? Tell me about it."

" With pleasure," said Kamnitzer, and while they strolled up and down the hangar he gave an account of his privately financed trips. Vossler, who made an attentive audience, eventually burst out laughing, and continued to do so even when a senior officer appeared.

"Excuse me a moment," said Vossler, turning to the officer. All the latter wanted was some technical information, which Vossler supplied with a total lack of ceremony and formality. By now, Kamnitzer would hardly have been surprised if the Inspector-General of the Air Force had turned up at Vossler's elbow.

"That's priceless!" said the warrant officer, returning to the subject of Kamnitzer's taxi-rides. He looked forward to retailing the story to Ahlers. "And well worth fifty marks," he added.

"Just to complete my pleasure," Kamnitzer suggested, "what about showing me over one of your crates?"

"You want to see one of our planes?" The warrant officer looked dubious. "It's not as simple as all that, I'm afraid. We'll have to get permission."

"Really? I was under the impression you owned the whole establishment. Strikes me you only have to wag your little finger and everyone comes running."

This was not the case, however. Kamnitzer was duly astonished to note yet another reversal of what he regarded as normal procedure. This time, the warrant officer approached a humble lance-corporal in oil-stained overalls. "I'd like to show our army friend a Noratlas—all right?"

"All these conducted tours!" grumbled the lance-corporal, but he gestured graciously to a big-bellied transport plane in the background. "Don't take any dirt in with you, though," he added warningly. "My mechanics aren't charwomen."

"Is it always like this here," Kamnitzer asked bemusedly, "or is this a special performance for my benefit?"

"Werner's only a lance-corporal," Vossler explained, "but he's acknowledged to be the best mechanic on the station. The same goes for flyers. When a warrant officer flies a plane his co-pilot may be a lieutenant and his navigator a captain—but they both have to obey the orders of the pilot, i.e. the warrant officer. They do, too. It comes naturally."

"But that's terrific!" Kamnitzer exclaimed with genuine

enthusiasm. "Performance before rank and ability before authority! I didn't know any outfit operated like that. Why don't we hear more of it?"

*

Like scores of others in the country, the local town was inhabited by solid and respectable citizens. When the military band played universal harmony reigned. It hadn't always been so, but what resistance there had once been had crumbled. Townsfolk now attended the band concerts in droves, and the residents of the market-place peered from their windows with evident pleasure at the sight that met their eyes. True, the bandsmen's uniforms were only slate-grey, and no weapons, accoutrements or medals glittered in the sun, but the hearts of the crowd involuntarily beat a little higher when the old marches rang out.

"Would you mind if I took Carolin for a stroll?" Martin Recht asked politely.

Frau Ahlers hesitated for a moment—not because she didn't trust Martin Recht, but because she was worried by the thought of Carolin being jostled by the crowds.

"Please, Mother!" pleaded Carolin. "I'd so like to go."

"All right, but be careful."

They heard the strains of the band from a long way off. It was blaring out the *Hohenfriedberger March,* though any tune would have suited their mood as well. Diffidently, Martin Recht felt for Carolin's hand, which she surrendered without hesitation.

In a sense, the band had helped to break the social ice on behalf of the garrison as a whole. It was an army band, and stationed elsewhere, but in response to public demand it now visited the town once every four weeks during the spring and summer months. Major Bornekamp made a point of showing himself at these concerts, accepting the band-master's salute with manifest pleasure and standing on the steps of the town hall to greet various notables—tradesmen mostly, but also civil servants, school-teachers and junior employees with social aspirations. Mayor Asch seldom attended.

"It beats me why those semi-soldiers have to spoil their programme with wishy-washy muck like that," Sergeant-Major Rammler averred to his dutiful listener, Sergeant Streicher. "Wishy-washy muck" referred to a Strauss waltz which had been sandwiched between two marches.

"They have to make allowances for the civillians, I expect," Streicher ventured. "They haven't reached the stage of knowing what they really like."

In actual fact, after years of aversion, mistrust and reserve, a constructively disposed minority of citizens—soon to become a majority—had recognised the signs of the times and come to terms with their community's special position. The town lay off the beaten track. Some might have described it as an idyllic spot, but the surrounding countryside was as bare of industry as it was of thriving agriculture. On the other hand, the town boasted numerous hostelries and large numbers of marriageable girls without prospects.

What was more, the place had always been a garrison town. In their time, the barracks on the north side had housed imperial troops, men of the Reichswehr and soldiers of Greater Germany in that order, and during the Second World War a subsidiary airfield had been built on the south side. Although the post-war garrison had not found it easy to capture the worthy citizens' hearts, the latter were at last beating in time to the bandmaser's baton.

"Look who's here," Rammler said, nudging Streicher, and pointing to the south side of the square. Martin Recht had just emerged from a side-street, attentively squiring Carolin Ahlers.

"Her father's a captain, don't forget," Streicher said cautiously.

"Anything he can do," Rammler said, eyeing Recht malevolently, "we can do better."

He was firmly convinced that, when it came to the pinch, a captain's daughter would know how to differentiate between a sergeant-major and a private soldier. Besides, he told himself, a lofty gesture of conciliation on his part might lead to the establishment of contact with the so-called upper crust, and there would be no harm in that.

"Nip across and tell 'em we've got a first-class view of the band here," Rammler commanded. "Say we'll be glad to share it with them."

After a moment's hesitation, Streicher obediently trotted off, worming his way through the listening throng until he reached Recht and Carolin.

He greeted Martin like a bosom pal and asked to be presented to his companion, assuring them both how delighted he was to see them.

"Why don't you come over and sit with us?" he asked. "We've got splendid seats."

Martin Recht felt almost honoured. Streicher was a good friend who tried, with his best interests at heart, to reach compromises, relax tensions and establish harmonious relations. Aptly, the band started to blare out the *Old Comrades' March.*

"Shall we?" he asked irresolutely.

"No." Carolin sounded friendly but firm. "I wouldn't want anyone to be saddled with a lame duck."

Streicher withdrew hastily and reported the outcome of his mission to Rammler.

"Thinks she's too good for us, does she?" the sergeant-major commented. "It's not surprising, the company these girls keep. Never mind, one day they'll realise what a bunch of miserable dead-beats they're going around with."

The band was now playing *The Glories of Old*—a march studded with fanfares and drum-rolls—much to the delight of the assembled citizenry.

*

For the time being, the varied festivities in the Hotel Asch were proceeding entirely according to plan.

In the Blue Room, air force cadets were piloting volunteers from the girls' high school round the dance-floor. In the Silver Room, the grenadier officers and their invited guests were embarking on a decorous social evening. And in the Green Room, also known as the Gun-room, the small but high-spirited party of young air force officers had assembled to celebrate the end of one of their many training courses.

The three parties shared the same cloakroom and lavatories, also a long ante-room which had to be traversed by anyone entering or leaving the three reception rooms. This ante-room was where the organisers of the various gatherings spent most of their time: Captain Ahlers for the air force, Lieutenant von Strackmann for the army, and Herbert Asch for the hotel.

"Everything seems to be going with a swing so far," Asch said contentedly. His own staff were working hard and the mess waiters seconded for the occasion were also doing their best.

"Let's hope it doesn't go with too much of a swing," said von Strackmann. "Our air force friends in the Green Room are making enough noise already."

"They're young," said Ahlers.

"Of course," von Strackmann agreed cautiously, "but I hope they won't become any noisier."

"It's unlikely for the moment," Asch put in. "The future heroes of the air have already absorbed so much alcohol that they've reached saturation point for the time being. Judging from experience, you won't hear much of them for the next hour."

"In that case I'll stand down until then," said Ahlers, winking at Asch. "Captain Treuberg can deputise for me in the meantime."

"We'll be in my office," Asch told von Strackmann as he followed Ahlers out of the ante-room.

The lieutenant stared after them uncomprehendingly, shocked at their casual attitude. Personally he intended to remain at his post.

All was going well in his sector. An atmosphere of tranquillity and well-bred decorum emanated from the Silver Room, which was in his charge. The guests were still dining, their needs assiduously attended to by a team of waiters and orderlies. Von Strackmann reflected that his system was functioning admirably, and the C.O. would be delighted.

The two other reception rooms presented quite another picture. An occasional babble of voices came from the air force cadets, who added insult to injury by bursting into vulgar applause between dances. Their band, which consisted of piano, electric guitar and drums, was altogether too loud, and the music it produced could only be described as "beat."

What struck von Strackmann as even more grave, however, was that the small party of air force officers was managing to produce considerably more noise than all the cadets, their partners and the jazz band put together. Alarmed by this, he decided to take precautionary measures.

His first move was to seek out Captain Treuberg, Ahlers's deputy. He found him sitting by himself at a table in the middle of the Blue Room, drinking cider and coolly scanning the enthusiastic throng for potential signs of misbehaviour.

Von Strackmann asked Treuberg to follow him outside. "Listen to that," he said when they reached the ante-room. "Quite a din, don't you agree?"

Captain Treuberg considered it important to demonstrate his inter-service esprit de corps. "You may be right," he conceded.

"Especially as Colonel Turner is honouring us with his presence this evening." Von Strackmann felt Treuberg to be a kindred spirit—the sort of man one could work with, even if he was wearing the wrong insignia.

The mention of his wing-commander's name settled the matter as far as Treuberg was concerned. Determined that Colonel Turner should not be disturbed by his own cadets, he issued the following decrees: subdued music only from now on, e.g. tangos, waltzes and slow foxtrots, but no more rock and roll, alcoholic drinks subject to authorisation only, and lengthy pauses between dances.

Treuberg's directives had a marked effect. In less than half an hour the party spirit was virtually dead and the first cadets drifted off with their high-school partners, ostensibly to escort them home. Only the best-behaved remained behind.

"What about the gentlemen in the Green Room?" von Strackmann inquired, concentrating firmly on his next objective and confident that Treuberg would again lend his support.

The young men in the Green Room seemed determined to extend the scope of their already nerve-racking activities still further. Not only did they grow noisier, but they visited the lavatory with increasing frequency, and when, as was inevitable, they encountered young ladies from the high school, they indulged in pleasantries which von Strackmann recognised as barely veiled propositions.

"We must do something about it," he decared stoutly. Captain Treuberg agreed, but added that it wouldn't be easy.

Treuberg was right. The young officers were a sort of closed society which drifted from course to course and station to station. Each garrison town offered a plentiful selection of bars but few unattached girls, so their craving for feminine companionship was intense.

"Do you have to make that frightful row?" Treuberg demanded of one of them, who was steering an unsteady course for the gentlemen's lavatory. "Can't you be a bit quieter?"

" 'Fraid not," he said equably.

"But Colonel Turner's next door," Treuberg remonstrated.

"So what? He's not disturbing us."

Unfortunately, this view was not reciprocated. At that moment, Colonel Turner was presiding over the festive board in the Silver Room like a decorative and much admired centre-piece. The whole brightly-lit room seemed to have been built around him, a handsome frame for an imposing picture.

His partner at the table was Frau Elfrieda Bornekamp, who sunned herself in reflected glory while he chatted to her with all the gallantry of the old school—though a trifle absently, since he was already pondering on his speech. General theme : the constructive values of social intercourse.

Major Bornekamp, meanwhile, sat there stiff-backed and correct, his eyes alert, his commanding voice subdued but clearly audible, his tone jocularly masculine when addressing the ladies, bluff and hearty when conversing with subordinates. Even here, he remained the Ironclad incarnate.

When the sweet—pineapple slices in kirsch—had been served, Major Bornekamp called for silence and handed the floor to Colonel Turner.

"Ladies and gentlemen—dear friends!" the Colonel began. "There was a time when real values and true dignity were conspicuous by their absence. That time does not lie very far in the past, but we can now congratulate ourselves on having seen the last of it."

Here the Colonel paused for effect so that those present might have time to absorb the significance of his words. The reverent silence that ensued was, however, shattered by the sound of male voices raised in song. The Colonel knit his brows, robbed of the power of speech less by the noise itself than by the realisation that the words issuing from a dozen lusty throats belonged to a ditty noted for its questionable taste or, to be more precise, its downright indecency.

"She was only a vicar's daughter!" roared the air force officers happily—and distinctly.

Turner preserved his poise with some difficulty. He glared accusingly at Major Bornekamp, who turned to relay the gorgon gaze to von Strackmann. Von Strackmann was not in the room, however, so Bornekamp had no alternative but to rise from the table.

"I'll soon put a stop to that!" he promised grimly.

*

Sergeant-Major Rammler was finding it an unenjoyable evening. "There's nothing to do in this dump," he announced to Sergeant Streicher, who retained the privilege of accompanying him. "They don't mind lining their pockets at our expense, these people, but they won't lift a finger to entertain us."

Sergeant Streicher essayed a nod which might have signified agreement. He knew that it was inadvisable to contradict Rammler unnecessarily.

"Dead as a door-nail, that's what it is," the sergeant-major pursued, as they strolled aimlessly round the marketplace. The town guide described it as "bathed in antiquity," but Rammler was blind to its charms.

"Not enough women, and the few there are just want to get married. It's a bloody awful state of affairs."

"Perhaps it's done deliberately," Streicher suggested, "so we won't get distracted from our work. After all, women aren't a standard part of military equipment."

This, however, was a subject on which Rammler felt strongly, especially after duty hours and at week-ends. To-day was no exception.

"It's lousy organisation, that's what it is! What do they think we are, stationing us here without any kind of safety-valve? It's a rotten trick, I tell you."

Rammler was a man of wide experience who had, as he put it, "sneaked" his way into the last war at a very tender age. "You can say what you like about the old days, but they knew how to organise things properly. There were brothels in the front-line, not to mention servicewomen and nurses, and every unit had a campful of women pioneers or German Girls' Leaguers attached to it. And that's not counting the local grass-widows."

Streicher thought he understood. The sergeant-major was smarting under all that had happened to him that day. The tough shell of his self-esteem had been punctured, but he had not abandoned hope.

" It's a dog's life," declared Rammler. " The only thing which might make it bearable at this moment would be a bottle of bubbly. One bottle—two at the most. How about it?"

He slapped his companion on the back without conviction and strolled slowly on. Then, outlined against the illuminated windows of a bookshop, he saw a figure which he recognised at once from fifty yards away.

" There's that little sod Recht," he said, slightly cheered by the sight. Raising his voice a degree or two, he summoned the grenadier over.

" Tell me, Recht," said Rammler, when Recht was standing before him, " have you been spreading atrocity stories about me?"

" No, Sergeant-Major."

" What about to-day, at the band concert?"

" Certainly not, Sergeant-Major."

" So when that—that young lady brushed us off like a couple of flies, she did it on her own initiative? Do you really think I'm stupid enough to believe that?"

Recht offered no answer to the last question. " Fräulein Ahlers is very shy," he said. " She's been an invalid all her life, so she isn't used to being with a lot of people."

" I can confirm that," put in Streicher, who was worried by Rammler's jaundiced mood and wanted to dispel it. " Fräulein Ahlers really is rather reserved."

Martin Recht rewarded Streicher's remark with a grateful smile. He was a good pal, there was no doubt about that, and Kamnitzer was wrong to underestimate him. For a few moments, Rammler, too, seemed disposed to listen to the voice of reason.

" What the hell!" he exclaimed, brightening suddenly. " Why should we let ourselves be kicked around by a bunch of stupid tarts!" His wrath embraced three women simultaneously—Helen Wieder, Gerty Ballhaus and Carolin Ahlers—but he seemed prepared to banish them from his memory. "A bird in the hand's worth two in the bush, friends. Let's pay a visit to the *La Paloma*."

"Would you excuse me, Sergeant-Major?" said Recht.

Rammler's face stiffened. "What's that? You don't appreciate my company, is that it?"

"I was just on my way back to barracks, Sergeant-Major. Besides, I haven't got an over-night pass."

"You don't want to, that's what it is." Rammler was outraged. That a wretched underling should have the effrontery to reject his friendly overtures was the last straw.

"I might have known it," he said bitterly. "When all's said and done, it's only what I'd have expected of you. It's in your blood, after all." His dull rage knew no bounds. Like a bull goaded beyond endurance, he now saw nothing but red. "Once a Jew-boy always a Jew-boy!"

Martin Recht turned pale and Streicher looked as though he had trodden on a nest of scorpions, but Rammler registered the satisfaction of one who inhabits a country where freedom of speech is an inalienable right.

"Don't look so bloody cretinous!" he cried. "If you haven't got that load of crap out of your system yet, it's high time you did. Right, you two! Buck your ideas up and try to behave like grown men. To the *La Paloma*, at the double—march!"

*

A hurriedly arranged conference was being held in Herbert Asch's office, those present being Colonel Turner, Major Bornekamp, Captain Ahlers and, naturally enough, Asch himself. The latter's prime function was to pour oil on troubled waters by dispensing the contents of a bottle of Iphöfer Kalb, vintage 1957.

The sole point under discussion was how to curtail the

activities of the group of young pilots whose singing of indecent songs had caused such an unpleasant stir and, as Bornekamp balefully expressed it, "interfered" with the Colonel's speech.

"The first thing to do," Herbert Asch suggested, with a covert wink at Ahlers, "is to establish whether the words were really objectionable."

"They were downright crude," said Major Bornekamp. Being well-versed in this field, he was qualified to give an expert opinion.

Lieutenant von Strackmann and Captain Treuberg had already encountered defeat at the hands of the airmen, some of whom were of the same rank and had greeted them like long-lost brothers. Having failed to establish a clear-cut position of authority, they had retired under a barrage of laughter.

"Strictly speaking," Bornekamp told Asch, "this is your problem. You're in charge here."

"You're absolutely right on the last point," Asch replied courteously, "but I'm in charge of a hotel, not a barracks, and there's a subtle difference. Military discipline is not my concern. There's nothing abnormal about people singing on my premises—it's an everyday occurrence in my line of business."

"What do you think, Captain Ahlers?"

Ahlers did not hesitate to say what he thought. "Fighter pilots are a law unto themselves. They travel around from one training course to the next. They're young, so it's not unnatural for them to let off steam occasionally. They're noisy, of course, but fundamentally harmless. The less notice you take, the less row they make. I recommend a little patience. That's all that's needed."

Bornekamp delivered a vigorous lecture on discipline and Colonel Turner advocated diplomacy, but no one seemed prepared to intervene in person. On the contrary, each endeavoured to pass the hot potato to the other, a game which might have gone on indefinitely if Lieutenant von Strackmann had not materialised. He looked agitated.

" One of the ladies has been molested ! " he announced.

" Physically? " inquired Herbert Asch.

" The lady involved was Frau Bornekamp," reported von Strackmann.

He had been standing with her in the ante-room, engaged in private conversation—he didn't say so, but Frau Elfrieda had hinted that she might allow him to escort her home later—when one of the fighter pilots appeared.

" He addressed her as ' doll,' " von Strackmann concluded.

" He probably meant it as a compliment," said Ahlers.

" Besides," said Asch, " Herr von Strackmann may have omitted to introduce them in time. That's probably how this unfortunate misunderstanding arose."

" It was a direct affront, for all that," Colonel Turner said coolly, satisfied that his well-judged remark would leave Bornekamp holding the hot potato.

The Major rose with an air of purpose and left the room. He descended one flight of stairs and strode majestically along the corridor until he came to the Green Room.

On entering, he found the party still in full swing. Some of the fighter pilots were, in his estimation, the worse for wear. Several had shed their jackets and ties and rolled their sleeves up, and two were actually squatting on the carpet like a couple of fakirs. The musician of the party struck three rousing chords on his guitar, and all eyes turned expectantly in Bornekamp's direction.

" I must ask you," he said sternly, " to terminate these proceedings. You're making a nuisance of yourselves."

The young officers regarded him with delight. The evening had been showing signs of flagging, so any distraction merited a hearty welcome.

An angular youth with carrot-coloured hair stepped forward, assuming the role of spokesman for the assembled merry-makers. " It remains to be seen who is disturbing whom," he said affably. " We like it here, anyway, and you're not disturbing us—yet."

" I am a major," Bornekamp said, not without dignity.

"I'm happy for you," the fighter pilot said with a cheerful grin. "Most of us are still captains."

"You will oblige me by calling it a day," Bornekamp insisted. "At once, if you don't mind."

"Did you hear what the man said?" demanded the red-haired youth, turning to his companions. "Was it a slip of the tongue—or did I just misunderstand?"

"Do you know whom you're talking to?" Major Bornekamp decided to throw the full force of his personality into the scales. "Clear out immediately, do you hear!"

The spokesman surveyed his friends with a twinkle in his eye. Everyone looked highly entertained. The party was proving definitely worthwhile.

"Listen, mate," he said, stationing himself in front of Bornekamp with arms akimbo, "—or Major, if you prefer it. May I point out that we're off duty now? That being so, we left our ranks behind in the cloakroom. Quite apart from that, you're in the army and we're in the air force—which is quite another kettle of fish altogether, in case you didn't know."

"How dare you lecture me! One of you molested my wife."

"There's no question of anyone having molested your wife. One of us may have used a term of endearment or admiration, but that's all. So either have a drink with us or shut the door behind you as you go out."

"You'll be hearing from me!" snapped Bornekamp, turning on his heel.

"A postcard'll do!" a jaunty voice called after him.

Bornekamp squared his shoulders and marched back to Asch's office, purple in the face with frustration.

"What—no luck?" Asch inquired blandly.

Bornekamp concentrated his face on Colonel Turner. "Disciplinary proceedings must be instituted at once, Colonel. Disobedience is a mild word for the behaviour of those young men."

"Gently, Major," said the Colonel, bowing his stately head in thought. "We mustn't be precipitated."

"Perhaps it would be best," Herbert Asch suggested, "if you yourself, Colonel . . ."

"I don't think that would be advisable," Ahlers said promptly.

"Why not?" Asch donned an air of surprise. "The Colonel is the senior officer present."

"Besides, Colonel, these officers are temporarily under your command," added Bornekamp.

Ahlers maintained a pregnant silence. Looking round, the Colonel saw the eyes of those present fixed on him in what he took to be a demonstration of confidence. He had no choice but to act.

"In that case," he said, not without misgiving, "I shall have to take the field myself."

*

Grenadier Martin Recht sat hunched in a corner of the Café Asch, staring moodily into space. He pushed his empty beer-glass towards the waitress who was serving him.

"Same again," he said. "Better make it two while you're about it."

He didn't notice that the waitress in question was Helen Wieder. He had no wish to see anything, neither the confused blur of tables, chairs, glasses and bright lights, nor the people that inhabited it.

"Aren't you feeling well?" Helen asked.

Recht gave no sign of having heard. He felt as if he were enveloped in a dense curtain of fog. Then the curtain parted, and Karl Kamnitzer appeared.

"What's up with you?" Kamnitzer demanded. "Why do you have to spoil my Saturday night just when it's shaping nicely?"

"I'm sorry," Martin said dully. "I didn't ask you to come. One more glass of beer and then I'll push off."

"What do you mean, one more glass of beer! You've got rid of three already—knocked them back almost before they were on the table, too. I'm well-informed, you see.

You've not only interrupted my dreams of a rosy future—you've alienated my girl-friend's affections. She seems to be far more interested in your welfare than mine."

Frau Elisabeth had accorded Kamnitzer the special privilege of sitting in the room behind the bar counter, where coffee was brewed and an array of bottles stood ready to hand. This, too, was where Helen Wieder spent her time when she was not actually serving in the restaurant—likewise ready to hand, Kamnitzer reflected, except that she kept eluding his playful advances and had insisted that his friend Recht needed him.

"I'm sorry," Martin said, again. "I didn't mean to disturb you."

"Well, you have, and here I am." Kamnitzer sat down and pulled his chair closer. "All right, let's have it. What's the trouble this time?"

Recht shook his head. "Nothing's happened, I tell you."

"Don't give me that," Kamnitzer persisted. "I can read you like a book."

Recht was silent for a moment. Then he gulped down the contents of his glass and said, almost angrily: "Haven't you anything better to do than sit here talking to a Jew?"

"Steady on!" protested Kamnitzer, pricking up his ears. He took a few moments to digest what Recht had just said. "What's that supposed to mean? Besides, you're bragging. You're only half-Jewish, aren't you?"

"I'm a Jew, all the same."

"Then be proud of it, man. Actually, it's a shame you're only half-Jewish. The Bundeswehr could do with a few genuine Jews. It'd be good for public relations."

Kamnitzer was familiar with Martin Recht's past history, though only vaguely. His father—a Jew—had served as a young but much-decorated officer in the First World War. He later married a non-Jewish woman and founded a successful business with numerous overseas contacts which proved extremely useful to him when he was forced to leave the country. He returned to Germany after the war, and died in his home town. He had never lost his affection for the army, and despite all his subsequent experiences he would probably have approved of Martin's decision to volunteer for the Federal army, had he lived.

"Someone's been getting at you, haven't they?" Kamnitzer demanded. "Who was it? Not Rammler, by any chance?"

Recht nodded mutely.

"When and how? Let's have all the details."

Martin Recht recounted what had happened, and the longer he talked the more relieved he felt. Eventually he even summoned up a faint smile.

Kamnitzer, however, looked more and more grave. "Well, what did you do?" he demanded finally.

"Nothing."

"You didn't knock his teeth down his throat? Didn't you even call him a moronic Nazi swine?"

"No, I just walked off. What else could I do? He's a sergeant-major, after all, and Streicher was there too."

"Fair enough," Kamnitzer said slowly. "Maybe you did right, under the circumstances. In any case, there's no reason why you should regard the word Jew as a term of abuse."

"Thanks," said Recht, laying a hand on his friend's arm.

"I see the whole thing in quite another light, of course," Kamnitzer said thoughtfully. "But that's my own affair. Tell me, where did friend Rammler go after his performance?"

"He said he was going to the *La Paloma.*"

Kamnitzer's shrewd eyes sparkled. "Not bad," he mused. "In fact, it may be the perfect place. How much cash have you got on you?"

"Just over forty marks."

"It'll have to do," Kamnitzer said firmly. "Hand over the lot. I need some working capital." He snapped his fingers impatiently. "Come on, there's no time to lose."

Recht obediently handed over the money, asking questions but receiving no reply. Kamnitzer added his own money to Recht's and began to count it, nodding happily to himself as he did so.

"I don't know what you're up to," Recht said, "but I don't want you to get into trouble on my account."

"Everything's risky these days," Kamnitzer said grimly. "It's a hard life for everyone—sadists included, even when they hide behind a uniform. The only problem is how to bring it home to them. Never mind, where there's a will there's a way."

*

Colonel Turner stood in the ante-room and surveyed the three doors behind which the social life of the station was pursuing its course. The remaining officer cadets and their high-school girls were still pounding the parquet in subdued fashion in the first room and a hum of lively conversation came from the second, but the occupants of the third were baying like wolves.

"No untoward incidents in my department, sir," Lieutenant von Strackmann reported in a courtroom, confidential, semi-official manner.

Captain Treuberg also hurried up, conscientious as ever, wanting to know if the Colonel needed anything.

All the Colonel needed at that moment was a brandy. Having fortified himself, he strode over to the third door, which Treuberg opened for him, and walked in. He was confronted by a jumble of chairs, a battery of empty bottles and a pile of broken glasses. Through the tobacco smoke and alcohol fumes he could make out a number of perspiring young men in their shirt-sleeves.

"Gentlemen!" Turner began.

"Welcome, sir!" called one of the fighter pilots, and his cry was taken up by the whole company. "Welcome!" they bellowed.

"Three cheers for the Colonel!" shouted another at the top of his lungs. "Hip-hip-hip!"

"Hurrah!" they roared with fervour.

"Gentlemen!" Turner said again.

He got no further because the guitar-playing officer leapt on to the table with a crash, knocking over several bottles and glasses in the process. "Friends!" he cried in ringing tones. "In the Colonel's honour we'll now sing *The Lodger and the Landlady*!"

This they proceeded to do, in so far as what emerged from their throats could be described as singing.

Colonel Turner stood there transfixed. He opened his mouth to say "Gentlemen!" again, but the din was so terrific that he abandoned the idea. Adopting the only course still open to him, he turned on his heel and left the room.

He re-entered Herbert Asch's office looking slightly distraught and gratefully accepted the glass proffered by Captain Ahlers.

"They welcomed me in unison," he said, with something akin to wonder, "and then they sang a song."

"Something obscene, I'll bet," said Bornekamp.

Turner could only nod. "Ostensibly in my honour, too, I never got a word in."

"It's an old dodge, sir," Ahlers said knowledgeably. "I was caught like that myself once. They're probably laughing themselves sick at this minute."

The last remark was somewhat ill-judged, as Captain Ahlers at once realised when the Colonel shot him a reproachful glance, clearly implying that no one laughs himself sick at a colonel.

"Anyway, something definite will have to be done now," Bornekamp said.

"What, for instance?" Asch asked curious
ly.

"Well," replied Bornekamp, with iron in his tone, "we could simply get together a scratch force, clear the requisite number of cells in the guard-room and lock the fellows up." Colonel Turner closed his eyes briefly and raised a restraining hand. He was always averse to any idea which might have unforeseen consequences. On the other hand, he could not think of a better one. He stared wearily into space.

"It's a hopeless situation," declared Ahlers.

Bornekamp controlled his rage with difficulty. "My officers would never dream of indulging in a musical performance of that sort," he said harshly.

Colonel Turner stiffened slightly and raised his eyebrows as if to convey that Bornekamp had exceeded the bounds of propriety. "In my command," he said in measured tones, "conditions of service are somewhat different."

"That's what I meant," said Bornekamp.

"In the air force," Turner continued, with a touch of condescension, "we have to master an extremely complex-weapons system, and that demands discipline of the highest order. But to maintain it outside the sphere of duty, let alone in the strictly private domain . . ." He paused. "There just isn't time."

"In my view," Bornekamp persisted, "discipline is inconceivable except as a whole. It must be present in any given situation."

"Even when you're on the bottle?" inquired Asch.

"Even when you're on the pan, for that matter," averred Bornekamp.

"I don't think we need go into details of that sort," Colonel Turner said with distaste. "Besides, we're straying from the matter in hand. The vital question at the moment is how we're going to silence those young savages without causing an unpleasant scene."

"If you'll allow me," Herbert Asch said suddenly, "I'll deal with them for you."

"Don't be ridiculous!" exclaimed Bornekamp. "If the Colonel and I failed to stop them, what luck are you likely to have?"

The hôtelier looked unabashed. "I can always try."

"Please do," Turner said. "You have my blessing."

Barely ten minutes passed before Asch returned. He resumed his seat with an air of satisfaction, raised his glass to the other three, and drank. "Well, that's that," he said.

"What's what?" Bornekamp asked belligerently.

"The noise. The young gentlemen have promised not to sing or accost the ladies."

"Remarkable!" Colonel Turner said admiringly. "How did you manage it?"

"It was quite simple, really." Asch winked at Ahlers. "I merely told them who I was and pointed out that a hotel-owner has certain rights, among them the right to serve whom he likes for as long as he likes and turn unwelcome guests out. What it amounted to was: either they piped down and behaved decently or they'd be ejected without getting another drop to drink."

"And it worked?"

"It always does. You've only got to make it clear that you know the rules of the game. Most of them are based on a bare modicum of common sense, and that, if you don't mind my saying so, gentlemen, is a quality which the services might well display to better advantage."

*

While Kamnitzer was setting off on his special mission, destination the *La Paloma*, Martin Recht remained sitting in the Café Asch. The thick fog round him had dispersed and Rammler's insult had assumed the reduced proportions of a misunderstanding. He was well looked after, too, first by Helen Wieder and then, after a brief interval, by Vossler and Gerty, who came over to his table. He greeted them delightedly. Vossler was part of Carolin's world, somehow, and anything that reminded him of her was a welcome distraction.

"We won't disturb you," Gerty said.

"We're not staying," Vossler added. "We've got plans for this evening."

"But we're going on a little outing to-morrow," Gerty continued, "and we wondered if you'd join us—you and Carolin, that is."

"I'd love to," Martin said gratefully, "but only on condition that Carolin—Fräulein Ahlers . . ."

"Leave it to me," said Vossler. "I'm one of the family, and a breath of fresh air won't do Carolin any harm. That's settled, then. I'll be outside the barracks in my car at fourteen hundred hours to-morrow, on the dot. Civvies and a cheerful smile to be worn by all."

They said good-bye and waved to him from the door before going out. Recht waved back, smiling. The last few minutes had banished his worries, but they returned with a rush when he caught sight of Sergeant Streicher.

Streicher hurried over to him with an earnest expression on his face. "I've been looking everywhere for you," he said. "I tried half a dozen bars and even rang the barracks to see if you were there. Thank goodness I've found you at last."

Martin Recht looked at his watch. "I'm pushed for time, I'm afraid. I've got to be back in barracks by midnight."

"Forget about that," Streicher said, sitting down. "What you need is a heart-to-heart talk. It'll do you good."

"Maybe to-morrow," Recht parried. "The last thing I want to do is get put on restrictions."

Streicher laid one hand soothingly on his arm and beckoned for two beers with the other. "You can't get shot of me like that. Don't worry about your pass—I'll see you're all right."

"What do you mean?"

"I've got contacts. After all, I'm a sergeant now, and the guard commander's an old pal of mine. I'll just tell him you left your pass behind—that'll do the trick."

Martin looked dubious, but Streicher reverted from the tone of authority to that of friendship. "You know you can always rely on me, don't you? You need advice, after what happened this evening."

Recht made a noncommittal reply, but he accepted Streicher's offer to sneak him past the barrack gates. "Get this straight, though. Don't ask me to apologise to Rammler for what he said."

Streicher looked shocked. "I wouldn't dream of it," he assured him, ordering two schnapps to go with their beer. "There was no excuse for his behaviour. He completely forgot himself. You just can't say things like that—it's unforgivable."

" He said what he thought."

" I told you, I condemn him for it."

" He meant to insult me. He used to word ' Jew ' as a term of abuse. You heard him."

Streicher drained his glass hurriedly. He knew that if Recht stirred up any mud—as well he might—he, Streicher, would find himself in it up to his neck, if not deeper.

" You've got to look at it in the proper light, Martin," he said, warming to his subject. " I'm not trying to defend Rammler—not in this subject. I'm not really anti-Semitic. Maybe he just meant it as a sort of joke."

" Oh, yes," Recht scoffed, " it was hilarious!"

" I admit it wasn't a proper subject for a joke, but he didn't insult you to your face. He just said : ' Once a Jew always a Jew'—more to himself than anything else. It sounds a bit different put like that, you must admit."

" What exactly do you want, Streicher?"

" I want to stop you doing anything stupid, that's all. Just think—if this business hits the headlines it could harm the reputation of the whole garrison—of the Bundeswehr itself."

" Rammler should have thought of that first, shouldn't he?"

Streicher lapsed into silence. After a pause, he said : " I take your point, Martin, but why make unnecessary trouble for yourself—and me as well?"

" I'm not making trouble for anyone, Streicher. Other people make it for me. But you haven't told me what you want yet."

" Discernment, understanding, generosity . . . I'm appealing to your common sense, Martin. Sergeant-Major Rammler will apologise to you formally, in my presence. How about that? Wouldn't that be the best solution?"

" Perhaps," said Recht, tempted to agree but mindful of Karl Kamnitzer. " Let's hope it's not too late already," he added almost inaudibly.

Streicher, who felt he was in sight of land at last, failed to catch the last remark. If Rammler wasn't completely demented he would apologise, which meant that his own responsibilities would be at an end.

"Leave it to me," he said confidently, and ordered two more beers. He laid his hand on Recht's arm again. "Just one more thing," he said in a low but purposeful undertone. "Could you do me a small favour?"

"What is it?"

"I wouldn't ask if I didn't feel we both trusted each other. I had to celebrate my promotion, see, and it wasn't cheap. One expense after another, and the bills are still coming in. To cut a long story short, I'm completely broke. Could you possibly slip me a fifty-mark note?"

"I'm awfully sorry," Recht said with genuine regret. "I haven't a pfennig left. Someone borrowed my last mark a few minutes back—word of honour."

"Blast!" said Streicher, deeply disillusioned. He went around solving other people's problems, and what thanks did he get? They left him in the lurch in his hour of need.

"Well, I've got to raise some cash somehow," he said, getting up. "I've already left my pay-book in one bar as a deposit."

"Don't forget you promised to get me past the guard-room," Recht reminded him.

"First things first," Stretcher called over his shoulder. "I shan't get in myself without a pay-book. Wait here—I'll be right back."

So saying, he vanished, not to reappear that night.

*

Meanwhile, Kamnitzer was launching Operation Reminder, as he had christened it to himself, in the *La Paloma*, or, to be more precise, in the "passion parlour."

"Hello there!" he called to the men round the bar counter, who were all Italians. "How about drinking a toast to international understanding?"

"We shit on it," said one of the Italians, with an admirable command of German idiom.

Kamnitzer was undeterred. "Let's drink to it all the same."

The Italians raised their glasses reluctantly. They were suspicious, and not without reason. The German weather didn't agree with them particularly, nor did German schnapps. They earned fairly good wages, it was true, but their private life was virtually non-existent, first because of the language difficulty and second because male competition in the small town was positively overwhelming. What with the army, the air force and an additional kennel full of Americans, there were at least ten men on the trail of every unattached girl.

"And now," said Kamnitzer, when he had ordered the next round, "let's drink to everything in skirts!"

The Italians, who were beginning to warm to Kamnitzer, laughed. The young soldier seemed to be a bit of a wag. What was more, he seemed to enjoy their company. Far from jeering at their clumsy German, he ventured an occasional word of Italian, which they found both endearing and entertaining.

By the time they had demolished a third and fourth round of drinks at Kamnitzer's expense, harmony reigned supreme. It was a harmony which appeared to extend even to their dislikes. To convince themselves of all this, all they had to do was glance at the mirror behind the bar. This reflected the furthest recesses of the passion parlour, where, wreathed in tobacco smoke and a haze compound of alcohol fumes and cheap perfume, sat Sergeant-Major Rammler, who had wedged himself between two girls.

The girls were stolidly waiting for him to make his choice in accordance with an unwritten law which stated that, in this garrison town, the military had first call on their professional services. Differences in rank played a role, but civilians and Italians came at the bottom of the scale.

"So you've taken a fancy to me, eh?" Rammler demanded with a grin.

"You could say that," one of the girls drawled wearily.

G

Her eyes flicked over the Italians as she did so, but she knew that a sergeant-major had considerably more to offer, financially, than a foreign labourer.

" We're being patient," said the other, " but you'll have to decide on one of us some time, or the other'll miss the boat."

" I'll go for you both," declared Rammler, hugging them possessively as if they symbolised womanhood in general. He seemed quite indifferent to what was going on at the bar.

Kamnitzer, who was still sitting there surrounded by his new friends, was telling them about a trip he had made to Italy. He had never been there in his life, but his perusal of the illustrateds and weeklies in the battalion reading-room gave him enough material to go on.

" Friends," he said, " what do I do when I go to Italy? Do I take a girl-friend along? Certainly not—I behave like an Italian."

" Does it work?"

" Every time," Kamnitzer said firmly. " It all depends whether you know how to adapt yourself. When I'm in Italy I act like an Italian, so when you're in Germany you must act like Germans."

" How do you mean?" asked one of the Italians, intrigued.

" Get used to the way things are done here. Adapt yourselves to local customs. Don't let yourselves be elbowed aside. Charm won't get you anywhere on its own."

As Kamnitzer discoursed in this vein, and round followed round, the Italians began to thirst for action. Their newly awakened pride was stung by thoughts of their defeat of a few days before, and they wagged their heads significantly when Kamnitzer concluded his harangue with the words : " Competition's there to be eliminated."

This they were determined to do, though how to put the idea into practice in the most effective way was less easy to see. However, prompted by Kamnitzer, they all recognised the figure in the corner as a symbol of the competition which had to be eliminated.

Thus, when Sergeant-Major Rammler rose in response to a call of nature, the most pugnacious of the Italians started to follow him. Kamnitzer held them back. "Not yet," he said, "not here. Wait for the right moment—I'll see you get your chance."

Ordering his new-found friends another round—this time of invigorating grappa—he slapped them heartily on the back and went over to Rammler's two female companions. He sat down between them uninvited. "I'll pay the normal price," he said without more ado, "plus ten marks special expenses, plus as many free drinks as you like—just so long as you don't work to-night."

"What if we want to?"

"I shall understand," Kamnitzer assured them. "In that case, I'll put my Italian friends at your disposal. All you need do then is take your pick." He eyed the door of the gentlemen's lavatory. "I must be going. We'll discuss details outside in the corridor."

Negotiations were brief but satisfactory. Kamnitzer paid the girls generously in advance and gave them precise instructions. With everything in readiness, Rammler was at liberty to make the next move.

*

Grenadier Martin Recht flitted through the streets like an uneasy ghost, looking for Streicher. His pass had expired hours before.

He visited all the hostelries round the market-place in turn—The Bunch of Grapes, The Wild Boar, The White Hart—inquiring everywhere for Sergeant Streicher, but without success.

Desperately, he combed the side-street locals patronised by the garrison—The Gay Dog, The Eagle and Child (affectionately known as The Bustard and Bastard), and The Black Horse. A sea of faces met his gaze, some stolid and contented, others staring into space like lost souls surveying the depths of their own despair, but the comradely sergeant's was not among them.

Recht was tired now, and far from sober, but still he roamed on. He saw a drunken man propped motionless against a wall, a woman dragging her husband home, a courting couple compressed into the shadow of an archway.

Above him the moon, pale as a corpse and tipsily indifferent, white-washed such house-fronts as it could reach and drew livid chalk-marks across the cobbles.

Then Recht found himself standing in front of the block where the Ahlers lived. How he had got there he had no idea. He stared up at the blank windows, behind one of which Carolin must be sleeping. He had a vivid picture of her lying there with her face buried in the pillow, her long hair flowing free, breathing softly and smiling at some tender dream inspired by memories of him. . . .

In reality, he couldn't see the window of Carolin's room at all. It looked out on to the courtyard where the dustbins were kept. Carolin wasn't smiling, either. She was breathing heavily, her face looked strained, and her hip was hurting. An enjoyable day was taking its toll.

It was not long before Recht's musings were invaded by the harsh realisation that he had to find Streicher and get back to barracks, come what may.

But Streicher was nowhere to be found.

*

" How much longer have we got to sit here?" one of the two girls asked Rammler. " It's time we were going. What about it?"

" I'm champing at the bit," Rammler assured her. " The only thing is, I'm a bit broke at the moment. Could you give me tick—just till next Saturday? I'll pay you interest."

" For you," said the girl, gently removing his hand from her knee, " I'd do anything."

Rammler felt flattered and, for the first time that day, appreciated.

"You carry on," said the girl. "I'll follow you in a minute. Meet me on the corner of Fasanenstrasse and Hobelweg."

"Done," said Rammler. He left the bar enraptured by the notion that no one could resist the power of his personality.

"Well, what about it, sports?" Kamnitzer said encouragingly. "This could be the chance you were looking for."

The Italians conferred quickly among themselves, putting their heads together like pigeons in the Piazza San Marco. Then five of them peeled off and left the *La Paloma* in quick succession. Kamnitzer ordered a glass of champagne. There was nothing to do now but kill the next quarter of an hour.

After about twenty minutes the Italians returned, looking as though they had recently indulged in some mild but exhilarating form of exercise. One of them rubbed his hands.

"That should do it," he said, winking at Kamnitzer.

Kamnitzer bought his energetic friends one more round in token of his appreciation, secretly hoping that they had done their work with a thoroughness worthy of their German hosts. Then, full of expectation, he left the *La Paloma.*

He strolled along the dark length of the Fasanenstrasse towards the intersection with Hobelweg. On the corner of the two streets stood a chestnut tree and an advertisement hoarding. There was no street lamp, and now that clouds had hidden the moon the outlines of the ruined fence and the scattered houses in the background were blurred and indistinct.

Kamnitzer casually lit a cigarette, threw the match through a gap in the fence and began to whistle, discordantly but with bravura. No particular tune was identifiable.

"Hey, you!" a voice called.

Kamnitzer interrupted his recital. "Who's there?" he asked.

"Me!"

The voice issuing from behind the fence sounded quite pitiable. Kamnitzer had been expecting it, but its unsergeant-major-like tone took him by surprise.

"What do you mean—me?" he inquired with relish. "Who's me?"

"Help," pleaded the man behind the fence, "I've been beaten up."

"Are you hurt?"

The man mumbled something inaudible. Then he called: "Hey, don't I know you? Of course! It's Kamnitzer, isn't it?"

"Herr Kamnitzer, if you don't mind."

"Thank God!" the voice cried unsuspectingly. "What a bloody miracle you came along. I need help."

"Who are you?"

"Can't you hear? It's Rammler, Sergeant-Major Rammler."

"Anyone could say that," Kamnitzer said in tones of deep suspicion. "Why don't you come out where I can see you?"

"I told you, I was set on. They tore all my clothes off—left me without a stitch."

"Then get dressed."

"Goddammit!" bellowed Rammler. "They pinched my clothes. Can't you understand, blast you?"

"Kindly moderate your language," Kamnitzer said reprovingly. "You're beginning to annoy me. If you really are stark naked, you're creating a nuisance. It's an affront to public decency. I'll have to report it to the police."

"Kamnitzer!" Rammler called despairingly. "Surely you can recognise my voice, can't you?"

The sergeant-major saw no alternative but to show himself. He emerged from the shelter of the fence. White as the belly of a fish in the light of the moon, which had uncharitably reappeared, he trotted towards Kamnitzer with one hand clutching his private parts and the other extended in supplication. Kamnitzer ignored both gestures.

"Do you recognise me now?" he asked.

The lance-corporal shook his head distastefully. "No, why should I?"

"So you refuse, do you?" Rammler's voice resumed its old menacing tone. "Right, this is an official order . . ."

" An official order? Don't make me laugh!" Kamnitzer sounded amused. " Since when do people issue orders in the altogether? Sergeant-Major Rammler would never dream of doing such a thing. That proves you can't be him."

" You rotten swine!" Rammler roared. " I see your game! You're mixed up in this business, aren't you, you filthy little sod!"

" Push off, you dirty old man!" said Kamnitzer. " That makes two offences you've committed—indecent exposure and masquerading as a sergeant-major in the German army. I'm going to call the police."

" Kamnitzer!" called Rammler, pleading again. " Be reasonable, for God's sake!"

But Kamnitzer turned on his heel and vanished into the night, whistling.

*

Martin Recht only meant to pause near the barrack gates just long enough to regain his breath, but ten minutes passed before he screwed up the courage to take the last few inevitable steps.

He leant back against a tree, worn out by his vain quest for Streicher, but exhaustion could not subdue his mounting anger.

Streicher had obviously broken his word, which meant that he was liable to be put on restrictions. If things really went wrong, he would not be able to see Carolin for some time to come. There was one last chance of retrieving the situation, and he decided to take it.

Drawing a deep breath, he walked up to the barrack gates and wished the sentry a polite good evening.

" What do you mean, good evening?" the sentry asked peevishly. " It's just on four a.m."

" Nice night," Recht remarked.

" Your pass," said the sentry.

Martin donned an air of desperate amiability, but the

sentry's bleary face remained sullen. " Sergeant Streicher of No. 3 Company has got my pass," he said, with as much charm as he could muster.

" Let's see your pay-book," said the sentry.

" Ask the guard commander," Recht said eagerly. " He knows Sergeant Streicher—they're old pals."

" If it isn't one thing it's another," grumbled the sentry. " It's beginning to get me down." Morosely, he locked the gates and slouched over to the guard-room with Recht.

The guard commander, who was engrossed in a whodunnit, did not welcome the interruption. He listened to the sentry's report, eyeing Recht with some perplexity.

" You say Sergeant Streicher's got your pass? Funny he didn't mention it when he came in. I was speaking to him only an hour ago."

" Perhaps he forgot."

The guard commander stared absently at his detective novel. He wasn't inhuman, but what could he do? Orders were orders.

Even so, he left no stone unturned. First, he rang No. 3 Company and spoke to the duty N.C.O., who tersely informed him that Grenadier Recht's name was not in the leave-book. Then he asked to speak to Sergeant Streicher.

No. 3 Company's duty N.C.O. swore under his breath and went to call Streicher. After a considerable lapse of time, Streicher came to the 'phone. He stated, drowsily but definitely, that he knew nothing about Grenadier Recht's pass.

" There must be some mistake," Recht said agitatedly. " Please ask him once more."

Frowning, the guard commander repeated his question, but Sergeant Streicher's answer was still the same : no, he knew nothing about it.

" That's it, then," the guard commander told Recht with genuine regret. " I'll have to report you. Leave your pay-book here."

Recht did so. Then, with shoulders sagging, he trotted along the road leading to No. 3 Company block. His legs felt as if they were made of lead, and he was on the verge of collapse by the time he reached Room 13.

Here he was greeted by Comrade Streicher, who stood there in his nightshirt with arms akimbo. "What do you think you're up to?" he demanded indignantly. "What are you trying to pin on me?"

Recht did not reply. He merely stared steadily at his self-styled friend for several seconds. It was a look conveying extreme contempt, and it annoyed Streicher immeasurably.

"This is the last straw!" Streicher protested. "What are you looking at me like that for? I go out of my way to help you, and what thanks do I get? You try to take advantage of me."

Recht restrained himself with an effort. "What about your promise?" he demanded.

"I promised you nothing—nothing at all! I'll deny anything you say, I warn you."

"Why don't you belt up?" called a sleepy voice.

It being the week-end, some of the beds were empty. Four men were absent, of whom three had week-end passes and the fourth—Kamnitzer, needless to say—was being crafty enough to delay his return to barracks until daylight. Normally speaking, the orderly sergeant did not carry out an early morning tour of inspection on Sundays.

"So you're running out on me!" exclaimed Recht.

"I've never run out on anyone," Streicher said, with increasing volume. "How dare you make such an accusation! Don't involve me in your troubles, that's all I ask."

"Christ Almighty!" called another inmate, wakened by the noise. "If you want a fight, clobber each other and get it over. I want some kip—I'm on guard duty to-morrow."

"Mind your own business!" Streicher yelled.

Recht advanced to within a few inches of the sergeant. "So you don't know a thing?" he demanded. "You heard nothing and made no promise?"

"Don't you dare lay hands on me!" screeched Streicher. "I won't be threatened, do you hear?"

" Why don't you go outside?" came a weary voice from yet another bed.

Neither Recht nor Streicher took any notice of these interjections. They stood confronting one another like two fighting-cocks.

" Perhaps you'll also deny that Sergeant-Major Rammler swore at me for being a Jew?" Recht asked quietly.

" I don't know what you're talking about. It's nothing to do with me."

" You're a dirty mealy-mouthed bastard," Recht said softly.

" What did you say?"

" I said : you're a dirty mealy-mouthed bastard."

The occupants of the room sat up in their beds and stared, intrigued by the scene that was unfolding before their bleary eyes. They looked with interest from Streicher's beetroot features to the unexpectedly menacing figure of Recht.

" Clout him, Martin," said someone. " Then perhaps we can get a bit of rest."

" Take that back," Streicher hissed, " or . . ."

But no one ever found out what the " or " portended because Recht pushed the sergeant aside. He only meant to clear a path to his bed, but Streicher must have been off balance. He staggered sideways and crashed against a cupboard. Rebounding, he cannoned back into Recht, who seized his nightshirt with both hands, tearing it, and flung him aside with a grimace of disgust.

Streicher crashed into the cupboard once more, lost his balance completely and sat down with a thud. He looked around him in outrage, but his furious protests were drowned by a peal of laughter.

*

The day that followed came to be known as " Mellow Sunday." Although it was not an altogether apt description, the sun dispensed its radiance lavishly and the earth seemed to glow with well-being. Even the barrack-room windows gleamed softly.

Everyone prepared to enjoy the day ahead, local inhabitants and members of the garrison alike. People were up and about early—whether to take the air, drink or pray— and in the Municipal Gardens the first courting couples disappeared into the willow-thickets round the so-called swannery, which only housed ducks.

Colonel Turner sat in his garden, lost in thought. His beloved *Critique of Pure Reason* lay open on his knee, but he was not reading it. He had never read any Kant in his life, but he enjoyed carrying the philosopher's books around. It gave him the sensation of moving in exalted circles, a sensation doubly agreeable after the distasteful events of the previous evening.

After two hours of exacting paper-work, Captain Ahlers took a short break. He used it to telephone Professor Martin about Carolin's forthcoming operation.

While they were still talking Captain Treuberg came in, ostensibly in search of a mislaid file. He listened with unabashed attention.

" That was a private call," Ahlers told the switchboard. " Put it down to me, please."

" Pretty expensive, these operations, eh?" Treuberg inquired, when his chief had hung up.

" Extremely. Still, you can't put a price-tag on a child's health."

" Anyway, the main thing is, you've got it—the cash, I mean."

" Yes, I've got it," said Ahlers, burying himself in his work again.

Lance-Corporal Kamnitzer, who had not got back to barracks until sunrise, was determined to enjoy a few hours' rest. The notice hanging at the foot of his bed—commandeered from a hotel and bearing the legend PLEASE DO NOT DISTURB in four languages—was merely there for decorative purposes.

Kamnitzer's room-mates were well aware that he seldom rose before lunch-time on Sundays.

When the lance-corporal finally condescended to sit up he saw Martin Recht sitting on a stool beside his bed. One glance was enough to tell him that his protégé had something on his mind.

" What's up now?" asked Kamnitzer.

" I overstayed my leave, Karl."

" Because of Carolin?"

" No, it was Streicher's fault."

" Then you're a stupid clot," declared Kamnitzer. " I can imagine getting into trouble for Carolin's sake, but not on account of that wet fish."

While Kamnitzer made a leisurely toilet, Recht told him the story in detail. He made no immediate comment, but demanded to speak to Streicher. The sergeant had left Room 13 at an early hour, however, and no one knew where he was.

" On lovely Sunday mornings like this," said Kamnitzer, " even the most hardened soldiers suffer from humane impulses. It's worth bearing in mind."

Major Bornekamp had not spent the night at home, which meant that his wife was able to breakfast with Lieutenant von Strackmann.

This meant, in turn, that the battalion and No. 3 Company were both deprived of their commanders, at least until lunchtime, a circumstance which guaranteed everyone else a relatively enjoyable morning.

Company Sergeant-Major Kirschke was resolutely applying himself to his favourite pastime. Indeed, he might have continued to enjoy his well-earned Sunday repose indefinitely but for the appearance of Kamnitzer, who drummed on the C.S.M.'s door until he was forced to open it.

" What do you want, little man?" Kirschke asked. He sounded irritable.

"I'll swap you a naked sergeant-major for a back-dated pass," Kamnitzer replied nonchalantly.

Kirschke looked suspicious. "Is that supposed to be a joke?"

"Not a joke, Sergeant-Major. It's a sad business altogether, but you might be interested to hear about it."

"Come in," said Kirschke, eyeing the lance-corporal curiously. "Anything's possible in this day and age."

Herbert Asch ate with relish. Frau Elisabeth had given him his favourite fish breakfast—salmon, russet-red and fragrant, smoked eel, fat, white and firm-fleshed, and Norwegian herrings, strong-flavoured and aromatic—but he found time, as he usually did at Sunday breakfast, to air his current preoccupations.

"You know," he told his wife, "it isn't that my time in the army has made me allergic to everything in uniform. That would be doing a lot of good men an injustice. It isn't that I dispute the army's right to exist, either. I'm prepared to regard it as a necessity, given the present international situation and the vast sums that are being frittered away on the arms-race all over the world."

His wife smiled. "If it's such a necessary evil, what are you worried about?"

"I'm worried by the suppression of the individual— I mean the civilian, the democrat, the citizen soldier— that's what he's often called these days, and it's a hopeful sign. But do we worry about him enough? Are we helping him to resist the tendency to turn him into just another digit in an endless column of figures? Politicians have gone back to their old habit of talking in terms of territorial rights, ethnic boundaries and spheres of influence—and the masses copy them like parrots."

"What's the answer then?"

"Give our two or three hundred thousand soldiers a genuine feeling of security and confidence, that's all."

"You always get so worked up, Herbert, but your fears

haven't been confirmed except in a few isolated cases, have they?"

" I know, Elisabeth, but it's the thin end of the wedge. We've got to do everything in our power to ensure that exceptions don't become the rule. It infuriates me to hear that a soldier can be bullied by his superior in a public place without arousing public indignation. It infuriates me when a soldier is ordered to jump off a ledge by a drunken N.C.O. and breaks his neck without inspiring anything more than a passing regret which is quickly allayed by the cheap excuse that such occurrences are a necessary evil. Soldiers are human beings, first and foremost, and they've got to be treated as such. It seems self-evident to me."

C.S.M. Kirschke had his own ideas about what was self-evident and what wasn't.

" I don't care how we arrange this," he told Kamnitzer, " as long as it's not at my expense."

" It's quite simple," the lance-corporal said firmly. " I forget I saw Sergeant-Major Rammler wandering about in the nude, and all he has to do is issue Grenadier Recht with a post-dated pass. I call that a generous offer."

The C.S.M. evinced neither agreement nor disagreement. " Wait here," he said. " I'll go and see which way the wind's blowing."

He found Rammler without difficulty. The sergeant-major was sitting in his room, in conclave with Sergeant Streicher. Both men regarded Kirschke expectantly.

Kirschke knew that there was no need to be particularly diplomatic with Rammler. He shooed Streicher into the passage, shut the door, and asked Rammler point-blank how he had got back to barracks that morning.

By the normal route, he was told, though not without difficulty. According to his own account, Rammler had fallen among thieves. They had torn his clothes off his back, but for the sake of the regiment's reputation he had not reported the matter to the police. His main concern had been to avoid attracting attention, and this he had suc-

ceeded in doing with the aid of a fellow-N.C.O. who had
turned up in the nick of time.

" But Kamnitzer saw you wandering around in the buff—
bollock-naked, as he put it."

" That bastard!" Rammler said accusingly. " It's ten to
one he organised the whole thing."

" Steady on," said Kirschke. " You might find it hard to
prove that."

" I'll hang it on him if I have to turn this place upside
down in the process."

" Will you?" Kirschke asked dubiously. " Do you really
think you can?"

Rammler knew he couldn't, but he wasn't prepared to
admit it. " If that little skunk dares to make anything out
of this, I'll dig up enough dirt to bury the lot of us."

This was just what C.S.M. Kirschke was afraid of. He
loathed paper-work, and von Strackmann was not in the
line of fire this time—unfortunately. If for this reason alone,
it might be advisable to save some ammunition for later.

Kirschke produced what he described as a suggested
compromise : first, Kamnitzer had not seen him in the nude;
second, Rammler had forgotten to issue Grenadier Recht
with an over-night pass; third, Grenadier Recht had been.
justified in assuming that his leave had been granted.

" Agreed," Rammler said at once.

Kirschke found the sergeant-major's prompt acquiescence
suspicious, but he could see no grounds for his instinctive
mistrust. The main thing was that his responsibilities had
once more been shelved and that the reputation of No. 3
Company—still his company, whatever von Strackmann might
think—had been safeguarded. Furthermore, Martin Recht
need have no fear of being reported. Rammler would vouch
for that.

" Everything went like clockwork," Kirschke reported to
Kamnitzer. " Rammler agreed at once, without any reservations."

" No reservations at all?" asked Kamnitzer, alarmed.

" What more do you want?" said Kirschke. " Rammler

knows he can rely on your word. A promise is a promise. I told you, everything went off smoothly."

"Too smoothly," said Kamnitzer in a worried voice. "If I know Rammler, he's got something up his sleeve. The only thing is, what?"

Herbert Asch received an unexpected visit from Major Bornekamp. Intrigued, he showed the C.O. into his office.

"We're all human," Bornekamp conceded magnanimously, bent on showing himself at his best. "Everyone makes mistakes sometimes."

It would have been unwise to discourage such a realisation. "I presume," Asch said politely, "that you've come about that interview you gave to the local paper."

"Is it going to be published?" Bornekamp asked apprehensively. "In full?"

"It's quite possible," said Asch, "but not probable, provided we can come to some acceptable arrangement. I have no direct influence with the press, of course, and everyone in this country has the right to express an opinion . . ."

"Guttersnipes included, more's the pity!" interjected Bornekamp. "But listen, Herr Asch—even if you can't bring pressure to bear, you can at least pull a few strings. Clear up these unfortunate misunderstandings for me. I know you can."

"I can't guarantee anything, of course," said Asch. "Besides, everything has its price."

"What do you want?" asked Bornekamp.

"I don't know yet," Asch said slowly, "but I'm sure I'll think of something when the time comes. We mustn't rush things, Major. If we can delay publication, that'll be something at least. It won't be in to-morrow's edition, anyway, I can promise you that."

Warrant Officer Vossler tucked Carolin carefully into his car beside Gerty Ballhaus and drove to the Grenadier barracks, where Martin Recht joined them.

They picnicked beside a sparkling blue lake, in a lush meadow encircled by pine forest. The day gleamed like a jewel, and the whole scene resembled an illustration in some glossy magazine: the spotless white cloth spread on the grass, the basket of fruit, the sandwiches, the cool bottles of *vin rosé*, the radiant sunlight and gentle murmur of radio music.

Later, when Viktor Vossler took Gerty off for a stroll, Carolin stretched out on a mossy bank. Martin Recht bent over her to adjust the rug. "Comfortable?" he asked softly.

"Very comfortable," she said, closing her eyes.

There was a long silence. Then Martin Recht said: "I wish it could be like this always."

"So do I," Carolin said happily.

Carolin was still feeling happy when the day departed in a blaze of glory. The setting sun bathed the sky in luminous colours, suffusing it with soft shades of pink and seeming to drown the scattered puffs of cloud in a sea of contentment.

"I love you," Carolin said, gently but distinctly.

"Mellow Sunday" drew to a close, and "Bloody Monday" took its place.

*

Karl Kamnitzer was the first to scent trouble in the Monday morning air. Climbing out of bed, slightly late as usual, he saw a circle of grey, weary, indifferent faces. This, of course, was a familiar enough sight on Mondays, but one particular face stood out from the others like a sore thumb: Streicher's.

"What's the matter, chum, swallowed a flag-pole?" he asked, merely curious at first.

"I'll thank you to remember my rank," Streicher said loftily.

Kamnitzer looked amused. "Bit hoity-toity this morning, aren't we?"

Streicher evidently considered it beneath his new-found

dignity to reply. He strode across Room 13 to the door as if he were traversing a municipal rubbish-dump.

"I reckon he's got a screw loose somewhere," Kamnitzer remarked, when Streicher had left the room.

"You're dead right," said another inmate. "Promotion seems to have gone to his head. Yesterday he behaved as though he was semi-human, but this morning he won't talk to us."

"Count your blessings," said Kamnitzer. "Let's hope he keeps it up."

"It's a pity Martin Recht didn't belt him good and proper the other night."

Kamnitzer froze. "What do you mean?"

"Your friend Recht and Streicher—didn't you know? Well, it's hardly worth mentioning. Recht wasn't the sort of chap to make a thorough job of it."

Kamnitzer hurried off to the wash-room to find Recht. "What's this I hear?" he asked. "You didn't tell me you'd clocked Streicher."

"I didn't," said Recht. "It's an exaggeration. I just pushed him aside a little—he was in my way. He slipped and fell, that's all. It didn't mean a thing."

"Not to you, maybe," Kamnitzer said, thoroughly alarmed, "but Streicher's the sensitive type, and now he's been promoted he thinks he's a superior form of life. Why the hell didn't you tell me about this?"

"Because I didn't think it was necessary," protested Recht. "I can't understand why you're getting so worked up. It wasn't a fight—it was a bit of a scuffle, that's all, and it's got nothing to do with anyone but Streicher and me."

"What did he say?"

"Didn't say a word—just sat there in his nightshirt looking stupid. It was quite funny, really."

"It's a hoot," Kamnitzer said grimly. "Have you spoken to him since?"

"No, I haven't had a chance."

"Did anyone else see this scuffle, or whatever you like to call it? I mean, were there any witnesses?"

" Everyone else in the room—there were five, I think."

" In that case," said Kamnitzer, " I suggest you shave and shine with more than usual care."

" I don't follow," Recht said uneasily. " What do you mean by that?"

" You'll find out soon enough, if I'm not much mistaken. I just hope for your sake that my brain isn't functioning properly—but I've a horrible feeling I'm thinking along the right lines."

*

Monday morning showed Company Sergeant-Major Kirschke in a new light. He was brighter than at any other time in the whole week because the previous day had topped up his reserves of sleep. He might almost have been called energetic, especially as Lieutenant von Strackmann did not put in an immediate appearance. For the moment, Kirschke controlled the company from his office like a captain on the bridge of a destroyer ploughing through calm seas without an enemy in sight.

He swapped jokes with the young subalterns who commanded two of the company's platoons, telling himself yet again, as he handed them their training schedules for the day, that they were quite nice chaps really. With von Strackmann out of the way, they struck him as thoroughly congenial types.

After the Y.O.s had departed Kirschke turned to Sergeant Streicher, who was waiting, in well-disciplined silence, for permission to speak.

" Well, my lad? " Kirschke asked brightly. " Not out with your platoon this morning?"

" I have a report to make, Sergeant-Major."

" That's splendid," said Kirschke, his composure concealing a pang of mistrust, " but reports have to be submitted in writing."

Streicher obediently produced a sheet of paper and tried to hand it over, but Kirschke demurred.

" What's it all about?"

" I have been assaulted, Sergeant-Major, physically assaulted."

" By whom?"

" By a subordinate."

Kirschke knit his brows and looked incredulous. He pondered deeply for a moment, and his first reaction was to clear the company office of all superfluous witnesses. His corporal clerk was sent off to the armoury and the civilian employee to the administration block, both on unimportant errands.

When he and Streicher were alone, he said: " Do you realise what you're saying? If your report is borne out by the facts, it'll mean a charge under Paragraph 25 of the Military Penal Code."

" I realise that, Sergeant-Major."

" Paragraph 25, Streicher, refers to physical assaults on superior officers. The penalty is six months' to five years' imprisonment—in particularly grave cases, twelve months' to ten years' penal servitude."

Sergeant Streicher apparently knew this too, for the revelation produced no visible changes in his demeanour. He had solemnly promised his friend Rammler to stand firm as a rock, and that was that. He held out his report once more.

Kirschke skilfully ignored the gesture. Since good advice seemed to be leading nowhere, he promptly went over to the attack.

" Were you injured?"

" No, but I was pushed—several times, too. I fell over."

" You didn't report to the M.O.?"

" No."

" So there's no visible evidence of this alleged attack on your person?"

" No, Sergeant-Major." Streicher was not easily shaken. He had obviously briefed himself thoroughly in advance. " But the law states explicitly that a punishable offence can be committed without inflicting physical injury. If I may take the liberty of quoting: ' It is sufficient for the superior officer to have been tugged by the sleeve or pushed to one side '."

Kirschke was silent for a moment. It was clear that he was dealing with a tougher nut than usual, and a lesser man than he might have hauled down the flag.

"A thing like this," he said, "needs to be considered carefully. Everything must be just so—not a comma out of place. What about witnesses, anyway? Have you got any?"

"Five of them, Sergeant-Major."

Kirschke did not give up, even then. The die was not finally cast. He was still unaware—officially—both of the incident itself and its alleged perpetrator.

The salient feature of the whole affair was that it lay outside a unit commander's jurisdiction. A case of this sort had to be passed on to the competent legal authority, and anyone who violated this rule automatically laid himself open to prosecution.

But things had not yet reached that stage. Everything in Kirschke revolted against the thought of handing one of his men over to justice prematurely. He eventually took the proffered report, but not because he had run out of ideas. He was merely looking for an excuse to shelve the matter temporarily, and he found one straight away.

"All you've put at the head of the report is 'Streicher, Sergeant'," he said. "That doesn't conform to the rules laid down for military correspondence. You've left out your Christian names and the precise designation of your unit."

Kirschke's practised eye had meanwhile taken in the essentials of the report. He now knew what had taken place and when, and he also knew the name of the accused, but he behaved as if he were still in the dark.

"You can take your effort back," he told Streicher casually, "and complete it in the proper way. If I were you, I'd write the whole thing out again. That'll give you time to consider the implications."

"Yes, Sergeant-Major," Streicher said, looking reluctant but dutifully taking the report.

"One more piece of advice, Streicher—just between ourselves. Don't take all this too lightly. Even if you've got witnesses, do you know for certain what their evidence will be?"

"They'll tell the truth," Streicher said. "It's a question of right and wrong, Sergeant-Major."

"Right and wrong?" Kirschke smiled sardonically. "Everyone's got his own ideas about that."

Sergeant-Major Rammler lent a sympathetic ear to what Streicher had to tell him. His first comment was: "That man Kirschke's anything but an ideal company sergeant-major. It's a pity the right people haven't cottoned on to him yet."

He demanded to know every last detail, and Streicher did his best to comply. Rammler had to admit that Kirschke was no fool. His allusion to the unreliability of witnesses carried some weight.

However, Rammler knew the meaning of the word system. First, he sealed off Room 13 and got rid of Recht and Kamnitzer. Then he ensured the absence of all who had not been present at the time of the alleged assault. This left five men, apart from Recht and Streicher himself.

"Listen, lads," Rammler told them. "We've all got responsibilities, and no bloke with any guts tries to shirk them."

He grinned encouragingly at the five blank, expressionless faces.

The fact that they betrayed virtually no reaction did not dishearten him in the least. It only made him more wary. He decided to preface his major assault with a brief lecture.

"We all know," he began, "that it's our duty to tell the truth where military matters are concerned."

This statement of principle could hardly be disputed, since it figured in half a dozen manuals of instruction. The five men reacted to it, predictably, by preserving an acquiescent silence.

"Under conditions of emergency, a lie can cost a fellow-soldier his life. Am I right?"

The five prospective witnesses nodded. Rammler scrutinised them closely, seeking out the weakest link, the man whom he could tackle most effectively. He identified him without difficulty, a grenadier who started to perspire at the slightest exertion and was already exuding timid docility. His friends called him Porky.

"What conclusion do we draw from this?" Rammler demanded, staring challengingly at Porky. "Well?"

"Lies must be avoided at all costs, Sergeant-Major," said Porky, breaking into a fresh sweat as it dawned on him that he was the sergeant-major's chosen victim. It was not the first time such a thing had happened. Some people seemed to find him an irresistible target.

Rammler concentrated on Porky with unwearying persistence. He bombarded him, in the kindliest possible way, with questions. Where was he when Sergeant Streicher was assaulted? What exactly did he see? What else did he see? Why hadn't he seen more? "The truth, lad, stick to the truth!"

After a vain attempt at prevarication, Porky's resistance quickly crumbled. He began by making a partial admission —"There was a bump, and Sergeant Streicher fell down" —but this was the thin end of the wedge. Rammler drove it home with sledge-hammer blows.

He plied Porky with further questions. What caused this bump? Who or what caused Sergeant Streicher to fall down? "What's the matter, lad? Trying to evade your responsibilities? Thinking of telling a lie, are you? They can put you in gaol for that, you know."

In the end, Porky could see no alternative but to confirm the contents of Streicher's report in broad outline. His superior officer rewarded him with a beamingly benevolent smile from which Porky derived no immediate satisfaction. For some moments he felt wretched, but a minute later he was already telling himself that the truth was the truth and a man must always do his duty, however hard.

"That's how it was, then!" Rammler said complacently. He turned his attentions to the other four, aware that now the break-through had been effected all that remained was a routine mopping-up operation.

"You lot must have seen at least as much as our friend here"—he indicated Porky—"if not more."

The other four were already looking uneasy. It was more than they could do to stand up to Rammler's barrage. Little by little, like snow beneath the spring sun, they succumbed. All they needed now was a final pep-talk.

"If I know you," Rammler said significantly, "you won't be irresponsible enough to accuse an N.C.O. of lying. I'm sure you won't leave one of your mates in the lurch, either, just because he's had the guts to tell the truth. And if that's not reason enough, lads—well, we'll be doing some field training later to-day. All right?"

*

"Your office," Lieutenant von Strackmann told C.S.M. Kirschke with comparative good humour, "looks like a pig-sty."

"I beg to differ, sir."

Von Strackmann allowed himself a superior smile. "You can differ as much as you like, but what I say goes round here, in case you'd forgotten."

"I'll pass your comments on to the appropriate department, sir. I'm not responsible for the cleaning-women. Besides, I'd like to point out that this is No. 3 Company Office, not my private study."

This conversation, the first of the day, took the place of a normal morning exchange of salutations. Both men remained calm, even cheerful, privately consigning each other to perdition and invigorated by the thought that their wishes might soon become reality.

Lieutenant von Strackmann disappeared into the inner office, leaving the door wide open so that he could hear what was going on outside. All that came to his ears, however, was a creaking noise as Kirschke settled himself more comfortably in his chair.

This provocative sound goaded von Strackmann into activity. Charging into the outer office like a bull into the arena, he saw Kirschke lolling back at his ease, toying pensively with a ruler.

" Haven't you got anything to do?" von Strackmann demanded.

" Of course, sir," replied Kirschke. " There's always something to do. At the moment I'm wrestling with a problem : whether one ought to take official note of every report that's submitted to one."

" No other worries?"

" Not at present, sir."

Von Strackmann's cheerful mood threatened to desert him. He longed violently for some excuse, some plausible excuse, to get rid of C.S.M. Kirschke. There were other, better, more loyal and trustworthy men—Rammler, for instance, despite his regrettable lapse of the other day.

For the moment, he decided to wear Kirschke down slowly, like water dripping on a rock, unaware that Kirschke favoured the same time-honoured method.

" I don't like the way the filing cabinets are arranged," he said.

" I like the arrangement," Kirschke retorted. " It's practical."

" They ought to be shifted round against the opposite wall."

" Impossible, sir," Kirschke said tersely.

" Of course it isn't!" snapped von Strackmann. " If you're short of men you can lend a hand yourself."

" Even if you lent a hand too, sir, it would still be impossible. The arrangement of this office was personally supervised by the company commander. It's quite possible he may be discharged from hospital in the next few days and take over the company again. He'll wonder what's been going on here soon enough, but there's no point in shifting all the furniture around as well, is there?"

Von Strackmann disappeared into his office again. There was no need for Kirschke to rub his nose in the fact that he was only acting company commander. He was well aware of it, but the last word had not been spoken on the subject.

Kirschke continued to toy with his ruler. He glanced at the door through which von Strackmann had vanished. It was still ajar, a potentially dangerous circumstance in view of Sergeant Streicher's imminent return.

Before long, Streicher reappeared. He held out his report. " Error rectified, Sergeant-Major," he said. " Christian name inserted."

" You didn't notice any other mistakes?"

" No, Sergeant-Major."

" Looked it through carefully, have you? What about your rank? Designation of unit? Name of station? Date? Month in full? Everything in order?"

" Everything, Sergeant-Major."

" You haven't forgotten the address? Did you just put in the name of the unit, in accordance with Mil. Regs. Para. 33b?"

At this point, Lieutenant von Strackmann re-emerged from the inner office like a jack-in-the-box, manifestly displeased at Kirschke's petty and uncharacteristic insistence on routine. " Form is important, Sergeant-Major," he said didactically, a company commander to his finger-tips, " but content is even more so."

Kirschke silently held his breath. Two alternatives presented themselves : either he could allow the lieutenant to plunge headlong into the mire in which he so richly deserved to wallow, or he could make a last attempt to save the company from a scandal of vast dimensions. With some reluctance, he plumped for the latter course.

With abnormal politeness and a deliberate observance of etiquette, he said : " With your permission, sir, I'll deal with this matter. It would be far better."

Von Strackmann, however, was unaware of his predicament. Kirschke had thrown him a life-belt and he mistook it for a stone. Resolutely, he held out his hand for the report, and Sergeant Streicher surrendered it.

" You can dismiss," Kirschke said resignedly. " Wait outside."

Lieutenant von Strackmann read the document with mounting agitation, seeming to swell like a rapidly inflated balloon as he did so.

" My God!" he said at length, breathing hard. " Were you trying to keep this from me?"

" Why should I?" inquired Kirschke, grieved by the acting company commander's stupidity. " I don't know what it says in detail, and anyway, it's not solely up to you to decide whether it should be taken seriously or not."

" What's that?" von Strackmann demanded furiously. " An N.C.O. is physically assaulted, and you don't know whether to take it seriously or not?"

" Sir," Kirschke said patiently but with a touch of weariness. " Making an allegation is one thing, proving it is another. It's too easy to burn one's own fingers in a case of this sort."

" What are you talking about!" von Strackmann exploded. " This is a most alarming incident."

" Possibly, sir, but not in the way you think."

" I'm not petty-minded," the lieutenant declared, " but if there's one thing I will not condone it's an attempt to undermine the basis of military discipline—and that includes physically assaulting a superior officer. No, I'm absolutely adamant."

" Does that mean prepared to see an otherwise decent soldier go to gaol for months or even years, just because of a stupid, drunken scuffle?"

" What do you mean, Kirschke? I don't understand you. What are you trying to hush up? Are you involved in this business in some way?"

Von Strackmann, who had been staring at Streicher's report as though spell-bound, looked up in sudden triumph. " So that's it!" he cried exultantly, convinced that he had put his finger on the sergeant-major's Achilles' heel. " You're partly to blame for this. The only reason why such a thing could have happened was that you failed to separate a newly promoted sergeant from his subordinates."

"The sergeant's quarters allotted to Streicher won't be free till to-morrow." Kirschke made this statement with almost yawning indifference. "Lack of accommodation and administrative difficulties often make it necessary for sergeants and other ranks to share the same sleeping quarters, but that doesn't mean they have to come to blows. Besides, sir, I've a feeling you don't realise the full implications of this business. The whole thing sticks in my craw. With your permission, I'll go and change my trousers."

*

Lance-Corporal Kamnitzer was one of the few people who could foresee the effects of Streicher's report, especially on Martin Recht, and a private chat to C.S.M. Kirschke confirmed his worst fears.

Accordingly, he decided to mobilise all available reserves. Although he had no very clear idea of how best to go about it, he knew that what had not occurred to him might well occur to someone else, so he made for the air force barracks.

This was comparatively easy to arrange. Kirschke simply ordered the lance-corporal to go into town on an official errand, and he pedalled off on the company bicycle.

The first person he asked for was Warrant Officer Vossler, for whose shrewdness and ingenuity he had a high regard. Vossler knew the ropes, but Vossler had just flown off to Crete and would not be back before nightfall.

Making up his mind swiftly, Kamnitzer went to see Captain Ahlers, who received his unexpected visitor at once and introduced him to Captain Treuberg.

"Playing truant?" Treuberg inquired in jocular tones.

"My presence here is strictly official, sir," Kamnitzer assured him, glancing urgently at Ahlers, who took the hint and asked his deputy to leave the room.

"Grenadier Martin Recht," Kamnitzer began without

further preamble, " has been accused of assaulting a superior officer. What's your reaction to that?"

Captain Ahlers thought for a moment. " My first reaction is to tell you that it doesn't concern me. The case lies outside my sphere of jurisdiction. I couldn't exercise the slightest influence on it."

" All right, sir," said Kamnitzer. " Let me put it another way. Do you believe that Martin Recht is capable of assaulting a superior officer?"

" I can't imagine him doing such a thing."

" He didn't." Kamnitzer endeavoured to explain what, in his view, had really happened. " But the report has been handed in and officially accepted. You realise what that means, of course."

Captain Ahlers knew only too well. " No unit commander is competent to deal with the sort of case you've described," he said thoughtfully. " Only a court could do that. The report will have to be passed to higher authority. It could lead to criminal proceedings."

" Could?" asked Kamnitzer. " Needn't it?"

" Not necessarily," Ahlers explained. " Not if it appeared subsequently that there had been a misunderstanding. That would show the charge to be groundless, but only if the plaintiff admitted that he had acted prematurely or without due deliberation."

" If I know the plaintiff, he's unlikely to do that."

" Then things look black."

" Can't you do anything, sir?"

" Be reasonable!" Ahlers said with genuine regret. " Your barracks and mine are two different worlds."

" Haven't you any influence—with Major Bornekamp, for instance? Our C.O.'s probably the only person to tackle, under the circumstances. Couldn't you breathe a word in his ear?"

" There wouldn't be much point, I'm afraid."

" Surely you won't abandon a decent lad like Martin Recht just because he wears a different insignia from yours?"

"Of course not," said Ahlers. "I'm prepared to adopt your suggestion and discuss the case with your commanding officer, but I can't promise anything."

"That would be something, anyway," Kamnitzer said gratefully. "It can't hurt to try." He looked worried. "Don't you know anyone else who could bring pressure to bear?"

"Yes—perhaps I do!" The captain seemed to have been galvanised by a sudden idea. "Come along, we'll pay him a visit."

Ahlers opened the door leading to the outer office and called: "Have my car brought round straight away, would you?" He had just picked up his cap and gloves when Captain Treuberg appeared.

"I gather you're going out. Shall I come with you?"

"No, thanks all the same," said Ahlers.

"Will you be gone long?"

"I don't think so, Treuberg. Probably an hour at the most."

"Where can I reach you?" Treuberg asked with manifest curiosity. "Just in case something urgent comes up."

"I shall be at the Hotel Asch."

When Captain Ahlers entered the hotel, escorted by Lance-Corporal Kamnitzer, the first person he met was Frau Elisabeth. She greeted him with restrained but perceptible surprise.

"I'd appreciate a brief word with your husband," Ahlers said, a trifle formally.

"It's something unpleasant, isn't it?"

"What makes you say that?"

"It's written all over your faces. Besides, it's an unusual time of day for you to come visiting."

"You can't call a thing pleasant or unpleasant until it's over," Kamnitzer interjected. "The great thing is to make it go the way you want it to."

Frau Elisabeth showed them into an adjoining room and went off to tell her husband, who materialised as if by magic.

"I'm most intrigued," Asch said brightly, by way of greeting. "My wife says you look as if you're carrying half a hundredweight of dynamite around with you."

"Herr Asch," Ahlers said. "May I begin by asking you a straight question? What's your opinion of Lance-Corporal Kamnitzer?"

Kamnitzer looked astonished. "If you gentlemen propose to discuss me, perhaps you'd prefer me to leave the room."

"Anything to avoid hearing the truth, eh?" chuckled Asch.

"Not at all," said Kamnitzer. "In the first place I'm thick-skinned, and in the second place I haven't got a particularly high opinion of myself—so what have I got to lose?"

"Lance-Corporal Kamnitzer has a story to tell you," Ahlers explained. "I shall be interested to know whether you believe it in every detail."

"Let's hear it first," Asch said with a grin.

Kamnitzer launched into his account, concentrating on essentials. Confident that Asch would be able to read between the lines, he avoided all unnecessary embellishments.

"Well," Asch said, when he had finished, "I'll let you know later whether I believe it or not, but one thing seems certain : it's not beyond the bounds of possibility."

"That's what I thought too," Ahlers said.

"Let's assume," Asch mused, "that everything Kamnitzer has told us is true and that his inferences are correct. What's to be done?"

"Streicher's report is a hot potato," Kamnitzer said. "C.S.M. Kirschke saw that straight away, but Lieutenant von Strackmann was stupid or, if you like, inexperienced enough to pick it up. In my humble opinion, the thing to do now is to prevent the C.O. from making a similar blunder."

Herbert Asch regarded Kamnitzer with growing approval. He was a man after his own heart. Why was he only a lance-corporal? He might even make a successful hôtelier.

"I usually feel at home in the bull-ring, I grant you," Asch said cautiously, "but before I let you prod me into it I'd like to clear up one important point—starting with you,

Captain Ahlers. Why are you taking such an interest in Martin Recht?"

"Personal reasons," replied the captain. "Recht visits my home and my daughter seems to think a lot of him. I'd like to keep him out of gaol."

"My reasons are purely personal, too," grinned Kamnitzer. "I like to see the puppets dance. You see—our motives are thoroughly suspect!"

"I beg your pardon," Asch said. "I shouldn't have asked such a question—I deserved that."

"It's quite all right," Ahlers assured him. "I understand your reasons."

Asch took a moment to collect himself. He should have known what had prompted the two men to take such a step—Ahlers, who had always championed a justice founded on generosity and common sense, and Kamnitzer, the gay rebel. He warmed to them both.

"I'll go at once," he said with sudden determination.

"You can rest assured that Martin Recht deserves to be helped," Kamnitzer told him, with a note of affection in his voice. "He always reminds me of a child who's got himself mixed up in something too big for him. If we can't stop children from playing soldiers, the least we can do is keep them out of the clutches of the law."

Herbert Asch jumped into his car and drove, slightly exceeding the speed-limit, to the Grenadier barracks. The sentry did not keep him waiting long this time and the C.O. ushered him into his office without wasting a moment.

"I've come to collect," Asch said unceremoniously.

"Is the paper going to abandon that article?" Bornekamp asked.

"Not only that. In order to turn the interview into a token of public esteem and appreciation, the draft will be submitted to you so that you can amend it, add to it, make cuts or round it off—exactly as you want."

"Splendid!" cried Bornekamp. "I feel I owe you a great debt of gratitude."

"That's just what I was banking on," Asch said.

"What can I do for you, my dear chap? Don't hesitate to tell me."

"Right, I'll come straight to the point. Have you received a report dealing with an alleged assault on an N.C.O.?"

Major Bornekamp started. "Certainly not."

"All the better." Asch looked pleased. "Then I need only advise you, for your own good, not to accept any such report."

"What are you talking about?" Bornekamp demanded with growing bewilderment. "What report is this? Who's responsible for it? How do you know of its existence, anyway?"

"These things get around," Asch replied coolly.

Bornekamp stared at his desk in dismay as though Asch had deposited a time-bomb on it. His eyes became almost glazed when he learned that Asch had—quite fortuitously—heard the story from Captain Ahlers and that the accused man was—no less fortuitously—not only a personal acquaintance of Asch but so well known to him that he had no hesitation in speaking up on his behalf.

"I've come here as much in your own interests as for any other reason, Major," Asch declared. "This accusation could stir up a lot of dust, especially as it's founded on what I judge to be extremely flimsy evidence. I can't imagine that you would embark on such a risky course of action. A badly bungled interview followed by an embarrassing scandal . . . Altogether too much of a good thing, don't you agree?"

"This . . ." the C.O. spluttered in agitation, "this is pure and unadulterated . . ."

"Blackmail, Major? Don't say the word," Asch remarked kindly. "I know, I know. What I'm asking you to do might be described as—how shall I put it?— beyond the bounds of legality, but I'm sure you won't worry unduly on that account. Besides, it's all between ourselves. You can take it for granted that Captain Ahlers's sole concern is the garrison's good name, so there's no likelihood of his communicating any details to Colonel Turner."

H

This was more than blackmail, Bornekamp told himself —it was downright impudence. The man was riding over him roughshod, but he could see no immediate prospect of extricating himself unscathed.

" Is there anything you're not clear about?" Asch asked.

Major Bornekamp closed his eyes for a moment. Then he picked up the phone and said : " Company commander, No. 3 Company."

Lieutenant von Strackmann announced his presence at the other end of the line, but his tones of loyal devotion were lost on the C.O.

" Listen to me carefully, Strackmann," he barked, " and don't interrupt. I wish to draw your attention to the following : any written report, whatever its content, must be formulated with the utmost precision. It must be checked —thoroughly checked—for accuracy. Every element of doubt must be eliminated. I rely on you not to bother me with efforts of any ambiguous, incomplete or controvertible nature. I don't care if it's a report on a damaged muzzle-cover or a pair of missing socks—or an assault on a superior officer, not that I can conceive of such a thing occurring in my battalion. Quite apart from that, I gauge the efficiency of any company commander by whether or not the men under his command keep their noses clean. Is that clear, Strackmann? Right, carry on."

Bornekamp snorted indignantly and replaced the receiver. " Is that good enough for you?" he growled.

" It ought to do the trick," Asch conceded. He felt that he had won a decisive, if not particularly admirable victory, but not even his acute eyes could penetrate the jungle of red tape, evasions and unhappy coincidences that lay ahead.

*

Lieutenant von Strackmann stood behind his desk like Napoleon on the outskirts of Moscow—billowing smoke and smouldering ruins met his eye at every turn. Even C.S.M. Kirschke's expression contained a glimmer of sympathy. Major Bornekamp's monologue had been delivered fortissimo.

" Hell and damnation!" von Strackmann said to himself. " What are we going to do now?"

" We, sir?" Kirschke asked ruthlessly. " It wasn't me who accepted that report."

" All right, all right!" the lieutenant snapped. " You've got your ear to the ground. You know which way the wind's blowing—all right, I admit it! What more do you want? It doesn't help me, does it?"

" No," Kirschke uttered the word without triumph. He was still company sergeant-major of No. 3 Company, even if von Strackmann was in command, and he felt responsible for it.

" There must be some way out," the lieutenant cried desperately. He had dismounted from his high horse and was staring at Kirschke almost beseechingly. " What if the charge turns out to be unfounded . . .?"

" As far as I can see," Kirschke said, " that's highly unlikely. Streicher couldn't back-pedal now, even if he wanted to. Rammler would never let him."

" What if I don't pass the report on? What if I simply chuck it into the waste-paper basket?"

" You'd be committing an offence."

" But what about freedom of discretion?"

" You haven't any. According to Paragraph 40 of the Military Penal Code, if I may draw your attention to it, an infringement of military discipline which also constitutes a penal offence may be dealt with by a unit commander, even when the facts are in doubt. That means you have to refer the case to the public prosecutor. If you don't, you're committing an offence punishable by imprisonment for a period of one month to three years."

Von Strackmann was in a cleft stick, there was no doubt about it. The report was in his possession, the C.O. didn't want it, and he couldn't simply hand it back. An N.C.O. had passed the ball to him, but if he tried to pass it on he would incur the Major's Olympian displeasure.

" Think, Sergeant-Major, think! Perhaps something'll occur to you."

" Plenty of things occur to me," Kirschke said with deliberation, " but you won't want to hear them."

" Speak up!" von Strackmann insisted. " The reputation of the company's at stake—our company, Sergeant-Major."

" The company's reputation?" queried Kirschke, wagging his head. " What's that? Reputation covers a multitude of sins. You can gain a reputation for efficiency by making men scrub the floor with a toothbrush or polish the nails in their boots . . ."

" All right, all right," von Strackmann interposed. " If the word worries you we'll let it pass. There's no point in arguing about trifles. We're both after the same thing, aren't we?"

" I'd like to think so, sir. But I don't regard a company primarily as a fighting unit which has been trained and equipped to kill. I look on it first and foremost as a hundred or more human beings."

" We're fundamentally in agreement there," declared von Strackmann.

Kirschke looked unimpressed. " With regret, sir, I dispute that, and since you've asked me to be frank . . ."

" I insist on it!"

" . . . I shan't hesitate to make myself plain. This seems to be a good opportunity. We're alone, and if you dislike anything I say you can always forget it. In the first place, sir, I won't disguise the fact that in my eyes you're what might be termed a first-rate soldier."

" Please, please! This is no time for flattery," said von Strackmann. He was agreeably surprised to receive commendation from such an unexpected quarter. "But I didn't mean to interrupt you. Please go on being equally frank."

"With pleasure," Kirschke replied. "As I say, I grant that you have a number of valuable professional qualities— for example, endurance, physical energy, initiative, military knowledge and a smart appearance. These count for a great deal, but are they enough?"

"I really don't know what to say, Sergeant-Major."

"But I do, sir. I say that professional qualifications of that sort, however highly developed, are insufficient in themselves. An officer needs human qualities as well, and that seems to be the point at issue here. When you assumed command of this company you quite obviously regarded it as a tool or instrument—though whether of national defence or personal advancement I won't presume to judge."

"Steady on, Kirschke! You're going a bit far."

Kirschke leant against the wall. He did not seem to be particularly involved in what he was saying, and his words matched his negligent stance. "Before you arrived on the scene, this company was a normal unit : the men were a willing lot, the N.C.O.s did their job and the standard of training was comparatively high. The system functioned and the unit performed its duties—that is, until you introduced your exaggerated notions of efficiency."

"I beg your pardon!" von Strackmann protested. "Do you know what you're saying?"

"I've thought of nothing else for weeks," said Kirschke. "From the moment you assumed command of this company, it became obvious that there had been a sudden reversal of standards. Your first step was to judge everyone by his attitude towards you personally. You mistook yes-men for devoted supporters of your theories. You couldn't tell the difference between discipline and bullying. To you, violent activity became synonymous with devotion to duty."

"That's enough!" von Strackmann bellowed. "We won't achieve anything like this."

"What are we likely to achieve?" Kirschke ventured. "It may seem far-fetched to bring all this up under present circumstances, I admit, but that report on your desk is only the tip of an ice-berg. Make a big issue out of it and you'll discover all kinds of things beneath the surface. You'll find, for instance, that a half-Jewish soldier in your company was sworn at for being a Jew-boy, that a sergeant-major was beaten up one night and wandered round the town in the nude, that one of your sergeants tried to borrow money from a subordinate, that a private soldier has been subjected to systematic persecution. Shall I go on? Believe me, this report of an assault on a superior officer is just a drop in the ocean."

"Stop!" von Strackmann cried in horror. "I won't hear another word!"

"I've finished. There's nothing more to say, anyway."

Von Strackmann sank back in his chair as though exhausted. "What can we do, Sergeant-Major?"

"Wait and see, that's all. Perhaps someone'll have second thoughts, though I'm afraid it's improbable, knowing certain N.C.O.s as I do. You've started something here."

*

Sergeant-Major Rammler was in full cry. His platoon stampeded through the countryside like a herd of wild buffalo, kicking up the dust behind them.

"There's a good reason for this," Rammler informed his gasping men at intervals. "I don't expect you to understand, but one day you'll thank me for saving your miserable lives."

Rammler knew that explanations to this effect could be found in every reputable infantry training manual. Fortunately, the general public had at last developed a broader understanding of the reasons for "rigorous training."

"To a real soldier," Rammler announced cheerfully, "obstacles don't exist. He presses on regardless with a stiff upper lip—and what else?"

"A tight arse-hole!" came the dutiful chorus. There was never a dull moment in No. 3 Platoon of No. 3 Company.

"Low flying aircraft on your left!" yelled Rammler. He might just as well have said "mortar fire dead ahead!" or "enemy M.G. on your right!"—the result would have been identical. The platoon melted into the ground, squirming into hollows, rolling between prominences or cowering behind boulders while Rammler stood erect, lonely and majestic as a war-memorial.

"Now work your way towards the river."

Rammler's men sprang to their feet to acknowledge the order. Then they pressed their bellies to the ground again and wiggled laboriously forward. Rammler could not repress an appreciative nod. They were shaping nicely.

"Disengage!" he announced in magnanimous tones. "But stay under cover."

Sergeant-Major Rammler looked upon himself as fair play personified. As long as the men toed the line they earned his approval. He even had a soft spot for them, provided they pulled their fingers out and kept them out. Anyone in his command who fared badly only had himself to blame.

"Shin up the nearest tree, Kamnitzer!" he commanded. "Watch out for enemy approaching from the east." He gestured in a south-westerly direction as he spoke, but it was one of his cardinal rules to say "east" whenever there was talk of the enemy.

Lance-Corporal Kamnitzer complied with this order willingly and with alacrity. He realised that he was being isolated from the rest of the platoon, but the thought was not unwelcome. Clambering up a chestnut-tree, he squatted between two of the thickest branches, where he had an excellent view of his surroundings but could not be observed from below.

"No. 3 Section, close on me!" ordered Rammler.

No. 3 Section consisted of the inmates of Room 13. Sergeant Streicher, who was commanding them for the first time, glowed with pride at his new status.

In the middle of the section stood Martin Recht, a motionless and seemingly composed figure, even when

Rammler's eye lighted on him. Recht, too, was isolated from the rest. He was given the task of crawling to the river and—like Kamnitzer—"observing the enemy."

"I want to see you worm your way forward like a stoat, Recht—like a stoat in the mating season." Here Rammler paused briefly to allow time for an appreciative titter. Three men obliged. "And keep your head down. You're not to stop till you've reached the edge of that water over there, so no faking tiredness—understand?"

Three other members of Streicher's section were told to dig in and the remaining five clustered round Rammler. They were the same five, headed by Porky, who had been selected as principal witnesses in the case of Streicher versus Recht, so Rammler eyed them with appropriate benevolence.

"You're the reserve," he told them. "You can take to the bushes for the next quarter of an hour. It may be half an hour—even longer, if you're lucky. Give your arses a treat, lads, but don't just lie there day-dreaming. I'm giving you a chance to think things over. I expect you'll find something to occupy your minds. All right, move!"

The first prospective witness dived into the undergrowth like fish into a clump of sea-weed. Each knew what was expected of him, and the prospect of an extended rest appealed to one and all.

Sergeant-Major Rammler now set out to demonstrate that he was not merely an exacting superior but a comrade in arms, a course on which he embarked all the more whole-heartedly because there was no potentially troublesome superior in sight. Lieutenant von Strackmann was still closeted in the company office with Kirschke, and the two young subalterns who commanded the other platoons in the company had their hands full elsewhere. Accordingly, Rammler felt impelled to set an example, to show that nothing could stand in a true Ironclad's path, not even a river.

The river, an innocuous little stream for most of its length, seemed at this point to have bowed to the requirements of the military. Its banks abruptly and obligingly converged, transforming it into a natural hazard which made it ideal for training purposes and might have been used as a course for canoe championships.

At the head of a chosen band, Sergeant-Major Rammler plunged into the river. The foaming water almost reached his chest but it failed to dislodge him. His sturdy legs were burdened not only with his own substantial weight but that of a light machine-gun and two boxes of ammunition. Nothing could have been more exemplary—or more conducive to stability.

Some twenty feet from the bank he halted with his legs planted firmly apart and stared imperiously at Martin Recht, who crouched in the bushes, looking wan with fatigue.

"Prepare to jump!" he yelled.

Martin Recht rose to his feet. He tensed his muscles and got ready to spring. A bare yard would see him in the water, he knew. He also knew that he couldn't swim, which added to his nervousness. The water was not very deep near the bank but it boiled like a maelstrom, and Rammler was heavier and steadier on his feet than he was.

Rammler was equally aware of all this, and proud of it. It was part of a leader's job to know his subordinates' weaknesses so that he could do everything within his power to combat them.

"Jump!" he called, adding, rather inappropriately: "At the double!"

Recht jumped.

Later, when pressed for "an accurate account," several platoon-members said that it had been a fine day and that they had welcomed the opportunity to cool off. They had positively enjoyed their dip and had splashed around happily. As for the current, the water hardly came up to their chests, so even a non-swimmer should have been in no difficulty.

But the water that hardly reached the others' chests seemed to grip Martin Recht's heart with chill fingers and constrict it. His legs turned to lead and his breathing faltered. He stumbled, lost his balance and went under, striking out desperately as he was swept away.

Still splashing feebly, he floated into the iron embrace of

Sergeant-Major Rammler, who tried to stand him on his feet—vainly, at first, because his limbs seemed to be made of rubber.

" That's what I like to see!" Rammler muttered grimly. " That'll teach you to lay your grubby paws on a superior officer. When it comes to the pinch, you youngsters are as soft as liver-sausage."

The other members of No. 3 Platoon said later that Recht had folded up like a jack-knife—the only one of them to do so. No one could have foreseen this, because although he had never been particularly tough he should have been able to manage the crosssing like all the rest. It was a mercy that Rammler had caught hold of him and pulled him ashore. Saved his life? Yes, you could put it like that.

" I should have let you drown, you wet streak," said the sergeant-major, bending over Martin Recht's heaving form. " We don't want softies in this outfit, especially the sort that lay hands on their superiors."

Rammler was confident that he had taught Recht a lesson —and the others, too. With luck, it should have beneficial results. Glancing round encouragingly, he saw a circle of submissive faces.

He also saw the approaching figure of Lance-Corporal Kamnitzer.

*

What is commonly called fate—or chance—can hinge on little things. On this occasion it hinged on a bottle of imported Scotch whisky which bore the name Red Horse and was stocked by Schlachtmann's Delicatessen. Frau Elfrieda, wife of Major Bornekamp, had expressed a desire to try some, which was how Lieutenant von Strackmann came to visit the shop.

With an arduous day behind him and the night still young, von Strackmann was yearning for solace and relaxation. Frau Elfrieda could be relied upon to supply both, and it occurred to him that whisky might be the best possible basis for a congenial evening.

But Schlachtmann's also stocked, among other things, a mixture of beer and German champagne entitled Champi and priced at DM 1.20 per bottle. This beverage was much favoured by sundry ladies of the local *beau monde,* among them Captain Treuberg's wife.

Thus it came about that there was a reunion between the air force captain and the army lieutenant—deputies both, both burning with ambition and both equally convinced that their professional ability was not sufficiently appreciated. This accounted for the mutual understanding that had blossomed between them during the supervision of the Ladies' Night and the cadets' dance.

"Glad to see you again," said Captain Treuberg.

"My pleasure," von Strackmann replied cordially.

"In actual fact," Treuberg said, dropping his voice, "I've been wondering whether to give you a ring all day." He piloted the lieutenant into a bay bordered by phalanxes of tinned fruit and fish. "I imagine you've been having a hard time of it."

"These things are sent to try us," said von Strackmann. "But how did you know?"

For a moment, Captain Treuberg forgot all about his wife and her ever-increasing reliance on Champi as a medium of oblivion. As a sensitive person, she was pained by the fact that her husband was still a captain, and doubly pained because he was deputy to Ahlers—Ahlers, of all people! —which meant that she did not enjoy the social status proper to her.

"I know quite a bit," said Treuberg, glancing round.

There was no enemy in sight, but he suggested that it might be advisable to find a place where they could talk undisturbed—The Brace of Pheasants round the corner, for instance.

They installed themselves in the farthest corner of the

tap-room with two glasses of foaming, golden-yellow beer. The smoke-blackened panelling around them was adorned with painted beer casks enclosed by oak-leaves.

" Tell me something, von Strackmann—just between ourselves. Are you aware that you've got enemies? Have you any idea why Captain Ahlers might be prejudiced against you."

" Is he?" the lieutenant asked, pricking up his ears. " I can't think why he should be."

It began to dawn on von Strackmann that this conversation might be important. He took a deep pull at his beer and asked for further details.

" I ought to tell you," Treuberg said slowly, " that I've always regarded Captain Ahlers as a first-rate officer. Unfortunately, I'm now compelled to admit that his conduct has not been exemplary in every respect—for instance, in the matter of divorcing official duties from personal considerations. I imagine you're familiar with the name Martin Recht?"

" Am I !" the lieutenant ejaculated. " What's he got to do with it?"

" Well, this chap Recht is always in and out of Ahlers's house. He's keen on his daughter—not that there's anything wrong in that. It may be entirely above board—serious intentions and so on."

" What you're implying," von Strackmann said with scarcely suppressed excitement, " is that Captain Ahlers has intervened on Recht's behalf, behind the scenes."

" I'm not only implying it—I'm stating it as a fact."

" So that's the way the wind blows !" von Strackmann exclaimed. " He went to the C.O. and put a spoke in my wheel—just like that !"

" Things are a little more complicated than that, I'm afraid. Ahlers is much too clever to have intervened personally. He brought up a big gun to do the job for him— Mayor Asch, no less."

" But it's scandalous—trying to pervert the course of justice for the sake of your daughter's boy-friend !"

"I wouldn't put it quite like that," Treuberg said cautiously. "Whether the man involved was a future son-in-law or Private X, Ahlers's motives for trying to protect him might be entirely honourable. It wouldn't be easy to prove the opposite."

"But the man's bound to be biased—any fool can see that."

"I shouldn't indulge in speculation of that sort if I were you, von Strackmann. There are other arguments which carry much more weight. I mean, anyone who poses as a champion of justice and morality must have a clean sheet himself."

"And Ahlers hasn't?" Lieutenant von Strackmann snapped at the bait like a ravenous fish. "In what way?"

"As you know, my dear chap, an officer has certain obligations where his private life is concerned. I don't mean affairs with women or anything like that—I mean debts. If an officer runs up debts . . ."

"And has he?" von Strackmann swallowed the bait whole. "Do they amount to much?"

"Several thousand marks at least." Treuberg sat back contentedly. His work was done. He had lent valuable assistance to a brother officer, and the rest would be plain sailing. "But that's not all. One of the people Ahlers has borrowed from is a warrant officer."

"A subordinate!"

"Vossler by name. He's had to fork out three thousand marks on Ahlers's behalf."

"And a bounder like that dares to stab me in the back! It's almost incredible. I'm very much obliged to you for the information."

"It was a pleasure, Herr von Strackmann. I've told you this in the strictest confidence, of course."

"Of course."

"I knew you'd understand. My position makes it impossible for me to act otherwise." Treuberg was Ahlers's deputy, after all. If he stepped into his shoes as a result of the ensuing complications his motives might well be misconstrued. "Besides, what I've told you will do the trick even if you can't name your source. Facts like these speak for themselves."

"Captain Treuberg," von Strackmann said solemnly, "I can't tell you how obliged I am."

*

"You there!" Sergeant-Major Rammler shouted as Kamnitzer trotted towards him. "You've deserted your post."

Lance-Corporal Kamnitzer did not appear to notice the sergeant-major. He hurried over to the sodden bundle of clothing that was Grenadier Martin Recht and knelt down beside it. Taking his friend's face in his hands he stared into the weary, apprehensive eyes and was rewarded by a gleam of gratitude.

"You had me worried for a moment," he said roughly, trying to disguise his evident relief.

"I'll be all right, Karl," Recht murmured faintly.

"Kamnitzer!" shouted Rammler. "Didn't you hear what I said?"

"What did you say?" asked Kamnitzer, without looking up.

"Kindly stand to attention when you're talking to me!" Rammler bellowed. "And look me in the eye!"

"Certainly, Sergeant-Major." Kamnitzer rose to his feet, stationed himself in front of Rammler and regarded him with a cool, appraising, almost imperceptible smile. It was a well-tried expression and guaranteed to have a provocative effect.

Its effect was not lost on Rammler, but he retained his composure—if only because of the numerous soldiers within earshot.

"Lance-Corporal Kamnitzer," he said with suppressed fury, "are you aware that you have left your observation post?"

"Yes, Sergeant-Major."

"You left it without being ordered to do so by me?"

" Yes, Sergeant-Major."

It was clear that Kamnitzer's stereo-typed replies were getting on Rammler's nerves. He couldn't fathom why an innately cunning individual like Kamnitzer was behaving so casually, when he, Rammler, had at last got him where he wanted him.

" Good God, man!" Rammler spluttered. "You could be court-martialled for this!"

" For what, Sergeant-Major?"

" For leaving your post in the middle of an exercise. Don't you realise what it could mean if this were the real thing?"

To the listening platoon, it looked as though Rammler was safe in the saddle and Kamnitzer up the creek without a paddle. However, Kamnitzer did not keep them waiting long for an answer.

" With respect, Sergeant-Major, you've made a mistake— several mistakes, in fact."

" Mistakes?" exclaimed Rammler, squaring his broad shoulders belligerently. "What mistakes?"

" To begin with, Sergeant-Major, I was sent up a tree, but no one issued me with any clear or comprehensive orders."

" You were supposed to observe the enemy!"

" I know, Sergeant-Major, but what enemy? What was I meant to do if I saw them? Where was platoon H.Q.? No one told me anything like that. Anyway, for want of anything better to observe, I observed you, Sergeant-Major, and in the process I saw a member of the platoon in danger of drowning."

" Shut your filthy trap!" yelled Rammler.

" Did I hear you say filthy trap?" Kamnitzer inquired politely.

" I said hold your tongue!" The sergeant-major was fuming with rage. "I've had enough of your lip for one day."

" There's just one more point, Sergeant-Major. When some-one looks as though he's in serious danger, I should have thought it was much more important to try and save him than sit back and watch, especially in default of definite

orders to the contrary. Isn't that what the C.O. means by
initiative?"

"Are you trying to teach me my job?"

"No, Sergeant-Major, just trying to save you from making
a mistake."

Rammler ground his teeth, but his nutcracker face remained entirely devoid of expression. It was past his
comprehension that Kamnitzer should have won yet another
round against him, this time in front of the whole platoon.

He decided to banish his audience to the bushes, but
before doing so he made an announcement which showed
that he realised what a dangerous corner Kamnitzer had
manœuvred him into.

"Once and for all," he said emphatically, "I'd like to make
it clear that no one was in any danger here. No one has
ever drowned in this river, nor ever will, while I'm in
charge." He paused. "Lance-Corporal Kamnitzer stand fast
—the remainder, dig in! Nuclear attack imminent!"

The men dispersed. They drove their shovels into the
ground with a will, happy in the knowledge that Rammler
was otherwise engaged and would probably remain so for
a considerable time to come.

Rammler fixed Kamnitzer with a baleful stare. The
bell had gone for the next round.

"We're going to have a little talk," he said significantly.
"Just the two of us."

"By all means," said Kamnitzer. On Rammler's instructions, he obediently loaded himself with a machine-gun and
several pounds of ammunition.

"To the clearing!" Rammler called. "At the double—
move!"

The others bent low over their work and delved away
with redoubled vigour for a few moments. They knew what
Rammler's order portended. The clearing was his favourite
place for "individual tuition," as he termed it. Kamnitzer
knew this too, but he trotted almost eagerly through the trees
to the ill-omened spot.

When they had reached it and were alone at last in the idyllic woodland glade, the sergeant-major made what he intended to be a brief introductory address.

"Do you know what I think of you?" he demanded, enunciating carefully. "You're a lousy mother-fugging bastard, a stinking little skunk, a shit-faced insubordinate swine. That's what I think of you."

"May I point out," Kamnitzer said mildly, "that expressions of that nature are not in current use these days? They're against regulations."

Rammler laughed scornfully. "You'll be asking me to apologise to you, next!"

"Not a bad idea, except that I'm not sure I'd be prepared to accept an apology from you."

"You're a degenerate little swine, Kamnitzer—a malicious little sod, that's what you are."

"Can I make a note of that?" asked Kamnitzer. "It'll look good in my report."

"Get stuffed!" shouted the sergeant-major. "We're on our own here, in case you hadn't noticed. Who's listening? Where are your witnesses? You can wipe your arse with your report—that's all it'll be good for."

"Thanks for the advice," remarked Kamnitzer.

The setting sun tinged the surrounding trees with gold and cast long shadows on the verdant grass which carpeted the glade. A belated bird was chirping to itself somewhere near at hand. The forest idyll was complete.

"Lie down!" shouted Rammler.

Kamnitzer did not move. He just stood there blinking at the soft evening sunlight.

"Lie down!" Rammler repeated.

"Why?"

"I'm giving you an order!" Rammler hissed. "If you don't comply with it immediately you'll regret you were ever born."

"Really?" Kamnitzer looked genuinely interested.

"I'll put you on a charge."

"Steady on, Sergeant-Major. You seem to have forgotten that we're on our own. Who's to hear? Where are your witnesses? You can take your charge and wipe your arse on it. That's all it's good for."

Although Kamnitzer had used the precise words which Rammler himself had uttered a few moments before, Rammler felt as if he had never heard them before in the whole of his military career. They sounded different when uttered by a subordinate. A whole world—his world—seemed to be tumbling about his ears.

"I could tell you to get stuffed," Kamnitzer continued, "but I won't. I could think of plenty of obscene things to call you, too, but they wouldn't do justice to a man of your calibre. I'll just say this : you're a despicable human being and a rotten soldier. I'm going back to the others now. Are you coming?"

*

The storm-clouds continued to gather as the evening wore on.

Carolin Ahlers sat in the kitchen on the bench beside the stove. A book lay open on her lap, but she was not reading it. She was a little uneasy. Martin Recht had promised to call, but there was no sign of him.

"Why doesn't he come?" she asked.

"Perhaps he can't make it," Frau Ahlers said soothingly. "A barracks isn't like an office, with regular hours. I've had to wait for your father often enough."

"That's different, though."

"Of course," Frau Ahlers said. "Your father never watches the clock when he's on duty. His private life comes second." Her voice contained no hint of reproach. "But Martin has to do what he's told. He can't dispose of his time as he wants to—you'll have to get used to that. Besides, I expect he doesn't want to disturb you to-night."

"Disturb me? How could he think that!"

"He knows you have to go into hospital to-morrow, so

perhaps he wants to spare you any excitement. That's what it is, I'm sure. You ought to be grateful to him for being so thoughtful."

Carolin was half-convinced for a moment, but she went on waiting.

Helen Wieder was not waiting for anyone. At least, she showed no sign of missing Kamnitzer's presence. She went on serving the customers as usual, and the fact that her eyes swivelled repeatedly in the direction of the entrance was, she told herself, purely coincidental.

Kamnitzer, meanwhile, was lying on his bed with a transistor set on the pillow beside him. He glanced across at Martin Recht from time to time with an expression of benevolent appraisal.

Recht was writing a letter to his mother. It was full of the usual assurances : he was well, he got plenty to eat, there was no need to worry about him.

Both Kamnitzer and Recht had been ordered to stay in Room 13 and wait, it was not clear what for. " In case you're needed," they had been told, and their room-mates were also on call.

In the meantime, von Strackmann and Kirschke were fighting shoulder to shoulder, to the surprise of the whole company. Both of them were doing their utmost to bury the charge alleging " assault on a superior officer." Kirschke, in particular, had brought his considerable powers of persuasion into play, but Streicher, with Rammler's hot breath fanning the back of his neck, remained adamant.

" Well, we've done all we can," von Strackmann declared at length. " You can confirm that, Sergeant-Major."

" I know," said Kirschke, " but we ought to have acted more promptly—more firmly, too. I'm afraid we're going to have to ride out the storm now."

" I don't give up so easily," von Strackmann said. " I'm going to make the best of the situation, however hopeless it looks."

" At whose expense, sir?"

"Not at the expense of this company, I can tell you that much."

"I hope, sir," Kirschke said, his suspicions suddenly aroused, "that you aren't confusing the interests of the company with your personal welfare."

They were back to where they had been a few hours before. The brief armistice was at an end.

"You don't know what you're talking about!" snapped the lieutenant, and he vanished into his office like a weatherman, slamming the door behind him.

Von Strackmann couldn't bring himself to leave the company block. He felt it imperative to remain at his post, if only to prevent Kirschke from stepping out of line. This meant that Frau Elfrieda Bornekamp had to wait, too, but she did not wait unsolaced. Von Strackmann telephoned his apologies and got an orderly to deliver her bottle of Red Horse.

Elisabeth Asch had no time to wonder where her husband was. Not only was she far too busy, but she had never felt neglected by him. If he kept her waiting he must, she was convinced, have his reasons.

She was right. Herbert Asch was engaged on what he termed "preventive measures." These consisted in conferring with Captain Ahlers and trying to persuade him to contact Colonel Turner.

"I don't know if that would be wise," Ahlers said dubiously. "The Colonel's a very punctilious man."

"That's just what we need," said Asch. "We've got to get the ball rolling. If we just sit back and wait, anything may happen. A lot of people could suffer, and in my experience it's always the little people that get hurt in these situations— i.e. Martin Recht. But that's just what we want to avoid, and that's why I'm in favour of clearing the air as soon as possible."

"Perhaps you're right," Ahlers conceded reluctantly. "I only hope we haven't overlooked anything."

The ball started rolling, just as Asch intended, though

not in the direction foreseen either by himself or by Ahlers, neither of whom was aware of Captain Treuberg's booby-trap.

The explosion was triggered off in the following way:

Phase One: Captain Ahlers telephoned Colonel Turner. "We shall hardly be able to avoid adopting a stand of some kind, sir," he said after a lengthy preamble, "particularly since members of the civil population are taking an interest in the affair. I would suggest that you consult Herr Asch. He's prepared to make himself available at any time."

"I don't want any fuss, Ahlers."

"Precisely, sir. That's why we ought to take preventive measures as soon as possible."

Phase Two: Colonel Turner telephoned Major Bornekamp. After the customary cordial assurances that he had no wish to give precipitate advice or meddle in the affairs of another arm of the service, he said: "But we shall all be forced to take official note of the affair, in view of the prevailing state of public opinion."

"Which will change again before long, sir, I trust."

"Until then, we must resign ourselves to the fact that it carries a certain weight. In any case, Major, I should be grateful if you would do your best to keep me up to date with developments."

Phase Three: Major Bornekamp telephoned Lieutenant von Strackmann. His introductory remark—"I've got better things to do than lose sleep because of my subordinates' incompetence"—was succeeded by a string of questions, namely: had von Strackmann dealt with a certain delicate matter? If so, was it settled for good? If not, why not?

The lieutenant took a deep breath.

"Don't beat about the bush, Strackmann! I'll give you precisely ten minutes to produce a final answer."

Phase Four: Lieutenant von Strackmann telephoned Major Bornekamp. "The matter has been investigated with the fullest attention to detail, sir. The charge is corroborated by the evidence of a trustworthy N.C.O. and five men." He paused for a moment. "With respect, sir, there's something fishy going on. I've been reliably informed in confidence that an air force captain named Ahlers has been trying to persuade the Mayor to intervene—for personal reasons. Recht is involved with his daughter. Captain Ahlers's private life doesn't seem to be above reproach, either. He's in debt to the tune of several thousand marks."

There was a lengthy pause. Then Major Bornekamp asked: " Is this fact or supposition?"

" Corroborative evidence can easily be produced."

" But you haven't managed to scotch this blasted charge of assault."

" No, sir. I'm very sorry."

Phase Five: Major Bornekamp telephoned Colonel Turner. He began by assuring the Colonel how grateful he was for his advice, how much he appreciated the confidence reposed in him, how receptive he was to suggestions of any kind—but . . . " But I very much fear that personal considerations enter into this. I'm referring to Captain Ahlers."

Apparently, Ahlers looked on the accused man as a future son-in-law. Even that might be all right, but . . . " But I submit that a man whose ostensible purpose is to defend the cause of justice and integrity ought to put his own house in order first. I'm told that he's heavily in debt—ten thousand marks is the sum mentioned. He's even said to have borrowed money from a subordinate."

" That," said Colonel Turner, consternation in his voice, " is news to me."

" I hope you'll treat my remarks as confidential, Colonel."

With that, Bornekamp was confident that he had shaken off the importunate area commandant and equally confident that this distressing affair had been shelved, at least for the time being. However, he had reckoned without the Colonel's punctiliousness where official matters were concerned. Turner would not tolerate any loose ends in his command. He summoned Captain Ahlers at once.

" Are you in debt?" he demanded.

" Yes, sir."

" Have you borrowed money from a subordinate?"

" Yes, sir."

" What do your debts amount to?"

Ahlers hesitated. " About twelve thousand marks, sir."

The Colonel stiffened. " This is not only serious," he said eventually. " It's quite incredible. I simply can't have that sort of thing—not in my command."

" If I might be permitted to explain how I incurred these debts . . ."

" There's nothing to explain," Turner said sternly. " No explanation, however ingenious, could alter the extent of your indebtedness. That is the only point at issue. Regretable as it may seem, I must draw my own conclusions. Only one course of action is open to me : you are relieved of your duties until further notice, that is to say, until a court of inquiry has reached a decision on your case."

" May I ask one thing, sir?"

" I'm sorry, no. I must do my duty, I've no other alternative. My decision is final, much as I regret it personally. You are relieved of your duties as of now, and will hold yourself in readiness to give evidence. Captain Treuberg will take over from you in the meantime."

The die was cast.

Summary proceedings were now to be instituted against two men : against Grenadier Martin Recht for assaulting a superior officer—probable sentence, with luck, several months' imprisonment; and against Captain Klaus Ahlers for excessive indebtedness.

Since the latter case automatically raised the possibility that Ahlers might have been employed as a paid contact by foreign intelligence services, Military Intelligence had to be notified at once. If his debts, at least one of which was incurred by borrowing from a subordinate, proved to be his own misdemeanour, it would probably mean dishonourable discharge, deprivation of rank and loss of pension.

The disaster seemed complete.

*

"We must do our duty unflinchingly," Lieutenant Dieter von Strackmann declared. "I'm extremely distressed by the whole affair, but it was absolutely unavoidable."

"You can do your duty, sir, if that's what you like to call it," the C.S.M. said wearily. "My duties are over for the day."

"You're not going to leave me in the lurch, Sergeant-Major?"

Kirschke avoided looking at his acting company commander. He found the sight embarrassing. He tidied the few things that lay on his desk and closed the drawers, one by one, as though oblivious of von Strackmann's presence.

"Listen, Kirschke," von Strackmann said, almost coaxingly, "I'm in a cleft stick, you must try to understand that. I've got to resolve the situation somehow."

"At whose expense?"

The lieutenant could have tried to explain his motives. He could have said that he meant well, that he was trying to do the decent thing, that he was a man of high principles, that it was only natural to defend oneself when everything conspired against one. . . .

But he said none of this, mainly because Kirschke sat there like a rock, motionless, craggy and unyielding. He looked contemptuous.

"I'll make one last effort," von Strackmann said. "I'll call the Judge Advocate General's office and speak to someone there."

"If you do that, it's as good as reporting the case officially."

"The J.A.G.'s people can dismiss it."

"They won't, though."

"For God's sake, Kirschke!" von Strackmann exclaimed with a mixture of rage and entreaty. "Why do you always have to know better?"

He picked up the 'phone and asked for the Judge Advocate General's department. Despite the lateness of the hour, he was put through to an official named Minzlaffe.

"A perfect prima facie case," was Minzlaffe's terse verdict, when von Strackmann had summarised the situation. "Kindly forward the appropriate particulars as soon as possible."

Von Strackmann registered dismay. "You don't see any possibility, under certain circumstances, after considering all possible interpretation of existing regulations . . ."

"I'm sorry, no," said Minzlaffe. He knew his trade, as his next words clearly showed. "You may rest assured that I fully appreciate your concern as unit commander, but in this case—believe me—the legal position seems quite clear. A moderate term of imprisonment is inevitable."

Von Strackmann replaced the receiver as though renouncing a crown. His face wore an expression of solemn resignation. "I didn't want to do that," he said.

"But you did," Kirschke retorted.

The lieutenant bowed his crew-cut head in an attempt to convey submission to fate. It was his lot to be misunderstood.

"The inevitable has happened," he announced. "We must take the appropriate steps."

"What sort of steps do you mean?"

"Well," said von Strackmann, squaring his shoulders, "in the first place, full details must be forwarded to the J.A.G.'s office without delay. Then there are certain precautionary measures to be taken, on the basis that Recht must be isolated from Streicher. The safest way of doing that would be to transfer him."

"Out of the question," said Kirschke. Coming to life again, he advanced on the lieutenant. "We must keep the case and the men involved under our jurisdiction, or we won't be able to exert any influence on the outcome."

"But the matter's settled, Sergeant-Major."

"Not for me it isn't, sir, nor for you. We shouldn't be under any illusions about that. There's still that chap Kamnitzer to be reckoned with, not to mention a number

of other people, including some whose existence we may
not even be aware of."

"Why do you always have to look on the dark side,
Sergeant-Major?" Von Strackmann stamped his foot like a
boy who has been forbidden to play ball. "I'm prepared
to put my faith in the court's judgment, anyway."

"You're welcome, sir," said Kirschke. "I trust you'll still
be as happy if their judgment happens to coincide with
justice."

*

"I regret this situation," Captain Treuberg said with an
air of genuine regret, "but there's nothing I can do."

"All right," Ahlers replied curtly. "What do you want?"

Captain Treuberg, yesterday Ahlers's deputy and to-day
his superior, stood unflinchingly behind his desk. It belonged
to him, now, as did the maps and plans on the walls.
Ahlers was his to command, but he preserved what he
hoped was a comradely attitude. "I can't tell you how sorry
I am about all this, Ahlers, but I must ask you—at the
Colonel's request—for an accurate and detailed list of your
debts."

"May I draw your attention to one not unimportant
point? Any liabilities I may have incurred are of a purely
temporary nature."

"However you regard them," Treuberg said courteously,
"I'm afraid it doesn't affect my instructions, nor yours
either."

"You'll get your list. Will you give me an hour?"

Captain Treuberg was magnanimous enough to grant this
request. He even placed a pad of paper and his own fountain-
pen at Ahlers's disposal. "If I can help in any way, please
don't hesitate to call on me."

Captain Ahlers retired into the outer office, squatted on
a window-sill and started to draft the required statement.

While still engaged on this depressing task, he was

interrupted by Viktor Vossler. " Just bear one thing in mind, Klaus," he said in a low voice. " A friend is a friend. Nothing can change that."

Ahlers looked up. " Don't overestimate the value of friendship, Viktor. Sober facts are all that matter now."

" I'm your friend, Klaus," Vossler insisted. " Don't ever forget it."

Ahlers gave a wan smile and returned to his calculations. The final figure was DM 11,350—in words : eleven thousand three hundred and fifty marks—nearly all of which had been spent on Carolin's medical expenses. Drawing a double line beneath the figure that symbolised the years he had spent in trying to prevent his child from becoming a permanent cripple, Ahlers took the complete balance sheet to Treuberg.

Treuberg accepted it with an impassive face, though his eyes glinted involuntarily when he had read it through. " Is that the lot?" he asked in mechanical tones. Ahlers responded with a terse affirmative. " In that case, I must convey this to the Colonel at once."

Turner laid aside his beloved but unread volume of Kant, stared at the total, impressed, and summoned Captain Ahlers to his office.

" How could this have happened?" he said, shaking his scholarly head in sorrow.

" I know how I can meet these liabilities in full, sir."

Turner looked up expectantly. He was always ready to act on his basic principle, namely, to avoid trouble as long as there was any possibility of doing so. " I'm open to suggestions, Ahlers."

" Well, sir, my late father left me and my sister a piece of land with a house on it. It's nothing very grand, but it must be worth forty thousand marks—perhaps fifty. I'll try to realise my share of it within the next few days."

" You really think there's a chance?" The Colonel was not inhuman. His face had assumed an expression of paternal benevolence. " How much time do you think you would need?"

"Ten days or a fortnight ought to do it."

"Right," said Turner. "I'll give you ten days' leave. If you've managed to clear this business up by the end of that time, I'll be the first to welcome it. But don't disappoint me, Ahlers. I should regard that as a sign of ingratitude."

*

"Certain things have come to my ears," Herbert Asch told Major Bornekamp, "but I can hardly credit them."

Bornekamp emitted an indignant snort. "Can I help it if one of my subordinates rushes in feet foremost and messes everything up? I've got to obey the rules, after all."

The C.O. was visiting Asch at the latter's invitation. They stood facing one another in the mayor's office with seven centuries of local history staring down at them in the shape of parchment scrolls, oil paintings and a heavy seal in a glass case. In a display cabinet lay a broken dagger, the property, so it was said, of a general of Nordic origin who had allegedly tried to drive it into the mayoral desk during the Thirty Years' War—without success, because the desk was constructed of stout and well-seasoned oak.

"In that case," Asch said quietly, "you've broken the terms of our agreement."

"What am I supposed to do, with subordinates like that?"

"But they are your subordinates, aren't they, Major?"

Bornekamp writhed, but only briefly. As commander of the Ironclads and a professed fighting soldier, he considered it beneath his dignity to give ground to a mere civilian.

"You've got a nerve, blaming me," he protested, going over to the attack, "after the egg you laid—Ahlers, I mean. The cheek of the man, sticking his nose into our business and stirring things up when he's got little enough to be proud of himself. Do you expect me to let a chap like that ride roughshod over me?"

"Kindly note the following, Major," Asch said, retaining his composure with an effort, "I'm not blaming anybody,

I'm merely stating facts. And as far as my friend Captain Ahlers is concerned, I'd go bail for him any time."

" For his debts, too?"

" If by that you mean his temporary obligations, yes—to the limit."

" It's probably too late for that." The Major looked into a pair of cool, appraising eyes. He was unused to being looked at in this way, and it irritated him. " Anyway, what do you know about our job and its difficulties?" he demanded. " You've no idea what we're up against— thwarted by little pipsqueaks and spat on by bastards who aren't fit to lick our boots! A lot of senior officers are weak-kneed these days, so don't expect any miracles from me!"

" All I expected was that you'd keep your promise."

" What did I promise?" Bornekamp demanded aggrievedly. " Go on, tell me."

" If you can't remember, there's no point in my reminding you."

" I made no promises."

" Very well, neither did I."

" Are you trying to threaten me?" Bornekamp scented danger in the air. " Come now, surely you're not going to crucify me for the sake of a private soldier? I don't believe it! You wouldn't do a thing like that, after the way we've always worked so well together."

The words started to gush from Bornekamp's lips like water from a fractured pipe. Herbert Asch let him run on, even though he regarded it as a sheer waste of time.

" Would you excuse me?" he said eventually, and walked out, leaving the Ironclad-in-chief standing there with a face that looked as though it had been daubed with crimson.

In the adjoining room, Asch called Flammer of the *News*. " This is it," he told him. " Go ahead and print."

" In full?" asked Flammer.

" As far as I'm concerned, Herr Flammer. In fact, I suggest you run the article in its original form—preferably to-morrow morning. Major Bornekamp's views deserve the fullest possible coverage and the widest possible public recognition. You follow me?"

"It'll be a pleasure," Flammer assured him. "But I hope you know who's going to carry the can for this in the end."

*

"Let's get to work, then," said Councillor Mathias von Minzlaffe, peeling off his gloves.

He sat down at the company commander's desk and opened a file containing nothing but virgin white paper. Unscrewing the cap of his fountain-pen with long, sensitive fingers, he glanced keenly at von Strackmann through his rimless glasses. "This seems a clear enough case. It shouldn't take long to master the essentials."

"You can count on my support," von Strackmann said.

"I'm banking on it," von Minzlaffe assured him with a thin smile. The Councillor, a civilian judge-advocate, was the ideal man for this case, which promised to be a model of its kind. He was, as so often before, in his element.

"First, the plaintiff," he commanded.

Sergeant Streicher made an excellent impression on the Councillor. His demeanour was a blend of modesty, determination, humility and readiness to co-operate. His answers came back pat and without hesitation. In short, he inspired confidence.

"You say you were assaulted by the subordinate in question?"

"Yes, sir."

"No possibility of a mistake?"

"None, sir."

"Will you stand by your evidence, come what may?"

"Come what may, sir."

Minzlaffe studied Streicher's earnest features with approval and then glanced at von Strackmann, who experienced a mild sense of pride at having such a subordinate under his command.

"Now the accused," said von Minzlaffe.

Grenadier Martin Recht appeared. His manner, the Councillor sensed at once, left much to be desired. He did not give a sufficient impression of candour or self-confidence. On the contrary, he betrayed signs of nervousness and diffidence, possibly engendered by a bad conscience. His face looked pale and worried.

"I'm not here to pass judgment on you," the Councillor announced. "That's not my function. My job is to handle the preparatory details. I hope—in your own interests—that you'll place the fullest trust in me. You will, won't you?"

Martin Recht hesitated for some seconds before replying. Von Minzlaffe's glasses flashed and he tapped the papers in front of him with his pen, spattering them with ink—not that he appeared to notice. His bland, unwrinkled face had gone as blank as a hurriedly wiped blackboard.

"Are you guilty?" he demanded sternly.

"No," Recht replied. "At least, I'm not aware of having done anything wrong."

Von Minzlaffe screwed the ink-spattered sheet of paper into a ball and tossed it into the waste-paper basket. His lips narrowed and he closed his eyes for a moment. It was always the same—they all denied it. They produced a string of worthless excuses and hoped that people would be stupid enough to believe them. What a world!

"Once upon a time," von Minzlaffe said, "men used to stand by what they said—and did. It was a point of honour, something which accorded with the basic principles of national discipline. People are impressed by a thing like that. It would be taken into account at your trial. Well, Recht?"

"I really didn't do what I'm accused of."

Von Minzlaffe frowned and glanced across at von Strackmann. The implied reproach was not lost on the lieutenant, who felt that he had been failed by one of his subordinates. "Come on, man," he urged. "Don't let the side down."

His exhortation was in vain. Recht remained stubbornly silent, and not another word could be extracted from him. Von Strackmann blushed with shame.

" I only hope all your men aren't like that," the Councillor said at length, when Recht had been dismissed.

This was not so, as the succeeding interviews clearly demonstrated. A string of witnesses, directly and indirectly involved, marched smartly in and out, compliant almost to a man. One or two of them expressed cautious reservations or succumbed, as von Minzlaffe put it, to a false confusion of loyalties, but these irregularities were soon ironed out. Von Strackmann's pride in his command revived.

He was proud, for instance, of Sergeant-Major Rammler, whose replies came back like neatly wrapped bars of chocolate emerging from a slot-machine. They tended to be a trifle crude and unpolished, of course, but this did not detract from their cogency. " Recht," he declared, " is a broken reed. Slackers like him always shit their pants when things get tough—everyone knows that." Or again : " Sergeant Streicher's still wet behind the ears, I grant you, but he'd bust a gut rather than let the company down."

Councillor von Minzlaffe smiled indulgently. Men like Rammler were a pleasure to deal with. The sergeant-major struck him as a rough diamond, a rude but stout-hearted individual, a martinet, perhaps, but endowed with an unschooled sense of justice.

Company Sergeant-Major Kirschke, on the other hand, tried to make trouble. His first words when questioned by von Minzlaffe were : " Why all this fuss? In the normal way, a case of this sort has to be forwarded to the public prosecutor's department—that is, if there's a case at all."

" You don't understand these things," von Minzlaffe said loftily, in a rash attempt to put Kirschke in his place. " We're merely exploring avenues of approach."

" Is that what you call it? It looks more like an encroachment on the functions of the public prosecutor, to me. In fact, some people might regard it as official interference."

Councillor von Minzlaffe bridled visibly. Donning an expression of grave concern, he drew von Strackmann into the far corner of the office and addressed him in an agitated whisper. The two men put their heads together and clucked like chickens, leaving Kirschke standing in solitary state like a rooster on a dung-heap.

"We needn't detain you further, Sergeant-Major," von Minzlaffe said at length, striving to sound firm.

"In that case I'll go," Kirschke replied. "I've got to change my trousers, and my hands could do with a wash."

When the C.S.M. had departed, von Minzlaffe turned to von Strackmann, who had gone pale. "Have you got any more men like that in your company?"

"Unfortunately—yes. A lance-corporal named Kamnitzer."

"Is he directly concerned with this affair?"

"No, not directly."

"Then we can dispense with his evidence. I trust your judgment implicitly on that point. There are some witnesses who only obscure the true issues."

"What if he insists on giving evidence?" Von Strackmann could not refrain from uttering a word of warning. "He's an unpredictable type."

"Come, come!" said von Minzlaffe, closing his file with an irritable snap. "Take an old stager's word for it, if a man isn't asked anything, he can't answer. Malcontents should be excluded on principle when it's a question of reaching a proper verdict."

Lieutenant von Strackmann was fully convinced of this. Von Minzlaffe was expert at preserving the interests of justice, he was sure, but had he come across a type like Kamnitzer? It was doubtful.

*

Carolin Ahlers was due for admission to Professor Martin's clinic, and Warrant Officer Viktor Vossler had decided that the occasion must not pass unnoticed. He organised a cortège to escort her there.

"I'm not touting for sympathy," he told Herbert Asch. "I'm merely inviting you to take a drive into town. I'll lead the way in my Mercedes and that big hotel saloon of yours can follow. All right?"

I

"On one condition. We'll make it a three-car procession, and I'll bring up the rear in my Porsche with Captain Ahlers."

"You're a blackmailer after my own heart," Vossler said gratefully.

He drove to the Grenadier barracks to see if he could winkle out Recht and Kamnitzer, which proved to be easier than he thought. A few words of explanation to Kirschke, and the C.S.M. put the two men on "stores detail."

"Don't look so surprised," Vossler said. "You've been assigned to me. You're under my command for the next few hours, and the first thing I want you to do is look cheerful."

"I'm an expert at it," Kamnitzer assured him with a grin, "but I can't vouch for the mental state of this youngster here." He crooked a thumb at his companion.

"Listen to me, lad," Vossler told Recht. "If you're dwelling on your own troubles—forget them. At least keep smiling until Carolin's safely inside the clinic."

"I'd do anything for Carolin," Martin said quietly.

"And remember," Vossler went on, "even if they do gaol you for a couple of months, you won't be the first innocent man who's done time. The main thing is not to worry Carolin. Concentrate on the idea that she wants to get well, and that you're one of the reasons why she wants to."

"Fair enough," said Recht. "But we're wasting time. Let's go and fetch her."

They climbed into the enterprising warrant officer's car and drove to Ahlers's house, where they got out and waited patiently until the procession had assembled.

"Right," said Vossler, when Ahlers had greeted him in the hall, "where's the beautiful victim?"

"I'm still wondering if this is the right moment for an operation," Ahlers said cautiously.

Vossler drew his friend into a corner. "What do you mean?" he asked. "You haven't told Carolin anything about your troubles, have you?"

"Of course not, Viktor."

Vossler looked relieved. "Forgive me for asking. I'm sure all you want is to see Carolin cured at last. What's it worth to you? Your uniform? Your pilot's licence? Your captaincy? My friendship?"

"You're just delaying things unnecessarily," Ahlers said with a smile.

"Carolin!" Vossler called gaily. His voice rang through the small flat. "Come here, girl! You're not nervous, are you?"

Carolin appeared. She walked over to Vossler, limping only slightly, spread her arms wide and flung them round his broad shoulders in a gesture of gratitude which made him feel how trivial his financial help was in comparison.

"First, a little refreshment," he announced, extricating himself carefully and with evident reluctance from Carolin's embrace. "No harm in fortifying ourselves before we venture into the lion's den. Are you scared, Carolin?"

"What of? Why should I be scared of being cured?"

Carolin was genuinely unafraid, Vossler realised. She would enter the clinic confidently, unconscious of the difficulties which threatened those nearest and dearest to her.

He walked to the window and opened it. "Come up," he called, "and bring that hamper out of the boot of my car while you're about it."

Within a minute, Carolin was surrounded by the party which Vossler had mobilised: Vossler himself and Gerty Ballhaus, now officially engaged to him, Herbert and Elisabeth Asch, Kamnitzer and Helen Wieder, her parents, and Martin Recht. Carolin went over to Martin and took his hand.

"I'm a bit worried," Kamnitzer declared. "If Carolin's operation is successful, bang go my chances of ever beating her at skittles."

There was general laughter at this. Vossler produced some glasses and opened two bottles of champagne, assisted—as to the manner born—by Gerty, who contrived to look quite housewifely.

"My dear friends," said Herbert Asch, raising his glass, "I often feel that we take a great deal of what we call life completely for granted. We accept things without sparing them a thought, and we find it only too easy to forget the simplest and most important lessons of everyday existence—things which can be seen on any street corner or road on the faces of our neighbours. . . .

" Must we go to gaol before we know what freedom means? Is personal experience of war essential to a genuine desire for peace? Do we have to be ill before we recognise the blessings of normal good health?

"I raise my glass to Carolin. May she walk, dance and play skittles to her heart's content. May she lead a healthy, happy, normal life. I challenge anyone to tell me what could be worth more than that."

*

Three days later, while Carolin was preparing for her operation, Ahlers doing his best to liquidate his assets and Martin Recht awaiting trial, a grey-green Volkswagen saloon purred through the air force married quarters and drew up outside the block in which Captain Ahlers lived.

Two men in civilian clothes got out. Their faces were set in a fixed, chilly smile that looked as if it had been frozen there, and they exchanged few words. In the normal course of events, each knew what the other was thinking.

Trotting noiselessly up the stairs on rubber soles, they rang the bell and waited patiently. When the door opened, one of them inserted his foot in the gap while the other inquired softly: "Are you Frau Ahlers?" Receiving an affirmative reply, he asked: "Where is your husband?"

" Away," Frau Ahlers told him.

" Ah," remarked the man who had his foot in the door. " So he's away. Not in the Eastern Zone, by any chance?"

Frau Ahlers recoiled as she recognised the menace latent in the question. Anyone who read the newspapers knew that, to some people, a suspected concentration camp murderer was a saint compared with someone who was allegedly contaminated with Communism. Absurd though such an insinuation was in her husband's case, she did not lose her temper. She knew that it would have been pointless. The two men were doing their duty. " My husband is visiting his sister," she said.

" Ah, and does she live in the Eastern Zone?"

" She lives in Bavaria."

" Why?"

" My colleague means, why is he visiting his sister?"

" To deal with some financial matters, I think."

" You think? Don't you know?" The man spoke in the unemotional tones of a gas-meter reader. " You're not trying to cover up for him, are you?"

Frau Ahlers eyed the two expressionless faces nervously. " I don't know what you mean."

" Bavaria," said the other, still with his foot across the threshold, " borders on the Eastern Zone."

Frau Ahlers could restrain her anger no longer. " If you're suggesting what I think you are, I strongly resent it. There's not a scrap of truth in the idea."

" As you wish, Frau Ahlers, but I ought to point out that we've made no insinuations—we've merely explored certain possibilities. From your attitude, you seem determined to withhold further information."

" Under present circumstances—yes, I am."

The two men, small-eyed, greasy-skinned and slightly corpulent—they might have been brothers—glanced at each other and nodded. Almost simultaneously, they turned and padded off down the stairs.

Frau Ahlers hurried to a window and peered out. The men stood motionless on the pavement outside for a few moments. Then, after exchanging a word or two, they separated, one going to the house next door and the other to the house across the road.

Their mode of procedure was identical. Donning an air of courteous inquiry, they requested permission to ask a few questions " in confidence." These questions could have been summarised as follows: do you know Captain Ahlers and his family? How long have you known them? How well do you know them? What do you know about their financial position? How would you define their political views? Are you aware of any debts incurred by the said Captain Ahlers or a member of his family? If so, what is their nature and extent? Have you noticed any unusual or suspicious callers recently?

Each interview concluded with the parrot-like formula: " I must ask you to treat our conversation as strictly confidential and to refrain from drawing any premature conclusions from it. Thank you for your helpful co-operation.'

Within a couple of hours, everyone in the officers' married quarters knew—or suspected—that there was " something fishy" about the Ahlers family. As the tide of rumour swelled, vague hints became transformed into concrete allegations and debts into criminal offences. Some spoke of desertion and others of contacts with Communist agents. The word treason was uttered.

No one knew the exact identity of the men who had asked such fateful questions. True, they had prefaced each interview by flashing a card bearing a photograph and a rubber stamp, but no one had scrutinised or read it with any care. There was talk of detectives and secret police—but no one doubted that they were officials of some sort.

Meanwhile, the men had moved on to the air force barracks, where they separated once more. One, whose long suit was discretion, went in search of Colonel Turner, while the other, a rather tougher type, strode into the offices where Captain Ahlers had worked until a few days before.

" Where's the boss of this outfit?" he demanded, eschewing any form of greeting or introduction and not deigning to produce his warrant card. He evidently felt at home, judging by the way in which he addressed those present—sergeant clerk and female secretary alike—as subordinates. Even Monika's full-blooded charms seemed to be lost on him, which not unreasonably annoyed her. She turned her exquisite back on him, but the sergeant clerk, who scented the presence of authority, cautiously moved closer.

" I asked you a question!" barked the civilian.

Adopting a half-informative, half-respectful tone, the sergeant clerk said: "Captain Treuberg's in the Mess and Warrant Officer Vossler's out in the hangars."

"Fetch them," commanded the civilian, adding, as if to reassure himself that he was in the right place, "This is where Captain Ahlers used to work, isn't it?"

"Yes, sir," said the sergeant clerk. "This is it."

He left the room and went in search of Vossler. "Can you come to the office a moment?" he asked. "There's a funny-looking civilian in there."

"If he's so funny why aren't you laughing?" Vossler inquired without interest.

"He asked if Captain Ahlers used to work in our office." Vossler's eyes began to glint. "A snooper, eh?"

"He may be someone from M.I., inquiring about Captain Ahlers. I didn't see his pass, but he smelt rather like it."

"That's my boy," Vossler said, setting off in the direction of the office.

The stranger, whose civilian clothes Vossler at once identified as camouflage, was leaning against the door-post puffing at a cheap cheroot and trying to blow smoke-rings.

"Hello, who have we got here?" Vossler inquired brightly.

"Who are you?" the stranger retorted with some asperity.

"I'm on home ground," said Vossler. "Anyone who barges in here has to introduce himself first."

"I'm here on official business."

"So am I—have been for years."

Monika and the sergeant clerk watched, enthralled, as the clash of personalities unfolded. Vossler stood with his legs planted firmly apart like a wrestler waiting for his opponent to spring. The mysterious civilian continued to lean against the door-post, but he had stopped trying to blow smoke-rings and his cheroot appeared to have gone out.

It was Vossler who made the first move. "Either you show me your credentials at once or I'll have you removed."

"What's the matter—got a bad conscience?"

"What makes you think so?"

"That's the impression you give," said the civilian. "In

my experience, people who make a lot of noise are scared of something, and anyone who's got a bad conscience needs thorough checking."

Vossler didn't know whether to be annoyed or amused, but his ears had detected at least one revealing phrase: "thorough checking" was one of the principal functions of M.I. or Military Intelligence.

At that moment the civilian condescended to produce his pass, and Vossler read: "Sergeant-Major Gross, Internal Security Division, Military Intelligence Service."

"I'm investigating the Ahlers case," the M.I. man declared, "and I must ask you not to be obstructive."

"That's crazy," said Vossler. "There isn't an Ahlers case."

"Kindly allow me to be the judge of that. Anyway, I've got to speak to Captain Treuberg and "—he consulted his notebook—"Warrant Officer Vossler."

"That's me."

The M.I. man looked incredulous. He even tried to step back to get a better view, but the door-post intervened. "In that case, I must ask you to place any information you may have at my disposal," he said uneasily.

"Come off it!" Vossler protested. "What's this all about?"

"There may have been an attempt to pervert the course of justice." Sergeant-Major Gross seemed to have recovered his self-assurance. "Whether it'll come to an arrest remains to be seen."

*

The proceedings against Grenadier Martin Recht in respect of offences against Paragraph 25 of the Military Penal Code—

Anyone who commits an assault on a superior officer shall be liable to imprisonment or detention for a period of not less than six months

—took their slow and laborious course. As the president

of No. 2 Court, Dr. Bohlen, repeated several times during the hearing: "We shall take our time. One cannot be too thorough or painstaking in a case of this nature."

The reasons for this cautious approach were fully appreciated by the two military representatives, a sergeant-major and a lance-corporal, who quickly recognised the delicacy of the issues involved. Counsel for the prosecution, on the other hand, did his best to hurry things along, confident that he had a clear-cut case and that the evidence at his disposal could not be more conclusive.

"Not even the accused can dispute the salient facts of the case," he asserted. "But I submit . . ." interposed counsel for the defence. He said this each time he interrupted the prosecutor's argument, glancing keenly but respectfully at the president as he did so.

Dr. Bohlen, a calm and impassive figure, leant back slightly in his chair. His eyes were friendly, and a suggestion of a smile seemed to play about his lips most of the time. His voice was that of a sorrowing father, and when he raised a restraining hand it was as though Jupiter were temporarily directing the traffic.

"Herr Recht," he said, deliberately echewing the word "accused," "if I understand you rightly, you were not aware, on the night in question, that the plaintiff was your superior officer."

"That's right, sir," Recht replied, heartened by a brief nod of encouragement from his counsel. "All I saw was a friend who slept in the same room, someone I'd shared my meals with."

"But you knew that the plaintiff had been promoted," prosecuting counsel interposed. "You had seen him wearing sergeant's insignia—you'd even addressed him by that rank."

"Yes, sir."

Recht was the worst conceivable champion of his own cause. He had a conscience, and his conscience persuaded him that he was not entirely guiltless. No one on earth can be that, he told himself. Even a person who does absolutely nothing sins, if only by omission.

Dr. Bohlen made a discreet endeavour to skirt this feature of the proceedings. He tried, as always, to dispense justice in the most humane and conciliatory way possible, though Recht's distressingly uncompromising attempts at objectivity made his task no easier.

"Herr Recht," he said mildly, "you must try not to indulge in speculation. We are not concerned with what would have happened or what might have been if you had or had not done this or that. We cannot assess your thoughts. Facts are the only things that carry weight here."

It was demonstrated by the prosecution that a physical collision had occurred. It was further demonstrated that a room-mate who should at least formally have been regarded as a superior officer had fallen to the ground as a result. (Evidence of one witness: "I thought he'd sprained his backside!") Finally, it was a proven fact that Recht made no attempt to deny that the incident itself took place.

"—which argues in my client's favour," asserted defending counsel.

"—which proves that the charge against the accused is well-founded," retorted counsel for the prosecution.

The president raised his hand for the fifth time since the start of the hearing, and silence fell immediately. "You are quite at liberty to entertain your own opinions about this incident, gentlemen, but I would ask you to remember that it is the function of the court alone to reach a finding. You can facilitate that function, but you cannot usurp it."

Counsel for the defence bowed. "I request permission to call a witness for the defence: Lance-Corporal Karl Kamnitzer."

Prosecuting counsel had been thoroughly briefed as to Kamnitzer's identity and knew what to expect from him. "Irrelevant and immaterial!" he protested. "This man was not present when the incident which forms the sole subject of these proceedings occurred. Consequently, he cannot supply any evidence about it."

"But he can supply evidence as to the circumstances

which led up to the incident," argued counsel for the defence. "I submit that Lance-Corporal Kamnitzer could make a substantial contribution to the court's understanding of the atmosphere in which all this took place."

"On the contrary," prosecuting counsel said resolutely. "From the information in my possession, the calling of this witness would only obscure the real issue."

This virtually clinched the court's decision. Dr. Bohlen, whose curiosity had been whetted by counsels' exchange, said: "I venture to suggest that the court is fully capable of deciding for itself whether or not a witness's evidence is admissible."

Once the green light had been given, Kamnitzer entered the small, bare, shabby courtroom with the same self-assurance which characterised his behaviour in barracks or in the Café Asch.

"How's the case going, sir?" he inquired unceremoniously.

Dr. Bohlen, who couldn't remember having been asked such a question in the whole of his career, had some difficulty in keeping a straight face. "Herr Kamnitzer," he said courteously, "if you ask me how the case is going, I must regretfully inform you that I myself have no idea at this stage. I shall only know after the close of the hearing."

"So it's not going too badly?"

"That depends, Herr Kamnitzer, on what you understand by too badly."

Those present regarded the strange spectacle with astonishment. Elderly judge and unabashed young man were smiling at one another in a positively familiar fashion. Indeed, they appeared to find pleasure in each other's company.

"And now," Dr. Bohlen went on, "may I ask you to abide by our rules? Before we continue our conversation, Fräulein Horn, our stenographer, would be glad to know whom she's dealing with. In other words, she has to record your personal particulars."

Kamnitzer readily supplied all the requisite details. "Now do we get down to the case, sir, such as it is?"

Dr. Bohlen concurred. "But I would ask you to remember that we are examining a case of alleged assault upon a superior officer, nothing more."

"You mean you want me to stick to the point?"

"Exactly."

"I get it," said Kamnitzer. He moved a step nearer as though about to embark on a private conversation. "I won't ask you, sir, if you've ever had one over the eight. I doubt if you'd appreciate the question, and it's none of my business anyway, but you can imagine being in that condition, can't you?"

"I can imagine, yes," Dr. Bohlen said with a smile.

"Very well," said Kamnitzer. "The question is : can one regard this incident as a single, isolated occurrence, divorced from everything else? When two people bump into each other in a confined space and one of them falls down on his backside, is that all there is to it? All kinds of things could have contributed—floor polish, for instance. You can see your face in the floor of our room."

Dr. Bohlen smiled. "That may speak well for the floor-polishing activities of your section, but it doesn't, unfortunately, dispose of the fact that one of the two men who bumped into each other was a subordinate and the other his superior."

"With respect, sir, that's the whole flaw in the argument," declared Kamnitzer. "In reality, they were just two people who'd lived together for months. They got up at the same time, cleaned their teeth side by side, ate together, worked together and spent some of their leisure time in each other's company."

"For months, you said?" Dr. Bohlen inquired.

"For the best part of half a year, if that sounds better." Kamnitzer felt that he was operating on the right lines. For a pillar of the law, Dr. Bohlen seemed to be an understanding sort. "And throughout that time, Recht, Streicher and myself have been living in our own little corner of the barracks—tucked up side by side, so to speak."

"Go on."

"I won't pretend I'm a model soldier," Kamnitzer said spiritedly, "but Streicher's no angel either, and Martin Recht isn't just a bone-headed lout who lets fly with his fists every two minutes. They've both got their failings, but who hasn't? I've kicked both of them in the pants before now, when occasion demanded. Things like this happen —and if it means someone has to be hauled into court every time, all I can say is, I pity the judges."

"We appreciate your sympathy," commented Dr. Bohlen.

"I haven't said a word against the regiment's reputation. I hope you've noted that, sir."

"It hadn't escaped me, Herr Kamnitzer."

"I've done my best to keep to the point, too, I hope."

"I wouldn't dispute that," said Dr. Bohlen. "Thank you for your remarks. They have been most informative."

This concluded the hearing. Although Lieutenant von Strackmann's name was raised, Dr. Bohlen deemed it unnecessary to call any further witnesses. He listened impassively to the closing addresses by counsel for the prosecution and defence, and then announced that the court would retire to consider its verdict.

"Well done," defending counsel told Kamnitzer. "You mustn't expect miracles from a court of law. A judge can interpret the law but he can't ignore it altogether. I forecast that young Recht will get away with a comparatively light sentence—six months is my guess. Dr. Bohlen is the sort of judge who thinks human beings are more important than the laws they're subject to."

Dr. Bohlen reappeared, took his seat, and announced:

"In the name of the people: the court finds the accused guilty as charged. He is hereby sentenced, subject to confirmation, to three months' imprisonment."

*

When Captain Ahlers returned from leave—two days earlier than foreseen—his wife told him what had happened in the interval. He at once reported to Colonel Turner.

"Highly regrettable, this whole business," Turner said, in a tone which dissociated him from it entirely.

"It's not only regrettable, sir—it's disgraceful!"

The Colonel shook his head indulgently. He could have avoided this embarrassing interview, but he never shirked responsibilities of any kind—or so he told himself. "This has been a great disappointment to me, Ahlers."

"While I've been away raising the money as agreed, sir . . ."

"Did you manage it?"

"Every last pfennig. I sold the house I told you about—the one jointly owned by myself and my sister. There wasn't time to get a good price, but my share comes to twenty thousand marks, so I shall be able to pay off all my debts."

"I'm very glad, from your point of view."

"But I'm told that I've been investigated in my absence. M.I. has been in action, spreading the most appalling rumours about me. The married quarters are absolutely buzzing with them."

"Most regrettable," repeated Turner, "but the propensity to gossip is a human failing which can never be entirely eliminated. In any case, M.I.'s action was inevitable under the circumstances."

"But I had your approval, sir. I had your promise that the matter would be allowed to rest until I'd managed to raise the necessary funds, and I've kept my side of the bargain."

"Is that meant to be a reproach?" Turner inquired icily.

"I had your word, sir!"

Turner drew himself up until he resembled an allegorical statue portraying integrity. "You're not, I trust, implying that I have broken my word? I can only assure you that the exact opposite is the case."

Ahlers ignored the warning contained in these words. He was conscious only of himself and what had been done to him. " M.I.'s investigations have discredited me, violated my honour and brought my family into disrepute. Even if I could tolerate that, there's my wife to be considered. She feels like a leper."

" I'm sorry," Turner said coolly, " but you only have yourself to blame for repercussions of this kind—can't you understand that? Captain Ahlers, you drew up an official list of your liabilities which put the total at eleven thousand three hundred and fifty marks."

" It was correct."

" I'm sorry, Captain, it was not." Turner looked stern. " Since then, it has transpired that your statement was inaccurate. To be blunt, it was false, which means that you wilfully deceived me, not to say, deliberately lied to me. I learned the full story from a reliable source, and there is ample evidence to corroborate it."

" I don't understand you."

" What about the three thousand marks you borrowed from Vossler—from a warrant officer who was your direct subordinate? You don't deny it, I suppose?"

" No, of course not, but that sum has nothing to do with my debts as such. Viktor Vossler is a personal friend."

" Possibly, but you are his superior officer."

" Who told you, sir? Or, rather, who denounced me?"

" That is immaterial."

" Captain Treuberg—it couldn't be anyone else! "

" Let's stick to the facts, Captain. They are as follows : you submitted a list of liabilities. I trusted you and gave you a chance to put your affairs in order. It turned out later that your list was bogus . . ."

" Incomplete, sir, at most."

" It was inaccurate, however you regard it. That compelled me to suspect the worst . . ."

" Of me, sir? You know me well enough to realise that's absurd! "

"Of course, Ahlers, of course! You are—or were—an officer endowed with very special qualities, nor shall I ever hesitate to draw attention to them or speak on your behalf. I know you, yes—but I also know the regulations, and one of them states that cases of excessive indebtedness must be reported to higher authority without delay. Surely you're aware of that? "

Captain Ahlers was not only familiar with the regulation —he approved of it in principle. Any man who incurred liabilities had to discharge them somehow, whether by tapping other sources of credit, by gambling or by selling himself. And the easiest way for a man in uniform to sell himself was to contact a foreign espionage organisation, which would pay up willingly in return for services rendered. Ahlers knew all this, but it had never occurred to him that anyone would suspect him of such conduct.

" I know that I've acted improperly," he conceded frankly, "but I'm unaware of having done anything inconsistent with my honour as an officer."

"Far be it from me to dispute that, Ahlers, but the court will have to decide for itself. Disciplinary proceedings have been instituted against you. Do you know what that means? "

"Yes," Ahlers said bitterly. " Temporary suspension from duty, a ban on wearing uniform and partial stoppage of pay."

"You're right, I'm afraid." Colonel Turner gave a nod which signified that the interview was at an end. " And I recommend that you consider seriously whether it wouldn't be advisable to submit your resignation from the service."

*

Dark, too, were the days that Major Bornekamp was compelled to live through, thanks to Herbert Asch. The newspaper profile of the Ironclads' C.O. was raising its anticipated cloud of dust.

"Can't a man express his opinion freely any more?" Bornekamp growled furiously. "Why should the malcontents and fellow-travellers have it all their own way?"

"All the same, sir," the adjutant ventured, "you are a representative of the State, in a sense. I realise that malcontents and half-witted intellectuals are given free rein these days, but in your position . . ."

"What did I say, then?"

It seemed to him that he had said a lot of highly commendable things, all of them officially sanctioned. Only one thing seriously disturbed him, and that was the misinterpreted analogy between conscientious objectors and convicts, or even concentration camp detainees. How absurd! He had never had the smallest connection with a concentration camp.

"These ridiculous misunderstandings have been deliberately exaggerated. My only regret is that I can't deal with the man responsible as he deserves."

The man responsible was, of course, Herbert Asch, but his attempt to spread the gospel according to Bornekamp had been an extremely laborious business.

"I eagerly await your readers' reaction," Asch had told Flammer, but for a while he waited in vain. The local citzens swallowed Bornekamp's effusions without a murmur, and there had been no immediate comment. This did not necessarily mean that they all agreed with the Iron Major, but even the more rebellious spirits had ceased to wonder at the patriotic, nationalistic, militaristic fare that was set before them. They merely frowned and shrugged their shoulders while the growing numbers of trusty provincial patriots

nodded their approbation: the Major had given them something to think about all right!

Accordingly, Asch did his best to ensure that Bornekamp's
warlike utterances reached a wider public than the readers
of the local paper. A leading illustrated, a radio com-
mentator and, finally, a member of the parliamentary opposition took the matter up. The result was a cloud-burst of
publicity which threatened to engulf Bornekamp and wash
him away down the plug-hole of political controversy.

Being confident of his own innocence, Bornekamp had
to find someone whose guilt was demonstrable. Several
candidates leapt to his mind. Chief among them was
Herbert Asch himself, but Asch was beyond his reach. For
want of a better scapegoat, he settled on Lieutenant Dieter
von Strackmann, whose appalling incompetence had been
ultimately responsible for landing him in his present predicament.

" I never want to set eyes on him again!" the Major
announced. " He's an utter failure."

"Dieter's not a failure," retorted his wife.

" What makes you so certain?"

" Have a guess!"

Bornekamp ignored the implication. " I'm surrounded
by incompetents. It's been one mess-up after another. That's
what comes of trusting people."

He was determined to put his house in order, to create
the sort of atmosphere in which a man with true iron in his
blood could breathe. Consequently, when headquarters asked
him to supply a sergeant-major, three N.C.O.s and twelve
men for service in a new unit which was to be stationed
in a dismal moorland camp, he passed the request to No.
3 Company.

Lieutenant von Strackmann seized the opportunity to rid
himself of certain troublesome and undesirable elements.

" Deal with it at once, Kirschke," he commanded. " Make
Rammler the sergeant-major and Streicher one of the N.C.O.s,
and get shot of the whole of Room 13—including Kamnitzer, of course." He added: " They don't need a C.S.M.

unfortunately. It would have been a pleasure to say good-bye to you."

"A mutual pleasure," Kirschke murmured, sitting down at his desk to draft the requisite list.

He wrote off Rammler and Streicher with pleasure, adding a few more equally pushful types but not including Recht, whose army days were numbered anyway, or Kamnitzer, who merely appeared on the top sheet which the lieutenant read but not in the copies which he signed.

Later, when it was too late to rectify the error, Kirschke alleged that he must have misheard. He was sure von Strackmann had said "Room 13—excluding Kamnitzer"—excluding, not including. "With respect, sir, it's essential to speak clearly in the army. Also, it's advisable to run a careful eye over anything one signs."

For the moment, however, Lieutenant von Strackmann was satisfied. "Good riddance!" he said, pushing the signed papers vigorously aside. "They can rot in hell, for all I care."

Twelve other unit commanders had acted similarly, sloughing off everyone who struck them as troublesome or incompetent. "A fine old shower that'll be," von Strackmann remarked, smiling complacently to himself.

"Officer commanding the new detachment," Bornekamp's concluding order read, "will be Lieutenant von Strackmann."

*

The case against Captain Klaus Ahlers, commanding No. 1 Squadron, Air Transport Wing, charged with conduct prejudicial to good order and military discipline, was heard by Disciplinary Court No. 4. The sessions, which were held in camera, took place on 12th-14th and 20th-22nd July. Those taking part included the president, Dr. Kruppke, two military observers, a lieutenant-colonel and a captain, an official from the Attorney-General's department acting as prosecutor, and a stenographer. Counsel for the defence was a Dr. Friedrich Stolle.

The atmosphere was cool, objective and utterly impersonal. Even the light that streamed in through the tall, slightly dirty windows looked grey and indifferent. The president, Dr. Kruppke, might have been conducting a board meeting.

"Let us stick to the facts, gentlemen," he said. "Kindly remember that we are dealing with a string of figures, nothing more."

No particular attention was lavished on what Colonel Turner felt obliged to say, namely, that Captain Ahlers had always shown himself to be a keen, competent and enterprising officer who enjoyed the affection and respect of subordinates and superiors alike.

"I'm afraid your remarks have little bearing on the points at issue, Colonel."

"I merely thought it my duty to draw attention to certain facts. I do not presume to suggest what inferences the court should draw from them."

Captain Treuberg's evidence followed a similar pattern. "I can state that I always respected Captain Ahlers. He was often referred to as the life and soul of the squadron, especially by personnel of junior rank, and I can only describe his working relationship with me, his deputy, as exemplary— all things considered."

"And you never entertained any suspicions about him?"

"How could I have, sir? He enjoyed the Colonel's confidence."

"No reservations or suspicions of any kind?"

"Absolutely none. Naturally, I was not in a position to foresee what has happened since."

Everyone extolled Ahlers. The sergeant clerk was so moved by his own evidence on the captain's behalf that he appeared to be on the verge of tears.

"I challenge the prosecution to produce any witness willing or able to say anything detrimental about Captain Ahlers," declared Dr. Stolle.

"Which makes it all the more disturbing," countered the prosecuting attorney, with a burst of rhetorical zeal, "that such a thing could have happened to an officer who inspired universal confidence and trust—sentiments which now prove to have been misplaced."

"No digressions, please, gentlemen," said the president. "The matter before us is one which can be assessed in terms of straightforward mathematics. We can dispense with emotional colouring, whatever its complexion. Kindly call Warrant Officer Vossler."

＊

Carolin Ahlers sat on a chair in the waiting-room of Professor Martin's clinic and stared dreamily into space as though the polished parquet flooring were carpeted with flowers.

In the doorway stood Martin Recht, dressed in a dark civilian suit. They were alone in the room, but he seemed reluctant to interrupt her day-dreams. He watched her solicitously for a few moments, noting how pale and fine-drawn she looked.

"Carolin," he said softly, without moving.

She looked up. Her eyes widened and a gentle flush rose to her cheeks. "Martin!" she cried. "Stay where you are—don't move!"

"I've come to fetch you, Carolin."

"That's wonderful. Don't move, though. I've got something to show you."

She rose to her feet unaided and stood there, erect and relaxed. Then, keeping her eyes fixed on his, she stepped forward with a sure, light, unhesitating tread. When she reached his side she halted, smiling happily.

"You walk like a dream."

"Yes—I can walk properly at last!"

She walked back to the chair, where she paused for a moment. Then she paced this way and that, almost pirouetting as she turned. "I'm not a lame duck any longer, am I?"

"You never were, Carolin."

" Not to you, Martin—I know."

She scampered across the room and threw herself into his arms. Her cheek felt burning hot against his and her breath came fast. They might have been two disembodied spirits, except that they seemed to hear the blood racing in their veins—though that, as the unromantic Kamnitzer might well have said, was probably due to some quirk of the clinic's plumbing system.

" I'm so glad you came to fetch me," Carolin said, gently freeing herself. " I hope you didn't find it hard to get away."

" Not at all."

" Are you on leave, then?"

" I'm not in the army any more."

Carolin shot him an inquiring glance. Then she said hurriedly : " All the better, Martin. I mean, one serviceman is enough in any family. Father's worth a dozen on his own, isn't he?"

" He's the kindest, most decent person I've ever met."

" Where is he?"

" He's been detained, Carolin."

" On duty?"

" You could say that." Martin avoided looking at her. He went over to the chair and picked up her suitcase. " We mustn't keep your mother waiting. She's outside in Herr Asch's car. Shall we go?"

" Martin," Carolin said, blocking his path, " there's something wrong, I know there is."

" Your mother's waiting."

She gripped his arm. " What's happened? Has father had an accident?"

" No, Carolin, nothing like that."

" What, then?"

" Just difficulties—trouble at work."

Carolin looked relieved and the pressure of her hands relaxed. " Is that really all?"

" Yes, really—but you mustn't forget how much his work means to him."

Carolin's eyes danced. "I'm sure I mean more. Don't you think so?"

"I not only think, I know. He's proved it."

*

Viktor Vossler strode into the courtroom as if it were a canteen and surveyed its occupants as if wondering which of them to invite to a glass of beer.

"I really don't know what I'm doing here," he announced. "This business has got absolutely nothing to do with me."

"Kindly allow us to decide that," said the president, adding, in matter-of-fact tones: "Have you ever lent the accused money?"

"You mean Captain Ahlers? Well, what if I have? That's my business, isn't it? I can do what I like with my own money. I can chuck it out of the window if I choose to."

"That's beside the point," Dr. Kruppke said wearily. "By all means regard yourself as a private citizen when circumstances permit—but in this case and under present circumstances you are a warrant officer from whom a captain —a direct superior, what is more—is alleged to have borrowed money."

"Who says so—or, rather, who's proposing to prove it?"

Vossler looked challengingly at Ahlers, but Ahlers did not return his glance. He had eyes for no one in the courtroom. The whole performance distressed him immeasurably. He was ready to pay the penalty for his foolishness, if penalty there must be, but he found it humiliating to have his private life subjected to the cool and appraising scrutiny of a roomful of strangers.

"Herr Vossler," the president admonished, "kindly spare us your irrelevant speculations and try to be completely objective."

"Very well," Vossler said indignantly. "If the court is absolutely set on prying into my personal affairs—for instance, into what I choose to do with my private resources—I can tell you, just for your information, that three thousand marks is chicken-feed to me." He paused. " And as I said, who's going to prove that I ever played banker to a superior officer? What happens if I flatly deny it?"

Dr. Kruppke heaved an almost imperceptible sigh. He found the witness's unreasonable attitude slightly irksome. " Why all these evasions?" he asked. " Why these superfluous and time-wasting attempts to rebut straightforward facts and figures with a lot of vague personal observations? The court has heard evidence from Captain Treuberg, among other people."

" That's worthless, for a start!" Vossler exclaimed belligerently. " I venture to dispute Captain Treuberg's ability to give objective testimony in this case."

" Please, please!" defending counsel exclaimed in dismay. " On my own and my client's behalf, I can only deplore such remarks."

" But why?" demanded Vossler. " I'm merely pointing out that Captain Treuberg never felt at home in the role of Captain Ahlers's side-kick. He was hell-bent on taking over the squadron himself—everyone knew that. He has never been a friend of Captain Ahlers, and if he's trying to incriminate him now, all I can say is, I smell a rat—and a man-sized one at that!"

For the first time during the proceedings, Ahlers looked up. He glanced at Vossler and shook his head reprovingly. Even if mud was being flung at him, he was not going to fling it back.

" Herr Vossler's personal views may be of psychological interest," the president said, totally unimpressed, " but they are not the decisive factor here. We are concerned with facts alone, one of them being Captain Treuberg's testimony that he actually saw the I.O.U. in question. Do you dispute that?"

" Certainly I do!" said Vossler, still under the impression that he had the upper hand.

" This I.O.U., addressed to you by Captain Ahlers, was typed by one of the civilian employees who work for your unit. Her testimony is already on record. She gave it reluctantly, if that means anything to you, but she gave it all the same."

" But, sir," Vossler protested boldly, " this so-called I.O.U. was meant as a sort of joke. It had no practical significance. People do indulge in jokes sometimes, especially when there's a ready-made butt like Treuberg around."

Dr. Kruppke suppressed a yawn. " The court is in possession of a cheque which was traced during the course of inquiries into Captain Ahlers's financial position—inquiries which were pursued without any objections being raised by the accused, I must add. This cheque is made out in the sum of three thousand marks. You, Herr Vossler, drew it, and Herr Ahlers presented it—of that there is absolutely no doubt."

Vossler retained his sang-froid with an effort. " It could have been I who was in debt to Captain Ahlers. Perhaps I was paying him off when I wrote that cheque."

The president waved a disdainful hand. " How do you propose to prove that? No, Herr Vossler, the facts are beyond dispute."

" Captain Ahlers," defending counsel pointed out, " is fully in a position to pay off all his debts."

" But he incurred them, did he not?"

*

Martin Recht took Carolin by the hand and led her into the restaurant's private room, with its flower-bedecked table and glittering array of bottles and glasses. Herbert Asch had announced his intention of celebrating his birthday six months early, in honour of Carolin's release from hospital.

" The others won't be here for a few minutes yet," Martin said. " I've got so much to say, but I don't know how to start."

" It can't be very important, Martin." Carolin slipped her hand beneath his arm and nestled against him. " I know the most important thing already."

He longed to put his arms round her, hold her close and tell her that she was the whole world to him, but he never got the chance because at the crucial moment Karl Kamnitzer appeared.

"Don't tell me—three's a crowd," he said jauntily. "Never mind, there'll be other times."

Interrupting their idyll in his usual unabashed way, he embraced Martin and seized the opportunity to give Carolin the same treatment. Then he held her at arm's length and looked her up and down. "Well, girl, did the surgeon earn his money?"

"She can walk properly, just like anyone else!" Martin assured him eagerly.

"I can even dance," Carolin chimed in.

"This I must see!" Kamnitzer bowed low. "May I have the pleasure of the next waltz?" he asked with a grin.

Carolin improvised a series of movements which might charitably have been described as a curtsy, and stepped forward. Kamnitzer started to hum a slow, leisurely waltz tune which bore a vague resemblance to something out of *Tales from the Vienna Woods*.

At first they rotated stiffly, like two figures on the lid of a rusty musical box, but before long their movements became lighter, looser and less constrained. Their bodies began to sway rhythmically. They floated apart, whirling and pirouetting, until Kamnitzer, apparently struggling for breath, came to a halt.

"Good heavens!" he gasped. "It's incredible! Next time we play skittles you'll wipe the floor with me. What have I done to deserve this sort of treatment?"

"Thank you," Carolin said happily.

Martin Recht walked over to her, put one arm tenderly round her shoulders and led her to a chair. They gazed at each other as if they were the only people in the room but Kamnitzer seemed totally unworried by this.

"What's it worth, Carolin?" he asked.

"What, Karl?"

"Everything—the fact that you can walk, dance, run—

play tennis, if you like, swim, ride a bicycle, climb mountains. What's it worth to you?"

Carolin looked perplexed. "I don't know what to say. I only know that I feel as if I were starting a new life— my real life, maybe."

"You mean, no price is too high to pay?"

"I suppose you could say that."

"You're thinking along the right lines, then."

"Karl," Martin interposed cautiously, "I don't think this is quite the moment . . ."

"Nonsense!" Kamnitzer retorted. "Of course it is." He turned to Carolin again. "Your father thinks exactly as you do, and the sooner you reconcile yourself to the idea the better."

"What do you mean, Karl?"

"Nothing in life is free, that's what I mean. Everything's got a price-tag on it, even happiness. They talk about fate being blind, but I reckon it's more like a debt-collecting agency than anything else."

✱

Dr. Kruppke, presiding judge of Disciplinary Court No. 4, read out the court's findings.

"In the name of the people!" The verdict was delivered with practised objectivity and a certain measure of dignity. It was obvious that the court had been uninfluenced by emotional considerations of any kind. All that had been evaluated were facts, and facts alone . . .

"On the basis of the testimony presented . . ." There was a rustle of paper. The president's face betrayed no trace of emotion and the military observers looked equally impassive, as though earnestly intent on banishing all feeling. Counsel for the prosecution looked round complacently like a winning jockey at the post. Counsel for the defence studied his well-tended hands, conscious that Dr. Kruppke had never arrived at anything other than a strictly proper verdict.

" . . . the court finds as follows . . ."

Ahlers did not look up, even then. He sat in the dock like an inanimate figure made of dry, dun-coloured clay, seemingly oblivious of what was being said.

He was satisfied of his own guilt, and would have said so in his closing plea to the bench. He and his counsel had worked out the following statement:

" I have always tried to do my duty throughout my twenty years in the service—successfully, as I believe. I can also state that I have always dedicated myself to my work, body and soul. I have never been punished, nor even reprimanded, for any offence. My debts were incurred for purely personal reasons. The fact that my assets were sufficient to cover them is no excuse. I realise that I have acted improperly, but I would ask you to accept that I sincerely believed myself to be motivated by force of circumstance. I regret what has happened.".

These words had been typed out on a sheet of paper but they were never uttered. Meanwhile, the president was announcing verdict and sentence:

" (i) The accused is guilty as charged.

" (ii) The accused is sentenced to be dismissed the service. In view of his record, however, there will be no deprivation of rank or pension rights."

" There you are! " whispered defending counsel. " Couldn't have been fairer if he'd weighed it out on a pair of scales. It was the best we could hope for."

With his career at an end, Ahlers still clung to what was for him the ultimate military virtue: selfless obedience. " I accept the court's decision," he said simply.

※

" Now you know everything," Martin told Carolin. " I'm a gaol-bird and your father has been dismissed the service."

" He's just bragging, Carolin," Karl Kamnitzer called from the other end of the room. He was inspecting the row of bottles on the sideboard with every appearance of interest.

" You're a fine one to talk," Martin said. " You never come up against any problems. You just sidestep them, or disregard them—or talk people into believing they don't exist."

" It's a method I can recommend to anyone." Kamnitzer studied the label on a bottle of old cognac with relish. " By the way, you needn't expect any interruptions from me for the next few minutes, if you want to make the most of it."

He turned his back on them and poured himself a generous glass of brandy, feeling rather pleased with himself.

" Martin," Carolin said softly. " When I was in hospital you wrote and told me you loved me."

" I know."

" Was it just to make things easier for me?"

"No, not just for that."

" Everything's all right, then. Nothing else matters."

" How I envy your sublime innocence!" Kamnitzer chuckled, draining his glass. He inserted himself between them and draped his arms round their shoulders. " I hope you don't look on love as a universal pain-killer, my children. Some things exist, and no amount of amorous rapture can banish them for good."

" Stop being such a wet blanket, Karl."

" I'm not—I'm just telling you the facts of life. Strikes me you're badly in need of enlightenment."

THE END

H. H. Kirst

Sometimes very funny, often bitingly satirical, Hans Hellmut Kirst's novels describe Germany and the Germans, from the Nazi era to the present day. 'Kirst's oblique, deadpan gaze is deeply revealing, deeply compassionate.' *Sunday Times*

The Revolt of Gunner Asch

Gunner Asch Goes to War

Officer Factory

The Night of the Generals

The Wolves

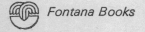 Fontana Books

Eric Ambler

A world of espionage and counter-espionage, of sudden violence and treacherous calm; of blackmailers, murderers, gun-runners—and none too virtuous heroes. This is the world of Eric Ambler. 'Unquestionably our best thriller writer.' *Graham Greene*. 'He is incapable of writing a dull paragraph.' *Sunday Times*. 'Eric Ambler is a master of his craft.' *Sunday Telegraph*

The Intercom Conspiracy

Journey Into Fear

Judgment on Deltchev

The Levanter

The Light of Day

The Mask of Dimitrios

The Night-Comers

Passage of Arms

The Schirmer Inheritance

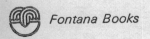 *Fontana Books*

Fontana Books

Fontana is best known as one of the leading paperback publishers of popular fiction and non-fiction. It also includes an outstanding, and expanding, section of books on history, natural history, religion and social sciences.

Most of the fiction authors need no introduction. They include Agatha Christie, Hammond Innes, Alistair MacLean, Catherine Gaskin, Victoria Holt and Lucy Walker. Desmond Bagley and Maureen Peters are among the relative newcomers.

The non-fiction list features a superb collection of animal books by such favourites as Gerald Durrell and Joy Adamson.

All Fontana books are available at your bookshop or newsagent; or can be ordered direct. Just fill in the form below and list the titles you want.

FONTANA BOOKS, Cash Sales Department, G.P.O. Box 29, Douglas, Isle of Man, British Isles. Please send purchase price, plus 6p per book. Customers outside the U.K. send purchase price, plus 7p per book. Cheque, postal or money order. No currency.

NAME (Block letters) _____

ADDRESS _____

_____

_____